BOOK TWO
DAUGHTERS OF THE KALI YUGA

JANABAI
SHEPHERD

BOB JENKINS

Daughters of the Kali Yuga: Book Two
Janabai Shepherd
Copyright 2017 by Bob Jenkins, all rights reserved.
First Print Edition: August 2017

Cover and Formatting: Streetlight Graphics

ISBN 978-0-9979960-6-7 (print paperback)
ISBN 978-0-9979960-7-4 (e-book)

Facebook: Daughters of the Kali Yuga
Website: daughtersofthekaliyuga.com

Janabai Shepherd is a speculative novel about a farm girl who grows up in the years after a cataclysm destroys civilization. Though set in the near future, Janabai's character was inspired by three fictional girls who grew up more than a century ago in classic works of children's literature. To those girls, and the authors who created them, this book is dedicated.

Heidi (1881) by Joanna Spyri (1827-1901)
Pollyanna (1913) by Eleanor H. Porter (1868-1920)
and, especially,
Rebecca of Sunnybrook Farm (1903) by Kate
Douglas Wiggin (1856-1923)

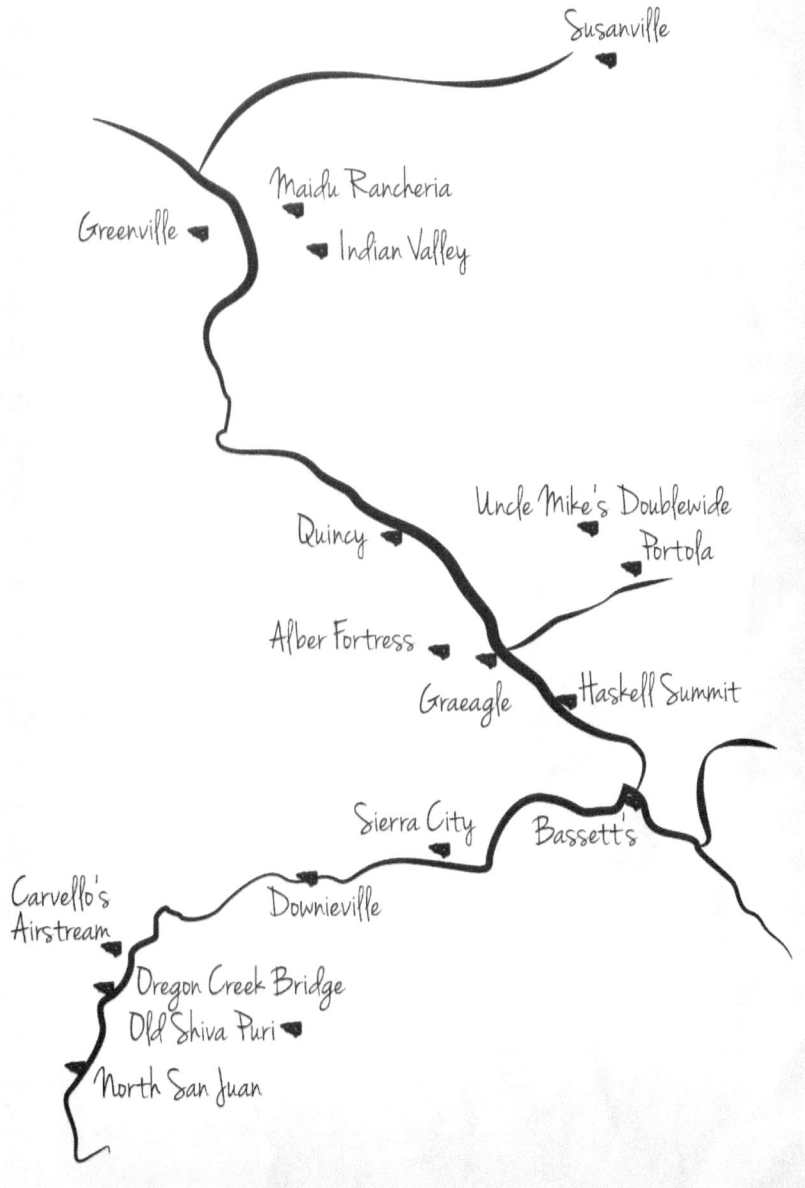

The World of Shiva Puri
5 Years After Kali Yuga

Susanville

Maidu Rancheria

Greenville

Indian Valley

Uncle Mike's Doublewide

Quincy

Portola

Alber Fortress

Haskell Summit

Graeagle

Sierra City

Bassett's

Carvello's
Airstream

Downieville

Oregon Creek Bridge

Old Shiva Puri

North San Juan

WARNING

Kali Yuga lit. "Age of the apocalyptic demon Kali," the last of the four stages of the world as described in Sanskrit scripture. The "Kali" of Kali Yuga (from the root verb *kad*, "to suffer, grieve, hurt; confound, confuse") is the reigning lord of the Apocalypse. This demon (his name pronounced with both vowels short) should not be confused with the goddess Kali (with both vowels long).

It is said that toward the end of his Yuga, the demon Kali will go to war with his archenemy, the Divine Parvati. The world will suffer a fiery end that will destroy wickedness, and a new age will begin.

Or not.
K.

Useful Translations

These terms, mostly Sanskrit, are used throughout *Janabai Shepherd*:

Dharma, the path of righteousness
Karma, the law of cause and effect
Siddhi, a supernatural power
Shakti, divine energy
Sanskrit, the holy language of ancient India
Nritya, spiritual dancing, kinetic yoga
Satsang, a gathering of people to worship
Seva, selfless service, work, a job offered to a devotee
Mandir, a temple
Amrit, a dining hall
Puja, an altar
Asana, a prayer rug
Lingam, the physical representation of male divinity
Yoni, the physical representation of female divinity

PART ONE

Prologue

"A GIRL," KERILYNN SAYS, "SURE AS shootin' it'll be a girl." She should know. Midwife, still, after all these years; two hundred good babies have slithered into her hands. "I lost track," Kerilynn says, "and anyways, I only count births here at Shiva Puri." She is mostly right with predictions; her mouth to God's ear. If the *thing* has to be something, let it be a girl.

I am writing from my comfortable cot, living in luxury, as I am reminded, often, by you-know-who. Everybody else, including you-know-who, is sleeping rough on the floor of the factory or out under the trees, and making do, while I whine away the hours on soft blankets, waiting, waiting, waiting on the birth of my "baby." I shouldn't complain; it's *unbecoming*, one of Mother's favorite barbs, but I do it anyway, complain, I mean. "Un-becoming Janabai," that's me, "Princess Priss of Shiva Puri."

Okay, Janabai, get on with it. Lord, yes, I am pregnant and punished for it. How could it be otherwise? Karma demands balance, and karma gets it, even when we don't know *what we're being punished for!* Karma, are you listening? You never tell us how you work, what you want, and only fools try to understand. So the sages say.

Grotesquely swollen and laid up since the end of May, now halfway to August, two miserable, sticky, itchy months, and I am, in a word... gross. I can't get comfortable. I can't move around. Kerilynn advises me, "Lie there and think, and sweat, and stink like an outhouse, and read something to improve your mind."

Think? Check.

Sweat? Check.

Stink like an outhouse? Oh mama!

Also, I don't feel like reading, so get *Huckleberry Finn* out of my face or I will sink my teeth into your thumb. Begging your pardon. My friends will swear I am good-natured, but these days I want to bite anybody who comes near. Imagine me a dog tick, swollen so tight I will explode if you touch my skin. Will this damned *thing* ever crawl out?

My lower back hurts so much.

The rash is driving me crazy.

I need to pee.

I want my sister to sing me a song.

I want Daddy to cuddle me like his sweet papoose.

The poultice for my prickly attitude is this *book* I'm supposed to start writing. Mother's idea. She suggested, no, *insisted*, I keep busy by scribing the story of my life at New Shiva Puri, and of the astounding things that happened to us in the twenty-two years since she founded the farm in Graeagle, California. Speak the truth, I didn't think I had the energy for such an undertaking, but you know what? I surprised myself. Twisting and turning through the endless, itchy night, I decided I liked her idea. My story; the only record of the Last Days of Humankind! How's that, Mother? I'll write your damned book! *The Story of a Girl at the End of the World* by Janabai Shepherd!

Propped against pillows stuffed with sweet grass, a fresh breeze blowing through the tent, no mosquitoes this morning, praise Shiva, and a glorious view of Lake Klamath, here I am, writing *The Book*, the *first* book, probably the *only* book, to be made in the New World, the world After Kali Yuga, the World of the Future. Mother says her diary does not count, merely the scribblings of a silly woman. Mother is many things, few of them agreeable, but *silly woman* is not among her defects. She's just trying to fluff my confidence with false modesty. Also, she has bribed me with this elegant, old-timey fountain pen, a Sheaffer Imperial Lifetime 3000 Fountain Pen, no less, and... *four*, count 'em, *four* unmarked spiral notebooks! Where has she been hiding these rare artifacts? The fountain pen is quite the nicest thing I have ever owned. I have filled it with ink, not making too big a mess.

I got no real training in writing, no education to speak of after I graduated from the Bigs, but I'm smart, let's get that out of the way; not a *wunderkind* like Suranjini Devi, but smart enough, and I studied with writers who still live in their books, Twain and Hemmingway and Austin and Leonard and Parker and Steinbeck. They are my teachers. Blessings on them.

Steinbeck is my favorite because he writes about people like us, farmers who don't have much and are just hanging on, though I don't get why Steinbeck's people are so ugly to each other. They'll grow more food if they all work together. Right? Everyone has to plow in the same direction. What's hard about that?

Sorry. No more stalling.

This is my story, the story of a shepherd girl, the First Child born in the year of the Kali Yuga. I will tell you everything that happened to me, and what happened to the village of New Shiva Puri as outside our walls, with hateful yellow eyes, the demon hunted us.

He hunts us still. He will never stop until he gets what he wants. Me.

CHAPTER ONE

First Born

DANIEL KUCINICH, MY SAINTLY FATHER, supervised the day-to-day affairs of our village, but deferred to my mother, Azriel Burke, to make the life-and-death decisions. Between them, Daniel, steward of the present, and Azriel, guardian of the future, they held Shiva Puri together through the first Fimbulwinter, a nightmare season "so cold pee froze before it hit the ground," or so said Vic Tretheway, boss mechanic, and always good for a laugh. Snuggled inside Mother's warm belly with Mirabai, my twin, squirming beside me, I was oblivious to the frigid world outside. Likewise, I was spared the horrors of the sickness that stormed our village walls, a disease Mother called "Rakshasa," her bitter homage to the demons who dwell in dank caverns, and whom Mother held responsible for the epidemic.

On New Year's Day, one month after Rakshasa laid us low, the plague retreated from its rampage, but not before sickening everybody, killing thirty-five, including most of the old-timers. The demon disease, sated with human flesh, required no further offerings; more might die before harvest, but it would not be Rakshasa taking us below. Lynda Cheng, once nurse practitioner to Dr. Mistry, and now our only trained medic, declared the rest of us would live. The surviving members of Shiva Puri numbered 183 souls, men, women, children, and two sixteen-day old infants — me and my sister Mirabai, whom they called "First Born," the earliest babies to survive after the Event that destroyed civilization, two faint, mewling hopes for the future, the supernatural twins, Janabai and Mirabai. Nobody guessed the supernatural part, not back then, on New Year's Eve, in the first year of the Kali Yuga.

CHAPTER TWO

Un-likely Twins

MY BIRTH NAME WAS BURKE-KUCINICH, Burke from my mother's side of the family, the Liverpool Burkes, and Kucinich from my father's side, the Jewish-Hindu-hippy Kuciniches. I took my adult name, my *seva* name, Janabai *Shepherd*, when I graduated the Bigs and began tending the herds. I shimmied out first, red-faced and wailing. My mother, Azriel, suspected she carried twins; Kerilynn predicted it from the beginning. My father, peacock proud, was holding me aloft when Mother screamed:

"I'm not done, dammit, pay attention!"

"With a wiggle and a jiggle," the midwife sang, "we'll just corkscrew the little booger right out of there."

Mirabai was a breech baby, not uncommon for the second of twins, but, with Mother stretched as wide open as she was going to be, the delivery posed little difficulty. A few seconds of midwifery sleight of hand, and Kerilynn tugged another slippery infant into the light, smooth and fast. Mirabai, my other half. She was as placid and composed as I was squalling and irritable.

One unusual occurrence marked Mirabai's birth: she arrived with a caul, her birth sack, draped over head and face, an iridescent wedding veil, the unmistakable sign that the infant was claimed by the gods. Mirabai Burke-Kucinich arrived into the world betrothed to a celestial husband.

Janabai and Mirabai, twin peas from an odd pod, who couldn't be more un-alike. Right from the beginning, we were different *from each other*, and later our people would discover we were just *different*. The midwife was at a loss to explain why both of us came with blue throats; not all the way around the neck, just on the front, sky-blue patches from just under our chins to just above our collar bones, as if gently caressed by angelic fingertips.

"Never seen the like," she said. "Pretty enough."

Something about the Kali Yuga, radiation, perhaps, must have changed us when we were embryos, or perhaps it was gas or germs, but whatever it was, we were unique. Mutations, some said. Mother preferred to call us *gifted*.

I was small, wrinkly, and dark-haired like my dad, and quickly grew to favor him in personality as well, being an active baby who needed to be into something at all times, newly hatched and full of beans.

Mirabai was plump, smooth, and flaxen-haired like, well... nobody knew who she favored... and blind. Yes, my sister came into this life with un-seeing pale-blue orbs instead of normal eyeballs. No irises, no pupils, featureless spheres, as if her eyes were cut from polished marble like those of statues you see in picture books from the ancient days.

As Mirabai grew older, her "baby blues" darkened to cobalt and gradually to indigo. Those with the courage to gaze into their depths said that Mira's eyes were full of movement, not at all featureless, but "swirling with currents of color." Some said, her eyes "twinkled with cerulean sparks," but everyone agreed, such eyes had never been seen in this world. They were right about that. Also, most people thought my sister profoundly disabled, that she would require constant care for the remainder of her life, a span nobody expected to last long. Oh, how mistaken they were!

CHAPTER THREE

A Curious Bond

ON THE FIRST ANNIVERSARY OF the Kali Yuga, March 25, *One After Kali*, or *One Ay Kay*, as it came to be known, we "unlikely" twins were three months old. My eyes had focused weeks earlier than the midwife predicted, or so I am told by Dad, who also said I was cute as a puppy wearing socks, so you can decide for yourself the accuracy of his opinion. My forehead crinkled up as if a skeptical old woman lurked inside my tiny skull. I showed a preternatural interest in the world around me.

Mirabai, village cherub, blind and happy, bypassed the colicky wails of newborns, to smile, sweetly and serenely, for everyone who came near, a smile that proved irresistible. Our people competed for the right to cuddle "Baby Meera." To pick her up was to be washed by joy. But one adult in particular muscled in as Mirabai's personal nanny. No, not my dad, who had taken me as his Special One. *He never would admit to such favoritism.* And no, not Mother, who was already back at work mapping our path to Paradise. Mirabai's guardian angel was none other than Maxine "Max" Flythe, sergeant, United States Marine Corps.

Between the angelic Mirabai and the hard-faced marine, a curious bond developed no one could explain, Max least of all. Out in the field, as she taught the arts of war to our fledgling band of badasses, Max kept Mirabai near all the time. She rigged a sling that kept the infant swaddled across her chest like a newborn assault rifle, tiny head tucked into Max's armpit. Mirabai and Max. Max and Mirabai. Find one, find the other.

In moments of deepest reflection, Max considered the possibility that the baby was a substitute for my mother, the woman Max had loved since the day they met. Perhaps Mirabai was compensation for not possessing the true object of her desire, but whether Mirabai was a little piece of Mother or a consolation prize, Max recognized something about the baby others would not understand for years:

Mirabai was *divine*.

What an exotic word for Sergeant Flythe to settle upon, *divine*, and yet it was the most accurate nomenclature the marine could express. Intuitively, Max knew the baby was connected to something magnificent, spontaneously and mysteriously attuned to the other worlds. Mirabai's true nature was far beyond Max's experience, but the marine had only to touch the child to feel at peace; one touch, and the tension drained from her body, her breath deep and long, her mind free from doubt and fear. For Maxine Flythe, combat veteran, virtuoso cynic, lesbian and drunk, the blind infant radiated ecstasy, a pocket-sized bliss-light holding back the horrors of the darkling plain and illuminating the marine's own ravaged spirit.

Never, of course, would Max say it aloud. She might admit such thoughts to a certain seven-year-old girl when she was drunk. Max, I mean, was drunk, not me. But never in public, or sober, would Maxine Flythe give voice to such bullshit.

Chapter Four

Peetee Essdee

O N THE FIRST ANNIVERSARY OF the Kali Yuga, having pried Mirabai away from Mother's nipple, Sergeant Max stood in her usual place against the back wall of the *mandir*, "Baby Meera" strapped to her hip. A keen observer of people, Max frowned at the muttering around the hall. Surely, she admitted, dangers surrounded our village, and heartache, and desperation, but there was also hope. Wasn't she holding that hope against her side in the miracle of this child? Didn't the joyous wedding between Bill Lemko and Simone Jackson augur happier days?

Spring was upon us. Shiva Puri, previously occupied with the business of survival, was unraveling in the small window of "downtime" between winter freeze and first planting. Now, we had too much time to remember what had happened to our world and what had been lost forever. Now, we had too much time to worry about the Herculean labors of another planting, another harvest, another winter, the inexorable dwindling of resources. We were running out of toothpaste, and shampoo, and laundry detergent, and antibiotic ointment, and a million other necessities and comforts great and small.

Dad was in the front of the hall attempting to lead a meeting that was rapidly devolving into communal bickering.

"How can we bring babies into this doomed world?"

"How can we *not*?"

"What about the Alber murders?"

"What about the gang of killers?"

"What if they come for us?"

"What if we have a bad harvest?"

"Do we fade away, last one alive, turn out the lights and lock the door?"

And on and on.

"We had a magnificent harvest." Dad raised his voice. "We

have seed for next year. We survived the Rakshasa plague. We have work, *good* work, in front of us. We have each other. What's the matter with us?"

"What's the matter with us?" From the middle of the room, Greg Pequinot, a bruin of a man, tallest and strongest in the village, rose to his feet and began to shout, his fear unleashed, his voice hysterical, arms waving wildly, rapidly coming apart.

"We're done. Finished. We're going to die, all of us. We never should of left Downieville. We never should of put you in charge. Who made you god? We need a new boss. And I'm not the only one who thinks so."

Low mutters of agreement rose from a cadre of Pequinot's friends sitting off to one side.

"I say we elect a new leader right now. Who's with me?"

Two men climbed to their feet.

Dad tried to pacify the man. "Please, Greg, take it down a notch. You're scaring the children."

"You stand there telling us to do this, do that, get to work, don't whine, don't think, while your wife, the holy bitch of the universe, tells us everything is hunky-dory."

When Max heard the word "bitch," she handed Mirabai to Mother.

"Take her."

Pequinot blustered on, working himself up into a lather. "Well, it's not hunky-dory. If we hold on another year, we'll be living in huts and crawling in the mud. I say..."

Dad put his hand on the man's arm. A mistake. Pequinot knocked his hand away and then shoved the smaller man in the chest. Dad backpedaled across the room, tripping over one of the kids and falling into the musicians.

"Don't touch me!" Spittle flew from Pequinot's mouth. "Don't nobody touch me!"

Vic Tretheway and Donnie Sims, two formidable men themselves, got to their feet, one on each side of the agitated man. Pequinot looked left and right at his new threats, both of whom had stopped in place to stare at Max, who was cutting through the crowd like a barracuda coming for prey. Before Pequinot could turn around, Max leaped on his back, wrapped both legs around his waist, whipped her forearm across his throat, and pushed his head forward mashing his windpipe against the unyielding radius bone of her right arm. Pequinot's eyes opened wide in surprise as he tried to take a breath, fluttered, rolled back in his head, and closed. He sank to his knees, Max on his back, a hag out of folklore, riding him to the ground.

"Bad manners to make a scene on a wedding day," Max hissed through clenched teeth. Pequinot's two henchmen took a few steps to intervene, until stopped in their tracks by Vic Tretheway, who wagged his finger in warning. They watched, along with everybody else, as Max choked Pequinot until he stopped moving. Releasing her grip and untangling herself, Max climbed to her feet, sauntered over to Mother and retrieved Mirabai, plunking the baby back against her hip as if nothing had happened.

Max looked around the sea of shocked faces. "He'll be alright in a few minutes. Just a touch of PTSD."

The hall was utterly silent, the people stunned by the violent turn of events, so sudden, so convincing. Dad broke the silence.

"PTSD?"

"We've got it, all of us," Max answered. "I've seen it a lot, had it myself. Hell, I have it right now."

"Please come up here where we can see you," Daniel said.

Max refused to move.

"Go on, pal," Mother said. "You started this."

Max sighed, rolled her eyes, and walked into the bright circle of lantern light.

"Is that my daughter on your hip?" Dad asked.

"Let me see," Max answered, making a comical display of examining the baby, confirmed, "Yes, sir, I believe this to be your daughter, by name, Mirabai Burke-Kucinich."

Though rocked by the vicious act they had just witnessed, the villagers could not help chuckling. Disaster averted, at least for the evening, by Max, their warrior goddess, softened by her care of the infant Mirabai, but still scary. Don't piss her off, and never, ever insult Mother in her presence.

"Post-traumatic stress?" Dad asked.

"That'd be my guess," Max answered.

"What do we do about it?"

"I'm not a shrink. Ask our resident witch doctor, the esteemed Dr. Simone."

"You're the most experienced," Mother shouted from across the hall.

"Positively," the esteemed Dr. Simone confirmed.

"So," Dad repeated, "what do you recommend?"

"Well, I think, we get the problem out where we can see it, then we name it for what it is, Peetee Essdee."

"PTSD."

"No. Not PTSD like some college degree. *Peetee Essdee*, like you nickname a red-headed kid. 'Hey, Peetee! Peetee Essdee. Come over here, boy.'"

Max's enactment earned another chuckle from the assembly.

"That's right," she said, gathering speed. "*Peetee Essdee, he's our boy*. You spiritual Hindoo types like call-and-response, so when I say *Peetee*, you say *Essdee*. Right? Okay, here we go... *Peetee*."

Embarrassed, a few people mumbled the response.

"Well, swell," Max said. "That was terrific. I tell you what, people, I'm going to give you one more chance to give me all you got, and if you don't, I'm going to walk out in the middle, grab the first two of you I come to, and smack your heads together like coconuts. So take a big breath, and get ready... *Peetee!*"

This time the villagers shouted back, "*Essdee!*"

"*Peetee!*"

"*Essdee!*"

"Das right," Max said, affecting a cornball accent, "we gots de *Peetee Essdee* real bad. *Real* bad. So bad. I mean we gots it so, *so* bad."

"How *bad* do we gots it?" Vic Tretheway yelled, tossing Max the ancient setup line.

"Thank you, Vic. How *bad* do we gots it? Well, let's see. Annabel, give me that E chord on your tiny piano thing."

Annabel pumped up the harmonium and played the chord.

"We got the Peetee Essdee so damn bad," Max sang.

She looked over at the musicians expectantly. Annabel provided the obligatory chord change.

"You know it makes us so damn sad."

The drummer tapped the stinger... *ba bum baba bum!*

"Give us the worst damn blues we ever had."

"Oh, yeah, honey chile, tell us," an exhortation from Simone.

"But Azriel here is gonna make us glad."

"I am?" Mother asked.

"Oh yes, mah sistah, you gonna get off your butt and take us dancing!"

The people of Shiva Puri Village whistled and cheered as Mother climbed to her feet, infant daughter Janabai (me) tight against her chest.

"Ganesha Sarinam?" Mother asked.

Her suggestion was met with applause and cheering. Max started to walk away, relinquishing the spotlight, but Mother caught her by the arm.

"Oh no you don't." Mother nodded to Annabel, who sounded the first notes of the sprightly bhajan, a fast chant to evoke the elephantinic power of Ganesha, Remover of Obstacles.

"I don't know this dance," Max said.

"If you can stand up in front of the village and jam the blues off the top of your head, you can do this. Don't worry, I'll lead." Mother leaned close and whispered, "What you just did was extraordinary. You are remarkable, you know?"

"Yes," Max answered, "yes I am."

Cradling me in her arms, Mother began the first steps of the Ganesha nritya.

Max, holding Mirabai, followed Mother's lead. Soon, every member of Shiva Puri, young and old, was dancing around the Shiva lingam. Even Greg Pequinot was on his feet, though from later accounts, he wasn't quite sure how he got there.

Did that really happen? Too good to be true? Did Max choke Greg Pequinot right in front of everybody? Did she make up the "Peetee Essdee Blues" off the top of her head? And sing it spontaneously in front of all the people? And cure everybody of post-traumatic stress something? I forget what the *D* is for. Disease? PTS Disease? Maybe it's a tall tale, though Simone Jackson, who told the story to me, swears it's Shiva's own truth. We still sing "Peetee Essdee" every Kali Yuga Day, so there must be something to it.

Of course, I was too young to remember Max singing and curing Peetee Essdee, but I like to pretend that dance with my mother is my first memory. I've heard the story so many times, I imagine it happened just like that. Max holding Mira, Mother holding me, swirling and twirling together through the flickering light of the great hall, round and round the lingam, pungent smudge smoking in abalone shells as the harmonium played and drums pounded our hymn to the Great Elephant.

CHAPTER FIVE

Seedlings

AFTER THE *PEETEE ESSDEE* DISASTER of the first anniversary of the Kali Yuga, Mother devised a new Kali Yuga holiday, a celebration of survival and hope, the centerpiece to be the ceremonial planting of twenty-nine seedlings in remembrance of the twenty-nine brothers and sisters who had fallen since the night when the skies above Old Shiva Puri exploded.

This is how Simone "Mama Witch" Jackson describes the scene to me. I warn you; it's not flattering, but it's going in the book just the way she tells it.

"We searched for superior trees, and we returned from the

fields and woods with hundreds of prospects. Jivan Bose, the only experienced arborist, selected the best from among the many offerings and transported the candidates to starter pots in our greenhouses. Galen Raether, as behooving his status as boss farmer, chose premium sites for planting. We started a new compost pile, and piled the best soils nearby.

"Galen said, 'These seedlings will have a better chance with autumn planting, but I reckon they'll do just fine with a spring start...' He paused to give everybody a stern look. 'Just fine as long as each tree is babied through the summer, shaded, watered, fenced and fed.'

"We all nodded.

"'Not too much fertilizer, just enough, I tell you what.'

"In the late winter when the ground was still soft, Galen assigned each seedling to a caretaker, a villager who was close to the person to be memorialized. The caretaker dug tree holes according to Raether's instruction.

"'Better to plant a five-dollar tree in a fifty-dollar hole, than a fifty-dollar tree in a five-dollar hole.'

"We dug fifty-dollar holes.

"I've never seen a dollar," I interrupted Simone, "but I know what they were from books, so I get the idea about fifty-dollar holes. Good holes, deep holes, the best drainage, lots of humus, light, and air. Like that?"

"Right. Anything else to add? No? Then, I'll go on with my story. On Kali Yuga Day we met at the greenhouse, all of us who weren't out on the guard posts. Your mother rehearsed a grand speech, but had to cut it short because you were wiggling around in her arms and generally acting like a spoiled princess. At one and a half years old, you had already figured out that your mother was your biggest rival for your father's attention."

"That's called an Electra Complex," I interrupted again. Simone gave me a warning look, the kind she's really good at. "Psychology talk," I added, unnecessarily.

"To this day I do not know why Azriel made the unfortunate decision to tote you along. Maybe she thought it made her look more maternal, the vision of Mother Nature or some such hoo-hah. Big mistake. You did everything you could to steal her moment."

"Like what? What did I do?" This was fascinating.

"Oh, you chatted away with your best baby nonsense while she was trying to talk. You pulled locks of her hair loose and sucked on them. You kicked your feet in her ribs. You grabbed at her nipples like you wanted to be fed. You banged her in the head with your favorite toy…"

"The plastic palomino horse with one leg chewed off!"

"Good memory. You blew spit bubbles, and laughed at your amazing feat. Weren't you the most darling little girl anyone had ever seen? Your mother tried to soldier on, she said, 'We plant these Great Trees to show our faith in the future. We plant them in devotion to the Earth, she who sustains us. We consecrate them as our promise to go on, to make a better life for our children. We adults will never sit in the shade of these trees, but our children will, as will their children, and our descendants in the years to come.'

"Azriel picked up an oak seedling and held it over her head. You tried to grab it out of her hand. She tried to ignore you.

"'Can you imagine this tree one hundred years from now? We will all be gone, but the tree will just be starting its long life. Can you imagine it in two hundred years? In five hundred years? In one thousand years? Imagine one million years from now, the descendants of our people will still be sitting in this same spot in the shade of the Great Trees we planted on this day in the second year of the Kali Yuga.'

I just had to butt in here. "No one can actually imagine one million years. Once I think I imagined a thousand years. How far can you imagine into the future?"

Silence.

"Okay," I said in a squeaky little chipmunk voice, "I'll just be quiet now."

Simone laughed.

"What's so funny?"

"That voice. When did you learn it?"

"I don't know. I could always do the chipmunk."

"No, you learned it from your mother. I remember a time before you were born, when Azriel said those exact words, 'I'll just be quiet now,' in that exact voice."

"Tell me about it!"

"Another time, honey chile. I believe I was rapping the great tree planting shindig."

"Please, go on, but don't forget you owe me the chipmunk story."

Simone winked, and continued, "So we dutifully closed our eyes and did our best to send our minds out to distant futures, to see people like ourselves still here, laughing and loving each other—and planting more Great Trees. Jai Shiva! What a perfect opportunity, this auspicious moment of silence, for you to demonstrate your advanced vocabulary!

"You drew in a deep breath and yelled, 'DA DA DA DA DA,' as loud as you could. Your mother had enough: 'Daniel, will you please take your child and drown her in the river.'

"Your Da Da Da took you in his arms, wherein you lay your head serenely against his neck, stuck your thumb into your mouth for a quiet little suck, and stared at your mother. Azriel shook her head in exasperation and said, 'She's not usually like that,' a hilarious thing for your mother to say, because you were *exactly* like that, and everybody knew it. Your mother took a few seconds to tuck drooly locks of hair behind her ear before resuming her speech.

"'Vic Tretheway, come forward.'

"Vic, waiting on the side, stepped up.

"Holding out the oak seedling, your mother said, 'Vic, will you accept this Great Tree in memory of Maitreya Gordon?'

"'I will.'

"'Will you plant it today and care for it tenderly in the same way you would care for Maitreya if she were still with us?'

"Vic managed to whisper, 'I will.'

"'Lead us to the place you have prepared.'

"In a long procession, we followed Vic Tretheway to the fifty-dollar hole he had dug for the woman he loved. The hole was behind the old resort, on a little bluff above the Feather River. Vic knelt down next to the hole holding the Maitreya tree in both hands. He looked up at Donnie Simms, who had also loved Maitreya.

"'Will you help me, Donnie? I can't do this by myself.'

"Donnie knelt next to his friend. Together they worked the compost into the soil with their hands, and packed it in tight, not too tight, just enough. As Vic watered the little Maitreya tree, the first of many, many waterings, Donnie placed a wire fence to keep away the wildlife.

"As the two men stood above the seedling, Vic said, 'I knew Maitreya Gordon. She was magnificent, everything good in the world a woman can be. She was tough and brave and smart. She was taken from us too soon. I will never forget her.'

"His knees buckled, but Donnie was there to catch him, though truth be told, Donnie was hardly in better shape, two men sort of holding each other up.

"The procession wound through the town of Graeagle, stopping at each hole for planting and sweet words of memory. All in all, twenty-nine Great Trees were started that day:
Douglas Fir
Hemlock
White Fir
Red Fir
Lodgepole Pine
Sugar Pine
Jeffrey Pine
Incense Cedar
Walnut
Maple
White Ash
Sycamore
Mountain Alder
Quaking Aspen
Ponderosa Pine
and
Many Oaks

"One tree for Maitreya Gordon, the first to fall, and three trees for Laksman, Levi, and Ajay, the brave boys who tried to avenge her, and nineteen trees for those who had been taken by the Rakshasa sickness, six trees for the refugees who had staggered in from Quincy only to perish within a week, and one tree for Baby Bose. who left this world the same day he arrived.

"In this way, Janabai, did the Great Trees of Shiva Puri become divine, not that you were aware of it at the time, having finally given up and fallen asleep, soaking your father's chest with your own divine slobber.

"At the evening program, the happiest prayers, chants, and dances were enjoyed, and afterward, nothing for it but Max to revive her 'Peetee Essdee Blues,' everybody joining in on the chorus, with Greg Pequinot, whom Max had choked unconscious the previous year, singing loudest of all. Together, with many of us making contributions, we recited the story of the first Kali Yuga, sometimes dire and tragic, occasionally heartfelt and nostalgic, but often comic.

"I performed a spot-on impersonation of your mother: 'I'm not leaving without my goats!'

"I was quite amusing, if I do say so.

"Your father jumped in to perform a parody of himself. 'You know I've tried to talk sense to her, but it's Azriel,' he lamented, drawing out her name into a wail of despair:

"'Aaaazzzzrrrriiiiiiiiiiiel!'

"Your mother was laughing so hard I thought she would hurt herself."

"*Mother?*"

"Let me tell you something, Janabai. When your mother was the same age you are now, she was the goofiest little flit in the village."

"My mother. Not somebody else's mother?"

"Your very own mamacita."

"Well, what happened to make her the way she is now?"

CHAPTER SIX

When Mother Danced

I DON'T LIKE MY MOTHER. LET me be clear on this. Mother is a woman of many parts. Some of those parts, I *do* like. A few of them, I *love*. But most of the time, she just rubs me the wrong way. Right from the beginning, I was jealous of her. I tried to get in between her and Dad, I mean, right in between their legs, like an unmannerly puppy. I blurted out the most stupid things in the middle of their conversations. I didn't like the way Dad looked at her, and said so, and most especially, I didn't like the adoring way he looked at her when she was *dancing*.

Picture this: Mother strides out into the dancing circle, goddess-embodied, long legs and big bosom. Face it, Mother's stacked. Ankle bells jingling, all business, she stands perfectly still, closes her eyes, and waits for Annabel to start the music. Her head falls back, and her eyes roll up. If you are close enough, and looking at just the right angle, you can see her eyeballs flicking back and forth under her eyelids. Hang on to your mind; Azriel Dancer is going to take you someplace you have never been. She moves, sometimes in slow circles, sometimes floating in great orbits around the lingam. The room gets brighter, no one knows why, but just ask anybody, and warmer. The drummers follow *her* tempo, not the other way around. She connects to some rhythm from beyond, and Annabel's earthbound music comes along for the ride. For a few seconds, just sit back and feel the Shakti.

Now, get on your feet and join the dance. Don't worry, you'll catch on, and besides, who's looking? You follow her around the mandir, or sometimes you spin in your own private world like the Dervishes of olden days. Sometimes there are no steps, just a sort of shuffle; sometimes the steps are so intricate you have to bear down and concentrate. Sometimes the dance is so slow it seems like you are hardly moving. Sometimes so fast, it's almost riotous. Tender, passionate, you never know what to expect, except this:

23

bliss is on the way. Undeniable, unmistakable *ecstasy*. You can be in an okay mood or down in the dumps, relaxed or uptight, it doesn't matter. Mother is going to bring you out of yourself and into a wondrous state where you are gloriously *That. Tat Tvam Asi. Thou Art That*, the state where you melt into the great Oneness. Every time. Every single time you dance with her.

Let me ask, how would you like to have *that* as your mother?

Except when dancing, Mother was never at ease in front of people. Oh, she handled herself well enough when she had to speak, or when she had a task to accomplish, a piece of work in front of her, but she said only what she needed to, no more. And I need you to understand this; to her credit, she never, ever wanted to be the guru, a burden she wore around her neck like an anvil.

Mother was astonished when Shiva Puri anointed her prophet. She never believed she was enlightened, or the village *needed* a living guru. To the contrary, she believed we would succeed if we relied on ourselves for everything. Whatever needed to be done, we did, or it didn't get done.

"We already have what we need, or we do without," Mother said, and also, "Don't look to me for *truth*; look within your own *self*."

But doubt it not, we acted differently when we were around her. Yes, we adored Mother, but we were afraid of her. Our elderly librarian, Odessa Piwinski, would stand up to her, and Simone Jackson, Mama Witch, our psychiatrist, could make her listen to common sense. Of course, Max, just as weird in her own way, was the only person Mother would take orders from.

Dad. Dad. Dad. And then there was Dad. Mother held herself aloof from him, looking out at him from behind her eyes, even as he ate her up with his own. How could she be so cold to him? Mother was sufficient to herself, set apart from the rest of us, not in any nasty way; maybe divine, but certainly remote, and she kept dad totally under her thumb. She put him in a pumpkin shell, and there she kept him very well. He needed more, and he deserved more. The way he fawned over her; it made me sick. In the olden days, I prayed that he would pay more attention to me.

These days, I pray he pays more attention to her.

CHAPTER SEVEN

Let the Dogs Bark

OUR VILLAGE LOOKED LIKE, SOUNDED like, and smelled like Noah's Ark; you know, the fable in the Old Testament? Have you read it? The Bible is one *maha* difficult book! Naturally, I have read it cover to cover. Some funny stuff in there, especially about the end of the world. Har-dee-har. Not even close! I have also read the Gospels many times. Wasn't Christ the sweetest? I wish I could have heard him preach the Sermon on the Mount. Swami Jesus could give Shaktipat initiation like nobody else! Oh, yes, he surely could!

What was I saying? Sometimes I distract myself, like now, with the *thing* twisting around inside me; and oh mama, it can kick like a donkey! Donkey! Oh yes, the Shiva Puri Ark. We treasured every animal, from Moxie the donkey, to the goats Mother rescued on Kali Yuga Night, to Bill Lemko's cattle, to the pigs and chickens and sheep and all the rabbits and turkeys and ducks we adopted.

Our most important passengers were the dogs.

When me and Mirabai were three years old, Hanuman was as much a part of our lives as our parents. He thought of us twins as his puppies. I would ride him around the village, hanging on to his ruff as he ran at full speed, careening around corners, hurdling over anything in his way, me screaming with excitement. Like Dad, I was smallish, and Hanuman weighed one hundred and twenty pounds, a huge white bear of a dog. He let me do whatever I wanted to him. Mirabai, being the way she was, couldn't play as freely, so Hanuman would hang out with her, gentle and affectionate. Mostly Mirabai just wanted to spoon up next to him, her arm over his great bulk, and the two of them would dream away the afternoon.

As far as we knew, Hanuman was the last Great Pyrenees in the world, the end of his kind. He didn't seem to mind, because he was too busy keeping the Shiva Puri goats in line to pay attention to his tragic circumstance. By the time Mirabai and I came along, Hanuman was seven years old, already past his prime, his thick white coat yellowing around the edges, behind his ears and around his butt. Like most of the enormous breeds, Hanuman's life expectancy was only ten or twelve years. He was probably on the short end of the expectancy stick because he had worked every day of his adult life. During daylight hours when Uncle Manoj and Uncle Raj were minding the herd, Hanuman was a lazy boy, especially in hot weather; just a big drooly, snoring lump.

But when the sun went down and the shepherds went to bed, it was a different story. Hanuman came alive, a creature of the night. He worked dusk till dawn patrolling the perimeter, walking unending circuits around the herd, sniffing, listening, watching for threats. Just the tiniest scent of something unknown, or even the sound of wind shuffling leaves, would set him off. He would bark the deep, unmistakable Pyrenees bark, a hard, scary boomer echoing through the countryside, over and over, all night long if he was worried. Dad said Hanuman's bark would wake up people in farms miles away, back before the Kali Yuga, of course, but we learned to sleep right through his ruckus. We were used to being guarded by the big boy and appreciated his vigilance.

One time I asked Dad, "Why does Hanuman bark so much?"

Dad answered, "That's his job."

"He's good at his job, huh?"

"Best damn dog in the world."

One night, Hanuman started barking, but there was something different about it, and scary, like he was screaming, a furious, frenzied call to war. I opened my window just in time to see Mother dash out of the Batch Shack where she had taken up living with the single women. I watched from above as she closed her eyes and cocked her head to listen, then grabbed the iron bar that hung next to the alarm bell and whanged away. Soon, alarm bells answered from guard posts out on the perimeter. People scrambled from their homes, shouted, and raced to assigned positions. Mother was checking the load in her shotgun when Max ran up. I didn't hear everything they said to each other, but one word cut through the air, a word I had heard before in stories, but never with the fear and hatred that lifted it up to the window sill where I perched.

The word was... *Kali.*

The demon? Mother and Max were acting like Kali was real.

Dad squeezed my shoulder. He was shaking.

"What's happening, Daddy?"

He took a deep breath and picked me up.

"Don't worry, Jana-Bee, everything will be okay."

"Why did they say 'Kali'?"

"Shhh," he said and tucked me back in bed next to my sister. "Go back to sleep. Hanuman did his job, and now your mother and Max will take care of that old Kali."

"Dad?"

"Hmmmm?"

"Hanuman is the best damn dog in the world."

"He is that, but maybe you should leave out the 'damn' word when you're around your mother."

"Okay, but you should hear all the stuff Max says."

Dad laughed, but he was pinching the skin of his neck, the surest sign that he was worried.

"Dad? What's out there?"

"Nothing for you to worry about, but I want you to stay close for a little while. Don't go wandering off by yourself."

"Is it the Kali Monster?"

"No such thing. Just a story."

But he kept pinching his neck.

Pinch. Pinch. Pinch.

The next day Max pulled the perimeter in tighter and doubled the guards on each post.

CHAPTER EIGHT

Tiger, Tiger Burning Bright

A FEW NIGHTS LATER, I WOKE up wondering where Dad was. We were sleeping in his bed. The reading candle was still lit, so he had to be close by. Even as a four-year-old, I knew we never left the house with candles burning. Leaving Mirabai alone, I went downstairs. Dad was coming back in from "doing his business," in the outhouse if he was taking a poop, or in the brush if he was making water. If you had to pee, you could do it on the ground as long as you were "three giant steps" off the path and you didn't use the same place over and over. Females were allowed to do all of their squatting in the outhouse, but most of the "ladies" were already used to the "three giant step rule" and preferred to drop their drawers wherever they were. Why dribble down a dark spidery hole when you could tinkle under the great sky?

Even in winter I liked to pee outside. Why not? It was just as cold inside the privy as out where I could melt the snow and maybe make a pretty yellow design, though the boys were much better than the girls at pissing pictures. Not fair, but later on, when we were teenagers, G-Mek pissed my name in the snow: *Jana*, not my whole name, because he ran out of pee before he could finish the *bai*.

"What are you doing up?" Dad asked me, brushing snow from his coat.

"Looking for you."

"Well, here I am."

"Where were you?" I asked.

"Outside, talking to the moon."

"No you weren't. You were pissing in the snow."

He laughed. "I was? How do you know?"

"You have peepee spots on your pants."

"So I do. You are uncommonly precocious, little miss."

"Pre-co-shush. What does that mean?"

"It means... ah... growing up too fast," he answered.

"I want to grow up real fast so I can be the boss."

"Oh, you do, do you?"

"Yup."

"Come over here so I can see how big you are."

I walked over to the door where Dad had measured my height in pencil marks on the jamb. I backed up and stood as tall as possible. Scratching his chin, Daniel looked at me, at the marks, first on one side, then on the other.

"Hmmm," he said. "I do see some growth. I think you have gotten taller since the last time we looked. When was that?"

"This morning," I answered.

"Yes, this morning. I have a great idea. Would you like to grow up even faster?"

"Oh, yes, Daddy. How?"

"Warm milk. Suranjini tells me warm milk accelerates bone growth."

"She does?"

Suranjini was the brilliant daughter of Gayatri and Abhinav Devi, the village scientists, a geeky teenager who had taken a liking to me, and vice versa. If Suranjini said a certain thing, well, in my estimation, it was unquestionably true.

"Would you like some warm milk?" Daniel asked.

"Yes, please," I answered. "Honey too?"

"Oh, I got all the honey you need right here," he said, swooping me up and blowing fart noises against my neck.

"Stop," I said. He thought I was fooling around and kept at it. "Stop, Daddy, stop." He pulled away, giving me a quizzical look.

"Something's wrong with Mira."

That's when three bad things happened at the same time.

Aaaaaaaauuuuuuunnnnnn!

A ferocious roar ripped through the village, followed by the shattering of glass in the upstairs bedroom and Mirabai's scream for help.

I didn't hear her scream with my ears; it was shrieking in my head, a single word. I echoed her scream aloud.

"*Tiger!*"

Holding me in his arms, Dad charged up the stairs and into the bedroom. The window glass was smashed to pieces as if someone had jumped through without bothering to open it. Mirabai thrashed around on the floor, entangled in bedding, hands slapping at her head, flames enveloping the blanket, her hair on fire.

Silently, without a sound of any kind, without crying, Mirabai fought the burning terror she could not see. Can you imagine? Four years old, blind, alone... and on fire? Gives me the creeps just remembering it. Dad put me down on the floor, snatched another blanket from the foot of the bed, and in two seconds flat, smothered the flames. He wrapped Mirabai up in a bundle.

"Stay here," he told me. "Tell your mother I took Mira to Nurse Cheng."

"I want to go. Mira says she needs me."

He gave me a strange look.

"Put on your coat."

We made our way across the dark clearing to the clinic, Dad walking fast, but not so fast he would trip; me racing to keep up with him. He must have asked me what I meant when I screamed "tiger," but that part gets blurred up in other questions he and Mother and the grown-ups were asking me, about how I just seemed to know things I couldn't possibly know, and about how the fire got started, and how the window got broke. Dad was freaked out and beating himself up because he left the house with a candle burning, never mind that the candle didn't just jump on the sleeping child, never mind the roaring animal sound that nobody but me seemed to hear, never mind about the tiger. Those parts just got shoved aside.

Except by Mother and Max, who took me aside after the excitement died down.

"Tiger. Why did you say 'tiger'?" Max asked.

"Mira said it."

"Mira doesn't speak." That's what Mother *said*, but what she *meant* was that I was making it up.

"Mira said it in my head."

"Okay, maybe I'll buy that. She said it in your head, but how could she know it was a tiger? She's never seen a tiger."

"Yes she has."

"How?"

"In our dreams."

"Dreams? You have dreams with your sister? The same dreams?"

"Mmm hmm."

"When was that?" Mother asked. "The tiger dream?"

"Before we was born. When we was still in your stomach."

CHAPTER NINE

Affinity

BESIDES HAVING THE SAME TIGER dreams, Mira and I had those identical birth marks I have written about, the blue "Shiva throats." We looked different from the other kids, and people were starting to notice other unusual things about us; well, about me at first, because Mira hadn't started talking yet.

When I was still a toddler, I learned how to understand what Hanuman was thinking and get him to do what I wanted. Hanuman taught me games like jumping and hiding and herding goats. I taught him all kinds of things like "Go get Mira's blanket." We were performing amazing, wonderful tricks no dogs had ever done. Everyone was amazed. Mother asked, "How are you doing that?"

"It's a secret," I answered, but I really wanted to tell her, to astonish her with my marvelous powers.

"Okay," she said, "a secret. I'll just lean down here and you can whisper."

Looking from side to side to make sure no one was close enough to overhear, I brushed her hair away and put my lips to her ear. I remember what she smelled like back then, her hair and skin. She smelled like herself, like heaven, my mother. I have not been so close to her in so many years. I almost forgot her smell. Wait. Where was I? What was I saying? Oh, right, I whispered my dog training secret in her ear.

"I put a thought picture in Hanuman's mind and he does whatever I want, one-two-three, but don't tell anybody, okay? Mum's the word?"

"I'm impressed," she said. She looked like she was impressed. I'm sure she was impressed.

One of my best tricks was to get a whole pack of dogs howling in harmony. Yep, *five*-part harmony. You should be asking yourself, "How did Janabai do that? What could a little girl know of harmony? How could she teach it to a pack of dogs?"

Here's the secret. Lean close and I'll whisper: *I didn't do the teaching; Mirabai did, but I took credit for it. Shhh.*

In the beginning I brought puppies into the house, but soon graduated to livestock. Dad pitched a fit. My room smelled like a pigsty because I loved to keep piglets under my bed so I could watch them running around my room. Anything cuter than piglets? Every baby animal is adorable... but piglets!

When I started going out in the woods by myself, I found animals of all kinds, and birds too, to bring home. No fish. I admit I do not love fish. I don't know why. I know they're important, they're fine, they're worthy of respect; I eat them when Cookie puts them on the table, and in principle, I do respect them, but I can't honestly say I've ever fallen for a particular trout.

Reptiles. One time I brought home a timber rattler. Dad pitched another fit. Mother laughed, picked up the snake behind the head, draped it over her shoulders. Together, we took it back where I found it and let it go free.

"It's better if you leave the wild animals where they live, don't you think?" Mother said.

"All wild animals, or just rattlesnakes?"

"All of them will be happier in their own homes."

"Even my baby skunks?"

"You have skunks?"

"Just four of them. Babies."

"Where do you keep them?"

"In a drawer."

"When did you get them?"

"Yesterday."

"Don't you think their mommy skunk is worrying about them?"

"I don't know."

"Yes, you do. If somebody took you away, I would be awfully sad and frightened."

"The babies are not scared. They like me."

"I'm sure they do, but what are you going to feed them?"

I had a ready answer. "Vegetables."

"They're not old enough for vegetables. They need their mother's milk. Do you know what will happen if they don't get their milk?"

"I could give them goat milk."

"It's not the same. Baby skunks need skunk milk."

"Will they die?"

"Most certainly."

I thought about that for a few minutes.

"We should take them back to their mommy skunk."

"Good idea," Mother said.

We carried the four baby skunks, one in each hand, out to the empty house we used for grain storage. The skunks lived under the porch. After we put the babies down near the steps where I found them, we walked away to a place where we could watch. Right away the mother skunk came out, looked around, sniffed her babies, decided they were hers in spite of the human stink. She scolded them back under the house. What fun! Mother and I laughed and laughed.

Mother had a way with animals, the affinity, as I have said before, even with reptiles and birds. She would sit real still and sparrows would fly down and perch on her shoulders, like they do on old Saint Francis statues. She could tell how animals were feeling or what they were going to do. She could calm them down with gentle words when they were scared or nervous. But she couldn't read their minds, or actually talk to them.

I could.

Yep, I "talked" to animals. The animals didn't talk back to me, don't be silly, because they haven't lips and teeth and the other things they would need to make human words. Right? What I mean is, I could sort of *blink* myself inside their minds, sometimes, and understand them, sometimes, usually in flashes of pictures or smells, but sometimes the animals would think almost like humans, and sometimes they would remember things that happened to them, mostly bad things. When I tried to explain what I was trying to do, Vic Tretheway said I was "strange as fur on a worm." Vic comes up with the funniest things.

Suranjini told me I was anthropomorphizing. She said there was no way for people to know *how* animals think, or even *if* they think at all. Suri should ride along inside of my head for a few minutes. She is a lot smarter than me, but she doesn't know diddlypoop about animals.

When wild creatures learned to trust me, I could usually make them do what I wanted. Not like special dog tricks, of course, but even wild animals would do simple things if I told them, things like "go away" or "stay out of the corn." I learned real quick not to say "come here" to every animal I met, because I never knew what a cougar, for instance, might do. Deer were okay, beavers were gentle, squirrels were totally crazy, but brave and funny.

My favorite wild animal? Wood rats. Old timers called them "pack rats" because they were always stealing bits and pieces and packing them away. Why? Decorating! Once, I opened up a gigantic pack rat midden. It was amazing, filled with pieces of glass and metal, shiny rocks, and pretty feathers. Positively artistic, you might say.

Nobody else knows this, but I will tell you a secret about pack rats. They are smart, really, really smart, much smarter than they should be because their brains are so, so tiny. Pack rats think more like people than any other animal, one thought and another thought and another thought, all in a line, like a story. One summer, I made two pack rat friends and gave them people names. I called one of them Scamper and the other one Scurry. They recognized their names, and they even had a name for me; not words, but a picture. If I had to put my wood-rat-picture-name into words, it would be "Big Blue Eyes." I was Big Blue Eyes. I liked that. Wouldn't you? Scamper and Scurry were my best wild animal friends. I also got to know their kits, but those little fuzzies were too young to have anything interesting going on.

I learned many other secrets about the animals, those who lived on the farm and those who lived in the forest beyond. Orphaned baby squirrels? Other squirrels will adopt them. No fooling. Goats have accents. Cows have best friends for life. There are so many astonishing things to know about animals. Sometimes I even get flits and flashes from birds, or maybe a snatch of something like a bird-song-that-is-also-a-moving-picture. How can I describe it? Think about the last light of sunset, the minute when everything turns pink. Pink sky, pink clouds, pink trees. You are sitting on a pink rock looking down at a pink pond. Take a pink pebble in your pink fingers and drop it into the pink water. Pink splash is the prettiest pink sound you ever heard. Pink ripple-song spreading in all directions. Listen and imagine. That's kind of like what a bird song *looks* like.

Now I will tell you about reptiles. Here's something you will find hard to believe. I understand snakes. Just a little bit, like an echo or a whisper from far away. Rattlers and kings, mostly, the bigger snakes, who are just sort of *there*, not evil or mean-spirited, just *there*, and aware of themselves, buzzing "*I Am I Am I Am*" all the time, like we sometimes chant "*So'ham So'ham So'ham*," which means the same thing. Wouldn't it be funny if snakes were highly evolved spirits getting ready to incarnate as people?

You know another animal I especially like?

Bears.

Chapter Ten

Janabai and the Bear

I didn't notice Max leaning against the tent pole. She's creepy that way. One moment she's not around; the next moment she's looking over your shoulder.

"Jana Bee, Jana Boo, how you hanging?"

"By a slender thread," I retorted.

"Over a bubbling caldron of sulfurous fire?" she embellished.

"Like a fat ugly spider."

"Oorah," she said.

"Max, whadda ya want?" I'm in one of those skin-crawly snits where there is no such thing as a comfortable position. Sarcastically, I ask, "How can I help you, *Maxine*?"

"Just checking on you, Jana *Bai*. What are you writing about this morning?"

"Bears."

"Bears?"

"About the first time I met a bear face-to-face."

"Out in the west meadow beyond Little Deer Creek?"

"Exactly! How did you know?"

"Your mother and I watched the whole episode."

"You did? Tell me about it."

"Oh no, this is your story."

"Please, Max, please, purple please with pleasing sauce, tell me your version of 'Janabai and the Bear.'"

Max, inveterate bullshitter, needed no further inducement.

"Well, let me clear off this convenient oil drum, and there upon deposit my aging but still attractive ass cheeks. Ah. Better. So, here we go. Your mother and I were hunting..."

"Mother hates hunting," I interrupted.

"Indeed she do, but she's always up for shooting her little pop gun, so I dragged her along without too much argument for some 'target practice.' We were up in the rocks above the meadow. Your mother, who was stretched out on her belly, watched the bear through the sniper scope, whilst I knelt beside her, spotting.

"'What kind is it?' yo mama asked me.

"'Black bear.'

"'It's brown.'

"'It may be brown, but it's still a black bear.'

"'Are you sure? Maybe it's a grizzly.'

"'Whatever you say, mighty woods woman.'

"'Don't be cheeky,' yo mama said. 'Okay, it's a brown black bear.'

"'Black bears come in all colors, but this bear does look a bit like a grizzly.'

"'Boar?'

"'Yeah, way too big for a sow.'

"'How far away is he?'

"'I'd guess six hundred yards. Just for practice, I'm going to adjust your elevation.'

"I bent over and made an adjustment on her scope.

"'And correct your windage, just a hair.'

"'What kind of hair?'

"'Funny girl.'

"I made the windage adjustment.

"'Why is he just standing there?' yo momma asked.

"That's when I saw you, Janabai.

"'Slowly, swing to your right,' I said.

"Your mother swung the rifle.

"'What? I don't see anything.'

"'A bit more, and up a bit. The gray rock pile.'

"'I got the rock pile.'

"'Now raise up,' I told her. 'Tell me what you see.' Suddenly, the world froze!"

"The world *froze*? *Suddenly*?"

"Just injecting a bit of drama, now be quiet."

"And then what happened to the suddenly frozen world?"

"Your mother couldn't breathe. All she could whisper was, '*Janabai!*'"

"'Yes,' I said, 'That is your daughter sitting on yonder rock.'

"'Does the bear see her?' she asked.

"'Oh,' I said, 'he sees her alright.'

"'*Janabai,*' she repeated.

"'Yes, we've already cleared up that point. Tell me what Janabai is doing.'

"'Talking.'

"'Talking? Talking to who?'

"'To whom.'

"'To whom. To whom is Janabai, your daughter, talking?'

"'She's talking to the bear.'

"'The big black almost-grizzly bear?'

"'Now she's climbing down off the rock and walking toward the bear.'

"'Okay, girlfriend,' I said, getting serious, 'This is the real show. Put the scope back on the bear and get ready to take your shot when I tell you.'

"'I'm back on the bear. Where do I put the shot?'

"'Right behind the shoulder where you can't miss. I'm going to release your safety.'

"'He's moving toward her.'

"'Right. I'll watch her. You just keep that scope tight on the bear.'

"'The bear's stopped.'

"'So has Janabai,' I confirmed. 'Stay on the bear.'

"'What's she doing?'

"'More talking. She's holding out her hands to him.'

"'I see the bear sniffing the air. I don't think he's going to hurt her.'

"'Horseshit. Get ready to take the shot.'

"'Not yet.'

"'Azriel, you need to take the shot. Ready? Do it now. Take the goddamn shot!'

"'Not yet. The bear's just standing there waiting. He's not making any threat.'

"'You don't even know what *kind* of bear it is, and now you're an expert on threat displays?'

"'I don't want to kill him if I don't have to. I'm going to wait until the last minute.'

"'This is the last minute… oh fuck.'

"'I know, I know, I've got both of them in the scope.'

"'What's she doing?'

"'Holding out her hand. The bear's smelling her. Now she's dropped down on her knees. The bear has his nose right on Janabai's face. I think she's laughing.'

"'God, I hope she doesn't try to touch him.'

"'She's touching him. She's scratching the bear behind the ears.'

"'What's he doing?'

"'Kind of twisting his head from side to side. Wait. He's stopped.'

"'Janabai's standing up, leaning over him. What is she doing?'

"'I can't tell. She's looking at something on his head. She's taking something off him, from behind his ear. I think she just pulled off a tick. She's showing it to him. He's sniffing it. He's rubbing his muzzle against her.'

"'Oh my god, does she have her arms around his neck? Is that what I'm seeing?'

"'That's what you're seeing. Janabai and Pooh, only Pooh weighs four hundred pounds.'

"Your mother lowered the rifle.

"'If I tried to shoot now, I'd be just as likely to hit her.'

"'You are crazy, you know, not taking the shot when you had the chance.'

"'Maybe. Give me a hand. I'm cramped up.'

"'Where?'

"'My wrist. Probably would have missed the shot anyway.'

"From a half mile away, we watched the bear lumber into the forest.

"'Can you make out what my daughter is doing?'

"'She seems to be imitating the bear. She's pretty good at it.'

"'Hmmmm,' yo mama hmmmmed, and that's the end of the story. Wipe the smile off your face, Janabai. Your mother should have taken the shot."

"Well, why didn't she?"

"I think Azriel was just figuring out that you had special juju with the animals. I mean, everybody knew you were good with the dogs and livestock, just like your mother, something you inherited from her, a natural gift, but your mother was beginning to suspect that you possessed something more, something beyond her, something supernatural. Maybe you been *changed* by the Big Kablooey."

"Mutated?"

"Yes, you were born an abnormal monster."

"Abomination in the sight of the Lord?"

"Precisely. Unclean creature of unnatural powers."

"Well, thanks, Max. You have really cheered me up. I feel so much better."

"My work here is done."

Chapter Eleven

Nibble, Nibble, Little Mouse

WHEN I WASN'T PULLING TICKS off bears, I was learning to read and write like any other Shiva Puri kid, but I have to tell you—well I don't *have* to tell you, but I'm *going* to tell you, false modesty is just more ego—I taught myself how to read by hanging around Dad, literally hanging around him, from his neck, slung onto his chest in a bag.

"Baby Larva" Dad says. He's here this morning, if you hadn't guessed, helping me with this part of The Book.

Yes, Baby Larva, in my snug cocoon. When I was tired, Dad would turn me around so we were chest-to-chest, with my soft little head under his chin. I would go to sleep, warm and comfortable, smelling his Dad smell, while he went about his duties. Most of the time he turned me outward so I was looking at whatever he was doing. My eyes came into focus the first month, so Dad bragged, and by the time I was three months old I was already "studying life in Shiva Puri." Dad called me the "World's Youngest Village Manager." Later, when I could sit up by myself, I perched on his lap or crawled under his feet while he worked on Shiva Puri business. You wouldn't think a village of two hundred people would need a lot of management, but you would be wrong. Dad, calling himself the "Big Spider," sat in the middle of his web, writing reports and calculating calories. Even with other council members doing their parts, Galen for the farm, Simone for stores, Olivia in the kitchen, Mother with security, and the Devi family with science, my father had to keep everyone moving ahead, the boss of just about everything in my childhood world.

One day I looked at the words on his papers and pretended I was reading.

"Hmmm," I said, just like he did, and pulled at the skin of my neck, just like he did.

"Do you have an opinion?" Dad asked.

"What do these words say?"

"Dairy Goat Production. Today I am going to calculate the dairy for the whole winter. Are you going to help me?" he asked.

"Yes, Daddy."

"Hmmm. How many gallons can we expect from the Alpines before the first snow?"

"I don't know!"

"The answer is right here on this paper. What do the words say?"

"Daddy! I can't read all the big words."

"Would you like to?"

"Ever so much."

"Okay. Break time. Let's go to the library and see if we can find some words just your size."

"The liberry? I've never been there."

"About time you started."

"I'm scared."

"Sacred of what, honeycomb?"

41

"Miss Pee-wee-skee."

"Odessa Piwinski, the librarian? Why?"

"She's a witch. She eats little kids."

"Who told you that?"

"Alma."

"Alma McGartland?"

"Uh huh."

Alma McGartland was three years older than me and liked to pick on smaller kids. Scaring me about Odessa Piwinski was just the beginning of the torments Alma would afflict during our childhood together.

"Miss Piwinski is not a witch. She's a nice lady."

Dad was stretching the compliment a teensy bit. Odessa Piwinski was many things, most of them admirable, but "nice lady" was not the first description that comes to mind. She was severe and stubborn, in the noble tradition of her profession, or so everyone believed, and she never married. Piwinski was one of the few elders who survived the Rakshasa sickness. People said when the demon came for her, she grabbed him by the ears and shook him until he begged for mercy. Could be true; she was tough as an old boot.

We walked down the street to a small building, now the village library, Dad holding my hand, me taking two giant steps to his one man step.

"Before you take home one of her books," he said, "Miss Piwinski is going to ask if you know your *ABC's*."

"I know my *ABC's*," I said.

"We better practice anyway, just to be sure. Ready?"

"Ready."

"Okeydokey, slow and pokey, let's go."

We stomped along, splashing through the puddles, shouting the alphabet with each stomp, the ancient melody that will probably be sung forever.

"*A-B-C-D-E-F-G, H-I-J-K, ELLEMENOHPEE, Q-R-S, T-U-V,* DOUBLEYOU *X, Y,* AND *Z.* Now I've said my *ABC's.* Next time won't you sing with me?"

"Perfect," Dad said, "I think you're ready."

We arrived at the library.

"What does it say?" I asked, pointing to a sign on the wall.

"Century 21 Resort Properties," he answered.

"What's that?"

"Stuff from the olden days. Doesn't mean anything now."

"How come?"

"No more real estate."

"What's that?"

"You are mighty inquisitive today."

"What's *inquisitive*?"

"It means curious, like George the monkey. Would you like me to get *Curious George* from the library for your bedtime story?"

"No," I said, "*Curious George* is a BABY BOOK."

"Alright, no *Curious George*, something more grown up for my big girl."

"Dad?"

"Yes?"

"What's real estate?"

"Do you ever forget anything? Real estate is houses. When people buy and sell houses."

"That's silly," I said. "Everybody has a house."

"Everybody does now."

"We had a house in the olden days, Mother says we had a house."

"Yes, your mommy and I had a house, a nice house with flowers and a bird named Benson, who could talk just like people."

"What did the Benson say?"

"He would say, 'Benson is a pretty bird,' and things like that."

"Like what?"

"Like, 'Let's find Janabai a grown-up book to read.'"

"Benson didn't say that."

"He didn't? Are you sure? I think I remember him saying exactly those words."

"Stop teasing. I wasn't even here."

"You weren't?" Dad scratched his head. "Where were you?"

I was confused. Where was I? Where was I before I was born?

"I was in Mother's stomach," I said.

"You were? How long were you in there?"

"A long time."

"Where were you before?" he asked.

I thought some more. "I was over the mountain."

"Ah," he said. "That's right! I forgot. You were over the mountain. What were you doing over there?"

Now that was a hard question. What was I doing over the mountain before I was born? I scrunched my face real tight. Scrunching helps draw forth reluctant memories.

"I was crying."

"Oh no. Why were you crying?"

"I was scared."

"You were? What were you scared of?"

"The tiger."

"The tiger?"

"The tiger was swimming through the air real slow and looking at me with his yellow eyes."

Dad stopped fast like he had been jerked back on a leash.

"A tiger? A tiger with yellow eyes?"

"His eyes were all glowy and creepy."

"Well, I guess so. Then what happened?"

"He would come close to me and show me all of his teeth. He had two giant teeth that came down like this." I demonstrated by making big fangs at the corner of my mouth with my fingers.

"Yikes," he said. "What did you do?"

"I called you, and you came and scared the tiger away and took me home and put me in Mother's stomach."

He smiled and knelt down in front of me. "Yes, I did. That's exactly what I did. I put you in your mommy's stomach until it was time for you to come out and be my little girl. Since I'm down here, you might as well give your dad a hug around the neck."

"How come?"

"Because your dad wants a hug, and you give the best hugs in the whole world."

While I was giving my father his hug, I saw a face peering out at us from the library window.

"Dad! Dad!"

"What?"

"The witch!"

The library door swung open and a wavery voice whispered, "Nibble, nibble, little mouse. Who is nibbling on my house?"

CHAPTER TWELVE

The Liberry

I SHRIEKED AND HID BEHIND MY father. "The witch! Don't let her eat me!"

Dad stood there shaking his head and rolling his eyes.

"Well come on in out of the rain," said Miss Piwinski. "I ate sooooooo many little children for breakfast."

"Just stop it," Dad said.

"I'm too full to eat this sweet thing."

"She's terrified," he said.

"No I'm not," I said, peering around his leg. "She's just fooling me."

Miss Piwinski winked at Dad. "Full of beans, isn't she?"

"You have no idea."

"Both of you sit down on the bench and take those muddy shoes off. I'll get you a towel. You can't come in here dripping all over my floor."

Odessa Piwinski protected her books like they were her own kids, if she had some kids, which she didn't. Before she allowed you to peruse the inner mysteries of her labyrinth, you had to remove your shoes in the mud room and show her your hands. Not clean enough? You did not get by her until they were.

"Go wash those grimy paws in the basin, and be sure you dry them well."

My first books, the beloved stories that taught me how to read, were *Goodnight Moon*, *Are You My Mother?*, and, yes, *Curious George*, which was fun for me to read to myself even though I had outgrown it as a bedtime story. I remember figuring out my first big words: "century," because Dad had shown it to me on the sign outside, and "library," a hard word for a kid because it should be spelled "liberry," like strawberry, which is how I spelled it the first time when I took a can of red paint and finger-painted "Liberry" at the bottom of the sign "Century 21 Resort Liberry," and made a mess of the sign, not to mention my hands and my clothes. Odessa says I was about four years old. She sent me to fetch my Dad. I thought I was in big trouble.

The next day Dad came back with Myron Jefferson, who was still a teenager, but already the best painter in the village. Myron painted over the entire sign with several coats of whitewash. When the paint was dry, he lettered, perfect and pretty in red and yellow, the words "New Shiva Puri Archives," and below in smaller black letters, "Odessa Piwinski, Librarian." He covered it with a tarp so nobody could see it, especially Miss Piwinski. Everybody in the village came the next day for the unveiling. When he pulled off the tarp, people caught their breath, clapped, and cheered. Miss Piwinski just broke down and cried. I was alarmed. Miss Piwinski should be happy, not sobbing her head off.

Myron's sign was more than just a library sign; it was an emblem of our future, our badge of courage. If we could have a library with red and gold words proclaiming our faith to the world, and to the gods, and to ourselves, wondrous times were still to come.

After the unveiling, no one could walk past the sign without smiling and feeling better.

CHAPTER THRITEEN

Pattycake's Club

E IGHT TEACHERS RAN OUR SHIVA Puri school. There were three grades, Littles, Middles, and Bigs, each with one teacher and one assistant. Patty Bose was in charge of the preschool, Pattycake's Club, and she also assumed the duties of principal. Her assistant was Robin Campbell, whom the kids called Miss Arcy (R. C.). Patty Bose was called Mama Patty, or Mama Pat, or Pattycake, by everyone, kids and grown-ups alike.

When I wasn't hanging around the library, "working" for Miss Piwinski, and reading my way through the stacks, or out in the pastures helping my Bannerjee "uncles" with the goats, I was in Pattycake's Club looking out for my sister. We twins might have been First Born, but by the time we started going to school, there were six other kids who arrived after the Event. Those Pattycake Club kids were Kelsey Raines (Taylor and Lindsay Raines were good at making babies), Bryce Chowdary, Nicole Loera, Evan Grunsky, Praveen Mehta, Masha Kolupaeva, and my best friend, Kavitha Bose, who had been born just before the Event.

Parents could leave their kids at Pattycake's or take them to work as they pleased. Club was full of kids during planting season and sparser during the winter when the parents were indoors to look after them. Mostly we played around at Club. It was not exactly a school, but we had plenty of singing and art and exercise and stories. We also had Healing lessons just like they did in the higher grades.

The big Healing lesson in Club was "Run! Find a Grown-up!"

I was Pattycake's big helper. She got me to read to the little kids and "keep an eye" on them, especially Mirabai, who liked to be around other children, even if she couldn't read or write. Excepting Alma Mendez McGartland, the Puri kids were sweet as pie to my blind sister. They ignored her disabilities and included her in play as much as possible. Whenever Max wasn't hauling

Mira around like a sack of turnips, I was responsible for her. I didn't mind. I liked being in charge of things, especially my first best friend, Kavitha Bose. Vitha, as everybody called her, was an infant when her parents died in the Rakshasa. Mama Pat adopted her and gave her the pretty name Kavitha because the baby's birth mother never spoke before she died. So, Mama Pat became Kavitha's "real" mother. We did everything together, me and Vitha, but I was the boss, even though she was almost a year older.

"You have to do whatever I tell you," I informed her.

"How come?"

"Because my mother is Azriel Dancer and my dad is the manager of the village, so I get to be the manager of you."

She scrunched up her nose, but had no argument to refute my logic.

Chapter Fourteen

Dear Old Golden School Days

AFTER SWELTERING IN THE FIELDS, working alongside the adults, we kids looked forward to the first day of school. Shiva Puri classes started in late autumn after the last crops were put up, after the roofs were swept of leaves and debris, after every log was stacked and covered, after all the equipment was cleaned and oiled, after the shutters were hung and the cracks caulked, after the doors were barred against the winter wind; then and only then did the children of Shiva Puri have time for study. As our sunburned bodies healed, our exhausted muscles refreshed, our flagging spirits restored, the teachers met in secret to think up wonderful new ways to teach us wonderful new things. First day of school! First day in the Littles! No more Pattycake's Club for

Janabai Burke-Kucinich! Six years old-almost, I am a Little! What a great day! Oh joy! Joy! Joy!

Kavitha, seven years old-almost, decided to wait for me so we could start school together as first year Littles. That decision made by a child might seem precocious, except that Kavitha's mother was Mama Pat, the school principal, which made Kavitha's urgent *need* to stay back with me a matter of bedtime conversation between the seven-year-old-almost and her mother, who spoiled her rotten.

Having engineered this artful feat, Vitha and I planned to make a big splash on the first day of school, a grand entrance with lots of makeup and stylish, grown-up hairdos. We would be Glamour Ladies. Giggling in the backroom of the "Liberry," we thumbed through faded magazines from olden times. The magazine we liked best was called *People*.

"I want to look just like Katy Perry," I said. "She has the smoothest hair."

"I want to look like Bee Yonce," Vitha said, "because she's tall and brown like me."

"Her hair is blond and smooth. You can't be Bee Yonce. Your hair is all black and crinkly."

"You could make it smooth," she giggled, "with some scissors."

What clever girls were we!

"Okay," I said, "but these scissors are pretty dull."

"Ow!"

"They don't cut straight."

"Ow!"

"What's wrong?"

"You're hurting me."

"Well your hair is tough and clumpy."

"Just be softer."

"Oopsy."

"What? What happened?"

After cutting Kavitha's hair, my handiwork left her less a beauty queen and more a frog with mange.

"We need a fancy dog," Kavitha said, "like the one Bee Yonce has in the *People*."

"Let's make Mirabai our dog!" I said.

"Goofy from comic books!"

We did our best to turn Mirabai into Goofy by painting her nose black and cutting off all of her hair except two hanks on each side we bound up to be Goofy's ears, the effect quite odd; and Mirabai, who of course let us do whatever we wanted, flapped her ears from side to side just like Goofy, a pantomime we thought terrifically funny. And after all these years I still think it was hilarious, but it never occurred to me at the time to wonder how my sister knew what dogs looked like flapping their ears.

Laughter and cheers greeted our grand entrance into the classroom, causing quite an uproar and launching our reputation for hijinks. Ted Kealoha was the teacher for the Littles. Everyone called him Mistah Tee. When he first saw his new students, Mistah Tee threw his head back and howled.

"Well, now," he said after composing himself, "who do we have here?"

"A frog!"

"A frog?" Try to imagine his expression. "What kind of a frog are you with all of those hair bumps on your head?"

"Just a regular frog."

"What about the bumps?"

"Oh, Jana just put them there to be funny."

"Funny?"

"Mmm mmm," Kavitha nodded. "I wanted to be Bee Yonce, but Janabai couldn't make my hair smooth no matter how much she cut off."

Mistah Tee squeezed his lips together, trying not to laugh.

"So I told her I would be a frog with lots of warts on my head, and my hair is *warts*," Kavitha said. "That's the funny part."

And he let loose. I don't think I ever heard a man laugh as loud, as long, as jolly as Mistah Tee on the first morning of school.

Mama Patty rushed in to see about the commotion. She raised her hands in the air.

"What's going on in here?"

Mistah Tee pointed to Kavitha, Patty's *daughter*, just in case that important point slipped your mind.

Mama Patty took those hands she had left hanging in the air and covered her mouth in horror.

"What. Have. You. Done?"

Mistah Tee sputtered, "She thinks her hair bumps are... are... fuh... fuh..." He couldn't get the word out before he was having another fit.

"FUNNY!" I yelled. "He thinks her bumps are FUNNY."

"Oh yeah, *wahine*, you one fine funny frog," Mistah Tee said in his cornball Hawaiian accent, a peculiar pidgin talk we would come to love.

Mama Patty didn't see one funny thing about it, and whirled out of the room, shaking her head.

Mistah Tee turned his attention to me. "Now who do we have here?" He looked me over head to foot, spending a long time examining my butchered blue curls.

"I'd say... I'd say... Hmmmm. A movie star?"

What! How did he guess? I knew nothing about movies, and I still don't, except from pictures in old magazines, but one "movie star" had smooth blue hair, and I liked the way she looked. That's not exactly what Kavitha, my personal beautician, achieved. To tell the truth, with my blue painted hair hacked into spikes, enormous dangling earrings, and grotesque red lip-sticked mouth, I looked more like a Curious George in makeup than a Glamour Lady. How did Mistah Tee get from blue-haired monkey to movie star? Was he a mind reader? All those years, I kept forgetting to ask him, until... until... oh bother, you know what's coming... until it was too damn late.

"And who is this?" he asked, turning to Mirabai.

"This is my little dog," I answered.

"Does she speak for herself?"

"No, silly, she's a *dog*."

"Oh."

Mirabai barked.

She didn't bark like a human being barks, trying to sound like a dog. She barked just the way Hanuman did when he smelled something he didn't like, big boomers that rattled your ears, big bass HOO HOOs improbably erupting from the throat of an almost-six-year-old blind girl.

"My my!" Mistah Tee said. "That's a lot of bark. Can you tell me your name?"

Mirabai smiled and scratched her belly like she had a flea.

"Her name's Goofy," I said.

"Well, Goofy, you go curl up over near the stove and stay warm, and you two beauties (meaning me and Kavitha) find a seat in the front where I can keep an eye on you. Noah Stickles and Kalina Simms," he said to two of the older kids, "remove yourselves backward into the seats we reserve for you Important Second Year Littles. Please, everyone, let's have a round of applause for the Second Year Dignitaries." We had no clue what he meant, but we clapped wildly. Already I loved Mistah Tee and his merry classroom.

"Now, how do we start the first day of school?" He fluttered his fingers. "I think... I think... maybe we should begin with... with... a... ?"

All the Second and Third Year Littles shouted out, "Song!"

"A song?" he asked, amazed anyone could think of such a wonderful thing. "Well, I tink dat one fine idee."

"Clementine!" someone yelled from the back of the room. I looked over my shoulder to the corner where we hung our coats.

Alma Mendez. What's going on? Alma was supposed to move up to the Middles. *Not fair!* A sentiment shared by both Alma and me.

When Kavitha and Mirabai and I joined Mistah Tee's class, the kids already there were Noah Stickles, Robert McGartland, Kalina Simms, George Sunkari, Hannah Reed, Jian "Gene" Cheng, and Jeremy Raines. The Raineses, as I have said, were baby-making machines. And... Alma Mendez McGartland.

Held back with the Littles in the hope fresh rain would fall on the bleak desert of her misery, Alma was far behind in reading and writing. Almost ten years old, and five feet two inches tall, Alma was now the oldest of the Littles. More significant to me, she was the biggest and meanest. The only good thing about Alma, in my opinion, was her truancy. She came to class when she felt like it, and rarely participated, which was why Mistah Tee was quick to seize upon her suggestion.

"Clementine!" he affirmed. "Da best kine song!"

We all liked "Clementine," especially the part about "ruby lips above the water, blowing bubbles, soft and fine, but alas, I was no swimmer, and I lost my Clementine."

> *"Oh my darling, oh my darling,*
> *Oh my darling, Clementine,*
> *You are lost and gone forever,*
> *Dreadful sorry, Clementine!"*

The last syllable hung sorrowfully in the air. Our woeful warble concluded, we readied ourselves for whatever musical wonders came next... except for Alma Mendez, who continued to rock from side to side, eyes closed, entranced by Darling Clementine's watery fate. Unaccompanied, Alma crooned her own reprise of the chorus.

> *"You are lost and gone forever,*
> *Dreadful sorry, Clementine!"*

In the silence that followed her solo performance, Alma opened her eyes to find us staring at her, open-mouthed and astonished. Taking the opportunity to cement my newly-forged reputation as class comedienne, I, Janabai Burke-Kucinich, Princess of Shiva Puri, and totally full of myself, piped in with, "Oh, Alma, are you having a BABY?"

Obligingly, everybody laughed. Alma stood there, face flushed, red, mottled splotches on her cheeks, her breath coming hard and fast.

"A baby?" she asked, bewildered by my question.

The laughter died away.

"That's what you sound like." I mocked with exaggerated agony, "CLEMENTINNNE!"

Alma rushed to the door, and stopped, turned, fixed me with one last expressionless look. Then she was gone. I waited, expecting my... what? Applause? Cheers of adoration for my dazzling wit? I got nothing. The other kids picked up writing boards and chalk, or found some small task to look busy. Most wouldn't meet my eyes. I turned to Mr. T. He just shook his head.

Now it was my turn to blush. In the awkward, unbearable silence, I looked to Kavitha for rescue. She did not disappoint me. Folding her hands against her chest as if in prayer, she sang, ever so sweetly,

> *"How I missed her!*
> *How I missed her,*
> *How I missed my Clementine,*
> *So I kissed her little sister,*
> *And forgot my Clementine."*

Everyone applauded. Mistah Tee grinned. I sat down, my disgrace averted, or at least postponed. Did I imagine for one moment that Alma Mendez was going to forget?

She got to me on the playground, formerly a tennis court next to the old Clio Golf Club. A chain-link fence separated the Little's playground from an adjacent field used by the older kids for soccer. Alma was on the other side of the fence. She called me over to show me a "secret."

"Come over here, Prissy."

"Why?" I was just six years old, but I was not stupid.

"So we can be friends. It's the Shiva Puri way, that's what your Dad says."

She was right. That's exactly what he said. Maybe this would be okay after all. And besides, there was a strong fence between us.

"I caught a lizard," Alma said, "with yellow stripes and a blue tail. It's called a skink. Have you ever seen one?"

I could tell Alma was holding something in her closed hand. I went over to the fence. Alma held her fist next to the wire and whispered.

"Get real close and I'll open my hand."

I put my face up to one of the holes in the wire. Slowly Alma opened her fingers. There was nothing in her hand. I started to say something, when Alma poked me in the eye with a stiff finger. Scared and stunned, I fell back on my rear end on the ground and began screaming my head off. Nobody ever tried to hurt me before. I was, Alma got that part right, a bit of a princess.

Mama Pat ran over and picked me up, checked me over, and took me inside, giving Alma a dark look over her shoulder. Mama Pat put a wet cloth on my eye and sent Marylouise, her assistant, to find Alma's mother, Sally McGartland, who complained Alma wouldn't listen to her, defied her, and walked out on her whenever she tried to "make a correction." Mama Pat told her to "keep trying." Sally McGartland, as skittery as she was tenderhearted, proved useless, and she was, truth be told, frightened of her adopted daughter.

For good reason.

CHAPTER FIFTEEN

The Littles

MISTAH TEE HAD NO CLASSROOM experience, but Lord Shiva, that man could sing and play the ukulele! He knew all the old Hawaiian songs, and when the weather was nice, he would take us out to the rocks by the river and teach music when we were supposed to be learning how to read and write. Together we would sing:

Aloha oe, Aloha oe
E ke ona ona noho i ka lipo
One fond embrace
A ho 'i a 'e au
Until we meet again

Saraswati! With Ted Kealoha in the lead, we Littles could sing! I didn't have much of a voice myself, but I loved every minute of those musical outings, knowing my classmates would carry me along.

Alma got her revenge, saying, "Where's the pain, Princess Prissy? Are you having a COW?"

"Splutz to you, Alma Mendez. I already know how to read and write better than you do, and it is ever more entertaining to sing with Mistah Tee than to do makeup work in Mama Pat's office like poor, dumb, nasty Alma McGARTLAND!"

No, I didn't actually say that. Not to her face. Not where she could hear.

But I can write about it now, how I felt about Alma, and about the Littles, and what we did in Puri school while outside our warm school room the long white winter drifted down on us. And of course, about Mistah Tee, the greatest teacher who ever lived in the universe.

Marianne Conroy, his assistant, was called Miss Conroy. That's the way she wanted it, no sweet nickname for her, nuh-uh, no "Miss Cee" for her! Miss Conroy disapproved of Mistah Tee's methods, but she always had her undies twisted up. That's unkind, and I apologize. Truth be told, if there was any "real" teaching going on, it was Miss Conroy who was doing it. She wasn't the most lovable person, but because of her devotion to teaching wild animals like us, I am able to write these words, so thank you, Miss Conroy; and let me add, years later, after we had become friends, Marianne gave her life for us, so I say, blessings, blessings on you, Miss Conroy.

What else? I almost forgot! Running! At Mother's insistence, we Littles started each day running unless there was a blizzard blowing outside. Paying homage to Tarahumara Indians, Mother set out to create a village of runners who enjoyed running and were good at it. She anticipated a time in the years to come when running would be our principal transportation.

"By the end of this first year, I expect each of you Littles to run your age in miles," Mother said. "Kavitha, how old will you be on Planting Day?"

"Seven," Kavitha answered.

"I challenge you to run seven miles by the end of school."

"I can run seven miles right now," Kavitha said.

"We'll just have to see with our own eyes, right, Max?"

"Oorah," Max answered.

Max taught Little Boot Camp. It was supposed to be called "Emergencies," but Max called it Little Boot Camp, and after a while, so did everybody else. The first part was learning how to hide.

"If there's trouble, what do Yard Apes do?" Max hollered.

"Drop to the ground and STAY THERE," we Yard Apes hollered back.

"What do you do on the ground?"

"We HIDE," the kids shouted.

"Who do you hide with?"

"Our THREE BEST FRIENDS."

"Who are your THREE BEST FRIENDS?"

"DARKNESS!"

"STILLNESS!"

"SILENCE!"

We would scatter around the training field until Max fired into the air. Real bullets, real bangs. She wanted us to learn what gunfire sounded like, and not to panic when we heard it. One eye blink after shooting, we dropped, and she better not see a kid anywhere, nor see the grass move, nor hear a sound. Nothing. We went to the ground and stayed there until Max whistled real loud with her fingers hooked in her mouth.

Little Boot Camp was like hide and seek, but serious, too. Max worried all the time about "bad guys" coming for us out of the forest, and especially about the *Kali Monster*, which we all knew was just a story to scare us into doing whatever she wanted, not that we dared say that to her face. Max didn't need made-up monsters to keep us in line. She was plenty scary all by herself, and if Max thought a kid was messing around, well, the kid hardly ever did it a second time.

Max was not the only Special Guest. Other adults came over to teach us Littles.

Lynda Cheng, the village medic taught Healing. These were her "medical" lessons for First Year Littles:

Send for Help if You Have a Friend to Send

Stop the Bleeding

Open the Air Passage

Cover for Shock

Go for Help If You're All Alone

Parker Adams, the boss weaver and Mistah Tee's partner, came over to teach painting, and penmanship, a skill highly valued at New Shiva Puri. Mr. Adams had been in the theatre before Shiva Puri. He was sweet and talented and sick. He tried to keep us from learning how sick he was, but we all knew it anyway. Mr. Adams was dying, but he still enjoyed being with the kids, and with me, in particular, with whom he shared an "essential fussiness," his little joke. Before he passed, three years later when I was nine, the two of us collaborated on several "fussy" endeavors.

Then there was my mother, Azriel Dancer, as she became known after the divorce. *I'll get to that later.* Mother taught Bush Craft. She taught us how to find water, how to stay warm, and how to get *un*-lost. She taught us that the sun rose in the east and set in the west. We learned to orient by going uphill, to find water by going downhill, and how to mark our trail with secret signs Max invented as fast as Mother needed them; and above all, she taught us how to stay calm and THINK for ourselves. "THINK!" was written in big letters on both sides of the door. We saw the THINK sign coming into the classroom, and the THINK sign going back out into the world.

THINK!

CHAPTER SIXTEEN

Goldilocks

WHICH IS EXACTLY WHAT I was *not* doing, THINKING, I mean, the afternoon I broke the most important rule for Shiva Puri kids: *Never go outside the wire.* It wasn't a real "wire" just an imaginary line we all learned to avoid. And beyond? Danger! Quicksand! Monsters!

We were exploring, Vitha and me, near Outpost 6, further away than we were supposed to go, but still, officially, "inside the wire." That's when I heard the rabbit scream. I knew what kind of animal it was because of the unmistakable "rabbitness" that exploded inside my head.

"Rabbit in trouble!"

"What rabbit?" Kavitha asked.

"Didn't you hear it?"

The rabbit screamed again, louder this time. In a single heartbeat, I *blinked* into the rabbit's head. Looking out through rabbit eyes, I saw what the little animal was seeing: a face, almost human, and something else, some kind of creature, with great curved teeth and glowing yellow eyes, coming down on me, closer, closer, the mouth stretching wide, hot, stinky breath, red pain, then… nothing.

Blink. I was back inside my own head.

"I'm going to save the rabbit."

I started running north, the direction I somehow knew would take me to the rabbit… and whoever, or whatever, was hurting it.

Behind me, Kavitha warned, "Don't go out there! We're not supposed to cross the wire!"

Over my shoulder, I saw her whirl and run back toward the village.

"I'm getting Max," she yelled, "and you are going to be in so much trouble!"

I slowed my hasty charge into the forbidden forest. Perhaps

I should practice the Boot Camp lessons we were learning from Max. Moving from cover to cover, low and hiding in the shadows cast by late afternoon sun, I tiptoed further into the bush, further away from safety.

Spotting a big sugar pine, I crept up behind it. Peeking around, I spied a girl a few years older and quite a bit bigger than me, a fairy-tale princess with a cascade of bright golden hair falling unclasped down her back to (almost) obscure her buttocks which were, I was surprised to see, quite naked, as was the rest of her, totally unclad but for that waterfall of blond curls. Her nakedness would have been strange enough by itself, but my shock at discovering such a remarkable sight was quite diminished by the ugly act in which the princess was engaged.

Squatting among the manzanitas, bare toes squishing into a pile of glistening entrails, the girl (whom I had immediately named "Goldilocks") was tearing a furry animal to pieces with her teeth and stuffing bloody gobbets of it into her mouth. Snapping bones, ripping sinews, smacking lips, and growls.

Then "Goldilocks" froze. I held my breath. Slowly, the flaxen-haired princess rose to her feet, cocked her head to one side, listened, sniffed the air, and, ever so slowly, turned toward me. For the first time, I got a clear look. The girl's mouth was decorated by a lipstick of bright red rabbit blood. Caught between crimson teeth, one greasy string of gristle hung to her chin. My sight slid down a glistening smear of gore over the girl's unexpectedly muscular chest, down over her smooth belly, and into a pubescent thatch of pubic hair out of which rose a stiff, upturned penis.

Not a girl! Uh-uh!

Growing up on a farm, I had seen my share of male privates, from goats to bulls, from my own dad's thing to the wee willies of my butt-naked playmates down at the swimming hole. But this boy's whackadoodie was pointed straight at me. Quite a different matter! Tearing my eyes away, I looked back up into her, rather, *his* face.

"Do you like what you see?" he hissed.

"Don't point that thing at me," I hissed back.

He looked down at himself, then back up at me, and grinned.

"Do you know who I am?"

"Some weirdo who ate a rabbit and got a stiffy."

Standing taller, the stranger seemed to expand in size. As if floating inches above the dirt, he drew closer.

"I am," he whispered, "Kali, Lord Enormity of Rakshasa Demons."

I put on my bravest face. "No such thing as Kali. Just a monster in a story to scare little kids."

He roared, "I am Eater of Worlds! Tiger of Lanka!"

I pulled my head back. Even from several feet away, his breath was awful. I wrinkled my nose, and said, "Well, Tiger of Lanka, put on some clothes. You look stupid."

His mouth fell open, his forehead crinkled in confusion. Again, he looked down at himself.

"Cover yourself up," I instructed as if I were his mother.

Having nothing but the dead rabbit head with which to conceal himself, he attempted to use that, a feeble effort I found quite funny. The raggedy remnant of the animal looked like a second ball sack, and the boy's tallywhacker, assailed by my howls of laughter, quickly deflated.

Goldilocks did not take kindly to my ridicule. He snarled, "Make ready, oh blue-throated goddess, for you are destined to be my wife."

"I'm not old enough to be a wife, and anyhow, I don't like you, and anyhow, I already got a boyfriend and he is a lot bigger and stronger than you."

"Look into my eyes."

"What's wrong with your eyes?"

The boy furrowed his brows. His eyes blazed with yellow fire. I found it impossible to look away.

"You will be mine," he said. "I will have you now and forever."

A ripple in the air, and somehow he was standing right in front of me, inches away, one hand around my throat. Not funny at all. I was truly frightened. I tried to think of something to say. Anything.

"I can't be your wife," I gasped, "because..."

"Because?"

"Because you didn't give me a wedding present."

For a moment he said nothing. I could see the thoughts whirring around behind those yellow eyes. Then he smiled and raised the dripping rabbit head in front of my face.

"Take this head as my token of love."

Having no choice, I took the rabbit head by the ears.

"Now kiss me to seal the bargain."

"No way," I said, trying to break his hold on my neck.

He leaned in closer.

"Kiss me."

I almost gave in, when I heard my name.

"Janabai!"

"It's Max," I said in relief. "Now you are really going to get it."

"Max? Mighty Max. The marine bitch?"

"We don't say that word at Shiva Puri."

Instantly he released his grip and flickered into something else, an animal, black and orange stripes, then flickered back into the golden-haired boy, then into a beast, huge and horrible, curved fangs like swords, blazing yellow eyes. He roared,

Aaaaaaaauuuuuuunnnnnn!

I squeezed my eyes shut and covered my ears.

———◆———

"Janabai."

Someone was shaking my shoulder. I opened my eyes. Max was there. And Mother.

Goldilocks had vanished.

Poof.

Max and Mother walked over to study the blood and guts by the manzanita bushes. When they turned their backs on me, I managed to hide the rabbit head under the sugar pine needles.

Why did I do that?

CHAPTER SEVENTEEN

Rabbit Head

ONCE AGAIN, MAX APPEARED LIKE magic, standing in the door of my tent. Once again, I didn't see her arrive, not surprising, Max padding around like she does, and me with my head down scribbling. I had sent G-Mek to fetch her because there was something I needed to say about the next part of the story, something I had been keeping secret since I was a little girl.

"I was wondering when you'd find the time to come by," I said with my best pout.

"I'm not your nurse."

"You did fine by Mirabai," I said.

"You're not your sister," Max said.

"True dat." I rolled my eyes.

Max threw her head back and howled. "You sound just like your mother." Her merriment was contagious.

"Stop it," I demanded. "Don't make me laugh. It hurts."

"Sorry, sport, I wouldn't want to cheer you up." Max pulled the barrel over next to the cot and sat. "So, what's on your mind?"

I paused. Well, am I going to do this or not? Okay, here we go.

"Do you remember the time Grimsman made animal ears for all us kids?"

"I remember you little Yoogies liked to play animals, always running around wearing animal parts, ears and tails and shit like that. Go on, tell the story, the way you remember it, and I'll help if I can."

Deep breath. Find a comfortable position. Not going to happen. Stop stalling.

"Okay. Grimsman was tanning deer hides, way out behind the alfalfa field."

"Where she hoped the stench wouldn't get into the village?"

"Right."

"Ah yes," Max said. "Now I'm beginning to remember. Continue."

"She was up to the elbows in a bucket, mashing deer brains into a pulp with her fists."

"Tiptoeing up behind her, I said, 'Whatcha doin', Grimsman?'

"She jumped, almost knocking over the bucket.

"'Don't do that!'

"'What?

"'Sneak up on me.'

"'Didn't mean to scare you.'

"'Yes you did, you little twerp.'

"I grinned. Grimsman shook her head in exasperation.

"'That's a funny word,' I said. 'Twerp. Twerp, twerp, I'm a little bird, twerp, twerp.'

"'You're a little bird, alright, a cuckoo bird.'

"'Cuckoo cuckoo,' I sang.

"'Cute, Janabai. What do you want?'

"'Like I said, whatcha doin,' *Grimsman*?'

"'Getting ready to tan this deer hide, if I can get some peace and quiet; and my name's Sandy.'

"'Max calls you *Grimsman*.'

"'Max is the boss. She can call me anything she wants. You, on the other hand, are a cuckoo bird, and you can call me Sandy.'

"'I like to call you *Grimsman*.'

"'Okay, okay, Janabai, whatever you say.'

"I stood up on my tiptoes.

"'What's this stuff?'

"'Deer brain.'

"I wrinkled my nose.

"'It stinks.'

"'It certainly does.'

"'Why are you squishing it?'

"'I'm going to use it on this hide.'

"I looked from the bucket of brain to a deer hide hanging limp over a piece of PVC water pipe. I gave the woman a skeptical look.

"'Why?'

"'Makes it soft and keeps it from rotting and smelling bad.'

"'Can I help squish?'

"'Sure. Put down whatever you are... what is that?'

"'Rabbit head.'

"'Rabbit head? Where did you get it?'

"Max, this is the part I need to tell you about, the part you don't know. I started to tell Sandy about how I got it from a boy with yellow eyes who called himself a demon, and how I hid it from you and Mother, but for some reason I didn't."

Max interrupted. "Why not, Janabai? Why didn't you tell us about the boy? Think of the heartache you might have saved yourself and everybody else."

"I know, I know. Don't rub it in. It has haunted me all these years. I knew he was... *wrong*. And dangerous. But there was something..."

"Something?"

"It's hard to explain. Like we were connected. Like he was important to me and I was important to him. And there was another thing."

"Which was?"

"I was just a little girl, but in that moment, in my heart of hearts, I wanted him to take me away and be my prince, my king, and I would be his."

"His what?"

"His... Goddess."

"Goddess?"

"It sounds so stupid, now, after all that's happened."

Max sat on the edge of my cot.

"It's not stupid, Jana. There are things in the new world, this Kali Yuga, that no one can explain; not me, or your mother, nobody. Mirabai, maybe, but probably not even her. Don't fret about it anymore. You said it. You got it out of your system. It happened just the way it had to happen. And now, here we are now, in this moment. Karma, right?"

"Karma. Thanks, Max, for listening."

"Sure thing, you bet. Now go on."

"Go on?"

"Finish the damn story."

"The story?"

"Okay. So you didn't tell Grimsman how you got the rabbit head. What did you say?"

"I lied. I told her I found it over by the ditch."

"'What happened to the rest of it?' Grimsman asked.

"'Maybe something ate it.'

"'I think you're right. Maybe a cougar.'

"'A coyote. I think I saw one this morning.'

"Another lie.

"'Maybe you did. They've been getting closer.'

"'How come?'

"'They want our chickens.'

"'They better not get near Hanuman.'

"'Or Jata. Now there's one dog that hates coyotes.'

"'Roger that.'

"Grimsman laughed. She had swallowed the whole fairy tale. She asked, 'What are you going to do with your rabbit head?'

"'Keep it.'

"'It's going to get maggots. Better throw it away.'

"'Can we tan it like a deer hide?'

"'I don't think so. We'd have to get all the skin off the skull, and when we finished it wouldn't look much like a rabbit.'

"'How about the ears? Can we keep the ears?'

"'Well, we could try. Maybe we could cure them.'

"'Let's do it, Grimsman. Let's cure up these ears.'

"'What will you do with them?'

"'Wear them.'

"'On your head?'

"'Of course, silly, where else would I wear them?'

"'Hanging off your elbows?'

"'You're funny.'

"'So I've been told. How come you want to wear rabbit ears on your head?'

"'So I can be a rabbit.'

"'Sounds like fun. How will you keep them from falling off?'

"'Maybe you can glue them?'

"'Won't work.'

"'Why not?'

"'The glue will get in your hair; then, when you have to take the ears off, the glue will pull your hair out, and it will hurt like hell.'

"'No it won't.'

"'It won't? Pray tell why.'

"'I'm going to leave them on for always.'

"'Don't think so. Annabel is not going to let you into the mandir wearing rabbit ears, I promise you. That's just for starters. You need to find a way to take them off whenever you like.'

"'Do you have any ideas?'

"Grimsman took a break from transforming the deceased deer's cerebellum into putrescent gunk.

"'As a matter of fact I do. Go find two hair clips, or one hair band, probably the hair band would work better. Go to Weavers' barn and finagle some thread and a big needle. Mind you, be careful not to lose the needle. Get some stiff wire.'

"'How much wire?'

"'As much as you are tall, or two wire coat hangers.'

"'Roger.'

"'Bring it all back to me after dinner, and I'll fix you up.'

"'You will?'

"'That's what I said. Now get going on your secret project.'

"'It's a secret?'

"'Shhhh. Do you want every kid in Shiva Puri to come around asking me for ears?'

"'Oh yes, Sandy, that would be wonderful! We could all get ears and tails and be animals of the forest. Wouldn't that be something?'

"'Lord Ganesha, what have I started?'"

Chapter Eighteen

Animal Manners

My circle of playmates, the youngest children at Shiva Puri, were called "Yoogies" by the older children because we were born *after* the events of the Kali "Yuga." We Yoogies played outdoors, games recognizable to kids from olden times: jump rope, hopscotch, building forts, hambone and patty cake, kick the can, hide-and-go-seek, and pretend.

Our favorite pretend game was Animal Manners, a great play I invented and for which I was the director (surprise!). Having led my band of Yoogies along "hidden paths" to the Big Blue Lingam, our secret place, I convened the ritual opening of Animal Manners, nodding to Praveen Mehta and Evan Grunsky, who began pounding on the bottoms of plastic buckets. From my woven "bush bag," I withdrew rabbit ears, and, having shown them around the circle, ceremoniously placed them on my head.

"I, oldest and wisest Rabbit, will now call role."

"Raccoon?"

"Present," Kelsey Raines answered, displaying a headband on which Sandra Grimsman had sewn a pair of raccoon ears. Kelsey settled the ears on her head.

"Cougar?"

"Present," Bryce Chowdary answered, adorning his head with cougar ears, a prize possession, as mountain lion kills were rare.

"High Mama Deer?"

"Present," Nicole Loera answered, setting a large pair of deer ears on her head. There were two sets of deer ears in the group, so each "deer" had her own name. Nicole became "High Mama Deer" because she was the tallest.

"Speckles the Baby Deer?"

"Present," Masha Kolupaeva answered.

"Possum?"

"Present," George Sunkari answered.

"Fox."

"Present," Evan Grunsky answered.

"Coyote?"

Mirabai answered with a series of yips followed by a howl that would have fooled a real coyote.

"Beaver?"

"Present," Praveen Mehta answered.

"Bear?"

"Present," Kavitha answered, removing from her bag our prize possession, the entire head and ears of a small black bear, meticulously cured by Sandra Grimsman. "Bear" was a prestigious animal in the game, and I might have been guilty of showing favoritism in awarding "Bear" to my best friend; but how could anyone object? I had badgered the hunters into providing and curing the totems in the first place.

"The Great Animal Council of Big Blue Rock is present. Stop drumming, Evan. We will now recite the Ancient Mantra of Animal Manners."

I intoned the "sacred words," and the other children repeated:

> These are the good manners of Big Blue Rock.
> The sharp teeth will hunt the flat teeth.
> The flat teeth will run and hide from the sharp teeth.
> No sharp tooth may eat baby animals.
> Every flat tooth is safe when she is touching the Big Blue Rock.
> If the animal has bad manners, he has to go away.

"How long?" Bryce asked.

"Forever until he learns good manners or tomorrow," I answered.

May Arjuna shoot me with his bow if I forget my animal manners.

"The great Rabbit, oldest and wisest, will now tell us the story," Kavitha said. "All hail the Great Rabbit."

"Hail the Great Rabbit!" the children shouted.

I began.

"This is a play called *Where's My Baby?*"

"*Where's My Baby*," the other children repeated.

"Once upon a time. Evan, STOP DRUMMING! Once upon a time, there was a mama deer named 'High Mama' because she was so tall, and she had a baby deer called 'Speckles' because she has spots all over her, and she stays here because she is safe here because the animals have good manners and do not hurt her at Big Blue Rock; so she sits here and never, ever, ever moves from this spot."

"That's stupid."

We looked up into the rocks at the source of the "stupid" remark. Alma McGartland was standing above us, smirking.

"What's stupid?" I asked.

"Your stupid game is stupid."

"No, it's not," Kavitha said.

"Do you want to play?" I asked. "I have some ears you can wear."

"I don't want to play your stupid Yoogie game, and I don't want to wear your stupid ears."

"These are real ears."

"They stink."

"No, they don't. Grimsman fixed them for us."

The mention of the hunter's name brought the older girl up short. The truth was, Alma McGartland was one of those awkward, uncoordinated girls, desperately insecure, and friendless. I didn't understand that at the time. I just thought she was horrible.

Alma swaggered over to my sister, still smirking, and leaned over her.

"Who do you think you are?"

"She's the coyote."

"She looks like a turd."

"Does not," I said. "Her name is Yip Yip."

"Her name is Mirabai. Mirabai the *turd*. She's blind and she stinks and she can't even talk."

"Yes, she can."

"Say something, turd."

Mirabai smiled even sunnier.

"See, just a stinky fat turd lying in the dirt."

"Don't call her a turd," Janabai said.

"What are you going to do about it, Princess Prissy?"

"That's not my name."

"What are you going to do about it, Princess Prissy?"

Unaccustomed to such rudeness, and taken totally by surprise, I began to cry.

"Leave her alone," Kavitha said, picking up a rock. Taking Kavitha's courage as their cue, the other children picked up rocks. Alma backed away into the trees.

"You have bad manners, Alma McGartland," Kavitha said. "You have to go away."

"My name is Mendez, Alma MENDEZ!" she screamed. "I hate you. Especially you, Princess Janabai. I'm going to find you one day without your little Yoogie turds around, and when I do, I'm going to beat your ass."

CHAPTER NINETEEN

The Mean Girl

"THERE'S THIS KID WHO DOESN'T like me," I told my father. "Who?" Dad asked.

"Alma."

"Alma McGartland?"

"No, Alma Mendez."

"Alma Mendez *is* Alma McGartland."

I gave my father a blank stare.

"Alma lost her parents, and Sally McGartland took Alma in as her own daughter and gave her the McGartland name."

"She lost her mom and dad? Where did they go? Will they come back?"

"No. She didn't lose them that way."

"How did she lose them?"

"It means they disappeared."

"Oh."

"You understand?"

"Like they... died?"

"We're not sure. Your mother and Max found Alma in the backseat of a car on the side of a road."

"They just *left* her there?"

"So it seems."

"Maybe they're still alive. Maybe they will come back and find her and take her away."

"Maybe."

"That would be a good thing. I hate her."

"Hate is an especially ugly word."

"I don't care. I hate her. I hate Alma Mendez to pieces."

"And she doesn't like you?"

"Uh-uh."

"How do you know?"

"She says mean things."

"Like what?"

"Like Princess Prissy and stuff about Mira."

"What stuff?"

"Like Mirabai's a fat little turd and she's blind."

"Mirabai *is* blind."

"She's not a fat little turd."

"No, she's not."

"Will you make Alma be nice to me?"

"Like I said, I'll look into it. In the meantime, I want you to do something about it yourself."

"What?"

"I want you to be as nice to her as you can be, that's the Shiva Puri way, and I want you to remember she doesn't have a daddy to love her like you do."

Janabai thought for a while.

"Okay, Daddy, I'll be nice."

"How nice?"

"Nice as berry pie."

CHAPTER TWENTY

Mirabai is Not a Turd

D ADDY'S IDEA OF LOOKING INTO it was having a chat with Alma's mom, who promised to have a chat with Alma, that accomplished 100 percent of nothing. Then he had another chat with Patty Bose and Mistah Tee in hopes their authority would bring Alma to her senses and make her start being nice to me.

Guess how well that worked.

But Mama Pat and Mistah Tee tried their best. They called Alma in for a scolding after school. Alma slouched in to find Mother and Dad, and Sally McGartland, Alma's mother, who looked like she was the one in trouble. Alma promised Mama Pat she would leave me alone and not talk to me ever again. Mama Pat told her she had to apologize for calling Mirabai a turd, an accusation Alma denied, claiming she was misunderstood and she only called Mirabai a "turkey" because we Yoogies were playing animals and she thought Mirabai was a bird. When Mama Pat threatened to call in the other kids to verify my version of the story, Alma said the kids would just lie to back me up because my parents were the village "rulers," looking Mother straight in the eye when she said it. I saw Mother's lips go thin and white.

Uh-oh.

Before Mother could speak or do anything, Mama Pat held up her hand and everybody bit back whatever they were getting ready to say. Mama Pat doesn't put up with ugly stuff, not in her school.

She said that the meeting was over and that she would handle it from here on with some "good old-fashioned school discipline."

Alma was punished by having to stay inside at recess for two weeks, and worse than that, sit in the "time out" chair next to Mama Pat in her office. And, the best part, or so I thought when Mama Pat was handing it down, Alma had to stay after school and write on the chalkboard, one hundred times, "Mirabai is not a turd."

How well do you think *that* worked?

Alma Mendez McGartland was not a good student. She was so slow, it took hours for her to write the sentence one hundred times; and because she was embarrassed by her terrible handwriting, she just got madder and madder every time she wrote the words... except for the word "turd." Alma liked writing "turd" and did a fancy job with it, adding little curlicues and making thick letters. She figured out to write the word "not" in small letters so it looked like:

Mirabai is not a turd.
Mirabai is not a turd.
Mirabai is not a turd.

When Mama Pat saw it, she made Alma erase all the little "nots" and rewrite them enormous.

Mirabai is NOT a turd.

Alma had to leave it up on the board overnight so it would be there when we all came to school in the morning. Guess what? In the morning, "someone" had come in and erased all one hundred "nots," so there it was on the board, one hundred times:

Mirabai is a turd.

Alma swore up and down and sideways she didn't do it, but she knew exactly who did, Princess Prissy Janabai, she said, pointing at me, because I would do anything to get poor misunderstood Alma into more trouble.

"Right," Mama Pat said. "Now you will stand there while we all watch you put one hundred 'nots' back in the sentence; not too big 'nots,' not too small, just the right size." Alma gave big sighs and sniffed like she was going to cry, but she went up front and started writing. When she finished the first sentence, she looked over her shoulder and gave me the meanest, scariest look you can imagine.

"Keep your eyes on the board, and keep them off Janabai," Mama Pat said.

I'm sure Mama Pat thought she was being helpful, but the room filled up with bad joo-joo, and I knew she was only making things worse.

Dad decided Alma would move into the single women's dormitory where there was a better chance of keeping her under control until somebody came up with an idea of what to do with her. Meanwhile, Shiva Puri would attempt to drown Alma Mendez McGartland with love, kill her with kindness, smother her with grace — and keep her too busy to cause mischief. When not in school she was "offered" seva in the mandir with Annabel Feuerstein, who felt steady work in the Divine Abode might heal the child's broken spirit.

"THAT'S ALL?" I screamed at Dad. "That's all the trouble Alma got into for hurting me and calling Mirabai a turd? You moved her into the bunkhouse?"

Dad told me to calm down, to "avoid" Alma, to stop trying to be her friend. Maybe if he had done something, I don't know, stronger and smarter, right at the beginning, things would have gone a different way.

But he didn't, and they didn't.

CHAPTER TWENTY-ONE

Mumbly Peg

IN A CORNER OF THE shed where she liked to hide when she was upset, Alma Mendez discovered a carpenter's toolbox. From among the rusty items tossed helter-skelter in the bottom, she selected a fourteen-inch screwdriver. Scraping angrily at it with a file, her mind filled with thoughts no eight-year-old girl should think. She worked for several hours, and when the tip had been sharpened to her satisfaction, she began to teach herself how to throw the screwdriver, knife-like, into the side of the shed, into trees, and into the ground. When, after days of secretive practice, she was confident she could throw it and make it stick wherever she wanted, Alma Mendez went looking for me.

"Hey, Janabai, wanna play a new game?"

Remembering the poke in the eye, I knew Alma was trying to trick me again. Too terrified to answer, I just stood there.

"Look, pal, this is a really easy game. Maybe you can even beat me. You'd like that, wouldn't you? To beat me just one time so you could brag about it to all your little Yoogies. Sure, I know, it would take a lot of guts to even try. Do you have the guts, Janabai?"

Well, she had me there. I really *did* want to beat her.

"If you can beat me, I'll give you my respect, and then we can be friends."

Max told me Alma was turning a corner, that she was doing really well in the women's barracks, that she was working hard, and that everyone was impressed with her improvement.

I wanted to trust her. I nodded.

"Hot damn!"

Alma explained how to throw the screwdriver so it stuck point-first in the ground.

"Hold it by the tip, like this, and flip it so it turns over a half way."

I watched Alma demonstrate. The older girl had been practicing.

Taking the proffered screwdriver, I attempted to throw it, and after several misfires, much to my delight, finally managed to stick it in the ground. I was thrilled, not only because of my success, but because Alma had been genuinely helpful, coaching me like a real friend. When I mastered the technique well enough that I could stick the screwdriver most of the time, Alma explained the game.

"It's called 'mumbly peg.' We stand face-to-face with our feet together. That's right, not too close, not too far away. You throw the screwdriver so it sticks in the ground just outside *your* foot. Now move your foot so it touches the screwdriver; then you bend down and pull it out and give it to me. Then it's my turn."

I threw the screwdriver so it stuck in the ground about eighteen inches away from my right foot. I grinned at Alma, who returned the grin with an encouraging smile. Glowing with pleasure, I extended my leg until my right foot touched the shaft of the tool, bent over, and retrieved the screwdriver.

"My turn," Alma said. "Give it to me." Taking the screwdriver, the older girl snapped it into the ground about six inches from her foot. "You want to throw it as *close* to your foot as you can."

"Why?"

"You'll see. It's part of the game. Your turn."

I took the screwdriver and spun it into the ground, again about eighteen inches outside my foot. This time I had to stretch to reach the blade, my legs at least three feet apart, almost losing my balance to retrieve it.

Alma threw again, another six inches, easily extracted the screwdriver, and handed it to me. I suddenly understood the game and realized I was in trouble. Too timid to throw the blade close to my foot, I worried if I threw it too far, I wouldn't be able to stretch all the way, but choosing the latter option as the wisest, I threw the screw driver almost twenty inches away from my foot. It stuck.

"Three in a row," Alma said. "That's good sticking. Now you have to stretch all the way out there and get it."

Nearly doing a split, I extended my leg toward the screwdriver, and almost made it, but in trying to stretch the last few inches, lost my balance and fell forward, right into Alma, who caught me and helped me back up.

"Too bad. I win," Alma said. "Want to play again?"

I did not find mumbly peg an especially fun game, but I was pleased with my ability to throw the screwdriver into the ground three times in a row (!), grateful for the improvement in my relationship with Alma Mendez.

"Sure," I answered.

"Okay! Now we're going to play the real way."

"The real way?"

"Yes. Put your feet together just like last time. You go first. But this time you throw it so it sticks outside *my* foot, and I have to stretch and get it. Be careful and don't stick me."

Dubiously, I took the screwdriver, aimed at a spot well away from Alma's foot, and threw. The screw driver landed on its side and skittered away.

"Bad throw," Alma said. She walked over and picked up the screwdriver. "My turn."

Holding the tip of the screwdriver between her thumb and index finger, Alma seemed to aim for a point well outside. She threw the blade hard and fast, straight down, right through my left foot. The sharpened point hit the bone in my big toe, ricocheted, punched through the outside skin, into the side of the adjacent toe and out the bottom, pinning my foot to the ground by two toes.

"Oops," she said. "I missed."

I looked down at my foot, the handle of the screwdriver sticking out at a crazy angle. For one shocked instant I froze, not breathing. The pain and horror of the spectacle screeched upward into my awareness. I screamed. And screamed again. And again.

My screaming wiped the smirk from Alma's face, which turned white as the blood drained out. The older girl whirled and ran for the safety of the forest, leaving me pegged to the earth.

Mama Pat, followed closely by Kavitha, was the first to reach me.

"Oh my lord, what have you done?"

The only word I could get out between screams was "Alma."

Mama Pat turned to Kavitha. "Go get Dr. Cheng and Azriel and Daniel and any other grown-ups you can find."

Kavitha, the fastest runner among the village children, loved any chance to show off. She streaked away.

"Pull it out, pull it out," I sobbed.

"I want you to calm down if you can, and take a few deep breaths. Do you think you can do that?" Mama Pat asked.

"I don't know."

"Give it a try."

I took a few hesitant huffs.

"That's right. Now I'm going to kneel down here and put my arms around you and give you some special Pattycake love. Okay?"

"I think so."

Mama Pat wrapped me in her arms.

"It hurts so much," I said.

"I know it does."

"I mean it really, really, really hurts."

"I know."

It seemed like a long time, but it was only a few minutes before Kavitha, followed by Kerilynn Fleenor, returned, gulping air with high drama as if she had just run thirty miles through the mountains.

"I couldn't find Lynda, but I found Kerilynn," Kavitha panted, bending over, hands on knees.

"Kerilynn will do just fine," Mama Pat answered.

"Let's see what we have here," Kerilynn said. "Patty, why don't you let go of Janabai and let me get in there?" Examining my foot, Kerilynn said, "I've seen some strange things, but this is one for the books." Kerilynn was the village midwife, a capable healer in her own right and not one to easily fluster.

"You done stuck yourself good, didn't you?"

"Alma. It was Alma who done stuck me."

Kerilynn snorted and looked up at Patty, who bit her lip and shook her head.

"Take it out. Make it stop hurting."

"Okay," Kerilynn said, "I'm going to pull it out for you."

"Do it slow so it doesn't hurt."

The midwife took a good grip on the handle, and with one fast, no nonsense pull, extracted the blade.

I screamed, "I told you to pull it slow!"

"Slow would hurt a lot more and hurt a lot longer," Kerilynn said. "Here, sit down now and get yourself together."

"It still hurts."

"But not so much, huh?"

I considered my foot. "Not so much. It's bleeding. Make it stop."

"I don't think so," Kerilynn said, examining the screwdriver. "This thing is pretty rusty. Probably better if we let the blood wash the wound clean."

"Is she going to get lockjaw?" Kavitha asked with a mixture of dread and delicious anticipation.

The two adults looked at Kavitha.

"Oops," Kavitha said.

"Lockjaw?" I asked.

"No, you're not going to get lockjaw," Kerilynn answered, "but just to be safe Lynda will probably give you a shot of Shakti-cillin."

"A shot?"

"Can I give her the shot?" Kavitha offered. "I've seen Lynda do it."

"Vitha," Mama Pat said to her daughter, "run find Jana's mom and dad, and don't come back without them."

"When I grow up I'm going to be a medic and give everybody shots," Kavitha added.

"Get going, your friend is bleeding."

"Yes, ma'am!" As she raced for the village center, Kavitha yelled over her shoulder, "I hope they don't have to cut your toe off."

"Cut my toe off?"

To my immense relief, Kavitha's alarming notion of amputation was ruled unnecessary, but I did get three injections of homegrown antibiotics in my rear end, each one hurting more than the previous. *Shakti-cillin*, concocted by the Devi scientists, was rough stuff; effective, but it rendered my butt cheeks sore for days.

Max and Mother searched the nearby woods for Alma Mendez, who was nowhere to be found and was not seen again until early morning two days later when, hungry and filthy, she sneaked into the back door of the amrit for breakfast. The girl posed a problem for the entire village. Had she been an adult, Max would have driven her miles beyond the village territory and dumped her on the edge of the highway with a warning that if she ever tried to return she would be shot on sight. But Alma was a child, and a damaged one at that. Nobody had the slightest idea what to do with her.

CHAPTER TWENTY-TWO

Judgment Day

THE COUNCIL OF SHIVA PURI convened to consider the "suffering" of Alma Mendez McGartland. Dad sent the "marines" out to find Mother and Max, who were still beating the bushes for Alma, then turned the sorry affair over to Galen Raether. Usually Dad took charge when one of us had issues that couldn't be handled by sitting down with Mama Witch or going out behind the barn for a smoke with Sergeant Max. But on this occasion, with a Burke-Kucinich (me) involved, Dad felt he had to step aside and let someone else preside. That "someone" was Galen Raether, who reluctantly agreed to do the dirty work even though he had his hands full bossing the farm.

Late in the afternoon, Mother and Max dragged in, bone tired, hungry, and radiating foul moods.

"Do you want to wait until after dinner?" Galen asked.

"No. Let's get this clusterfuck over and done."

I had never heard Mother say a word like that.

"I tell you what," Galen said. "Well, then... meeting will come to order. Simone, will you jot down a few notes?"

"I'll sit over here and jot away, Your Honor."

"Alright. We'll start with you, Alma. What do you have to say?"

Alma denied any intention to hurt me, said it was just as much my fault as hers.

"The screwdriver slipped out of my hand. It was an accident. Janabai wanted to play. She said so."

"That right?" Galen Raether asked me. "Did Alma invite you to play?"

"Yes," I answered.

"Did you accept her invitation?"

"Yes."

I was too young to see where this was going. I was telling the truth, and Alma was lying, so I was sure she would be punished for hurting me and for lying about it.

"Okay," Galen said. "First, the mumbly peg game is forbidden for now on, as are sharpened screwdrivers." He looked at Alma. "Do you understand me, young lady?"

"Yeah," she muttered with her head down.

"A little louder, please," he said.

She snapped her head up, locking eyes with him, and yelled at the top of her voice, "I HEARD YOU!"

Galen shook his head. "Given the testimony heard here today, I have no choice but to recommend Alma be acquitted. We can't prove it was an accident, and we can't prove it wasn't."

Alma looked at me with a kind of dead fish look in her eyeballs, scarier than if she had sneered at me.

"But," Galen went on, "I have no doubt that you, Alma McGartland, in your heart of hearts, did intend to hurt another child. Therefore, I am going to require you to meet every week with Simone Jackson."

"Why?"

"Just to talk, and maybe she can find out what's troubling you."

"Princess Prissy is troubling me," Alma said. "I don't need no meeting to figure that out."

"That may be, but you will still meet with Simone, every week, on Sunday afternoons, for an hour, and have a conversation."

"Or what?" Alma asked.

"Or you will be in more trouble than you ever imagined, I tell you what."

Galen was bluffing, and Alma knew it. She laughed at him, actually laughed in Galen Raether's face.

"Can I go now?"

Galen nodded at Alma, one curt nod, and she spun on her heel and walked out.

He turned his attention to Max.

"Keep her on a short leash."

"You bet I will."

CHAPTER TWENTY-THREE

Snot Locker

"MAX?"

"Hmmm?"

"Can I talk to you?"

"You're already talking to me."

"Are you teasing me?"

"Whatever gave you that idea?"

"I don't like it when people tease me."

"Okay, sorry. What can I do for you, Janabai?"

"Tell me what to do so I can be like you."

"Like me?"

"Nobody picks on you."

"What has gotten into you this morning? Wait. Don't tell me. Alma."

I nodded. Her face softened.

"What should I do?" I pleaded.

"What does your father say?"

"He says to ignore Alma and she will get tired of picking on me and stop."

"That's what he says, huh? Just suck it up and hope she gets bored?"

"Uh huh. But what if she doesn't stop?"

"You are going to have to fight her."

"I don't know how to fight. Will you teach me?"

Max blew air out of her lips and thought about it.

"Okay, I'll give you this. Get up close to her and get in the first lick, a quick, fast punch in the nose. Put everything you've got into it. Try to break her nose. Do it right, and she'll back off and leave you alone. Do it wrong, and you'll just make her mad. Remember. Quick. Hard. Right in the snot locker."

"Snot locker!"

"Oh, you like that, do you?"

"Snot locker," I repeated.

"You won't get a second chance, get me?"

"Pow! Right in the snot locker."

"Don't you dare tell your father."

"Pow!"

CHAPTER TWENTY-FOUR

The World According to Galen

BRAHMA THE CREATOR MADE THE universe, Vishnu the Sustainer preserved Brahma's creation, Shiva destroyed it all so the cycle could begin again. Finally, Galen Raether, the Farmer God, whose agricultural wisdom was supreme, came along to feed the people.

That's a Shiva Puri joke.

In his ragged overalls and a floppy straw hat, Galen looked more like a scarecrow than a god, but when he spoke of farming, his words were divine. He made the decisions that kept the village alive: when to plant, how to plant, what to plant, where to plant.

He tested the soil by tasting it, smelling it, spitting on a handful and squeezing it between his red, rough fingers. He dug holes, filled them with water, and watched to see how long it took for the water to drain away. He stood on the high ridge to feel the direction of the prevailing winds. He marked where the sun rose and set every day of the year.

Then he shocked the village by announcing that the soil at Graeagle was failing, the fertility declining, the farm unsustainable, and relocation to a new location inevitable.

Who could argue with Galen Raether?

Everybody argued. Of course. That's the Shiva Puri way. We had invested a half decade in the farm, and in the hard-won comforts of the new village, and in the safety of our isolation, and in the lovely customs and gentle life rhythms we enjoyed, in the sanctity of the beautiful mandir we had built together and where we gathered in the evening to pray, and chant, and dance. Leave it all behind?

But Raether was firm, his evidence right in front of our eyes. We had seen for ourselves how it took more work, more time, just to match the previous year's harvests, and, as Storekeeper Simone confirmed, this year's harvest was less than the previous year, even though water had been plentiful and the weather cooperative.

"What about farms all over the world that have been there for generations?"

"These are the Sierra foothills, stone and clay, not the San Fernando Valley or the Ukraine. It all comes down to soil. That's our real crop. That's what we grow: soil."

Someone shouted, "What about all the compost and manure we plow into it, day after day?"

"Yes," Raether answered, "those inputs are good, and necessary, but they're not enough if the foundation is lacking, if there just isn't enough topsoil to work with. We need a much bigger area, where we can rotate the crops more often, where the livestock can move from pasture to pasture without overgrazing. We are fighting a losing battle here, especially if our numbers keep growing. How many are we today?"

Dad answered, "Two hundred and thirty."

"Even with our losses to the Rakshasa..." Raether stopped, closed his eyes, took a breath, as did everybody, remembering Beth Raether, his beloved wife. Composing himself, Raether went on, "Even with our losses, we are twenty-five more, twenty-five stronger, twenty-five hungrier than we were on the night we fled Nevada County. And Azriel says our biggest need is more and more people."

Galen's mention of Mother's worry was true, but not the complete picture. In Mother's vision, Shiva Puri was always on the march, a nomadic people responding to the vagaries of climate change and available resources, moving from place to place, often returning to familiar ground, much as Galen rotated the fields from active to fallow. Recognizing our great need for stability after the chaos of the Kali Yuga, Mother kept that part of her vision to herself for more than five years, but she knew survivability depended upon Shiva Puri's willingness to pack up and move quickly. And in the skill to do so. Now we had to figure out how to accomplish such a move.

"We move, or we starve to death."

Raether's proclamation of doom struck Mother as providential, but horrified many of us, especially the children. Looking across the hall, she could see me crying, my hands over my face.

Dad stepped up to steer the discussion onto the practicalities. Where would we go? And when? Did we try to take everything, using all of the remaining gasoline, or did we take a bare minimum, saving our gasoline for use at the new village? Mother caught my eye and motioned to the side door with a tilt of her head.

Outside, in the crisp autumn night, mother and daughter conferred.

"What do you think?" Mother asked.

"Why? Why, Mommy, why? I like this place. I don't want to go."

"Moving away from your home, the only home you have ever known, is scary. But you heard what Galen said, and you are smart enough to know what he means. Right?"

86

I refused to answer.

"Janabai, I know you don't like this, but we have made a decision, the right decision. When we ran from the Kali Yuga, we had no choice, and we got lucky, or maybe someone was looking out for us, to give us a chance. But this time we have a choice, and we have made it all by ourselves because it's the right thing for us to do so you and all the other children will have a good life and a safe life in the years to come. Do you understand?"

"That will be a good thing?"

"Yes, it will, and you know something else?"

"What?" I sniffed.

"If you pull your bottom lip back in, I'll tell you."

I gave her a little snort, but retracted the offending lip.

"What?" I repeated, sounding more like an exasperated adult than a five-year-old.

"I think it's going to be fun."

"Fun?"

"Probably."

I put on a brave face to impress my mother. "It's important we keep on the move and learn new things, don't you think?" I asked, as if I was now in charge of the conversation.

"Your mouth to God's ear," Mother answered. "Now, come over here. I need to dry those tears. Your face is a mess."

Mother knelt down to blot my eyes with her sleeve. Putting her arms around me and drawing me close, she whispered, "Now I want you to do something hugely important."

"What?"

Mother pushed away, hands on my shoulders, face-to-face, she looked into my eyes.

"I want you to get all your Yoogies together and help them understand why we are moving. Some of them may be scared to go, but if you are brave in front of them, and tell them all about it... ?"

"They won't be scared anymore."

"Exactly. So will you accept this seva? Will you take care

of the young ones? Will you be our shepherd for those little Yoogie lambs?"

"Roger that!" I answered, and saluted just like Max.

Mother threw her head back and laughed out loud.

"Perfect. Now, let's go back inside and watch how your brilliant father pulls this adventure together."

I remember that night as clear as spring water. Galen's big surprise announcement, and Daddy's leadership, and all the people learning their lives were going to change again, yelling and arguing and afraid, but most of all I remember when my mother took me outside the mandir and trusted me to be her shepherd.

CHAPTER TWENTY-FIVE

Moving Day

IN MID-FEBRUARY, WHEN IT BECAME possible to plow the roads clear of winter snow, Dad took a team of thirty-eight mechanics, farmers, potters, and cooks north to Indian Valley to build new barns and communal housing. Every other day, Donnie Simms transported supplies and livestock on the flat bed of Prasad, the indomitable village truck. Load up one day, drive north and unload the next. Drive back south. Do it again.

With few habitable buildings in Indian Valley, only the bigger families would have private quarters; everybody else would bunk together in the new eight-person "hooches" Vic Tretheway and his construction crew, the "SeaBees," he called them, were fabricating. These weatherproof shelters, he bragged, his "Bees" could pop up, complete and ready for occupancy, in a single day. Rough, these "hooches," but they would keep us up out of the mud, and with scavenged metal roofs, dry during the rainy season. In summer, shutters could be opened on all sides to catch the cooling breezes, though without insulation, and heated by the most primitive wood-burning stoves, Vic's "hooches" were going to be "butt puckering cold when the north wind blows up your crack," so sayeth hilarious Tretheway.

Down south, I spent my last day in Graeagle avoiding the relentless Alma Mendez, who had been stalking me. Keeping a sharp eye peeled, I wandered through the congested fields where Shiva Puri was assembling for its risky relocation to Indian Valley, a scene that reminded me of wagon trains I read about in picture books, ox-carts piled high with supplies, cattle lowing, drovers shouting back and forth, farmers stomping through a slush of mud and snow, a rollicking scene that should have sparked adventurous swagger in every step, but inspired more gloom than excitement. Our village, now at its most vulnerable, was split into Dad's Advance Team and Mother's Bottom Enders, forty-six miles of emptiness between them.

Though it was late afternoon on Kali Yuga Day, March 25, 7 AK, there would be no ceremony this evening, no bandhara feast of gratitude for deliverance. My people, still in distress from uprooting our lives — a decision many thought ill-advised — distracted by worry, exhausted from packing, were in no mood for gaiety.

I watched the last bundles loaded, covered, and strapped down. Every inch of every passenger car, pickup truck, golf buggy, ox wagon, and goat cart was packed high and tight. The cattle were bunched across the highway in an adjacent pasture, and beyond them, the smaller herds of goat and sheep. Bird coops with their irritable occupants, and the families of lesser livestock, pig pens and rabbit hutches, even the bee hives, were already north in their new home.

Forty-six miles away! An inconceivable distance to a girl who had never been more than five miles from the place she was born. The adults who were not busy with the vehicles were still in town, closing up Graeagle, locking the doors, many of us weeping, devastated by the hard reality we were bidding farewell to our beloved foothill refuge, the little town that had kept us safe since the awful afternoon, a half decade before, when the sky exploded over California.

On this, the evening before the departure, every house in Graeagle was cleaned, yards raked, windows washed; every barn, stable, and pen mucked out. Shiva Puri would leave Graeagle sparkling. Chores finished, the "Bottom Enders," singly and in small groups, made their way to the mandir, where Mother was waiting. I saw her give a nod to Annabel Feuerstein. Striking the first chords on the harmonium, Annabel led us in prayers of thanksgiving to the little town that sheltered us, and to the citizens of Graeagle, who had built the homes and barns, to the pastures that had provided grain and forage to our herds, to the river that had quenched our thirst, and to the fields from whence all sustenance flowed. Chanting completed, Mother locked the front door.

"This is it," she said, turning to face our people. "No coming back for forgotten teddy bears."

If Mother had intended her quip as a joke to lighten the mood, it fell flat.

"Well, then. Lord Shiva's blessings on us all. Let's get some sleep."

Taking deep breaths, the shepherds headed out to the pastures north of town to watch over goats twitchy with anticipation and sheep snoozing away as if it were any other night. In town, the Bottom Enders found places to bed down, sleeping rough or snuggled together in the lobby of the former Feather River Resort. I went searching for my mother and found her behind the resort, having a pow wow with Max, and Bill Lemko.

"Yes, punkin' pie, what do you need?"

"What about the sign?" I asked.

"What sign?"

"The liberry sign. We can't leave the liberry sign."

"We can paint another one when we get to the valley."

"But this is the *real* sign. Myron painted it. We have to take *this* sign."

Mother was losing patience.

"We don't have the time or energy to take the sign down, much less find a place for it."

"But, Mother, Miss Piwinski will be sad."

"Did you just hear what I said?" Mother snapped.

I started to argue, but, biting my bottom lip, swallowed my retort and stomped off, not before catching Bill Lemko's wink. Hmmmm. What did that mean?

Before sunrise, I crawled out from under my blanket, shook Mirabai awake, and, before anyone else began to stir, dragged my sleepy sister down the dark road to our vehicle, the school bus assigned to the younger children. I wanted to be first on the bus so we would have the best and safest seats, in the front row where I knew Max would be sitting. I settled Mirabai right behind the driver's seat and put our lunch pails in the adjacent seat to save it for myself.

"Stay here," I said to my sister. "I'll be back soon. Don't let anybody take my seat."

Mirabai made no reply. She looked so vulnerable and small. I left her sitting alone in the dark school bus and went off to "manage" the younger children as I knew my father would want. An hour later, the entourage "managed" to my satisfaction, I returned to the bus. The first sight to greet me as I climbed the steps was the driver, Donnie Simms, snoring in the driver's seat just in front of Mirabai. The second sight was down the aisle to the back of the bus: Alma Mendez, sprawled on the middle of the rear bench, eating the lunch from my pail.

"That's *my* cheese sandwich," I said.

"Come and get it," Alma said. "It's so good. Uh-oh. This is the last bite." The older girl chewed with exaggerated relish, licking her lips and dribbling food down her chin.

"Mmmm mmmm. Tasty."

Alma stared down the aisle at me with an unpleasant smile on her face as if to say, *"This is going to be a long ride — for you."*

I said the first thing that came to my mind, "Snot locker."

She scrunched up her nose and licked her lips as if trying to taste something foul I might have put in my sandwich. Ha ha. I thought quickly.

Shaking his shoulder, I yelled in our driver's ear, "Donnie! Wake up!"

"Huh? What? Janabai? What's wrong?"

He was so funny waking up, but this was no time for jokes.

"I forgot to tell Mother something. Keep an eye on Mirabai; you-know-who is on the bus."

He looked down the center aisle at Alma and nodded to me.

"Both eyes," he said.

I told my sister, "I'll be along later. Don't worry."

Swaying back and forth, Mirabai hummed a little melody. She didn't seem worried. Mirabai never worried.

I kissed her, too, spun around, and jumped down the bus steps, right into Max.

"Where do you think you're going?"

"Uh... Mother said... I could... uh... ride with Bill and Simone on the wagon if they said it was okay, and I asked them, and they said it was okay." The last part came out in a rush. I was not an experienced liar, and I didn't fool Max for a second. A tiny smile on her lips, she looked down at me.

"Well, if that's what your mother said, I'm not going to argue with her. Get your butt down the line and check in with Simone. Don't go wandering off anywhere else, you get me?"

I swallowed. "Yes, Max." I started to turn away. "Oh, Max?"

"What?"

"Will you tell Dad I'll be along later, with Mother, and not to get mad."

"I'll tell him, but you know what he's going to do."

"Pitch a hissy fit?"

"The world's hissiest."

"Thanks, Max. You're the best."

"Yes I am. Now, give me a hug."

Max bent down for me to put my arms around her neck. I whispered into her ear.

"Look after Mirabai. I already asked Donnie to keep an eye on her, but you can't be too safe. Don't let Alma hurt her."

Hugging me tight, Max whispered back.

"You know I won't. Now, git!"

I let go of her neck and ran further down the line, to the rear cohort where Mother was waiting with the goats. When the bus with all the kids finally rumbled away and it was too late for her to do anything about it, Mother turned around and saw me standing over on the side with my hand resting on Hanuman's shoulder.

"Your father is going to go crazy."

"I can be a big help to you, Mother," I said. "The woolies do whatever I tell them to do. You need me."

"I do?"

"Yes, you do. I'm just as good with the herd as Uncle Raj 'cause I love them woolies so much and they love me."

"You're probably right. Are those your sturdiest shoes?"

"Yes, Mother."

"I see you're wearing your winter coat."

"Yes, Mother."

"You'll need it. It's a long, cold walk to Indian Valley."

"I can do it."

"Well, if you get tired, you can ride on one of the carts."

"I won't get tired."

"Does Max know where you are?"

"Oh, yes, she thought it was a good idea."

"Daughter, you're not very good at this, you know."

"Good at what?"

"Lying."

"Oh."

"So stop trying, okay? It's unbecoming."

At first light, Max fired a green flare into the brightening sky. Up and down the line, we cheered. With a rattle of decrepit engines sputtering to life on barely ignitable ethanol, the dregs of the fuel reserves, the "Grand Cavalcade of Shiva Puri" rolled out of Graeagle bound for Indian Valley, the village "tank," a 1959 Plymouth station wagon in the lead, a gun port cut through the roof with a washing machine drum welded around the hole, Donnie Simms with an M60 machine gun standing tall and alert in the "turret," the driver and three other armed hunters inside, the windows bristling with guns, sending the unmistakable message, "Don't mess with us."

Tucked in close behind the "tank," the ancient school bus chugged along, still reliable after seven years of Vic Tretheway's tender ministrations, three more hunters inside, one on the right, one on the left, one in the rear, and Max riding shotgun up front, leading twenty-seven children, Shiva Puri's most precious treasure, in spirited Marine Corps marching songs.

> *Bullshit, it makes the grass grow green*
> *Bullshit, it makes the best marine*

The kids loved to scream "Bullshit" at the top of their lungs; Max loved to demonstrate her prowess at inventing new couplets.

> *Bullshit, in flops and little beans*
> *Bullshit, eat it from soup tureens*

The kids had no idea what a "tureen" was, nor cared, except it had to be some kind of disgusting method for eating cow pies, and it rhymed with "beans."

To keep the school bus sandwiched between "armored cars," a Cadillac known fondly as "The Bomb," one of the two working passenger vehicles, rumbled into line, belching black smoke from the tailpipe, gamely facing its culminating and most important journey, Tretheway's mechanics making wagers at which of the forty-six miles it would burn its last cylinder and roll to its final resting place. The other passenger car, a Buick, gutted except for the driver's seat, and afforded the best suspension system, followed with the most sensitive and fragile of the laboratory equipment, though not the scientists themselves, who, like everybody else, would make the trek on foot or in one of the ox carts. Three pickup trucks piled high with supplies came next, followed by Prasad, the beloved flatbed, stripped down and empty, its duty to pick up stragglers, mechanical and biological.

As soon as the cars and trucks were underway, the fleet of twenty-three solar-powered golf carts, sagging under the weight of seventy-two adults, would roll out, and later, on the same day, with a bit of luck, no more than six hours after departure from Graeagle, they would glide, grind, or be towed into Indian Valley.

Further back, the ox wagons, laden with tons of farm and ranch equipment, personal possessions, and furniture, creaked into motion. The lead wagon, encumbered with the irreplaceable bags of seed, also bore a suspicious-looking object wrapped tight and strapped to its side. The Liberry sign! Bill Lemko wrangled this wagon himself, Simone Jackson at his side, comical in an oversized "prairie bonnet" she had whipped up especially for the occasion. The cattle herd, pushed along by drovers on foot, and the heavy ox wagons were expected to take four days, perhaps five, averaging nine or ten miles a day, a formidable challenge.

If all went well, the first wave of ethanol-powered vehicles would make the forty-six-mile trip in less than two hours, at which point, journey completed, Max would transfer to Prasad and rattle back down the line to bring up the rear with Mother and the goats, arriving just in time, Vic calculated, for the old truck to suck down the last drops of ethanol in the known universe, and expire. Max, along with her most trusted hunter, Sandra Grimsman, would have the dubious honor of enjoying the final automobile ride of her species.

The goats and sheep would amble along at their own pace. Working with the Bannerjee brothers, now grown men, and the other shepherds, Mother estimated twelve days to get the mixed herds north. On bicycle tires, four light goat carts would roll along behind the herd; one cart bearing medicine, another food, the third bedding, and, last but not least, the fourth cart would transport the cobalt blue *bana lingam,* the soul of Shiva Puri, the strange oblong boulder Dad had pulled from the Downie River in those first days of the exodus.

Bringing up the rear, Max and her five best hunters would walk the entire way, providing security for "Azriel's Goat Parade."

And no Alma Mendez!

CHAPTER TWENTY-SIX

A New World Unfurled

CRUMBLING ASPHALT STRETCHED AHEAD INTO the unknown. I, Janabai Burke-Kucinich, age seven, took my position on the left wing of a herd consisting of 63 sheep and 138 goats. Six bucks and four rams were already ahead in Indian Valley, a comfortable ride in the flatbed for those gentlemen, out of sight (and smell), far away from trouble with the ewes. In the weeks before we left Graeagle, the shepherds tried to keep the lads away from the ladies, but bucks will be bucks, and Shiva Puri bucks in rut are not to be turned away. A dozen ewes were already pregnant and likely to drop before completing the twelve-day journey.

Turning up my nose at Mother's offer to ride in one of the goat carts, I trekked from Graeagle to Indian Valley in a state of continual delight as the new world unfurled itself. For most of the journey, my mother strolled along on one side, Hanuman on the other, Max and the hunters singing rowdy songs, the Bannerjee brothers cracking jokes. It was the most stupendous adventure any girl could ever have. Could life be sweeter?

Out on the road, everything was fresh and exotic, worthy of commentary, and comment I did, a ceaseless, never-ending torrent of babble.

"Look over there. What is it? Is the sky bigger here? What kind of flower is that? Listen to the bird. Can you make that whistle like a bird? See the coyote? He wants to eat Blackeye's baby. I'm going to call him 'Skinny Skulker'."

Returning to the camp one afternoon after a long shift on the left wing, I introduced Mother and Max to my new friend, a pack rat, who seemed quite at ease riding on my shoulder.

"Does your pet have a name?" Max asked.

"He's not a pet," I answered. "He's a friend."

"Excuse me. Does your friend have a name?"

"Yes, but I can't say it in people talk."

"Why not?"

"It's more like a picture."

"Can you give him a people name?"

I thought for a moment. "I guess we could call him Nuzzle because he likes to rub up against my ears."

"Nuzzle. Good name," Max said, and turning to Mother, added, "Mr. Nuzzle will probably give fleas to your daughter."

I shrugged, just like Mother does, and using my best Mother voice, said, "What else is new?"

Mother fell over on her side howling, her reaction to my joke more comical than the joke itself. Max found herself caught up in the hilarity, plopped down on the ground, laughing, tears running down her face. It was one of those moments nobody can figure out why everything is so funny. The laughter comes to a stop, then someone chuckles, and everyone goes off again.

"Why are you laughing so hard?" I asked Mother.

Between gasps she managed to say, "You (gasp) remind (gasp) me of someone…"

"Who?"

"Me!"

"You?"

I reminded Mother of herself? Then I was laughing as well.

"We are just three women having the time of our lives," I said.

"What?"

I repeated as if I were many years older, "We are just three women having the time of our lives."

That set Mother and Max off again.

The Bannerjee brothers wandered over to check out the commotion. The confusion on their faces was the funniest thing of all.

CHAPTER TWENTY-SEVEN

Hanuman

"GET AS MUCH SLEEP AS you can." Mother addressed the footsore survivors of the Great Goat Parade. "We're pulling out before dawn and pushing hard. Max figures we're only five or six miles out."

"Seven at the most," Max added.

"I don't know about you," Mother said, "but I want to sleep warm and dry tonight in my own bed."

Whistles and applause. Two days of rain and fog had dampened our enthusiasm. Everybody was ready to get to our new home in Indian Valley.

Sometime in the middle of the night, I had a dream so vivid that even writing about it today sends rivulets of sweat running down my skin. I sensed someone near me, someone who shouldn't be there. I was scared, and I didn't want to open my eyes. I pretended I was still asleep, but whoever, or whatever, didn't go away. When I couldn't stand it any longer, I opened my eyes and looked. In the dying glow of the campfire, I saw someone bending over me, a face inches from mine, a beautiful boy with flowing blond hair. I knew him from somewhere, but I couldn't remember, maybe another dream. I wanted to say something to him, but I found myself transfixed and stupefied by his eyes, glittering, yellow eyes. My mouth would not form the right words. He smiled. It was a glorious smile until fangs slid down from his upper gums and elongated into wickedly curved tusks. I tried to move, but those eyes sucked me down, swallowed me, suffocated me, deeper, deeper, spiraling, down and down and...

I jerked awake to an earth-shattering roar.

Aaaaaaaauuuuuuunnnnnn!

Mother jolted upright next to me, her head cocked, listening, sniffing the air like an animal, and on my other side, Max, weapon ready, shooting finger in the trigger guard. Shaken by my nightmare, but now fully alert, I heard goats and sheep bleating, hooves on the hard ground, neck bells jangling, the rustle of wooly bodies crowding close to each other, and dogs... every dog in our pack howling.

"What the fuck was that?" Max asked.

We crawled out from under the tarp, pulling on our heavy coats. The other shepherds likewise climbed to their feet. Uncle Raj materialized out of the mist like a spook, walking toward us with a torch in his hand.

"There's something you need to see," he said.

"Hanuman?" Mother asked. I think she already knew.

He nodded, turned around, and led us back the way he came. The animals, nervous and upset, milled around in a mob. Out in the middle, Jata, her massive Pyrenees-shepherd head thrown back, bayed at the sky as if her heart were broken. Around her the other herd dogs whined and paced, sometimes stopping to bark or join Jata's lament. Where was Hanuman's big booming voice?

We pushed our way through the herd until we came to a small open space in the middle. At first, in the flickering torch light, I couldn't figure out what I was seeing. A big lump of something lay on the cold, soggy ground. Then, I made sense of the horror.

Hanuman.

Something had ripped out our Hanuman's throat.

I turned inside out; my guts climbed up my throat, gagging me. I couldn't catch my breath, low black clouds spun over my head, my legs gave way, and I fell. Someone caught me. Max. She lowered me to the ground.

"Sit right here for a minute," Max said, "and breathe."

I was panting so hard I thought I would break something in my chest, and then it came up, from the bottom of my soul: pain like I had never experienced, a wail of abject misery. I wasn't the only one crying. Above all the others, my mother screamed, and I will tell you, I never want to hear that sound again if I live a thousand years. I crawled over to where she was kneeling next to Hanuman's body and put my arms around her waist. We wailed together. The other dogs, unnerved by our lamentation, threw their heads back and howled even louder. The sheep and goats got into it, and we were all bawling, human and creature, together in our grief.

Max was the first to snap out of it.

"Everybody, listen to me, look at me. Manoj, look in my eyes. All right. Everybody, locked and loaded, tight perimeter, herd in the middle, Janabai in the middle of the herd. Jana, can you build up the fire really big?"

I nodded.

"Eyes moving, people; find a shadow, get in it. Stay low. Nobody talks, nobody moves until I tell you. Now go."

The shepherds and guards disappeared into the dark to find their positions.

"What could do that to Hanuman?" I asked Mother.

"I don't know," she answered, but I saw her mouth a certain word at Max, who just shook her head. Mother held out her hand to me, and you can be sure I took it. "Come on, baby," she said. "Let's get that fire going while Max checks on the guards."

"What was it, Mom? What killed Hanuman?"

"Probably a bear."

"A bear wouldn't do that to Hanuman," I persisted.

"Okay, Janabai, maybe a cougar."

"Why didn't we hear anything? Hanuman would put up a fight. We would have heard something."

Mother didn't have an answer for that.

Just one more day, just one more day, and Hanuman would have made it to his new home. Maybe Mother should have put him on one of the vehicles to keep him safe, and I'm sure she was thinking the same thing. But he wanted to come along so badly. Herding goats, and being with Mother, that's what he lived for. No way he was going to miss this journey. I thought back over the days since we left Graeagle. As Hanuman limped along, the goats followed, and he did his duty, from morning rollout to evening camp; but it was clear he was slowing down, day by day, which was why we were so long on the road and already overdue.

"Let's make room for him in one of the carts," Mother said, her hand on my shoulder.

Max made a bed of aromatic pine needles and early daffodils. I wove a garland of fern and wildflowers for his neck. Mother brushed his thick white fur until it lay upon his worn-out doggie body like fresh snow.

On the sixteenth day of the march, we stumbled into Indian Valley. The shepherds drove the animals up the long hill to get them settled in their new pens before our funeral procession started the climb. Mother, Max, and I waited for an hour at the bottom with the last goat cart. And Hanuman. By the time we arrived at the upper village, everyone had gathered at the barn that was to be our temporary mandir. Those who didn't have time to change clothes, at least washed their faces and hands and slicked down their hair. Annabel placed the harmonium on a picnic table, and the drummers tuned their instruments. As we drew near, Annabel sounded the opening chords of the "Hanuman Chaleesa," and two hundred voices joined to sing the forty beautiful verses:

> *Bhajelo ji Hanuman!*
> *Bhajelo ji Hanuman!*
> *O Friend, Remember Hanuman!*

Now that I am a grown woman, it's easier to embrace his passing, but back then I only knew my doggie was dead and was no more. Sometimes, I think I see him, in the corner of my eye. I walk out to the herds and expect to find him. One of the ewes gets cantankerous, and I whistle for Hanuman to bark her back into line. Why doesn't he come?

CHAPTER TWENTY-EIGHT

Boo!

I WAS A HERO AMONG CHILDREN.

"I could march forever, a nomad of the open road, a wanderer in the wilderness."

Thus I proclaimed to my envious Yoogie audience, though secretly I was relieved to be back with Dad and Mirabai, and happy enough to unroll my mat under a pine tree and fall asleep at the first opportunity. So deep my exhaustion, I did not rouse when Dad picked me up and put me into the bed next to my sister. I slept through the night, and through the next day, waking up just in time to stumble into the new amrit for dinner.

Now the work began, so much to be done before Planting Day: building and painting, digging canals, clearing boulders from the fields; not to mention the daily chores of a large farm: milking goats and cows, feeding ducks and chickens, trimming hooves and horns, weeding and sprouting, fetching eggs and slopping pigs. The older kids shared in that work, but we littles were mostly underfoot and sent off to Pattycake's Club. All of us kids were warned to stay close. After the horrible murder of Hanuman out on the road, Mother was worried sick. Max assigned armed hunters to keep their sights on us.

Come on, too many kids, too few hunters. After a few weeks, with no sign of trouble, supernatural or otherwise, the guarding got sloppy, then stopped altogether. Mama Patty took charge of our safety, but she could not keep tabs on every kid all the time, and us Yoogies, accustomed to playing by ourselves in the woods, drifted farther and farther away from her watchful eye.

I was off in the high pasture trying to find Butterbean, the little pest, who had wandered off from his mama and got lost. Alma Mendez tiptoed up behind me, leaned down close, and shouted:

"Boo!"

I squealed, whirled around, tripped, and fell on my bottom.

Seeing who surprised me, I got on my feet, face flushed, spitting mad.

"Why did you sneak up on me?" I demanded.

"I was worried about you."

"Worried?"

"Out there, all alone, Kali gonna get you."

"Kali?"

"Yeah, the monster what killed your dog. Him's what all the grown-ups are whispering about, whispering so you Yoogies won't get scared; but I heard 'em, and I know. It's the Kali Man, and I seen him for myself."

"You've seen him? You've seen him with your own eyes?"

"Maybe he talked to me and told me what he was going to do to you."

"No such thing as Kali. Max said so."

"Oh yeah, Kali Man said he gonna find you. Gonna hold you down with those yellow eyes of his; then he gonna sex you. You know what I'm talking about?"

"Of course I do! I know all about sexing."

"Yeah, he say he gonna open you up and put his thing in you. Then, he gonna eat you alive, eat you raw while you still watching, gonna start with your feet and eat his way up. Last part he gonna eat is your head. One snap with his big monster teeth, and he's swallowing you down, down, down his wet, squeezy neck into his hot, steamy stomach, and there's no air for you to breathe, and you're dissolving away into nothing, and you can't see because it's totally dark down there, and you try to scream, let me out, let me out, but nobody can hear you, and your mouth fills up with hot, black slime, and you choke and die."

"Don't say those words," I screamed.

"That's why I'm worried about you, Janabai, out here all alone."

"Kali Man's not coming around here."

"Why not?"

"Because he's afraid of my Mother and Max; everybody knows that."

"Your mother ain't so tough, and Max is all talk."

"I'll tell her you said so."

"You open your big mouth and I'll knock your teeth down your throat."

Chapter Twenty-Nine

Is Kali Real?

"Max," I asked, "tell me the truth. Is Kali real?"

Max was leaning against a live oak, her M16 field-stripped on a tarp. She glanced up at me, continued to run a brush through the rifle barrel, took her time answering.

"Your mother thinks so, ask her."

"I'm asking you. Did you ever see a demon? I mean for real?"

"We'll talk about it later, when you're older."

"I need to know right now."

"Why?" Max asked.

"Someone said the Kali Man was going to get me."

"Who?"

I remembered what Alma said about knocking my teeth down my throat. "Somebody."

"Well, *somebody* is trying to scare you. You just stay close like I told you, and do not talk to strangers. There's nothing around here can hurt you except bears and cougars and rattlers and wild pigs and skunks and rabid bats and shit like that."

I was not ready to let go of my question.

"Old Ben Gray Horse says there is a *kohuneje* that eats people."

"Old Ben says a lot of things."

"Mother says you saw a dwarf turn into a tiger."

"She told you?"

"Well, not me, but other people, and I heard it."

"I bet you did. You and your rabbit ears."

I touched my head and realized I was wearing my furry headdress. I giggled.

"Well?"

"Well, what?"

"Did you see a dwarf turn into a tiger?"

Max set the rifle barrel down on the tarp. Took a breath and blew it out.

"Okay. One day when your mother and I was out on patrol, she felt something was watching us and told me to stop the car."

"How did she feel it?" I asked.

"I don't know how, but she is almost always right."

"So what happened? Was she right?"

"Yes. I snuck around through the woods until I spied this little man pointing a gun at your mother. I sighted in on him, but somehow he knew I was there."

"Was he a dwarf, a real dwarf? I've never seen a real dwarf. What did he look like?"

"He was tiny, like a boy, and he had a skinny little braid of hair hanging down his back like a rat's tail."

"He was tattooed, right?" I asked.

"That's right."

"Like you?"

"Yeah, like me, only the dwarf had tattoos everywhere: his neck and face and arms, everywhere I could see."

"What happened?"

"I aimed and fired, but he was already ducking, and I missed or maybe just winged him, because I heard him scream."

"What about the tiger? When did he turn into a tiger?"

"Well, he disappeared, and a couple of seconds later I saw something that looked like a big cat with orange and black stripes, or maybe it was just a cougar and my imagination. I was pretty scared."

"You? Oh, Max, you're trying to fool me. You don't get scared."

"Everybody gets scared."

"But not you."

Max laughed and began to reassemble the weapon.

"Did you see the yellow eyes?" I persisted. "Everyone says the demon has yellow glowing eyes."

Max didn't answer right away. She looked up into my face.

"Like I said, go ask your mother."

I found Mother in Science looking over Suranjini's shoulder, both women's faces covered with masks. Suranjini was stirring a glass container filled with amber goo.

"Be with you in a minute, honey," Mother said. "What do you need?"

"Ask you a question," I said.

"Big question or little question?"

"Um, big."

"Sit down over there, we're almost finished."

I clambered up on a tall stool and watched as the two women capped the container and carefully stacked it among others inside one of Shiva Puri's most treasured assets, the solar-powered refrigerator Vic somehow kept working. Mother and Suranjini removed their masks and thoroughly washed their hands with precious soap. Drying her hands, Mother looked over her shoulder.

"So what's your question today, Miss Curious Georgette?"

"What are you and Suri doing?"

"Making a new batch of Shakti-cillin. Is that what you came here to ask?"

"No, Mother, something important."

"Ask away," Azriel said.

"Should I leave?" Suranjini asked.

"No, stay here and keep at it," Mother answered. "We'll go for a walk. Okay with you?" she asked me.

"Roger!"

Mother chuckled.

"Where are we going?" I asked.

"It's still an hour until lunch, so I think we should walk up the creek and find a place to cool off. What do you say?"

"I say yahoo!" I was delighted. Private moments with my busy mother were rare treasures. Meandering up the path, Mother found the place she was looking for. We took off our clothes and

106

waded into the water. The spot Mother chose was upstream from the village center, soap not permitted, and no peeing in the water! We swam among the boulders, playing the tag game where you're safe as long as you were underwater. Mother let me catch her. She thought she was putting one over on me, but I knew what she was doing. Sometimes it's better when grown-ups let kids win. We climbed out on a sunlit rock shelf to warm ourselves.

"You see these holes?" Mother asked, pointing at a cluster of depressions in the rocks.

"What are they?"

"In the old days, the Indian women would come here, right to this spot, to grind acorns in these holes."

"Why?"

"They were making acorn flour for their food. They would gather here every day. Each woman had her own spot, and they would work together, and sing, and laugh, and gossip."

"Gossip about what?" I asked.

"About men, of course!"

I laughed. It was so nice to be joking around with my mother, relaxed and enjoying each other. It didn't happen often enough. Mother was thinking the same thing. We shared a few moments of silence, letting ourselves dry off in the midday sunshine.

"Alright, Janabai, what is your big question?"

"Mother?"

"Yes, Daughter?"

"Is Kali real?"

"What do you mean?"

"I mean, does Kali walk around and find people and eat them and kill their dogs?"

"We can talk about this when you're older."

"We can talk about it now."

Mother stared at me.

"Sometimes you sound so grown-up you scare me."

"Scare you?"

"I don't mean scare in that way. I mean that you are growing up so fast, I just don't know what you are becoming."

"Is it a bad thing?"

"No, it's a remarkable, wonderful thing. I'm proud of you."

What a surprising thing for her to say! Mother rarely gives compliments.

But I refused to be distracted. "You didn't answer me. Do you believe Kali is real, I mean really, really real?"

Mother laughed.

"Oh yes, he's real enough."

"Have you seen him?"

"Let's see." Mother thought for a moment. "Two times I can be sure of. And many more times in visions. And once, I knew he was nearby, and I didn't see him, but Max did."

"When he turned into a tiger?"

"She told you? Strange. Max doesn't like to talk about it."

"I pestered her until she told me about it to get rid of me."

"That sounds about right."

"Where did Kali come from?"

"Some say he came from another world."

"The world of the gods?"

"That's right, and some say the old demon has always been here with us."

"Did he make the Kali Yuga and make the whole world go kablooey?"

"That's what I believe."

"Then I believe it too."

"Slide over here and let me put your arms around me. I'm getting a little chilly."

I snuggled up next to her.

"There," Mother said, "that's better."

"Why doesn't Lord Shiva just get rid of him?"

"Now that is an interesting question. Why do you think?"

"Maybe Lord Shiva is afraid of him?"

"I don't think so."

"Maybe Kali is stronger than Lord Shiva?"

"I don't think so."

"Maybe Lord Shiva needs Kali for some secret plan?"

"Aha, Daughter," Mother said, giving me a squeeze, "now you are on to something."

CHAPTER THIRTY

Googlers

W E YOOGIES LEARNED THE HARD way we had been demoted from Patty Club Alpha Dogs, to the back of the pack. The Googlers pushed us around whenever they felt like it. This was not the Shiva Puri way! We called them "Googlers" because they were always bragging that they could talk to the Almighty Google. These big kids were old enough to mourn the technological wizardry lost to them: television, smartphones, PlayStations, and the Internet. I didn't care about any of that stuff, and most of what they said was made up to impress Yoogies.

We seldom played together. Googlers played indoors, where their favorite games were Dungeons and Dragons and other stupid dramas they invented. Fantasy worlds, super heroes, and supernatural powers, or imaginary episodes played in front of dead computers; that's what they liked. Oh wow, sound like fun?

Their unhappiness came from memories of their lives before the Kali Yuga fell down on us. They were old enough to remember what it was like—civilization, I mean—but they were not mature enough to deal with the loss. We Yoogies didn't know any of that Before-the-Event glory, so we didn't miss it. Our lives were just the way they were supposed to be, and speak the truth, we were spoiled rotten by the grownups. We were the HOPE FOR THE FUTURE!

The Googlers thought we needed to come down a peg, and they made sure we knew our place: bottom of the dog pile. I could already read and write better than any of them, a fact that did not endear me to my older classmates. I was reminded on a regular basis that I was full of myself. In truth, I spared no effort in letting everybody know how special I was.

Kids do ugly things to each other. I suspect it has always been that way and always will be that way, but at Puri School the one rule, the most important rule was "No hurting": no hitting, no biting, no noogies, no physical stuff of any kind tolerated, no matter what awful thing was said. When older kids insulted me, I turned it around and sent it right back in their faces, twice as fast, twice as sharp. But Mirabai, blind and good-natured, was defenseless. Alma Mendez, forbidden to talk to me, took it on herself to become Mirabai's personal tormentor. I tried to protect my sister with words and tattling to the teacher, but one day, when there was no teacher around, Alma started singing a song she had made up all by herself.

Blind as a worm,
Dumb as a rock,
Mira-butt the moron,
Can't even wipe the turds off her butt

It was so stupid, and it didn't even rhyme. I listened to Alma go on and on until I just couldn't stand it. I ran over and slapped her. Even as I was doing it, I knew I should have punched her right in the snot locker like Max had taught me, but at the last second, I chickened out and landed a weak slap across her cheek. Alma stood there for a few seconds in shock. Then, smiling, she came after me, just like Max said she would.

Alma beat me up pretty bad. She was ten years old by then and so much bigger than me. Also, I take after my Dad, who is skinny and not at all good in a fight. So, Alma whipped the stuffing out of me, and this time we both got in trouble—but me more than her, because I started it. Mistah Tee called both of us up front.

"Do you have anything to say to Alma?" he asked.

"I'm sorry for slapping you," I said.

"Do you mean it?" Mistah Tee asked. I considered it. Did I mean it? I remembered Alma was Mendez, not McGartland, and both of her real parents had died or wandered off, leaving Alma in the back seat of an automobile, alone and in the dark. How would I feel? How would I act if my daddy and mother died and left me and Mirabai all alone.

"Yes, I mean it. I'm sorry, Alma."

"And you, Alma, are you sorry?" Mistah Tee turned to Alma.

"I'm sorry I said mean things to Mirabai, but I'm not sorry I beat up Prissy, who hit me first. Just stay out of my way, Yoogie."

Alma decided she had gotten away clean and resumed taunting Mirabai whenever Mistah Tee wasn't paying attention... until Max heard about it. How did Max find out? It wasn't me, if that's what you're thinking.

The same afternoon of the fight, Max came to get Mirabai. She picked my sister up in the air over her head like she was still a baby. Usually Mira laughed her happy Max-is-here laugh, but this day my sister hung quiet and limp. Something changed in Max's face. She stopped smiling and lowered my sister until she was looking into her face. Max shifted Mira over to one hip and looked around the room. Nobody said a word, not even Mistah Tee. It was so quiet. Max walked over to me, bent down, and examined my swollen lip and bruised cheek.

"You're going to have a real shiner tomorrow morning," she said, and nodded as if my wounds were somehow admirable. I started feeling better right away. Max stood up and looked around the room. Her eyes stopped on Alma.

"You still sleeping in the women's barracks?"

Alma didn't want to answer.

"How are they treating you over there?"

Alma answered in a teensy whisper, "Good."

"I'm glad to hear it," Max said. "You come see me from time to time. I'm always around, keeping an eye on you, in case you need anything."

Alma nodded.

"Can you say, 'Roger that'?"

Alma said, "Roger that." Another teensy whisper.

"Well, oorah," said Max. She shifted her attention away from Alma, who was, I'm quite sure, peeing down her leg. Max walked to the door with Mira still on her hip, stopped and turned around.

"Can you Yard Apes say oorah?" she asked.

We Yard Apes shouted, "OORAH!"

Max left.

At home Max grilled me about the fight.

"Did you punch her like I showed you?"

"I kinda slapped her, but not too hard."

"All you did was make her mad."

"I wanted to hit her in the snot locker, but I chickened out."

"Don't say 'chickened out.' Fighting is just not in your nature."

"What's my nature?"

"Well, you're a strange little duck, you get it from your father, and don't tell him I said so; and you're a caregiver, because that's who you are, and you get that from your father too."

"But I want to be a warrior, like you."

"Have you been listening to me?"

"Yes. You said I'm a duck, a strange little duck."

"That's all you heard, the duck part?"

"Can I be a duck and a warrior? A mighty warrior duck!"

"Aaaaiiieee," Max wailed, holding her head as I flung myself around the barn, punching and kicking, self-accompanied by an expectoration of mighty quacks.

"QUACK QUACK QUACK!"

"Enough," Max shouted. "Okay, Janabai, I mean, Janaduck. If you get into another fight, a real fight, you need to put the other person on the ground and out of the fight with your first punch if you can. Remember?"

"QUACK I remember!"

"Very well. Show me how you should have punched Alma."

I demonstrated.

"No good," Max said. "You're arm-punching, like a girl."

"I am a girl, QUACK, a duck girl."

"Yeah, sure, but not when you fight."

"What am I when I fight? A boy? A duck BOY?"

"No, you're not any kind of a duck. You're a warrior. So when you punch, you punch like a warrior, from the shoulder with all your weight and power behind it, twisting in, like this."

She demonstrated.

"Now you punch."

I tried again, aiming for Max's open palm.

"Better, but your fist is too loose and you'll just hurt yourself. Make a hard fist, like iron. Harder. Now, hard fist, from the shoulder, right into the palm of my hand. Do it."

I punched again.

"Better. Try it again. Spread your feet a bit wider. Left foot a little bit in front. Yes. Do it."

I threw my best punch.

"Ow," Max cried. "You hurt me."

I grinned.

Max grinned back, "And you are a still a strange little duck."

"No I'm not."

"You're not? What are you?"

"I'm a rabbit, a strange little RABBIT."

"You certainly are."

CHAPTER THIRTY-ONE

Safe Haven

THE MONTHS WENT BY, SCHOOL let out, and we went back into the fields. In Mistah Tee's classroom, I had gotten pretty good at avoiding Alma, and now that spring had arrived, it became even easier. Whenever I wasn't out in the sheds taking care of my goats, I worked in Odessa Piwinski's "liberry," a safe haven where you can be sure Alma Mendez would never stick her nose. I was almost ten, and Odessa was seventy-something, but in spite of the difference in our ages, we became friends because we both loved books. I loved what was *inside* them, the people and adventures, as did she, but Odessa loved the things themselves, the *books*. Among the thousands of volumes rescued from private homes, or "borrowed" from school and public libraries, there were

113

a few books Miss Piwinski treasured above all others, not for the content, but for the fine craftsmanship.

"You may never see another book of this quality," Piwinski would say. "Just feel the paper."

I would gently touch the page.

"It's magical."

"Yes, it is. Look how it's made. The pages are hand-sewn, not glued."

"We could sew the pages," I said.

Piwinski gave me an appreciative smile. "Yes, we could. We could, indeed. Let's see, I know we must have something here telling us how to make our own books."

And off we'd go, intrepid explorers, searching together through the stacks for books to teach us how to sew our own new books.

Before our move to Indian Valley, we made "liberry" cards for every volume at Shiva Puri, more than four thousand books. There was not enough room in her "hooch,", so Miss Piwinski annexed two nearby homes. In one she kept all the old magazines and newspapers. In the other she kept the "less interesting" holdings, including pornography. I have looked at pornographic pictures and read the words. I will tell you, it's pretty silly stuff, and it's boring. Mother wanted to burn it all, but Miss Piwinski said over her dead body.

"No book of mine, no matter how much you dislike it, Missy, will ever be burned in this village, so you can just stick your fascist book-burning matches up your holier-than-thou ass."

Besides Max, Odessa Piwinski was the only person at Shiva Puri who could get away with speaking to Azriel Dancer like that. The business about the pornography wasn't the only conflict between Mother and Miss Piwinski. The other disagreement was about history books. My mother lived in the future. She was the beacon and hope we might survive our current hardships and reach the Promised Land. Chosen by the gods to keep us moving forward, Azriel Burke-Kucinich channeled the Shakti, the divine energy. Her authority far exceeded her duties as "Security Chief"… and she was unpredictable. She would show up anywhere, at any time — in the warehouse, in the field, in the lab — looking over your shoulder and rendering her opinion.

Shiva Puri trusted Mother. Treasured her. Loved her. Feared her. Everybody knew she had killed somebody. Simone said she saw Mother stand over a man and put seven bullets into his head at close range. Simone wouldn't make up something like that. Mother would do anything, *anything*, to protect Shiva Puri, and you crossed her at your peril.

When Odessa Piwinski stood nose to nose with Azriel Dancer over the history books, it must have been a startling moment. I wish I had been there to see it myself, but it happened in the first summer before Mira and I were born. Our scavenging teams were raiding the countryside around Graeagle for everything that wasn't nailed down. Then they went back and dismantled the rest. Every house and building not being used for something else was stuffed with civilization's leftovers, but each seva boss had a list of priority items. Not Miss Piwinski. She wanted it all. Every book and scrap of paper with words or pictures on it. Mother countermanded Piwinski's request.

"Leave the history books where they are, or get rid of them."

Odessa tried to reason with Mother. "Why would we do something like that?"

"We don't need the history of what came before. History brought us to where we are. History destroyed the world."

"She who ignores history…" Odessa began. Mother cut her off.

"Is doomed to repeat it? Yes, so I've heard. It's not true. History weighed us down. It paralyzed us. It killed us with ancient hatreds. Palestinians and Jews and all the rest. We never escaped history. Now we can. We have a clean slate, a fresh start. The weight of that karma has been lifted from us."

"You're wrong, Azriel," Odessa said, "and you sound like all the fanatical nut jobs of the past, the ones we still have to look out for to make sure they don't take over again."

Well, that brought Mother up short. There is nothing Mother values more than the truth, even when she's the one who gets pinned by it. In our tradition, we haul our egos out of the cracks where they hide, and expose them to the light. Mother took a few moments to reconsider her opinion.

"This is a library," Odessa continued. "It may be the *last* library in the world. These may be the only books left. Every book, even the most deplorable, is rare and special."

Mother sighed. "Maybe you're right, Odessa. We'll compromise. You get your history books, but you keep them safe and out of my sight until I think this through more clearly."

They made the deal. History books were safe, back in the "annex," and people were free to read them, but they were not flaunted or displayed out in the main library. Miss Piwinski won the day, because you can't take the history out of stories. What is fiction about, all of those novels on the front shelves, if not stories *set in time*? Nor could you separate history from the non-fiction books, the volumes of science and geography and so on.

Mother took her war on history in another direction, and this time her attack was irresistible. History would never be a subject taught in *school*. The books were there in the library if you wanted to dwell in the past, but most of our people did not.

Decide for yourself which of those two she-wolves had the better of it.

In the winter, when it was too cold for her to keep her old bones warm in the library, and too wet for people to check out individual books, Miss Piwinski would bring our boxes of library cards to the Village Center. People would thumb through the cards and make their selections. Odessa would send me to trudge through the snow with a sled. I would find the books, wrap them up in waterproof bags, and drag them back to her winter desk in a warm corner of the amrit. Odessa called her cluttered little nest the "Branch Library." There, people would line up to await her inspection of their clean hands, present their bookmarks, and check out their literary treasures.

"Cliff Stoval has reserved *Salem's Lot,*" she said.

I would examine the holdings on the temporary shelves, locate the volume, and hand it to her.

"*Salem's Lot*, hmmmm?" She raised her eyebrows and looked over the top rim of her eyeglasses.

Cliff Stoval, standing tall and nervous, squirmed, awaiting Miss Piwinski's opinion of his taste.

"Early King," she said. "Not his best. Still, scare your pants off. One of my favorites. Be sure you have garlic in your pocket before you open this. You are about to summon the Vampire. Think you're up to it, Mr. Stovall?"

"Yessum, Miss Piwinski."

"Very well. You may have your book, and good luck. Next."

Mr. Stovall breathed a sigh of relief and scooted away with a big grin, saved again from Piwinski's bite.

Yes, not only my first seva leader, Odessa Piwinski became one of my dearest friends. She hoped I would become her successor when I graduated from school. That was not to be, but I am so happy to tell you that she is still my friend, and just as feisty, guarding her beloved books fiercely, though the library holdings are much reduced from those early days. Nobody dreamed Odessa Piwinski would survive the march across the Klamath Desolation, but she kept right on walking when others, much younger, dropped and died. Dharma to her books kept Odessa going.

CHAPTER THIRTY-TWO

Da Fine Idee

I'M IN SUCH A SENTIMENTAL mood this afternoon. Perhaps pregnancy, even unwanted pregnancy, makes every woman feel like this. But how would *I* know? This is my first time around, but it seems reasonable. Today the temperature is a bit cooler, and there's a nice breeze blowing through the tent. I think I will write something special in my book to honor Ted Kealoha, Mistah Tee, the gentle Hawaiian who taught us so many of our early lessons: how to be kind to each other, how to tell jokes, and how to sing the old sweet songs of faraway islands he would never see again.

Mistah Tee built a stage at one end of our classroom. Well, "stage" is a bit of an exaggeration; it was just a curtain he could hide behind and work his hand puppets. His partner, Mr. Parker Adams, costumed the puppets to be so lifelike it was easy to tell who they were supposed to be. The first puppets? Max and Mother. Mr. Adams called them Punch and Judy, perfect in every detail from "Punch's" tight Marine Corps bun to "Judy's" long wavy curls, hair so long it disappeared below the edge of the stage, a funny sight in itself. Judy also had a red bindi mark, just like Mother always wore, right between her eyes; and humongous bosoms, ha ha, just like Mother's. Punch had barbed-wire tattoos around her bulging biceps and always wore camouflage. Mistah Tee played Punch, and Mr. Parker Adams played Judy. They tried to get Miss Conroy involved, but she was too snooty to get down behind the curtain and "act the fool."

The two men performed the adventures of Punch and Judy, and they did a passable job, until two new volunteers stepped forward to don the puppets and show everybody how it was done. Max and Mother, playing themselves. The two old friends were astonishing. Who could have guessed Mother could do so many comical voices? And Max? After years of barracks banter back in the "Old Corps," Max could dish sarcasm fast and hot. Together, the two women would try anything, and afterward pretend it wasn't them, it was the puppets, and "we don't know what came over those creatures; some days they seem to have a life of their own."

We waited for the moment in every episode when Judy would do something wrong, or say something stupid, and bend over while Punch gave her a thorough spanking—something not condoned at Shiva Puri, so the sight of the puppets whacking each other was the height of naughtiness. One day, as usual, Judy was getting into trouble. Punch was slapping boxes down in front of her, and Judy was supposed to be putting candy in the boxes, and she couldn't keep up except by throwing the candy behind her. She made a mess of things until Punch caught her and, you guessed it, told her to bend over for a spanking. Whack! Ow! Whack! Ow! Whack! Ow!

It gave me an idea.

"What if we had a Kali Demon Puppet with big teeth and yellow eyes," I suggested to Mistah Tee, "and you played Kali and you came down in a fireball and you had a big fight and Punch and Judy spanked *your* bottom for making so much trouble."

Mistah Tee gave me one of his enormous smiles.

"Wahine, you git da fine idee!" he said, Hawaiian-style, what he called *pigeon*, I don't know why. *Pigeon?*

Then I had the biggest "fine idee" of all.

"What if we made a whole puppet play and kept it a secret and did it for the whole village on Kali Yuga day for a surprise, and we could all be in it, and the teachers too, and the Middles and the Bigs?"

The adults, Mistah Tee and Mr. Parker Adams, Mother and Max, and Miss Conroy, looked at each other, at our excited, eager faces, except Alma, who rolled her eyes. Mr. Parker Adams proclaimed, "Come springtime we shall thrust Janabai's Kali Yuga play upon the unsuspecting sensibilities of our audience!"

We didn't know anything about "unsuspecting sensibilities," but we clapped and cheered!

Every kid in the school, and all of the teachers, were invited to be in the Great Play, but there were few takers. Not one of the Middles volunteered, though their teachers, Nithinya and Leann, helped Mr. Parker Adams with costumes. None of the Bigs stepped forward — except one. Skyler Jones, in his first Big year, was the coolest kid in school, so cool that when he joined the Little kids to do the play, he became even cooler than he was before.

Of course, I had known Skyler Jones all my life. In a village like Shiva Puri, everybody knows everybody, but I will never forget the exact moment I saw his big shoulders framed in Mistah Tee's door.

"If you don't mind," he said with that slow drawl of his, "I'd like to help with Janabai's play."

Janabai's play! Well, he knocked the sass right out of me. I might have been a second-year Little, but I loved Skyler Jones from that very moment. I couldn't take my eyes off him. Lord Shiva's grace poured out of that boy, some aura of divinity; not to mention his good looks, which he possessed in abundance. Everyone liked to be in his presence, me most of all. When he smiled at me, well... I could hardly breathe. Have you ever met someone who made you feel like that? Anyway, Skyler Jones stepped into the room, and into my heart.

Then there was Alma.

Though she showed up less and less, Alma was still counted among us Littles, and was the only one of Mistah Tee's kids who did not participate in the play. She wanted so desperately to be accepted, but she was caught in between, too young to be a Googler, and too old to be one of us Yoogies, and never comfortable in either group.

One cold, gray January day I saw her standing outside in the snow, peeking in through the window at Kali play practice. When she noticed me looking at her, the saddest expresssion came over her face, helpless and lonely. I could have reached out to her *right then* and invited her inside, and I think she would have come, and everything that happened later might have been different. But I missed the moment. Maybe I was too afraid of her. Maybe I just hated her for hurting me. Maybe unkind thoughts kept me from acting as dharma required, and I did nothing but stare at her until she dropped her head and turned away to disappear into the snow.

And so the preparations for the Kali play went forward without Alma Mendez.

We tried to keep our plans secret, but more and more community time was spent on the production. Vic Tretheway and his mechanics tore out one side of the mandir and rebuilt it as a stage for the play, including a big hole in the wall for the puppets. Mistah Tee called it the "proscenium"; high enough off the ground for the puppeteers to operate the characters over their heads. Out in front of the "proscenium," Vic built the "apron," a platform for the live actors to be seen from the back rows.

Two months later, on March 25, the children of Shiva Puri, with a little help from our teachers, and featuring Azriel and Max as themselves, presented the first Kali Yuga play. The show was raggedy. Our props fell over, we forgot our words, people in the back had trouble seeing and hearing. It was a spectacular mess, and a more spectacular success. Before we finished taking our bows, the audience took up the chant:

"Do it again! Do it again!"

What could we do? Nothing, except to perform the whole thing all over again.

Two more times.

CHAPTER THIRTY-THREE

The Kali Yuga Play

Azriel dances around the Blue Rock

Kali falls from the sky with Fireball Dancers
(played by the first year Littles)

Azriel saves the pack rat

Galen the Farmer takes the villagers to Downieville in the old bus

Azriel brings the goats

Hanuman the Great Dog saves Azriel and the goats from the bear

Manoj and Raj bring the truck back to rescue
Azriel and Hanuman and the goats

The goats dance with joy (played by the second year Littles)

Daniel takes over and tells everybody what to do

Azriel meets Max

Max teaches Azriel to shoot

Azriel messes up and Max spanks her (the funny part)

Kali kidnaps Maitreya, Laksman, Ajay, and Levi (the sad part)

Azriel and Max go after Kali

The gunfight at the crossroads (the exciting part)

Kali begs for mercy (more funny stuff)

Azriel and Max spank Kali (more funny stuff)

Kali gets away and runs around the mandir
chomping with his big teeth (the scary part)

Azriel and Max chase Kali away

We all live happily, happily, happily ever after

The end

CHAPTER THIRTY-FOUR

The Middles

WHEN ALMA GRADUATED TO THE Middles, I hoped my life would get easier, but that wasn't to be. We graduated into the Middles at the same time. Alma and me, together again. Swell. At least I got to bring my sister along. Mirabai just sat in the classroom anyway, listening, but not saying anything. She couldn't read or write, of course, but Mama Patty decided Mira would be happier being with me.

There were twelve kids in the Middles, thirteen if you count my sister. Besides Alma Mendez McGartland and me, Evan Grunsky and George Sunkari also moved up. The other middles, the kids already there, were Austin Minard, who was one of the refugee kids from Quincy and adopted by the Magalskis; Aaron Magalsky (Austin's new brother), Tiffany Staab, Robert McGartland, who now had to put up with Alma, his adopted "little sister"; Kimberli Prymak, Ashdep Mondul, Dalton Cassio, and Annie Raines. What would a classroom be without a Raines kid in it? I know you won't remember all those names, but Mother said she wanted a thorough record with *all the details*, so there you go.

Miss Nithinya Varanasi, affectionately dubbed Miss Vee, was in charge of us Middles, poor woman. We were aged nine to twelve, a pack of brats if you ask me. Nobody but Miss Vee would put up with us. I already adored Nithinya Varanasi from when she came down to the Littles to teach arithmetic when Mistah Tee went up to the Middles to teach music. Every kid should have a big sister, and Nithinya Varanasi was mine. From the beginning I was horrible in arithmetic, and I believe the only reason I passed was because Miss Vee dragged me through it.

When I couldn't talk to Mother or Dad, Miss Vee was my confidant and champion. She listened to my complaints, endured my petulance, steered me away from making a fool of myself, and stood up for me even when I acted like the spoiled princess Alma Mendez accused me of being. When I first arrived in her classroom, Miss Vee was not much older than I am now, twenty-two or twenty-three. I worshiped her, and so did every unattached man at Shiva Puri. They were always finding excuses to come around just in case she needed help with any "little old thing." Nithinya Varanasi was the goddess of love, and I looked to her for instruction in the mysterious subject of boys.

Miss Vee also taught science. She would teach Basic Science to her Middle students and then go down to the Littles and teach Critters and Collards, then go all the way up to the Bigs and teach Practical Science. We lucky children of Shiva Puri got Miss Vee from the time we started school when we were six until we finished school when we were sixteen. She knew her arithmetic and science. By the time we graduated, so did every kid in the village, except two dunderheads. The first dunderhead was me, duh. I was just as horrible in science as I was in arithmetic.

123

The second arithmetical dunderhead? Guess. Alma Mendez refused to learn anything as worthless as "arit-matic." She almost never came to school. Thank the gods. No one knew where she was or what she was doing, or who she was doing it with. That was a mistake, not keeping a weather-eye out for Alma. We would learn to regret our inattention, bitterly regret it. But at the time, every school day without Alma was a blessing.

Leann Mills, nicknamed Miss Lee, was Miss Vee's assistant and taught composition and penmanship. Paper, pencils, and pens were far too precious for day-to-day school work, so we used chalkboards the Meks made for us, and smaller slates at our desks. We did get paper for the important reports and for the final drafts of our original stories we presented in February at the Mahashivaratri Book Faire. Miss Piwinski felt these projects were a valuable use for our precious paper.

"Our children's perceptions of the circumstances in which we find ourselves," Piwinski said, "are indispensable contributions to the archives." Something like that. At the end of the term, each kid was issued five sheets of paper upon which we anxiously recorded our stories in the teensiest handwriting you can imagine. *Both* sides of each sheet. We would meticulously sew our five sheets between cardboard covers. After the Faire, Miss Piwinski would collect every one and add them to the village archives.

Dad supported Miss Piwinski's Book Faire and authorized the supplies. Mother did not agree with the extravagant use of paper, but she and Dad were having another of their "estrangements," and Mother didn't want a public fight over the matter, so she just walked away. In private, if Mother said, "Don't you come in here with those dirty feet," Dad would argue, saying, "All the children have dirty feet." If Mother said, "I love your dirty feet," Dad would argue, "Don't you come in here with those dirty feet." That's the way I remember them, arguing over everything.

Max taught more Boot Camp, this time Gun Safety and Marksmanship, which I never did take to. *Sorry, Mother, I just never liked it.* I couldn't hit the target if "the muzzle was touching the bull's-eye," as Max said. Hunting? Me? Killing an animal?

Forget it. But I did whatever I was instructed, because we Middles were learning that Max's Boot Camp was not a game. Something dangerous was out there, beyond the wire, and Max was getting us ready.

Every morning, or whenever we went outside, or before leaving for school, we kids tied on the *bush kits* that held our flint, magnifying lens, signal mirror, and knife — Mother's rules. Mother also insisted we run everywhere and go barefoot except in winter. She said we had to grow up "tough as old leather."

She was right. As always. What a pain.

CHAPTER THIRTY-FIVE

Songsinger

FOR THE FIRST TWO YEARS of her life, everyone thought Mirabai was stupid as well as blind. She would hum to herself and make little grunting noises, like "hunh hunh," but that was about it. Around me she would say things aloud, like "go swimming." I assumed everyone knew she could talk. For the most part, she didn't have anything she wanted to say. To this day, she doesn't chatter, but when she does speak, it gets so quiet you can hear trees grow.

People began to catch on when she started singing aloud, just before we turned nine years old. Mira could sing every song she ever heard. That was amazing in itself, her musical memory, but nobody could guess just how good she was going to get. They were about to find out.

Mistah Tee used to come up to the Middles to teach advanced singing: harmony, ensemble, and *bhajans* (sacred songs). These sessions were Mirabai's favorite. She would sit on her rug and sway and hum along, and nobody paid any attention, until, one

125

November day, Mirabai started singing along. Astounding. She sang perfectly, note for note, word for word, never forgetting a lyric, never wavering on a melody, never going out of tune. Right away Mistah Tee realized she was sensational, better than he was ever going to be. Mirabai only had to hear a song one time and she had it. Mistah Tee would sing or play the song, then turn it over to Sis, who would sing it so beautifully everyone just naturally wanted to sing along.

One sunny Sunday morning, Mistah Tee interrupted satsang to announce he had a "surprise guest" who was going to lead us in singing the Shiva Stotram. Nobody groaned, aloud anyway, though privately most folks cringed. Shiva Stotram was not a village favorite, being our most demanding chant, 278 Sanskrit verses long, no repeats, with mystifying melody changes and fluky shifts from one key to another. Annabel Feuerstein, harmonium virtuoso, had to play the Stotram from a written score. Drummers spent years trying in vain to master the troublesome tekkas. All in all, Shiva Stotram was a divine pain in the butt. Rewarding it was supposed to be, if, and that's a big if, we ever got through it without messing up, which, in the days before Mirabai, was never. The long, long chant usually fell apart at verse 90, again at 215, and anyplace else where we faltered. Musicians as well as singers dropped out and hoped to catch up later. Cymbal fingers blistered, drummer shoulders ached. At our best, Shiva Stotram took almost two hours, and everyone was drained when we finally stumbled through the last verse.

Mistah Tee gave me the sign. I led Mirabai up in front of the sangam and left her standing there all alone while I took my time carefully unrolling my asana and placing it *just so* on the floor next to her and sat down with a mysterious smile. There was a tension in the mandir like something excruciating was going to happen and nobody could stop it. Annabel (Mistah Tee had tipped her off earlier) played the opening figures of the Shiva Stotram on the harmonium. Everyone scrambled to get out their chanting books.

Let me stop here and give my people a deep bow of respect. When the Kali Yuga happened on that awful night in March, twenty years ago, and everyone had to grab the few possessions they could carry in their hands, of the 209 souls who fled Old Shiva Puri, 124 of them brought their chanting books with them.

Sharing those precious chanting books, they opened to the beginning page of the Stotram. The hall monitors scurried around the hall opening the curtains so the people could more easily read the complicated Sanskrit text where, it seems, each word is about fifty letters long, and only one of the letters is a vowel. Dad gave me his "what's going on" face. I grinned back at him.

Mirabai began to sing the Shiva Stotram.

Stunned, at first nobody could do anything but watch and listen… and wait for my sister to mess up. Not one waver, not one false note, not one mispronunciation. Utter musical perfection, astounding of itself, but here's the truly phenomenal thing: Mirabai *understood* what she was singing. She unquestionably got it — not the literal translation of the Sanskrit verses, of course, she was just a kid, but the ultimate divinity within the words of the chant. She understood that the *words themselves* were divine, and what's more celestial, she was somehow able to convey that divinity to us, to wrap us within its reality. We got it too. The Sanskrit. The Shakti. All of it.

Gradually, our more experienced chanters began to sing with her. Soon everybody joined in. Miracle upon miracle, what had been unattainable was now effortless. Grace flowed through Mirabai, through the sacred words and celestial music, into us and through us. At the door, Max stood in her usual place, guarding us, but not *one* of us. She was holding on to the door jamb, trying to steady herself, tears in her eyes, the big marine softie.

Mirabai drove the chant faster and faster, verses soaring by of their own accord, until we reached the end in climactic shouts of "*Shiva! Shiva! Shiva!*" Over and over. "*Shiva! Shiva!*" A moment of silence, catching of breath, and people were clapping and yelling and laughing and jumping to their feet, hugging each other.

My sister became the lead chanter for our ceremonies and the music teacher for our school. That's how she got her seva name: Mirabai *Songsinger.* Age nine.

Chapter Thirty-Six

Darshan

Before the drone of the tamboura faded into silence, Simone Jackson came up to take my sister's hand.

"Oh, chile," Simone said, "I want..."

At this point, she froze, swayed back and forth, fell to her knees, and toppled onto the floor. *Thump.* Lynda Cheng, our medic, suspecting a heart attack or some other dreadful event, rushed to render aid. Others crowded around.

"Are you okay?" Lynda asked. "Just lie still. Somebody get water." And so forth.

Simone opened her eyes and stared up at the circle of concerned faces.

"My, oh my," she giggled, giving us her best shuck and jive, "Laws a'mercy! Hep me up."

On her feet, Simone stared at my sister.

"What's going on?" Mother asked.

"The Shakti be going on," Simone answered. "Touch that chile, but mind yo'self."

Mother put her hand against Mirabai's cheek, closed her eyes, took a deep breath, then several more. Eventually she stepped back and gestured for Dad to come up. He didn't quite faint, but he needed Mother to steady him. One by one, everyone came forward to place a hand on Mirabai. Everyone got zapped.

But it was Greg Pequinot, ashram *asshole*, who stole the show and started the whole darshan thing. Remember Greg? Max choked him out for calling Mother a bitch? Can't remember? Just take my word, Greg was absolutely the last person you'd expect to re-kindle the ancient spiritual practice of darshan.

Pequinot sashayed up to Mirabai. Everybody expected him to do something crass, and he was surely planning to oblige. Yawning like it was such a bother, looking around to make sure everyone was watching, he offered his fingers for her kiss. Putting on my best scowly face, I tried to stare him down. Uh-oh. Like a rattler sensing prey with heat pits on the side of her head, Mirabai struck, grabbed his hand, and held on. How did she know where to grab? Pequinot yelped, tried to pull away, then stopped, the puzzled look on his face melting into the silliest grin. His eyes rolled up in his head, and he would have fallen if Vic and Donnie hadn't been there to catch him. Oh-ho, that was pretty funny.

After the next satsang, Greg Pequinot was first on his feet, first to approach Mirabai. He presented her with a remarkable gift, days in the making, a wand of eagle feathers bound up in a haft of soft rabbit fur. I couldn't take my eyes off it. Mirabai reached out to accept the feather wand. How did she know where it was? She rubbed the feathers against her face, laughed, and whacked Greg on the head, on the shoulders, and against his heart. He didn't faint this time, though he was on the verge.

Later, Greg's swoon made perfect sense. Of all the people at Shiva Puri, Greg was the most grateful to Mirabai, because he was also the most insecure, the most doubtful, the greatest pretender. When Mirabai tagged him, when she opened her heart and gave him everything she had, his doubts flew away like frightened sparrows, and he knew, really *got it* for the first time, that he was *worth* something, that he was brilliant, breathtaking, bodaciously beautiful.

But, the episode still puzzled me. And it became even more mysterious.

In the months following Greg's offering, the people of Shiva Puri came at the end of every satsang to touch Mirabai, and be touched by her, to have her darshan, to "cop a buzz," as Max said, and to bring her little presents: baskets of wild mushrooms, ripe peaches, bouquets of flowers. Naturally, the mushrooms went into morning omelets, peaches into pies, and bouquets placed on the amrit tables to grace our evening meal. I sat next to her to identify her visitors and describe the gifts.

"Nithinya is giving you a perfect red apple," I might say.

Mirabai would hold out one hand to take the offering, and, with the other hand, whack Nithinya with eagle feathers. She would hand the gift to me, and I'd put it in a basket. If a visitor came empty handed, I'd reach into the basket and find a gift for Mirabai to present to the visitor, so don't get the idea that you had to bring something. She had a happy smile for everyone and never got tired of darshan. How could she? Get tired, I mean. She wasn't really *doing* anything. She just *was*.

Oh yes, everyone came for Mirabai's darshan. Except me. I hung back, hiding in my seva as her "attendant." Why? Because I was jealous of her? I mean, here's my twin, giving our people irrefutable, undeniable, personal experiences of their own divinity. That's a badass superpower, if you ask me. Great. Me? What's my badass superpower? My heavenly gift?

Dog tricks.

And goats follow me around.

Mostly.

Goats be goats.

And if Mirabai's darshan wasn't miraculous enough, by and by, she began to speak before I could get the words out of my mouth. She would say, "What a pretty apple. Thank you, Nithinya." How was she doing that? One morning satsang, my mind drifted away on the pleasant breeze blowing in through the mandir window.

"Jana?"

Someone calling my name? Mirabai.

"Jana, who is this?"

Snapping my attention back, I focused on the person in front of my sister. Marianne Conroy was staring at me with that disapproving frown I had grown so used to in Mistah Tee's class. Before I could speak, Mirabai said, "Miss Conroy, what a lovely daffodil. Thank you."

A certain thought, a tiny carrot seed thought, took root in my mind. Easy enough to see if that seed would grow. I watched visitors come up for darshan, as usual, but say nothing. Mirabai would say the person's name, thank them, and whack, whack with the eagle feathers. But from time to time, I would look away, and my sister would have to ask me who was standing in front of her.

So, that's her trick!

My eyes. She's using my eyes.

CHAPTER THIRTY-SEVEN

Twin Sight

M IRABAI IS KEEPING ME COMPANY *this afternoon, her left hand on my swollen belly. It feels so very nice. We don't say much. We don't have to. It's not a secret anymore, but it was back then. We're telepathic. Okay, exaggeration, but I learned that word in a science-fiction novel, and I think telepathy is sort of close to what we do, so I like to say it aloud. Telepathy. Tehhhhh... LEP... athy. It's not like Mirabai thinks: "Janabai, what's in that book you're reading?" and I answer with a complete thought; but if she wants something, I hear her, no matter how far away she is. Or maybe I need her. How can I describe it? A bell rings, and I know she's there.*

Okay, here, in a cosmic nutshell, is how I see for my sister. And how she sees for me.

In the summer between our second and third year of Middles, we were ten years old going on eleven, and Mirabai had been giving darshan for a little more than a year. One perfect afternoon, we were out in the fields tending the herds. That meant Mira sat on her blanket in the shade, hour after hour, humming songs to herself while I did the work. She always smiled when I took my rest. I'd come sit behind her with my legs spread so she could lean back into me. I'd wrap my arms around her "to keep her safe." So there we were, sitting together, me leaning against a willow, her leaning back into me, our eyes closed, almost napping. I snapped awake. My eyes were wide open, or so I thought, but it was dark — not pitch-black like inside a cave, but hazy dark, like the last glimmers of daylight painted with swirls of purple and rose sunset. Waves of blue luminescence swept over me. I could feel myself leaning back into my sister. No. Wait a minute. She was leaning back into me. Which was it? I couldn't tell if I was me or I was my sister, the leaner or the leaned upon. She laughed and clapped her hands in delight.

"I see," she said. "I see *everything*."

She was seeing what I was seeing, not just flashes of faces and apples. She was looking at the whole world through my eyes.

All these years later I still come up behind her and wrap my arms around her, putting my chin on her right shoulder, my head pressed against hers, cheek to cheek, temple to temple. We look in the same direction so we have the same view, no more than a few inches between my eyes and hers. More distance than that, and I get dizzy. We breathe together, inhale and exhale, *apana* and *prana*, *ham* and *sah*. I close my eyes. Breathe in deep, breathe out long, hold, repeat, our heartbeats pulsing in perfect time. Our bodies blend together. When I get up the nerve, I *blink* myself inside her mind. It's not a slow, gentle entry. One hard push, and *blink*, I'm inside.

At first, I keep my eyes closed, but I will tell you there is plenty to *see* inside Mirabai's head: colors you simply cannot imagine, if "color" is even the right word; light radiating from every direction, if "direction" is the right word. Inside my sister there is much more than visual phenomena — indescribable sensations. It's also true what they say: those born blind develop extraordinary other senses. While I am in her mind, I taste astonishing new flavors, layered and nuanced. The sweetness of the cherries she ate for breakfast is still rich and heavy on her tongue. Every sound in the village, or in the forest glade a mile away, is magnified hundredfold. The brook, a deer grazing in the meadow, the beat of bird wings a thousand feet overhead, the conversation down in the amrit, each sound distinct, clear, and complex. Every smell is potent and suffused with information about the world, olfactory knowledge without judgment of pleasant or unpleasant. Every inch of her skin absorbs the universe. Her fingertips are truly remarkable, sense organs in and of themselves, receiving the outside into her Self.

After I have blinked myself inside her, and after I have calmed down, because it's disorienting, as you can imagine, only then do I open my own eyes. I am dazzled as a flood of shape and color, mass and shadow pour into me, as if being in a dark cellar and opening the shutters to the noonday sun. It's a shock for both of us, and it takes a moment to adjust. When I first started seeing for my sister, we could share our *twin sight* only for the briefest time. The experience was too harsh. Gradually we built up to it by increasing the duration, little by little, day by day. It's exhausting and takes tremendous concentration to stay in sync with our breathing and our heartbeats. Dad, who is quite the scholar, thinks our brain waves align with each other when we do this. Mother just grins like she is in on our big secret.

Merging with my sister's mind, sharing and blending our sensation, was intense. That's a word too feeble to convey the heart-stopping plunge into her *other-ness*. For our communal seeing to work at all, I had to sacrifice my precious ego, my exalted idea of who I was; not easy for me because I was, as you know, quite full of myself. My little self. I had to find a way to give it up. Mirabai taught me, or rather she opened a safe space inside of her mind for me to surrender little Janabai to my real self. I smelled and tasted and heard and felt and gazed with wonder at the celestial realms, exhilarating for sure, but I begin to "glimpse" a minuscule light, "blue" being the closest word I have to describe the indescribable, a self-illuminating radiance no bigger than a sesame seed. It grew larger, or perhaps I grew closer to it, until I was absorbed by the tiny light and all my busy thoughts dissolved. I *became* the blue effulgence, without separation or isolation, or boundary, or distance. I was light itself, and I was also my sister, and I was also everything there is, and I was also my Self. I was *existence* and *consciousness* and *ecstasy*. *Sat* and *chit* and *ananda*.

There is no other way to become *one* with another. First, you surrender who you *think* you are, in order to become who you *really* are, and that's when you discover you and the other are *one-in-the-same*. This is not an easy lesson. So much of what I *think* I'm seeing is shaped by my opinions. I have lots of them, you know, opinions. I see a certain man. I don't like him. He is six feet tall and wears a red shirt, and he has an unpleasant look about him. He irritates me. Mirabai sees the same man through my eyes; he is still six feet tall and wearing a red shirt, but she sees him as beautiful. When I experience the man from inside Mirabai's

133

consciousness, I see through all the layers of his personality to his true being, and that his inner self is perfect.

> *Om Poornamadah*
> This is perfect
> *Poornameedam*
> That is perfect
> *Poornat Poornamudachyatay*
> If you add the perfect to the perfect, the sum is perfection
> *Poornasyah Poornamaadaayah*
> If you take away the perfect from the perfect
> *Poornahmevaah Vasheeshyahtay*
> Only the perfect remains.

Over the years I drew closer to Mirabai's way of "looking" at things. I learned to see the perfection of the world through her "eyes," most of the time, except when I am dealing with this thing-inside-my-womb-that-keeps-dragging-me-away-from-my-center. On a certain level, I understand my pregnancy is also perfection, and a great opportunity to pursue my spiritual work, my sadhana, *my* karma, *my* dharma.
But it still disgusts the hell out of me.
Shanti Shanti Shanti
Peace, Peace, Peace
Please stop kicking.

CHAPTER THIRTY-EIGHT

The Bigs

WE WERE TWELVE YEARS OLD-ALMOST-THIRTEEN when Mirabai and I moved from Middles to Bigs. Kavitha Bose, Kimberli Prymak, and Ashdep Mondul came up with us at the same time, and Elle Shergill and George Sunkari followed in late January. Annie Raines moved up from Middles in my second year. Three other kids, Austin Minard (Magalsky), Aaron Magalsky, and Tiffany Staab, came up the following year, so in my third and final year of Bigs, there were eleven of us in my class. Yes, I know, too many names, but you can always come back here if you forget; and besides, all these kids really like having their names in my book, so just move along, please.

Connor Doering (Mister Dee) and McKenna Klockenbrink (Miss Klock) taught the Bigs. Our morning was devoted to Practical Skills (drafting and mechanics) followed by advanced courses in Music (harmonium, violin, lead singing, long chants) and Healing (CPR, snake bite, stretcher making and carrying). The teachers figured that if you didn't know *readin' and writin' and 'rithmetic* by the time you were thirteen, you were on your own.

In the afternoon, Mister Dee went down to the Middles to teach intermediate science, and other folk came in to teach their specialties, from wheelwright to pastry chef. We were being exposed to all the village sevas, so when it came time for Offering, we would make a wise decision about the seva we would be joining as adults. Sevas were always "offered," never assigned or forced. How could you be happy doing something you didn't like for the rest of your life? I'm not talking about farming, of course. We were all farmers. If you wanted to eat, you farmed. Don't want to farm? No problem. Pack your kit. Good luck and blessings upon you! When we see the turkey vultures circling, we'll come find your bones and bring them back for fertilizer.

I'm exaggerating about vultures and fertilizer. Only one person ever refused to farm. Take a guess.

Almmmaaaaaaaaaaaaaaaa.

I poked my nose into every seva, from kitchen to kennel, weaver to potter, school teacher to cobbler. Everyone knew Kavitha was going to take seva with the medics. I got it in my head I would be a medic as well, so we could work together for the rest of our lives. Nope. Too much time indoors. Vic Tretheway called on me to help work on one of the super-secret mechanic projects I'm

135

not supposed to write about, so I won't, except to say, how do you think Vic keeps our bullets working when nobody else can? Hmmmm? Maybe I should be a mechanic? No, but that reminds me, bullets, I mean, I was also supposed to check in with Max to see if hunting seva was right for me. She took one look at my face and said, "Who are you trying to kid?" Max made her mark on my assignment board and told me to get lost.

Dad wanted me as his successor in management, but we both knew my pathetic arithmetic "skills" were not good enough. The same with science. I liked most of the sevas well enough, and I could have chosen any of them, but two seva bosses were leaning on me: Patty Bose wanted me at the school to teach reading, and Odessa, near-eighty, expected me to take over the library when she was no longer able.

Also, you should know, I got real interested in *boy* seva, as in offering myself to the boys. No, no, NO! That's not what I meant. Ha ha. I didn't even have my menarche until I was fourteen. Kavitha started two years before me. Even Mirabai, *my twin*, started before me, and that motivated Mother to come to us for "The Talk"—you know what I mean, the big pow wow about growing up and our woman's body and how it worked. Oh, *puh... lease*, Mother. I grew up on a farm. Not to mention, we live close together. I'll tell you, I have seen some fascinating things out in the barn. And anyway, Nithinya Varanasi, the goddess of love, had already filled me in on the particulars. Mirabai and I listened politely to "The Talk," and we thanked Mother when she finally ran out of steam, and assured her we would THINK before doing anything, and promised to be good girls. There must have been something in the tone of my voice that earned me a sharp look.

"You are just too full of beans for your own good," Mother said.

I made a little bean fart noise with my mouth.

"Ha," she said, and made a juicy fart noise back at me.

Well, when my period finally came, I swear the boys could smell me like bucks smell ewes. Hanging around, sometimes showing off, and sometimes acting mopey and stupid; and not just the boys in school, but a few who had already graduated.

Kavitha and I decided I should "like" George Sunkari, who had the nickname of Packy, that came from pachyderm because his ears stuck out like an elephant, and it bothered him, though he was a good sport about it. His ears never bothered me and were handy to hang on to when we were making out, which we did at every available opportunity. I thought he was a good kisser until Kavitha asked if we were "frenching," to which I answered "of course," but she knew I was lying, so she told me about opening my mouth and using my tongue, and when I tried that on George, he said I was the best kisser in the world. How would he know? Sometimes when George and I were sticking our tongues down each other's throats, I got hot and bothered in my you-know-where, but he was too scared to go all the way. Once I grabbed his hand and put it on my breast, not much there yet, not like Kavitha, who already had womanly balloons, which totally got every boy's attention because the rest of her was so tall and lean, but I was proud of what I did have and thought myself quite shapely. When "Packy" didn't do anything but give me a little squeeze, I said:

"Don't tease me, George."

You would think he could take a hint and get on with it, but he just got moonier, telling me how much he loved me and how much sexing we were going to do *after* we got married. Married? I don't think so. Why not? I cared for George, I did, and I enjoyed smooching with him, but there was somebody I had my eye on, that certain older boy who had already graduated and accepted hunter seva.

Skyler Jones.

I worshipped Skyler ever since he came down from the Bigs to help with the first Kali Yuga Play. He was handsome and strong and kind and cool and smart and funny and totally wonderful. And the boy could *run*! He was almost as fast as Kavitha and just a little bit faster than me, sort of right in the middle between us girls, so we three did a lot of running together, out in front of everybody else, our own little pack. Surely Skyler Jones was one of the gods, reincarnated in human flesh for the purpose of making Janabai Burke-Kucinich happy for the rest of her life.

When Offering Day finally rolled around, I planned to take off all my clothes and throw myself on Skyler Jones

CHAPTER THIRTY-NINE

Offering Day

OFFERING DAY! THE ACTUAL DATE changes from year to year, depending on the weather, but it usually comes during the last week of April or the first week of May, always falling on the day before Spring Planting. In the year 17 AK, Offering Day was set for May the first, an auspicious date, May Day. I, Janabai Burke-Kucinich, entered adulthood with my fellow "senior," George Sunkari, a class of two. For graduates of the Bigs, the celebration was the most exciting and most fun holiday of the year. Not only were we offered our adult sevas, but we formally dedicated our lives to the village. Offering was something like an initiation, and something like a marriage ceremony wherein we graduates take the name of our seva as our own.

George Sunkari became George Mechanic, or G-Mek, as he was now called. As I have told you, G-Mek and I "went around together," and we kept that up after graduation in spite of my promise to hurl myself at Skyler Jones. G-Mek was a better friend than I deserved, and to this day, I care for him deeply.

George and I sat in the back of the mandir wearing light blue robes to symbolize we were ready to walk the Dharma Path as adults. George had slicked down his spiky black hair with grease, which just made his ears stick out more. We were scrubbed clean and smelling nice. Have you ever had a hot shower? We did, me and G-Mek. The first hot shower of our lives. To honor us graduates, our families and friends went to the trouble of heating tubs of water, hauling them to the bath house, climbing to the roof, and dumping tub after tub into the trough while we stood underneath and let the hot water pour all over us. Glorious. Hot shower. You should try it at least once in your life.

Also, I had a new hairdo. My unruly curls were trimmed and tamed by Kavitha, personal beautician to the princess of Shiva Puri. To give compliments where due, she had improved since the day she cut my hair and painted it blue so I could make a big impression on Mistah Tee, which, as you remember, I did. Those curls were bouncing and flouncing as I walked down the center aisle to the front of the mandir and faced the assembled village. I took my own sweet time. There were only two of us to be offered seva, so what's the rush? And, I wanted to milk as much drama as possible out of the occasion.

Looking around the hall, nodding to this person and that person, particularly Skyler Jones to make sure I had his full attention, my eyes came to rest on Mother, who gave me a certain look: "Just get on with it, Janabai."

"I, Janabai Burke-Kucinich, offer myself to... (pause)... the seva of... (pause)... (pause)... (pause)... shepherd."

Now that got the communal gasp of astonishment I was hoping for. Hee. I let it sink in. I saw confusion on the faces of many people, especially from Odessa, who planned for me to follow in her footsteps as librarian, and Mama Patty, who begged me to join her at Puri School. Even Kavitha secretly hoped I would join medicine. Max slapped both hands on her cheeks and opened her mouth in a big *O* as if to say, "What? You're not going to be one of my hunters?" Ha ha. Max cracks me up.

Mother threw her head back and laughed out loud.

I continued the ritual.

"To work among the flocks and herds, to guard and care for our animal brothers and sisters as if they were my own self. If you find me worthy, I shall be known henceforth as Janabai Shepherd. Will you accept my offering?"

My "uncles," Raj and Manoj Bannerjee, stood up and said in unison:

"We find Janabai worthy of shepherd seva and do offer it to her in the name of Lord Krishna, first among shepherds."

Odessa started to say something, but Mother shushed her. Afterward, she told me she was proud of me, and she wasn't surprised with my decision, or, anyway, that's what she said, but it makes sense when you think about it. Years before, working side by side, Mother taught me everything she knew about the goats. I had more natural talent, more affinity with animals, than she ever would; she said so often enough. It gave Mother much happiness to know I was following her childhood seva, and her pleasure gave me joy in return.

CHAPTER FORTY

Bigfoot

AND WHAT OF ALMA MENDEZ? Which seva was she offered? Which seva did she accept?

When I moved up to the Bigs, leaving Alma behind in the Middles, she just stopped coming to school altogether and nobody did anything about it. I was twelve and moving fast; she was fourteen and still stuck in the mud. She started disappearing for days at a time, to everyone's relief, but duty compelled the council to search for her. Max discovered Alma's secret hideaway southeast of the village along a creek, an old miner's shack. At least the council knew where she was. As time went by, they just let her do what she wanted, to live there by herself. The council stopped trying to civilize her, just gave up, I guess.

Sometimes Alma would show up at school, peeking in through a window like a ghost. She didn't make faces, just stared at us kind of creepy. Sometimes she would sneak in the back door of the mandir for satsang, but always after the program had begun, and she never joined in, just watched and made us feel weird. She always left before it was over so she didn't have to talk to anyone. Once in a while she would come around to the back door of the kitchen, holding out a bag for food, never saying a word, and Cookie would always fill it for her. Sometimes she would raid the farm and take what she wanted. She never worked in the fields, but nobody seemed to mind, at least nobody said anything or did anything.

The only person she would talk to was Max, who went out from time to time to check on her. To the rest of us, she muttered and mocked, rolled her eyes and gave mean looks to those she could pick on and mean looks behind the backs of those she couldn't. The council offered her seva with the cattle herds, and it seemed as if that might work, until the day Bill Lemko found her poking a sharpened screwdriver, over and over, into one of the calves,

"Are you out of your goddamn mind?" he yelled, wrestling the screwdriver away.

"Maybe," she muttered.

"What do you think you're doing?"

"Sticking this calf."

"No screaming shit. Why?"

"We have to chop up the baby cows so we can eat them," Alma explained as if speaking to a slow child.

"That's enough. You're fired," Bill said. "Get out of my pasture and stay the hell away from my cows."

When they heard about it, the council sent Max out to talk to her.

"Is there anything at all that interests you, anything you'd like to try?" Max asked.

"Be a hunter and get a gun so I can shoot stuff," she answered.

"Yeah, right," Max said, unable to hold back her sarcasm. "That's not going to happen."

"You're the worst of them all," Alma said. "You pretend to be my friend. 'What do you need, Alma? Just ask your buddy Max,' and first time I do, you say fuck you, Alma. Well, fuck you, Max. Go away and leave me alone."

After burning her last bridge, Alma got lonelier and stranger. We rarely saw her, just an eerie glimpse, usually after dark, of a scraggly shape shambling through the trees. She scared people. The grownups called her Sociopath. The kids called her Bigfoot.

CHAPTER FORTY-ONE

Skyler to the Rescue

LATER, WHEN IT WAS ALL over, Kavitha had to admit responsibility for going out to pinch basil and mint behind Bigfoot's shack, but it was mostly my fault for sneaking us closer, just a little closer. For me, gathering herbs was just an excuse. I was spying. Not a sound or sign of life came from inside.

"Okay," I whispered, "I think she's gone."

Not true. My old adversary was waiting for me.

Alma burst out of the front door, a badger from her den, brandishing the sharpened screwdriver; she hurtled into me, taking me to the ground. Raising the screwdriver high above her head, she drove the sharpened point down, aiming for my face, but midway through its vicious descent, Kavitha tackled Alma from the side, rolling her off me and into a clawing, screaming catfight. Alma was stronger and heavier; Kavitha faster and more athletic. I knelt in the dirt as if paralyzed, too afraid to go to my friend's aid. Alma's screwdriver was just lying there, right over there, a few feet away. I could have picked it up. I could have jumped on her back. I could have kicked her or hit her. What did I do? Nothing.

Not impressed, are you?

Using her weight, Alma rolled on top, pinning Kavitha beneath, and began pounding down with her fists. Kavitha managed to parry most of the blows with her arms, but not all, and the tide of battle turned in the older girl's favor.

"I'm going to kill you," Alma snarled.

"Leave her alone," I screamed. "Help! Help! Help!"

Miraculously, help did arrive. Someone ran up behind the combatants and grabbed Alma by the hair, dragging her off Kavitha. Skyler Jones, my hero, now journeyman hunter, along with two other hunters, both armed, had come to the rescue.

Alma screamed, "Let me go! She's a filthy Yoogie. Let me go. I'm going to kill them all."

"You're not killing anybody," Skyler drawled, calmly, still holding Alma by the hair.

"Why not?" she snarled.

"Well, Alma, let's just say, it's not the Shiva Puri way."

"You're yellow. That's what you are, yellow pussy boy."

"Maybe I am, but I don't hurt little kids." Letting go of her hair, Skyler said, "Hold on to her."

Amber and Praveen, the other hunters, took Alma by the arms. He, Skyler, my Skyler, walked over to Kavitha and bent down.

"Are you okay?"

"I'm fine," Kavitha said, "and I'm not a little kid."

"No, of course you're not. Let me help you up."

Skyler pulled Kavitha to her feet. He turned back to Alma.

"If you ever touch one of these girls again, I'll deal with you. Got it?"

No answer.

"Let her go," Skyler said to his companions.

Humiliated and furious, Alma snatched her screwdriver off the ground, ran into her shack, and slammed the door.

"I hate you. I hate you all. I hate everybody," she screamed from inside.

Skyler walked a few feet away from the shack and stood in thought. Even in my distress, I admired how handsome he was, tall and war-like, his hair in the tight hunter's bun at the nape of his neck, just about the most beautiful thing I had ever seen, like the naked David statue in the library art books, except Skyler wasn't naked, though just for a moment, I imagined he was. I felt something drop in my chest.

Oh, silly girl. Open your eyes. Skyler was looking to Kavitha for something, approval, I guess, to help him make up his mind about Alma. I saw her give him a little nod. What? Wait a minute, this was going too fast.

Skyler turned back to Alma's shack and kicked the door in.

"From now on," he said, "nobody talks to you. Nobody listens to you. You are invisible to us. There is no more Alma. Poof. Listen up, everybody. I, Skyler Jones, hunter of Shiva Puri, say this: We shun you, Alma. Until you get a grip and start acting like a human being, you don't exist."

Silence from inside the shack.

"Do you understand me, Alma?"

"Fuck you, Skyler, and all your Yoogie turdlets."

"Get out of here, Alma, and don't ever come back."

"Or what?"

She walked out of her shack and into the clearing, her middle finger raised, a gesture we do *not* do in Shiva Puri.

"What are you going to do if I come back and stab Janabai in the eye when she's sleeping?" Alma asked, moving right up on Skyler, poking toward his eye with her stiff middle finger.

"Come on, Skyler, (poke) what are you going to do? (poke) Are you going to shoot me? (poke) Are you going to kill me?"

Now he was spitting mad.

"Yes, Alma, that's what I'm going to do."

"Say it, pussy boy, say the words."

"The next time I see you, I'm going to kill you."

"You don't have the stones."

"He doesn't need stones," Amber Braidman, Skyler's second hunter, said, "and I never had any stones to begin with, but I tell you this, Alma Mendez, you made my life hell when all I wanted to do was be your big sister and help you, and now, out here where there's nobody but us chickens, I would love to put a load of buckshot right in your face. Can I do it, Skyler, can I blow her head off right now?"

Skyler stared at Alma, stepped back, pulled his pistol from his holster, and cocked the hammer. Behind him, he heard the members of his team spread out to have clear fields of fire. He heard Amber cock her double-barreled 12, and Praveen chamber a round in his deer rifle. Skyler didn't have to look to know the muzzles of their weapons were locked on Alma. He didn't need to ask if they were ready to cut her down in the dirt.

"Let's do this now and get it over with," Amber repeated, "once and for all."

"Okay, Alma," Skyler said. "I'm going to count to three, and before I finish you better be running for the woods. If you're still in my face, I'm going to shoot you where you stand.

One..."

Alma didn't wait for "two" before she ran for her life. We watched her disappear into the brush.

Skyler hung his head and took several breaths; walked over and stood next to Kavitha. From the ground where I was pouting, I looked up at Skyler and Kavitha. My first thought: they are standing too close together. They were, I realized, standing *way* too close. Their arms were almost touching, just about the last thing in the world I wanted to see.

"Is anybody going to help me?"

Kavitha knelt down and tried to comfort me. "Show me where she hurt you. Is it bad?"

I snapped at her, "I can fight my own fights. Why did you have to butt in? I was getting ready to hit her with my hard fist."

"Well," Kavitha said, startled by my bad manners, "it looked like Alma was going to stick a screwdriver right through your head, and, by the way, why don't you try, 'Thank you, thank you, Kavitha, for saving my ass,' instead of whining like a princess."

"Don't you dare call me *that*."

Kavitha took a deep breath to compose herself.

"Okay, you're right, I'm sorry," she apologized.

"And in case you didn't notice," I said, "Skyler had to haul your ashes out of the fire."

145

"Yes, he did." She got to her feet and turned to Skyler. "I do thank you for coming to my rescue, sir hunter."

She stepped toward him until they were standing inches apart, face-to-face, her big Kavitha breasts actually brushing against his chest.

"My honor, brave lady."

"You don't have to stand so close," I said. "She can hear you perfectly fine."

Staring into each other's eyes, Skyler and Kavitha ignored my stupid remark.

I raised my voice, so shrill and nasty I sounded like a sharp-toothed little shrew.

"I SAID YOU DON'T HAVE TO STAND SO CLOSE!"

CHAPTER FORTY-TWO

Frontier Justice

RANDHIR SHEPHERD BURST INTO AMRIT, where most of our people were eating breakfast.

"Alma Mendez was ripping up them Memorial Trees."

"Where?" Dad asked.

"Over where Cook Creek comes out of the gully."

"My wife's tree?" Galen Raether asked.

"Yessir, I'm sorry to say."

"What did you do?" Max asked.

"I yelled for her to stop, and started running at her."

"What did she do?"

"She turned and run down the hill."

"Which way?"

"Toward old Ben's rancheria."

"Okay," Max said. "Grimsman, take a squad out toward the

rancheria and see if you can find her. Donnie, you take a squad over to her shack and see if she's there. Listen up, people, she's a big girl with a lot of problems, and she carries that pig sticker wherever she goes. Treat her as dangerous. Got it?"

"Roger," Grimsman said.

"We'll convene council right after lunch," Dad said. "Bring her there."

"Just a minute," Skyler Jones interrupted.

Everyone turned to look at the young hunter, two pink spots flushing his cheeks.

"You have something to add?" Dad asked.

Skyler let out a breath and closed his eyes, gathering his nerve. "There was a fight yesterday afternoon."

"A fight? With Alma?"

"Yes."

"And who else?"

"Well, me and Kavitha and Janabai."

"What happened?"

Skyler told the story of the fight, efficiently and modestly, in the fewest possible words and with no mention of his own heroism.

"What did you do then?" Max asked.

"We had words."

"What words? Don't make me drag this out of you, Skyler."

"Aye, aye." He blushed even redder. "She, I mean Alma, said she wanted to kill the girls, and I told her we had had enough of her bad vibes, and if she ever tried to hurt them again, I was coming for her, personally. She said some other things, and I told her she was outcast and she didn't exist anymore."

There was a long silence as the Council of Shiva Puri digested Skyler's story. To this point, Mother, who had been listening without speaking, rose from her bench. It seemed to me Mother just kept coming up and coming up, unfolding until she was much taller than her actual six feet. Now in her late thirties, Mother had put on weight, most of it muscle. Her already-broad shoulders looked more like those of a lumberman. People sitting to her sides adjusted their positions to give her more space. At this moment, there was no doubt in anyone's mind who was in charge of Shiva Puri.

As if her look was a pin and the terrified young man a butterfly about to be impaled, Azriel Dancer fixed Skyler Jones with a cold stare.

"Let me make sure I understand this. Alma Mendez McGartland beat up Janabai and Kavitha Bose and threatened to kill them, and you took it upon yourself to punish Alma with, what? Shunning? You decided, on your own, you would keep all of this to yourself? You somehow neglected to tell me someone tried to KILL MY LITTLE GIRL?"

"Yes, Dancer. I mean, no."

"And all of that happened yesterday?"

"Yes, Dancer."

"So Alma Mendez has had all night to prowl around our village making whatever vile mischief she can think of."

"Yes, Dancer. I'm sorry. I thought..."

"The last time I checked the seva roster, you were a hunter, not a thinker."

"Yes, Dancer."

From across the room, Kavitha shouted, "Stop it!"

All eyes turned to my friend, who was on her feet defying my mother.

"You have something to say?" Mother asked. "You're not out of this either. Nor you, Janabai. Why didn't one of you speak up last night and tell us what happened?"

"What would you do anyway?" Kavitha asked. "What would you do if we had come to you crying one more horrible story about horrible Alma Mendez? The same thing you've always done: nothing. Alma has been hurting Janabai since she was a little girl, picking at her, bullying her; and Mirabai, too, pinching her and burning her. And you knew it, don't pretend you didn't, and you did nothing except tell us to love Alma. Poor Alma, she lost her mother, she has problems, be nice to her, understand her; and Alma just kept coming, each time more hateful, more hurtful, until yesterday somebody finally had the guts to do something

148

about it: that man right here, Skyler, who had a bellyful of Alma Mendez like all of us, but he tried to fix it. So don't you dare point your fingers at him like he's some kind of a bad dog. Skyler Jones is the best and bravest man here as far as I'm concerned."

Silence.

"Well, Kavitha," Mother said, "what a pretty speech." Looking at me she asked, "Anything you'd like to add?"

"You council members knew Alma was crazy." Dad started to correct me, but I had my teeth set, and I was going to have my say. "I know we don't say *crazy*, but I am saying it now, and you have said it too, or at least you thought it. You all knew she was crazy, but you didn't do a thing about it."

"Don't act so naïve," Mother said. "You knew just as well as anybody to keep clear of Alma, and now you're pretending to be stupid and trying to blame us because you played with a snake and got bit."

"Janabai, what would you have us do?" Dad asked. "Put Alma down like a dog? Execute her? How? Hang her? Tell Max to shoot her?"

"Anytime," Max interjected.

"Skyler, do you have something you'd like to say?"

"I was caught," he answered, "like Arjuna in the Bhagavad Gita, not that I'm comparing myself to Arjuna, just that I had the same dilemma. Harm someone to protect someone? I thought it was my duty as a warrior."

"Oorah," Max said.

Mother ignored the marine. "Skyler, did you say those exact words to Alma, 'I'm going to kill you'?"

"Yes, ma'am. I did."

"Did you point a loaded weapon at her?"

"Yes, ma'am."

"Do you have anything else to add, before we decide what to do with you?"

"Haven't you done horrible things to protect us? Did you check with Daniel before you did it?"

Mother chewed on that, but didn't answer the question.

"Okay, boss lady," Max said, "get it done."

Skyler and Kavitha moved closer together, now side by side, shoulders touching. Kavitha took his hand, lacing her fingers with his, and if I wasn't certain before, I knew now, those two were together — you know what I mean, together. Like beavers and geese. My heart dropped to my feet.

"Let me line this out for the record," Mother said. "First, you took it upon yourself to threaten Alma Mendez with death because of the council's failure to take action, our... what? Incompetence? Cowardice? Second, you were compelled to do what you did by reading scripture. Finally, you shame me by pointing out I have done equally horrible things. Is this your defense?"

"Yes, ma'am."

"Very well. I like it. Good defense. Okay, Skyler, you're off the hook."

Everybody in that room let out a woof of relief except Dad, who was looking around like, "What just happened?"

"And one more thing, young Arjuna. Thank you for saving my little girl."

Skyler pressing his hands together in anjali mudra, bowed to Mother, and refrained from further comment. Probably a good idea.

"Alright," Mother said, having, once again, usurped control from Dad. She turned to Donnie Simms. "Get some people together and go to see how many Great Trees we have lost and any other damage we might have taken."

"Will do," Donnie replied.

"Simone, will you see if anything is missing from stores?"

"Right on, honey bun."

"Everybody else, go to work. Keep your eyes peeled for Alma and treat her like a rabid skunk. Council will meet again after lunch. I want all of you who were at yesterday's fight to be back here. You hunters grab a bite, then get here early for your instructions. You, too, Donnie and Simone."

"And me," Max asked, "just in case?"

"Oh yes. You most of all."

Chapter Forty-Three

Who Speaks for Alma Mendez?

Before Randhir Shepherd scared her off, Alma Mendez McGartland tore up nine of the Great Trees. As a farewell present just for me, she slaughtered one of my newborn lambs, puncture wounds too numerous to count, a blood sacrifice to her rage. Members of the council debated the symbolic meaning of the little murder, but I knew exactly what message Alma was sending.

"This is what I will do to you."

Mother agreed with my interpretation.

The council met in the afternoon to formalize the exile. Sally McGartland, Alma's foster mother, was given an opportunity to speak, but declined.

"Skyler, please escort Sally to the door," Mother said. "Her participation in this matter is concluded."

Sally departed, relieved.

Dad spoke: "It is the judgment of the Council of Shiva Puri that we will not hunt for Alma Mendez. Having fled from the scene of her own crimes, she has exiled herself and saved us the trouble. Alma Mendez McGartland shall be removed from our roster, cast off forever, never to return, or face the harshest consequences."

"And what would those harshest consequences be?" Max asked.

"We would need to meet and decide in the event she does return."

"Give her another chance?" Max persisted.

"We would take the option of another chance under consideration."

"Yeah, I bet we would consider the hell out of it."

"You're out of line, Max. You are here at Azriel's invitation, but you are not a member of the council."

Max raised her eyebrows at Mother, who sat stone-faced, unresponsive until Dad resumed speaking, drawing the attention back in his direction, at which time Mother gave Max the slightest wink, returned by Max with the tiniest nod. No one saw the interchange except me. Max and Mother were up to something.

Dad concluded: "Alma Mendez is dead to us, as if she never existed."

While the council members and guests reflected on his words, I tried to sort out my own feelings.

"Will we plant a Great Tree in her memory?" I asked.

Silence. No one had considered such a thing.

"Janabai's right," Simone Jackson said. "Alma is dead, dead to us, just as if we executed her. Yes, as if we just shot her down like a rabid coon, because make no mistake about it, folks, exile means death to that girl. If we can do that, we can at least give her the funeral rites any member of this village deserves. It's the Shiva Puri way, right? *Right?*"

The assembly looked to Dad for his response.

"This is our failure," he said. "But none of us have ever practiced frontier justice. We're making it up as we go along. What kind of ritual would we perform for someone we just threw out to die? How would we begin?"

"Like always," Simone sighed. "We ask, 'Who will speak for Alma Mendez?'"

No one said a word. Truth be told, Alma didn't have a single friend in the village. The silence went on and on. Oh, come on, somebody say something. And on and on. Unable to stand it one second longer, I stood without the slightest notion of what I was going to say, looked around the room, and took a breath.

"I knew Alma Mendez."

People nodded. Good start.

"She was older than me. She had a hard life."

More nods.

"She was always afraid."

I slammed to a stop. What else?

"Alma was always afraid of what?" Kavitha prompted.

"Afraid of not being accepted by the Yoogies, or being made fun of by the Googlers for playing with little kids, and all she wanted was to be cool."

What next?

"Talk about karma," Kavitha whispered loud enough for everybody in the room to hear.

"Alma, your karma was too much for one soul to bear. I wish I had taken some of the load from you. I wish I had taken better care of you. I wish I had been your friend. I wish I had invited you to play with us one more time, just one more time. Maybe if I had, you would have said 'yes.'"

I looked over at Kavitha for more help.

"Reincarnation?" she shrugged.

"May you reincarnate as something beautiful like a sleek river otter. I think you would like that."

Mother nodded. It was enough.

"Blessings on Alma Mendez-McGartland," I said, and added, "The girl could punch like a mule."

People laughed.

"*Jai* Shiva."

Everyone answered, "*Jai* Shiva."

Mirabai sang a pretty song I had never heard. It was called "In the Sweet By and By."

CHAPTER FORTY-FOUR

Bug Hunt

E*XILE FOR ALMA? AFTER THREATENING to kill me? You think Mother was just going to let her walk away? Not a chance. This is how Max tells the story.*

Mother and Max met before dawn and readied their kits for the chase. They didn't tell anybody where they were going, or what they planned to do, so as to skip out on some bullshit argument with Dad. Max asked Mother why she was so sure Alma was heading north.

"I *sense* her up there."

"Can you be more specific?"

"Not yet, but I can tell you this. Something is... *pulling* her north. Alma probably doesn't even know she's being pulled."

"Mystical truths from beyond?"

"Maybe. Just trust me."

"Trust you? You don't ever need to say that. Ever. I don't like it. Got me?"

"I got you. I'm so sorry," Mother said in abject sarcasm.

"Fuck you," Max graciously replied.

"I'm sorry, really, and, by the way, fuck you back."

"That's what I had in mind, but later," Max said. "Meanwhile, here we go, Azriel and Max, off on another totally screwed-up bug hunt."

"Ready?"

"Let's go kill a cockroach."

They found Alma just before dawn, a few miles below Susanville, covered in pine needles, sleeping rough, curled up on the ground, the glowing embers of a campfire her only warmth. A tiny noise and Alma was instantly awake, sitting up in one motion, pulling the screwdriver out of the ground. Across her campfire, in the dim light of dawn, she saw the sight she least expected — or wanted: Azriel Dancer, all six foot of her, double-barreled shotgun pointed at Alma's face. Before another thought crossed Alma's mind, Max whipped a hard forearm across her throat. Alma felt Max's hand pushing the back of her head forward, crushing her windpipe against the forearm, ears roaring, unable to catch a breath, strength pouring into the ground, tattered black edges of her world closing in like a murder of crows, her vision narrowed to one bright spot, but before the spot could flicker out, Max let up on the pressure. Alma gulped for air, found some, not enough, but some. Mother pushed the twin apertures of her shotgun barrels against Alma's forehead.

"Look at me, Alma."

Alma slid her sight up the slot between the two barrels and into the eyes of the shooter.

"Get out of the way," Mother instructed Max.

Max loosened her choke hold, rose, and circled behind Mother. For several long seconds, nothing happened. Not a motion, sound, or breath.

"Are you going to do it or what?" Max asked.

Mother let out a breath, shook her head, took a step back.

"This is the judgment of the Council of Shiva Puri. I will say it one time. You will keep moving north. You will never come south. If I ever see you again, I will kill you dead without warning. Do you understand what I'm saying?"

Alma glared, but nodded.

"Let go of the screwdriver."

Alma dropped it.

"You tried to kill my little girl. Even after you did, Janabai was the only one who spoke up for you. She blamed herself for not being a better friend to you. She thinks it's her fault you turned out this way."

Alma didn't respond.

"Do you have anything to say?"

"Tell her she didn't try hard enough. Tell her a stronger girl might have saved me. Tell her, she's weak. Tell her that."

"Sure. I'll be sure to tell her. Okay, get the screwdriver," Mother said.

Max picked up the screwdriver. "I'll keep this."

"Lots of screwdrivers," Alma said, rubbing her neck.

"Yes, but you won't have *this one*. Pick up your bag."

Alma crawled over to the fire and retrieving a metal cup and other odd items, dumped them in a sack and then climbed to her feet, damp from a long night on the ground, bedecked in leaves and filth, face mottled with insect bites, hair hanging in greasy strings, a woebegone hag of eighteen summers.

"Get out of my sight," Mother said.

"You heard her. Move."

Alma looked back and forth between them and smiled, the

lunatic leer of the true psychopath. Saying no human word, she hissed through her teeth like a serpent, turned her back, and slowly, swaying her bottom from side to side in a manner she thought insolent, waddled into the gray shadows of her hereafter and was seen no more.

"Well, that was swell," Max said. "You should have killed her. You really should have blown her fucking head off."

"I have another plan."

CHAPTER FORTY-FIVE

The Path Not Taken

"AHA, KEMOSABE. THAT'S WHY YOU get the big bucks. So, just how much of a head start do we give Bigfoot?"

"Until... ?"

"Until we follow her."

Warming her hands over the remains of Alma's fire, Mother took her time before answering.

"We don't. Not yet."

"Wait a fucking minute. You said 'something' was drawing her north. And now, we follow to see what that 'something' is. Right?"

Mother studied the embers as if seeking an oracle.

"Well?"

"What?"

"When do we go find the mysterious 'something'?"

"No rush. Whatever it is will still be there in a few days or a few weeks. Meanwhile, Daniel is probably freaking out."

"Since when did you start giving a rat's ass about Daniel's freak-out."

Mother laughed.

"I know. But we're not going off half-cocked. We'll put a proper expedition together after harvest."

Max looked skeptical. "Are you sure about this?"

"No, I'm not sure, I'm not sure about anything, but that's what we're doing."

They took a final look into the shadows where Alma had vanished. Then they turned around and started the long trek home.

"Anything to eat?"

"Gopi Gorp."

"Gimme."

That was Max's recitation of how they ran Alma to ground... and how they let her go.

As summer blended into autumn, another bountiful harvest taken and stored, our village hunkered down for the winter. The urgency to discover the source of Alma's magnetic pull northward faded. Mother's reconnaissance was relegated to the jumble of postponed projects. How could she just let it slide? She knew the demon was still out there, somewhere, probably up north. She had guns and a few people trained to use them. Max was itching to mix it up with the bad guys, and kept needling her.

"Sitting around here on our spiritual asses ain't gonna make that 'something' up the road go away. Ain't gonna make it easier to deal with. Let's go, Wonder Woman, while we have the chance. Shock and awe, baby, shock and awe!"

Azriel Dancer prided herself on recognizing critical choices, on picking optimum paths to the future, but she misjudged this fork in the road, and her failure to follow up the chase, to see for herself the cancer festering in Susanville, was a mistake that would torment her for the rest of her days.

PART TWO

PROLOGUE

B ELLY TIME. KERILYNN SAYS IT's the best part of midwifery, the "hands on the belly" time. Here, at the thirty-seventh week, she's going to turn, to *attempt* to turn, my baby from breech to *anterior*, as she calls it. I will feel some pressure, she says, but not much pain. What she doesn't tell me is how *pleasurable* it is. I love having her hands on me. She says she loves it too. And so does the baby, she thinks.

"The baby will do her best to cooperate," she says, but she's not sure — an "old midwives' tale." She winks at me.

The tale must be true, because the "old midwife" is successful. The baby turns. I will swear here and now Kerilynn Fleenor is a goddess. She performs miracles, which is what I think this must be, this "turning," something *good* for a change, a happy augury for better times ahead. I am more comfortable, that's for sure, and the baby seems to have settled down in her newly arranged cocoon.

"Help me sit up a bit higher, please," I ask her.

"There." She wedges another pillow behind my back. "How's that?"

"Perfect."

"How's Big Book of Janabai Shepherd coming along?"

"I'm just getting to the good stuff."

"What's that?"

"The Days of Grace."

"How old were you? Fifteen?"

"Sixteen. The summer of 17 AK."

"Ah, yes. Indeed. The good stuff."

CHAPTER FORTY-SIX

Muster

S TRANGERS SHOWING UP ON OUR doorstep was no longer a big deal. Most of the bad eggs had long since stumbled into the Great Beyond, starved to death, or been shot to rags. The good eggs were drawn to Shiva Puri by Myron Jefferson's hand-painted signs nailed to trees up and down the roads of northern California.

> *Come to Shiva Puri*
> *Trading*
> *Dancing*
> *Fresh milk*
> *Leave your weapons with the guard*
> *Do NOT approach the dogs without an escort*

In 17 AK, we closed all the guard posts except Crescent Mills along the old highway, and Crescent Mills had become more of a welcome station than a military position. Max decided it wasn't worth the calories to keep the posts going day and night, guarding against a golden-haired cannibal boy long since dead or gone elsewhere.

We were surprised how many vagabonds or small groups still wandered up Highway 89 or down 36, coming from nowhere, and heading toward the same destination. They were searching for something, hope or a hot meal, or just someone to talk to. These drifters might see the Crescent Mills outpost, or our livestock, or they might find one of us working in the rice field, our most distant acreage. We would look up in delight as unexpected company squelched toward us through the mud. If the strangers were polite, we would feed them and provide for their needs such as we could afford, with medicine or a coat or blanket, then send them on their way.

Or we would adopt them.

Shiva Puri was set high in the valley, beyond a narrow opening we called the Pinch, and behind a jutting outcropping we called the Spur. You couldn't see the village itself until you passed through the Pinch and circled around the Spur. Before you even got that far there was a smaller valley, Foreman Ravine, which opened to the south. Many of our barns and storage buildings were down in the ravine because it was much closer to the lower fields. Strangers were led to believe those buildings were the village itself. They never suspected what we had hidden above the Spur. Unless they passed muster, they never, ever got higher than the Pinch. But if they did, we considered them for adoption.

Yes, we recruited good people, strangers and stragglers, who somehow managed to hold on to their humanity. Often these folks brought useful skills. Tracey Sutter had been a baker, and Bob and Linda Bonnett had been cattle ranchers, and Aaron Weigle had been a machinist. The others we invited to stay on worked the farm until they were called to their proper sevas.

We worried these newcomers would not take to our spiritual life, but we needn't have worried. After years of suffering in the wilderness, without hope, without family, our "foster children" were euphoric to find themselves in a community that reassured them a happy future might be possible. We never had to explain "grace." They got it right away. From my sister.

Mirabai would drift down to Foreman Ravine holding onto Max's arm, though she easily could have walked it by herself. She arrived to "welcome" the new prospects temporarily housed in the lower bunkhouse while "the council determined their status." So we said. But it was Mirabai who decided who was welcome, and who was welcome to keep moving down the road. She didn't give sermons or whack the visitors with her eagle feathers. Mostly she just seemed to mind her own business, sitting silently in meditation under a tree, in the shade, Max standing nearby, packing, of course—Max was always packing.

The day's work done, we who worked the lower fields gathered in Foreman Ravine to sing with Mirabai before the evening meal. She led us in old songs most people knew, or maybe call and response chants. We introduced the newbies to her; always fun to see. She would hold out her hand to shake, they would take it, and, well, you never knew how people would react when they got the full force of Mirabai's Shakti. Men would cry like babies; women would give their babies to Mirabai to hold. People collapsed unconscious at her feet. Some folks laughed; a few fell into a trance. Some were terrified. They jerked their hands away like she was a rattler. Those people moved on.

When the audience was over, when grace flowed from Mirabai and into everybody near, Max would help her up, and she would sort of float away, Max holding on like she was a butterfly. When Mother moved it was like *the elephants are coming, the elephants are coming*. When Mirabai moved it was like a zephyr, a soft breeze drifting past your cheek.

Mirabai never had to say this person was acceptable, and that person wasn't. She knew, and we knew, and the people who came to meet her knew. Some felt, deep in their being, our gods were perilous, unendurable, and alien. They departed before morning. We helped them slip away into the night with food and blessings. Sometimes the departure was awful, when one spouse needed to go away and the other spouse needed to stay. Couples parted company right there in Foreman Ravine. Other times they would walk away together with one of them looking down and the other looking back over her shoulder, as if being sundered from her true family. And sometimes, before too many days passed, that one might return to be escorted up the valley, through the Pinch, around the Spur, and into Shiva Puri. Into our lives. Into our love.

I always wondered if Mirabai, being divine, made us more godly. Or did we project divinity on her and thereby make her so? Let me say this another way. Did Mirabai connect us to the truth within ourselves through her divinity, or did we, by telling her she was godly, make it happen?

We said, "Thou art God."

And Mirabai said, "Okeydokey."

CHAPTER FORTY-SEVEN

The Prodigal Joe

CURLED UP WITH A DETECTIVE novel, Robert Parker, my favorite, in the shade of the Crescent Mills outpost, I was wearing my old rabbit ears, a comfortable affectation I enjoyed when alone, though I would never, *ever* let anyone see me in such childish array. Fuzzy bunny ears make a girl feel right with the world, that's all I know. And lots better than a firearm, if I had one with me, which I didn't: Max decided I was more likely to hurt myself with a gun than make any good use of it. No, I was absent-mindedly stroking the fur on one rabbit ear while I kept one people eye on the goats. I didn't need both eyes because Vibisan, grandson of the great Hanuman, was doing the real work of guarding the herd. Actually, Vibi was snoring in the middle of a pile of La Manchas, likewise snoozing away the day. The hard life of Shiva Puri shepherd dogs. To tell the truth, we were both slacking off.

I was supposed to be on guard. Yep, that's me. The guard. The guard *extraordinaire*, scrunched down in the shade, my back to the road, my nose in my book. I didn't see the man approach. He made no noise, so he was right behind me when he cleared his throat. I just about jumped out of my drawers.

"Sorry," he said, "for scaring you."

"I'm not scared," I said. "But you shouldn't sneak up."

"I didn't see you there in the shadows until I was right behind you; then it was too late. I knew no matter what I did, I was going spook you. Again, I'm sorry."

"Apology accepted."

Well, the stranger was certainly polite. Good-looking, too, in a leathery, older-man kind of way. By now, Vibi had stalked over to see what was going on. When he saw the stranger, the ruff on his back stood up and his lips curled. He bared his teeth and began to growl his dangerous German shepherd warning. Vibi was big like his grandpa, Hanuman, and mean like his grandma, Trijata. Don't mess with him when he starts rumbling.

"Easy, Vibisan," I said, "He's okay. Maybe. Let's find out."

I gave the stranger my most intimidating glare of suspicion.

The man was heavily-armed, and Vibi could smell it. That dog knew exactly what firearms were, and he didn't like them. The man carried a rifle and a shotgun on his back and a handgun in a holster across his chest. He didn't make a move toward any of his weapons. Good thing, too. Vibi would have been all over him. I was sure the man knew this. Slowly, both hands held out, palms down, the man knelt. He didn't stare at Vibi, just knelt quietly, calmly, breathing.

"Vibisan," I said. "Go make friends."

The dog walked over to the man, one careful step at a time. He sniffed one of the man's hands, sniffed the other, his tail wagged, his ruff settled down, not all the way, just a bit.

"It's okay. You can stand up, but I wouldn't come between me and the dog until he knows you better."

"Good plan," the man said.

Outpost guards are trained to be wary of strangers until they prove themselves safe and friendly, and there is still the matter of a demon skulking around, somewhere, but I had already come to the decision that this man was one of the good guys.

"Want something to drink? I have some milk, fresh as can be."

"I'd love some milk," he said.

"Sit down over there, I'll get you some. Do you read?"

"I do," he answered, "whenever I get a chance."

"You can read my book while I'm getting the milk. It's a mystery. Robert Parker. Ever heard of Robert Parker?"

"I have, indeed," he said.

"This one's a 'Jesse Stone,' my favorite."

"I haven't heard those words in years, Jesse Stone, but yes, I remember Jesse Stone. Small town cop, right? Has a drinking problem?"

"That's right. And a woman he can't forget."

"Susan, right?"

"No, that's Spenser."

"Right, Spenser and Hawkeye."

"Hawk."

"Sure, Hawk. And Jesse Stone's girlfriend?"

"Ex-wife."

"Jessica?"

"Jenn."

"Of course, Jenn. You know your Robert Parker, don't you?"

"I should. I've read every one in the library about a zillion times."

"Library?" he asked. "You have a library?"

I realized I was talking too much.

"Maybe," I said. Just one clever response after another. I liked this man, this Robert – Parker-reading man, but I was getting uncomfortable with his questions. I should ask a few of my own.

"So, what's your name?"

"Joe," he answered.

"Nice name," I said. "Joe what?"

"Downing."

"Downing? Joe Downing? *Major* Joe Downing?"

"Nobody's called me that for a long, long time, but yes, I used to be Major Joe Downing."

Oh my Sweet Lords Shiva Brahma Vishnu! Joe Downing? The legend? The prodigal motorcycle major returns! And he's here at my guard post? Wait till I tell Kavitha about this. And Max! Another marine for Max! And Mother and Dad! Wait until everybody finds out who I'm bringing to dinner! This was the most exciting thing since... *ever*!

Now it was his turn to be suspicious.

"How did you hear about me?" Downing asked. "How do you know my name?"

"Stories," I said, grinning my face off.

"Stories? About Major Joe Downing? Who told you stories about me?"

Uh-oh. I bit my lip. I was talking way too much. We have rules for greeting strangers, and I was breaking most of them.

"Some people," I said, squinting my eyes. Cagey and cool, that's me.

"Okay," he said. "I'm making you nervous. You were getting me some milk, but before you go, let me ask you one more question... don't worry, it's a question I ask everyone I meet."

I looked at him for a moment, right into his gray wolf eyes.

"Go ahead," I said. "Ask your question."

"Have you ever heard of a woman named Azriel? Some folks called her Azriel Dancer. Have you ever heard of Azriel Dancer?"

"That's not her name. It's Azriel Burke-Kucinich."

"You know her?"

"Nobody really *knows* her, but yes, sort of. She's my mother."

He stood stock still.

"Azriel Dancer is your mother?"

"Yep. Lucky me."

"She's still alive?"

"She was this morning."

I made a quick decision.

"You stay right here, right here, and do not move, and do not try to follow me."

"Whatever you say, Lady Rabbit."

"Lady... ? Oh my God!" Blushing crimson, I snatched the rabbit ears off my head and stuffed them in my bag. I gave Downing a hard look. He raised his hands and made a face.

"Yikes, I'm sorry. It's not every day I see a rabbit reading a detective novel."

Deeply embarrassed, I ignored him.

"Vibi. Get the goats."

The dog barked up the herd, and I pushed them uphill as fast as goats get pushed. Times like these I wished I had a donkey or a llama to hurry them along. I saw Kavitha, moving one of the flocks down from high pasture. She was training to be a medic, but in the middle of the summer all of us work the farm. Kavitha was barely able to handle sheep, and a total loss with goats, but now at seventeen, with those long brown legs, she was unarguably the fastest runner in the village. Just what I needed.

"Find Mother," I said. "Fast as you can. I'll watch your sheep. Tell her it's an emergency. Tell her to meet me at Maitreya Hill."

Seeing the excitement in my face, Kavitha took off without asking questions. It seemed like all day, but it was probably no more than a half hour before I saw her and Mother running full speed through the Pinch. Mother, at thirty-six, was still fast, and her long legs ate up a lot of ground, but nobody kept up with Kavitha. By the time they reached me, Mother was gasping. Kavitha was hardly out of breath.

"What's wrong?" Mother demanded.

"Just follow me," I said. What a surprise this was going to be!

"Where?"

"You'll see. It's hard to explain," I lied. Hee! I knew Joe Downing was a special friend of my mother. I didn't know, then, just how special. "Follow me," I informed Mother. "Kavitha, you got the animals?"

"Got 'em."

I took off running, Mother beside me.

"How far are we going?"

"Crescent Mills outpost."

When I mentioned the outpost, Mother knew right away the emergency involved a stranger. It took the two of us about ten minutes to cover the mostly downhill mile and a half to the outpost. Joe Downing saw us running down the road, side by side. He walked out into the sunlight. Mother saw him and began slowing down.

"Don't worry, Mother, he's okay. I've already talked to him."

Mother came to a stop.

"It's Joe Downing, Major Joe Downing. He's been searching for you."

Frozen in place, Mother and Downing stood looking at each other, not moving or speaking.

Uh-oh, I thought. Something is wrong. Did I do something stupid? I wish Vibi was here.

"Mother, is it okay?" I asked.

Mother walked toward Downing and him toward her. Slowly,

then faster. They didn't hesitate. Before I could make sense of what was happening, they were in each other's arms kissing harder than I had ever seen anybody kiss, grabbing each other like they were trying to pull each other to pieces. I didn't understand what I was seeing. What was going on? The world tilted sideways. There was no air to breathe. I have read about passion in books, but I never got it until I saw them kiss.

Eventually they stopped and just stood there looking at each other.

"Why are you kissing Major Downing?" I asked.

Mother turned, paused, and in that moment, I could see her lips were swollen where she had crushed them against Joe Downing's. That's what I remember most, her swollen lips.

"Go find your father. Tell him Joe Downing is home."

Chapter Forty-Eight

Homecoming

MOTHER INSISTED JOE'S HOMECOMING BE moved from the amrit into mandir as befitting such an auspicious occasion. Dad rightfully objected.

"Welcoming Joe Downing into the mandir, our heart of hearts, is *not* appropriate nor is it safe."

Our folk had met Joe only once, and that was many years earlier. Dad pursued his argument.

"The major has not been initiated, has not been approved by the council, has not received Mirabai's darshan."

"Fine," Mother snapped. "Get Mirabai."

I led my sister into amrit, took her over to the table where Joe was eating, and left her standing there. No twin sight for this man, not from yours truly. Mirabai was on her own. After a few seconds, she held out her hands. Joe knelt down and took them in his own. Neither said a word. Mira didn't know any more about the major than I did, than anybody did, except for the story about Downing and the marines who rode in one day on machines, stayed for a while, and then vanished into the far north, pausing only long enough to clean out a nest of snakes down in Quincy. Whatever information Mirabai was getting about him, she was getting from somewhere else, another realm perhaps. She must have liked what she found there, because she broke into a huge smile, pulled him to his feet, and grabbed him in a long, sweet hug.

That was that. Joe Downing was officially approved, but there was still a nasty vibration between our guest and my dad. I caught the flinty look between my parents. Not good. Dad was wearing his snotty sneer, the sign that he was really upset and trying to hide it. Joe Downing could not take his eyes off Mother. Joe. Mother. Dad. Mother. Joe. Mother. Joe. Dad. I may have been the only one to see the passionate welcome Mother had given the major, but everybody in the room picked up on the weirdness. Mother was flushed and radiating heat. She was staring at him with such longing, my stomach twisted into a knot. What was I thinking? I'd run to her with such excitement, thinking I'd found the long-lost folk hero. Instead, I'd taken my father's usurper by the hand and delivered him to our door.

I have always been a daddy's girl, and I am ever so loyal. Whatever happened, I was going to take Dad's side. But face facts. My parents were not lovey-dovey. They did not even sleep under the same roof. But they were married, or something, weren't they? Mother simply could *not* treat Dad like that. I ground my teeth, working myself up into a lather. Really! Mother, act your age!

After Arati and the waving of lights, Mirabai led a brief call-and-response, "Jaya Jaya Shiva Shambo." A chair was brought up and set down in front of the puja, a singular honor for someone the old-timers barely knew, and we youngsters not at all. Major Joe took a seat and looked around at us and at our temple. It must have been overwhelming, the lingam and the yoni, the smudge and candles, the portraits of our deities, most of them hand-painted by Myron in vivid colors, adorning the walls. More than two hundred people filled the room, sitting expectantly on their cushions. Yes, it must have made quite an impression.

Mother spoke: "Eighteen years ago, Major Joe Downing and the Growlers passed through Graeagle. You may be too young to remember, or you may be new to us, but I know you have all heard the story. He only stayed a few days, but in that brief time, we learned to trust him. Before he rode away, we promised we would always be friends. He made the same promise to us. We hoped, I hoped, he would remain with us, but dharma took him and his marines north. I invited Joe to return to Shiva Puri when he had discharged his duty. I invited him to begin a new life with us. Now, he has returned. He has come home. Joe, will you tell us your story?"

"It's a long story," he said.

Everybody cheered and clapped.

"Why the applause?" he asked. "I haven't even started."

"We love long stories," Mother said.

Joe sat there for a few minutes, getting his thoughts in order. Finally, he decided on his beginning. He reached down and took something out of his pack, unwrapping the object from several layers of tattered plastic.

"This is the duty log of the United States Marine Corps." He opened the book and thumbed through it until he found the page he wanted. "Sergeant Flythe, make your report."

Max stood up. She had chosen the simple wool dress most of the women wore for evening programs. With her glossy chestnut braid and shawl around her shoulders, she looked more like a farm wife than a sergeant of marines. "We're still here, sir."

"Well done, Flythe. At ease."

He picked up the stub of a pencil hanging from the "duty log" on a piece of grimy string, opened the book again, and wrote:

"Sergeant Maxine Flythe is officially commended for outstanding service as the commander of Shiva Puri security forces. Effective this day... does anybody know the date?"

Galen Raether said, "July twentieth, 18 AK. I *believe* that is the right date."

We were amused by his, "I believe." If Galen Raether said it was the twentieth, well, it was scripture. Joe Downing caught the humor and smiled.

He entered the date in the log book and held it high for those in the back to see.

"It's all in here, the story of the Growler Motorcycle Club and what happened after we parted ways, but if it's alright with you, why don't I just tell you the way I remember?"

Two hundred heads bobbed up and down in approval.

"Very well. We rode out of Graeagle and up to Quincy, where we cleaned out a bunch of bad guys. Did any of the Quincy people make it down to you?"

"One small group, but only the three children survived the winter," Mother said. "Myron, Austin, Kavitha, stand up."

The three young people got to their feet.

"This man saved your lives," Mother said, shooting another quick look at Dad.

"Sir," Myron, the oldest of the surviving children, spoke, "I don't know what to say. We never thought we would see you again."

"Say 'thank you,' stupid," Austin said.

Myron glared at the younger man. "We don't say 'stupid' in front of guests."

"It's alright, son," Joe said. "And you are welcome. It was our privilege to help you, and let me tell you, my boys had a lot of fun rousting out those creeps."

"OORAH," Kavitha shouted.

I wanted to slap the stupid smile right off her stupid face.

CHAPTER FORTY-NINE

The Last American Air Base

"WE WORKED OUR WAY NORTH, sticking to back roads, heading toward the Whidbey Island Air Base above Seattle. Whenever we could, we scrounged a meal from people just trying to hang on, mostly good people like you folks. A few bad ones, too. We siphoned gas from abandoned cars, and there were a lot of them. More cars than people. The main problem was our rides. Motorcycles are finicky. When they broke down, even a simple problem was disastrous. There were no repair shops, no spare parts. The bike became another pile of metal junk on the side of the road. So one cycle would go down, and the marine would ride with another marine. By the time we crossed the Washington state line, a couple of us were already riding double.

"You're right to wonder why we didn't commandeer passenger vehicles. There were plenty of abandoned cars and trucks. There was fresh gasoline to be siphoned. You have to understand, these were our *cycles*, our customized, personalized war horses. They were as dear to us as members of our families. Our cycles had names, personalities, history. They were our connection to better days. They held us together. We were the Growlers *Motorcycle* Club. We rode together, under the sky, not crammed in mommy vans. The thought of dumping our cycles never crossed my mind.

"We came to a little town called Wenatchee. Wenatchee, Washington, doing better than most. We stayed a couple of weeks helping those people get in a wheat crop. Some of my guys met *women*."

Downing paused to give us a comical look. Even I laughed, but I caught myself and bit it back before anybody saw me. He went on:

"The people of Wenatchee, just like you folks, wanted us to stay on, resident marines, I guess, but I told them the same as I told you. We had a duty to report to base. So I gave the orders to mount up and ride. The men were not happy about it. Another mistake on my part."

Here, he looked directly at Mother.

"Definitely a mistake. I should have been doing more listening and less ordering. I was caught up in the mission, in being the major, being in charge. I didn't think it through. When the cycles started to break down, what were we going to do? We were going to be in a fix. Were those of us still riding going to leave comrades behind? To follow on foot? What about the breakdowns to come? Another two of us left behind? It didn't take long for my mistakes to catch up with me."

Again, Joe looked over at Mother when he mentioned mistakes. This time he smiled and gave a little shake of his head. Mother inhaled deeply. His remark meant something powerful to her, some memory from before. The two of them were connecting on their own vibration. I looked over at my father, but his head was bowed. I didn't think he was praying.

"The first day out of Wenatchee, it happened, the inevitable catastrophe. One of the cycles blew a gasket. No repair possible. I made a speech, like, 'If some of us ride on four wheels, all of us ride on four wheels. Strip your cycles and put your kits together. Top, see what kind of trucks you can requisition from these town folks. Be ready to rock and roll at dawn.'

"Around our camp, I could see the men talking together and clamming up whenever I got close. Mutiny? Was I looking at a mutiny? No surprise when Top Cunningham came over for a private chat. The men were going back to Wenatchee, and if I didn't like it, well, I could shout orders until I turned green, but they were done with my fool's quest, and don't try to stop them. Top had worked out a deal. The men would go back to town and make the best lives they could. I would take my cycle, all the gas I could carry, and go wherever I wanted.

"I asked Top, 'What are you going to do?'

"Cunningham looked at me like I was out of my mind.

"'Going with you, sir, what do you think?'

"'Anybody else?'

"'Fahey.'

"'Three of us?'

"'Glad to see the major can still do arithmetic.'

"The men didn't have enough cycles to get all of them back to Wenatchee, but that was their problem. The next morning, they tried to say something conciliatory, but I wasn't having any. Top Cunningham, Sergeant Fahey, and I fired up our motors and rode away. I didn't look back.

"Top's bike went down that same afternoon, so he and I rode double. The next morning Fahey's bike froze up, so the three of us started walking. A couple of days' worth of blisters, and enough of that hiking crap. We found a pickup truck we hot-wired. Siphoned gas from the two bikes, jammed ourselves into the front seat, and continued our scenic drive along Highway 2 through the Okanogan National Forest. I guess you could call it the Okanogan 'Wilderness' now. We skirted Seattle completely. Maybe we should have gone into the city for a look, I don't know; easy to say now, but at the time I decided we would check in at base first and recon Seattle later. We never did get around to it, and we learned later there wasn't much left to see after the tsunami came up the sound."

At this revelation, people all over the hall gasped. Kelly Cassio, who was born in Seattle and had family there, used to have family there, cried aloud and fell into her husband's arms. In that moment, it really dawned on me how little we knew about the world beyond our perimeter. Max had sent scouting teams out in the early days, but no more than about fifty miles in each direction. That was our world, a circle one hundred miles across. Joe's story was the first real news since the night of the Kali Yuga, almost twenty years before.

"I should have realized we would have trouble getting to Whidbey Air Station. Deception Pass Bridge, the only way to drive onto the island, was gone. I found out later we had taken it out ourselves, by "we" I mean fighter pilots, bombing it to keep refugees off the island. The ferries were gone, too, probably to the bottom of the sound with harpoon missile holes in their hulls. Top opined that our difficulty getting to the air base might be a 'cosmic sign' that we should head back down to Wenatchee and rejoin the lads.

"'Bad joo-joo,' Top said. 'The gods are telling us something.'

"I thanked him for the spiritual guidance, said I would 'take it under advisement,' but I was thinking along the same track. Enough. I've done enough. Why not turn around right now and head back here, to Shiva Puri? The thought gnawed at me for days, but then we got lucky. I guess you could call it luck, for Top and Fahey, as it turned out. We were working our way along the shore, on foot, making one last effort to find a way over to Whidbey Island.

"Fahey leaned over and whispered, 'We're being followed.'

"Sure enough, that night at camp, four men and two women walked into the firelight, armed and alert, but not hostile.

"The spokesman said, 'Semper fi, marines.' Encouraging beginning.

"I answered, 'Semper fi.'

"Our visitors were the elders of an extended family of Swinomish Indians. We were, we didn't know it at the time, on the Swinomish reservation. We invited them to sit down for a cup of tea, best we had, and they contributed a slab of dried salmon. I asked them how they knew we were marines.

"'Takes one to know one.'

"The spokesman, George Kalla by name, told us many of their young men had joined the Corps at one time or another, including himself, shot up in the Middle East and retired on disability. The brotherhood of the Green Machine saved our bacon with these folks. As they say, 'Once a marine.'

"When we asked what had happened to all the people in Seattle, they snapped shut. After a long, uncomfortable silence, a woman, George Kalla's niece, spoke.

"'The big wave came. Most of the city people died,' she said. 'Some tried to come out here and take our food. We would not let them take our food. They got angry with us, so we made them go away.'

"That's all we could get out of her. Well, this is the funny part, that's not all Top Cunningham got out of her. Her name was Marie. Good woman. In the years that followed, he spent more and more time with the Swinomish, and eventually married Marie, and they started having babies. As far as I know Top's still there. I think of him often. Best marine I ever served with."

"Blessings on Top Cunningham," Mother said.

"Jai Shiva," we responded in unison.

Joe Downing startled at the interruption. He smiled.

"Thank you," he said. "Maybe I should stop for the night. I must be boring you with all of this painstaking detail, trying to cram fifteen years into one sitting."

The people of Shiva Puri disagreed, and demonstrated with calls of "Don't stop," and "Please, go on."

"We tell stories at night," Mother encouraged. "That's what we do. And we know how fortunate we are to hear a new one, especially a true one, and one that means so much to us. We'll stay here all night, if that's what you need to tell the whole thing."

Joe smiled. "Well, it won't take that long, but I'm grateful to hear that you will allow me to get it all out. Where was I?"

"You were telling us about Top Cunningham and the Swinomish woman, Marie."

"Yes, but I'm getting ahead of myself. The Swinomish offered to ferry us over the bay on their fishing boat, an offer we reluctantly accepted. I think we had our hearts set on heading back south. They invited us to stay with them if we didn't like what we found. We didn't. The air station was deserted, though it had been left in good order, like somebody had locked the doors and gone on vacation, but everything airworthy was gone. There were a few disabled hulks in the maintenance hangers, engines stripped for parts, and one crashed Growler towed off the end of the runway. There was nobody there to report to, no squadron to join, no assignment to take, no orders to carry out.

"Top asked me what we were going to do.

"'Settle in and wait, I guess.'

"'That's wonderful news, sir,' he said. Top was even better with sarcasm than your Sergeant Flythe. 'I'd like to point out something to the major, something so obvious I'm sure the major has already considered it with his marine-issued wisdom.'

"'Spit it out.'

"'The major ain't ever gonna fly again. This card house done blowed down.'

"'Probably right.'

"'In that case, what are your orders, sir?'

"'See if you can find a generator and some gas fresh enough to run it. Get Fahey fixing some chow.'

"'Aye, aye, sir. Then what?' he asked.

"'Wait,' I answered.

"'Why is that, sir?'

"'Because we took an oath. Because we are the United States Marines. Because the president might come by one day and ask where his air base went and why we didn't do our duty to keep it safe.'

"'Oh, *that* why.'

"For five years, I kept the base in good order. Now, it just seems crazy; but I was caught with the idea that Whidbey might be the only place in the country where there was still... how can I put this?... a sense of order."

I stared at Mother. She sat there stonefaced. Dad smirked. Max looked like she had bit into a sour apple. Even at fifteen, I was having trouble following his logic. To heck with his "sense of order." If he loved my Mother so much, why didn't he just come back to Shiva Puri?

"In the beginning, I would move through each day expecting someone to walk in the door. I kept thinking I would turn a corner and bump into someone. Or maybe the phone would ring. The radio would crackle to life. A carrier jet would line up for an emergency landing. But there was nobody there but ghosts. After a few weeks, even they departed.

"There's good farm land on Whidbey Island, plenty of empty houses, few people. After a while the Swinomish moved over from the mainland to make new homes. The island was, when you think about it, their ancestral land. So why not take it back? The Indian dream come true. And the island was secure as anywhere else.

"The Kallas were the first to come. As I mentioned, Top married into that family — he didn't waste any time — and six months later Fahey married Lorraine Critz after her people moved over. The Indian families came together to make a new village they called 'Swinomish.' Top and Fahey moved into the village with their new wives, and I had the base to myself, the commanding officer and sole occupant of Whidbey Island Naval Air Station. As far as I knew, I was the only functioning government of the entire United States of America.

"In time, I became the un-elected justice of the peace, arbitrator of disputes, and, from time to time, mafia don. If someone was causing trouble, I rounded up Top and Fahey and some brawny Swinomish lads. We straightened things out. So, the years went by while I flapped in the wind like the forlorn American flag I raised every morning. I performed maintenance such as I could on the buildings and cut the grass around the admin center. When my military chores were done, I would head over to Swinomish and get to work on my real jobs, farmhand and handy man.

"Then, one day I just woke up and decided I had done enough. Five years, and what had I accomplished? The time was long overdue to accept your generous invitation."

Chapter Fifty

Joe Downing's Quest

"Top and Fahey and their families came over for a farewell ceremony. We lowered the American flag for the last time, folded it per regulations, and placed it on the commanding officer's desk. Goodbye, America. God bless America. Last man to leave America, lock the door and turn off the lights."

Joe stopped his story for a moment to wipe his eyes. He wasn't the only one. He shook his head to clear it and went on.

"Over the next few days I put my kit together. Weapons and ammo, as much food as I could carry, poncho, extra socks, first aid pouch, this and that, a second pair of shoes hanging by the laces. I figured there would be houses along the way where I could sleep dry most of the time and where I might replenish my supplies. I would hunt when I could, and work for food when I could. My Swinomish friends sailed me back across the bay. I said goodbye, a tough bit, knowing I would never see any of them again. Top and Fahey knew exactly where I was going. They wished me well and sent their greetings to you folks. They hugged me, hard, both of them. I thought Cunningham was going to break my ribs. It's touching to have your first sergeant crying on your shoulder with his nose running like a little kid.

"I headed south to California, walking all the way, again making a wide detour around the drowned city that used to be Seattle. I retraced my steps along Highway 2 through the Okanogan Wilderness and down to Wenatchee to see what had happened to my men. I'm proud to say they were still there, all but two who had passed on, one from pneumonia and one in a logging accident. The community was hanging on, doing better than most. They received me politely, but I could tell my marines still felt uncomfortable about deserting me. I told them it was okay; I was pleased to see them doing so well. I told them stories about Top and Fahey, which made them happy. I told them these were different times. No hard feelings. I tried to let them off the hook, but when it was time for me to move along, they were relieved, though they said otherwise.

"Further south, I heard about bad things in Susanville, so I detoured west toward Mount Lassen. I had always wanted to climb it again. I had done it once before with my father. It's just a day climb, I'm sure you all know, and the views from the top are indescribable, especially now the air is so clean. One thing made me nervous: lots of fissures on the north face, with steam venting up. I clambered down the southeast face, circled around the bottom of Lake Almanor, caught old Highway 89 and headed for Graeagle.

"Here's the part that really hurt, the screwup that would cause me so much heartache. I walked right past this place. Right past it."

How could he not notice us? I thought back to that time. We had just moved up from Graeagle. This was years before we put up the signs to welcome people. Mother was afraid Kali was still skulking around. We were hunkered down in the upper valley, keeping our heads low. Okay, I guess it makes sense. Still… he walked right by and never knew we were here!

"I was moving fast, not stopping to look around, anxious to get to Graeagle and find you. Well, that was a miserable surprise, as you can imagine, getting to Graeagle and finding it empty. No sign of you or any clue to where you had gone. A ghost town, and the ghosts were not friendly, to me anyway. I never should have left you. I could have been with you all these years."

Joe was looking right at Mother when he said this. Now everybody was getting it, the heartbreaking thing between Major Joe and Azriel Dancer. You could hear whispers all over the mandir. It was just about the most awful story anybody ever heard. I knew Mother wanted to go to him, but she nodded to Simone Jackson, who she counted on for a soothing touch. Simone went up behind the major and put her hands on his shoulders. She didn't say anything, none of that "it's okay stuff." She stroked his shoulders softly, one human being to another. I wondered how long it had been since he had been touched by a woman. After a while he reached up and patted one of Simone's hands. He wiped his nose on his sleeve. Simone returned to her cushion. Joe continued.

"I knew you had come up to Graeagle through Downieville, so I walked down there. Another ghost town. I remembered something you said about your original home across the Yuba, so I kept moving south on 49. When I got to the river, I saw the cars shoved on the bridge blocking the way. Your spray-paint warnings were still there. I knew then you had not come back that way. I hadn't figured out what I was going to do if I didn't find you."

I may have been a teenager, but I was old enough to understand that there were two stories going on at the same time, the story Joe was saying to all of us, and the story he was telling to one person alone. When he said, "I never allowed myself the thought that you might not have made it," the "you" he was talking to was the woman he had loved and left behind: my mother, Azriel Dancer.

"I camped at the Yuba for a few days trying to get myself moving again. When the food ran out, my only choice was to move along, or starve, and believe me, I gave starving serious consideration. I shouldered my pack and set off west, walking a line, like a tightrope, with untouched wilderness on my right and the incinerated earth on my left. This was, let's see, five, no, almost six years after the Event. The burned lands were coming back, coming back strong. No big trees, but green everywhere: saplings fifteen, twenty feet tall, and plenty of undergrowth. There, along the dividing line, I saw animals in astonishing numbers: mule deer by the thousands, bears, coyotes, you name it. It would have been a hopeful sign, if I cared.

"For days I drifted toward the coast. I didn't know where my journey was taking me, but had some notion the route would eventually deposit me like driftwood on the shore of the Pacific Ocean. I might find a cave along the cliffs. I would crawl inside like a bear, go to sleep. Never wake up. That was my plan."

He laughed, but there was nothing funny about it, not to me or anybody else. Everyone could see he was holding a whole world of pain.

"When I stumbled into Colusa Town over near the Sacramento River, I asked the people if they knew where I could find Shiva Puri. I don't remember if they answered me. I don't remember anything at all for weeks. The Colusa people fed me, cleaned me up, got me back on my feet. When I felt well enough, I worked with them in the wetlands, miles and miles of marshes and shallow lakes, some kind of wildlife refuge back before. It was a perfect land for growing sugar cane and rice. In the winter the Colusans shared their rice with millions of water birds flying south, ducks of all kinds, and snow geese in such numbers when they rose you couldn't see the sky. Every bird you can think of came to Colusa. The birds ate the rice, and the Colusans ate the birds. One odd thing about those birds got my attention. Not all of them wintered there; some just dropped by on their way to Mexico and points south. That's something to think about, isn't it? The birds headed south, found their ancient destinations intact, and flew back. I had been thinking that there was nothing left below the edge. The birds knew otherwise.

"I stayed in Colusa for five more seasons, good people there, and no reason for me to leave except I was restless and wanting to find something, I don't know what, but it wasn't in Colusa. After five years I had gotten past the pain of not finding you in Graeagle, but I was still sick at heart. Not much use to anybody, and not pleasant to be around. The Colusans didn't make much of an effort to stop me.

"On the coast, Mendocino was a ghost town, cold and windy. I turned north to Garberville, Eureka, Arcata. I walked from one small community to another, to farms and forts, family compounds and hermit huts. I asked everyone I met if they had heard about Shiva Puri. One man, a kind of naked guru, I'd guess you call him, tapped me between the eyes and told me to be happy. He had a tattoo of a face on his chest that said the same thing: Don't Worry, Be Happy.

"Another man told me about a big farming village east in Redding. Could it be? I headed over that way. As I got closer to Redding, I began to find bodies, lots of bodies rotting in the fields."

Here, Joe looked over at a gaggle of kids sitting in their usual place, right up front.

"I think I should stop now, and pick up this next part at another time."

Mother agreed. She told the parents to tuck the little birds in bed, a chorus of objections from the peepers, as you can imagine, and for the rest of us to stretch and get a snack and "something to drink," she said, looking at Vic Tretheway meaningfully. An hour later, we were back on our cushions munching popcorn, a village favorite of which we have an abundance, and sipping Vic's Best from ceramic cups. Joe fortified himself with a long chug of spirits and nodded gratefully to Vic.

"Eventually I found the community, what was left of it, but

it wasn't you. These folks called themselves "Reds," mostly Mexican migrant farmers and a few Asians who had escaped captivity over in Redding. The Reds told me their story, things that had happened to them so horrible that, well, let me give you a cleaned-up version."

"No sanitized version," Mother interrupted. "Tell us the whole thing."

"The Reds told me that a huge mob, an 'army' might be a better word, an army of marauders, came down the old Interstate 5 riding bicycles, maybe five hundred of them. They murdered many of the Reds right where they were working in the fields, and forced the rest of them into slavery, and worse. Rabid dogs, killers, and rapists. Their leader was a giant of a man named Kumbakarma, a sadist and a stone-cold killer. He had a consort who was just as vile, a kind of witch queen they called "la Hiena," the hyena. But worst of all was a kid, just a teenager, but some kind of a cannibal. The Reds thought this kid was actually calling the shots. They didn't see him often, and they didn't want to. Goldilocks, that's what they called him, Goldilocks because of his long blond hair. They said to look into his yellow eyes was death. Whoever went into his place never came out except as bones he threw off the roof, a pile of carnage growing higher and higher."

Mother and Joe Downing stared at each other. Nobody said a word.

"Shall I go on?" Downing asked.

Mother closed her eyes and nodded. Downing continued:

"One night when the outlaws were drunk, the Reds slipped away toward the coast. When I came upon them, they were still hiding and waiting for the "Rakshasa," as the outlaws called themselves, to come after them. I asked them how long ago they had escaped. More than a month, they said. What happened to the Rakshasa? Nobody knew. I said it would be a good idea to find out, and besides, I had nothing better to do. That sounds cavalier, I know, 'nothing better to do.' It's true. I had nothing better.

"Four nights later, at five in the morning, we crept into Redding, me and three Reds. We wore black, head to toe, with black grease on our faces and hands. We went unarmed except for straight razors and piano wire. If we got caught, firearms were not going to help us.

"The town was empty and dark except around the old city hall where the Rakshasa had made their camp. A few oil barrels burned low, the only light. No one on watch, no challenge. They were all asleep, dead drunk. We circled around the edge of the encampment. When we found one of them sleeping a little ways away from the others, I slit his throat with a straight razor. We worked in teams of two. One of us muffled any sound while the other one sliced. Altogether we took out about fifteen of them. The Reds wanted to keep slitting throats, but I gave orders to withdraw, and they pulled back with me. No need to push our luck. I figured the bad guys would be freaked out enough when they woke up and found a dozen or more of their bedmates grinning through a second mouth below their chins.

"We waited another week before I crept back for a look-see. The Rakshasa had vamoosed, whereabouts unknown.

"The Reds moved back into their city. For the next seven years I lived with them, helping them rebuild their homes and secure their defenses. We destroyed all but one bridge across the river and fortified that one. When the work was done, they renamed the town 'Rio Rubio,' Red River.

"I liked the people, a lot, these Reds, and they liked me, and they were grateful for my help as much as I was grateful to them. I felt useful again. My head was in a much better place, during the day, anyway, when I was working. But at night, I couldn't sleep. I couldn't settle down. When I finally told them I was moving on, they pitched a fit. Why didn't I take a wife? Why didn't I start a farm, or a ranch, and raise some kids? Where did I have to go that was better than Rio Rubio? I didn't have good answers. I just knew that I was too restless to stay. I needed to keep moving, keep searching.

"I headed east again, this time planning to walk all the way across the country to the Atlantic Ocean. I thought I would stop one more time in Graeagle, I'm not sure why, to take one more look, maybe just to say goodbye, a final torture, and move on. I

186

got to Graeagle, spending the night in the same room in the same lodge where I had slept so many years before. I woke up when I heard talking outside. A boy and two girls were walking down the road. I shouted to them, which was not a good idea, because they spooked and ran, but I hollered that I was friendly and just passing through. They stopped and waited for me. The kids were scared of me, and not polite, snotty is more to the point. They spoke to me, when they answered at all, in monosyllables. I asked them my usual question, had they ever heard about Shiva Puri. No, never heard of it. What is it? I said that it was a farm village that used to live here.

"'Oh, you mean the Hindoo *idol-aters*. They're going to hell, you know.'

"For a moment, I swear I couldn't breathe.

"'Yes,' I said, 'the Hindoos. What do you know about them? Where did they move?'

"'I don't know,' one of them said.

"Another one said, 'Up north, somewhere.'

"'Where?' I asked, 'Do you know?'

"'We don't know and we don't care.'

"'Maybe your parents will know?' I said, 'Where are they? I'll ask them.'

"The kids looked at each other with some alarm. Obviously they didn't want me taking my questions to the adults. Maybe they were not supposed to be here, or they were supposed to be somewhere else, or maybe they were never to talk to strangers. All I know is they didn't want me talking to their parents.

"The oldest, one of the girls, said, 'I hear they are up in Indian Valley.'

"'Where's Indian Valley?' I asked.

"'Up near Greenville, but if you get to Greenville you've gone too far.'

"'They don't like strangers. Probably shoot you dead.'

"'Don't tell them we told you.'

"'Why not?'

"'Maybe they won't trade with us no more.'

"'Maybe they'll come down and kill us.'

"'They will not,' said the boy.

"'You ever see the Devil Max? Shoots hellfire out of her eyes.'

"'Does not.'

"'Does, too.'

"'You are such a baby.'

"'Anyways, we got to go now,' said the oldest girl. 'Like I said, don't be telling them we told you where they was.'

"The children darted into the undergrowth like rabbits.

"That was that," Joe finished. "My story. Here I am."

"Here you are," Mother said. "Where you belong."

Chapter Fifty-One

Small Measure of Comfort

THE NIGHT AFTER MAJOR JOE'S recitation, Azriel Dancer, my mother, stood before the assembled membership of Shiva Puri and divorced my father, Daniel Kucinich. In the fewest possible words, she expressed what everybody already knew. Their marriage had been over for a long time. I had never seen a divorce before, but I knew what it was from books. Now it was done. Snap.

Mother had been living in Hunter House since I was six, but when Joe Downing showed up, they moved in together in a loft up at the number three barn. I didn't see much of them from then on. What was happening? I don't mean *that*, I know *that* was going on. I mean what was happening to my mother's life, to my life? I needed to talk to someone about Mother and our new, what would you call him? Guest? Member? Officer? Well, I certainly couldn't talk to my cast-off father about it. He was moping around like a sick puppy.

Not Max, that's for sure. She always took Mother's side. If you asked Max something about what Azriel Dancer was thinking or why she was doing something, Max would always say "You don't *need* to know."

Annabel Feuerstein, most devout of us, was willing to listen, but what you usually got was a pithy spiritual proverb, or if you were really, really lucky, an entire sermon. I needed something more down-to-earth. Practical advice. Okay, Janabai, stop the dillydally. Find Mama Witch and get on with it.

Besides being the village shrink, Simone Jackson was one of Mother's closest friends. In the first days after the "divorce," when Mother was on the outs with the rest of the village, Simone backed her and told everybody else to slack off. You could always depend on Mama Witch to serve it plain without honey.

I stood in the doorway of Storehouse Three and watched Simone work among the beeswax candles.

"Chile," she said, "don jes stand there loafin, hep me out."

She was in one of her shuck-and-jive moods.

"Do what?"

"Cut each a'dese foh footers in half. Tie foh pieces together with two pieces a'twine."

Every October, after harvest, grownups received a personal allotment of candles for the winter. The portion was measured in inches. Use your candles as wastefully, or frugally, as you wanted. There were one hundred and seventy-one grown-ups which equals... which equals?

"Thirty-three thousand inches a candles," Simon supplied. "How many inches foh each folk?"

"Uh... uh..."

"One hundred and ninety-two inches each."

"One hundred and ninety-two."

"You gots it. See? Yo kin do de numbahs jes fine when I heps. Now, I jes gonna sits over chere on de bench and do de real work."

"What's that?" I asked. "The real work?"

"Checking off de names wid dis heavy feather quill."

"Do you think I will ever be able to do such a hard job?"

"Prolly not. Only de wisest woman gets dis seva."

"Gee, Simone, I want to be just like you when I grow up."

"Fat chance," she said.

We worked together until I bundled a winter's worth of candles, stowed them on the rear shelves, and rotated last year's reserves to the front. We always went into the cold months with enough supplies to ride out a second winter if the harvest went bad.

"Okay," Simone said. "Les rustle up a cuppa and you can tells ol' Mama Witch whas on yo mind."

We walked over to the kitchen, wheedled two cups of mint tea with honey (!) from Radha, and found corner seats in the empty amrit. Folks, it may seem hokey, and too good to be true, but we try to settle most of our problems by sitting down with Mama Witch and a "cuppa," Hey, that's life at Shiva Puri. We're not perfect. We do what we can to keep on the dharma path, even when it comes to fixing bullies like Greg Pequinot... and even when we fail miserably with crazies like Alma.

"Spill it," Simone said.

I spilled. For hours, I complained how much I was hurt by Mother's distance, her coldness toward me. I whined about my confusion about the divorce, and my hatred of Joe Downing for tearing Mother and Dad apart.

Simone dropped the jive and reverted to her natural dialect, upper East End London where she was born, not the cotton fields of the "Old South" like she put on. "First of all, Janabai, 'hatred' is not a word that becomes you, and second, you are using it to shock me, and third, it's not true. Joe Downing did not tear your mother and father apart, as you very well know."

I looked at the floor. Simone reached over the table and took my hand.

"Listen to me, baby. Your mother loves you very much, and Mira, and all of us, and in her own way, she still loves your father."

"She has a funny way of showing it."

"Your mother is a most complicated woman. And most unique. There is no one in the world better with the animals, except you. It's a gift from the gods that comes to you through her. Why do you think you chose shepherd as your seva?"

"Trying to please Mother?"

"Good guess, but no, I don't think so. More than that. It's your birthright."

"My mutation?"

"Where did you hear that? Never mind, don't answer. It doesn't matter. Mutation, perhaps. We have certainly discussed the possibility. Maybe some kind of radiation changed you when you were an itty-bitty microbe. But if your gift is a mutation, it's a great mutation, and we hope you pass it along to your own daughter along with your mother's talent for prophecy."

"Do you have faith in her far sight?"

Simone laughed. "No, we don't have *faith* in your mother's visions. We don't *need* faith because we know her visions are *real*."

"How do you know they're real?"

"Well, right after the Kali Yuga, we found your mother in the mandir where she had been all night in some kind of a trance. She was dancing by herself when we came in. Max went up and put her hand on your mother. The next instant, Max was flying across the room like she had been shot out of a gun. It's pretty funny now, but it scared the willies out of us. I will tell you this, Jana. There is power in your mother, or maybe it comes *through* your mother, but however it happens, the gods have chosen Azriel Dancer as their own, chosen her to lead us, her alone, to show us where to go, what to do. Would you like to carry that weight?"

I didn't answer.

"So, if your mother finds some measure of comfort with Major Joe, don't you think she should have it?"

I didn't answer. Drifting away into a most delicious revenge fantasy, I began to cook up a plan. I was going to frame Joe Downing with some horrible crime and get rid of him. No, that's not right. Good guys get framed. What do bad guys get? Oh, yes, they get *set up*. That's what Spenser and Hawk were always doing in the detective novels. They set up the bad guys. I was going to set up Joe Downing. He was going down, baby, and when he realized who set him up for the fall, it would be too late. How I would laugh! Mother would kick him out and go back to Dad. Maybe Max would kill Downing in a shootout.

You see, reading detective novels is useful after all.

How should I go about it? What would Spenser do? I could shoot somebody, maybe Kavitha, not kill her, of course, just a flesh wound, and then plant the gun under Joe's bed and then lead the searchers to it, accidentally of course. Too much? Okay, I could steal some loot and hide it in his room. That would probably be enough. The main problem is that we don't actually have any loot. What about some of these candles? Yeah, that's it. The candle count comes up short. Oh no! Candles are missing? Where could they be? Let's look in Joe Downing's backpack!

"Janabai, wake up!" Simone was trying to get my attention. "Where you been?"

Good question. Where had I been? Out in Private Eye World hatching dumb plots to frame Joe Downing. But all I said, was:

"I wish he had never come here."

"Maybe. But, before you do whatever you're scheming, I have one suggestion for you."

"Hmmm?"

"Go to your sister. Do whatever it is you two do together, that joo-joo thing. Try to see Joe Downing through her blind eyes."

I didn't want to, because if I went to see Mirabai, I knew she would make me see Major Joe as he really was and not like the bad guy in the novel I was writing in my imagination, and then I would have to let go of my resentment.

But I went to see her, and she did, and I did.

CHAPTER FIFTY-TWO

Good Times

How could I have been so wrong? Joe Downing brought grace to Shiva Puri; as if karma had directed his footsteps to us. The land was fertile. The rains came. Women delivered healthy babies.

I even came to like Major Joe, who was a great guy. You have to admire a man who would carry a torch for eighteen years.

The year after Joe returned was the best of my life. I'll tell you one thing about Shiva Puri, we worked hard, and we played harder. During winter we skied and went snow shoeing and ice skating; we played patty-cake games and hambone. When it was warm enough, we went fishing and swimming and exploring and singing and dancing and holidays and goofing with the new babies and pulling practical jokes on each other. Reading! I worked my way through the "adult" books in the library and went back through all the ones I have read a second and third time.

What did I forget? Oh my Lord, the weddings!

Simon Johns, who was sweet on Ann Schultz, finally persuaded her to marry him, something we never thought was going to happen, because she had her eye on Vic, who, I am sure of this, never got over the murder of Maitreya, his one true love. That was a long time for a man to mourn, but Vic never showed any interest in settling down with anybody else.

Donnie Simms married Nithinya Varanasi (*ta dum!*), and those two adopted a refugee baby they named Maitreya. All on the same day! Instant family. Donnie asked Vic to be the girl's godfather. Of course, both men got all choked up, and so did everybody else.

Hmmmm? Did I forget anyone? Oh yes... Dad! It wasn't a wedding, not yet, anyway, but after the Prodigal Joe re-entered our lives, Dad started keeping company with Kathy Keen, a widow who was now managing the apiary with two grown kids. He seemed to have accepted the new way of things, and, anyway, he was often seen helping the lonely (and lovely!) Widow Keen, with the hives, not that he knew anything about bees except they made the honey we depended on for sweetness. So, hurrah for Papa! That's what I say. Getting a bit o'honeycomb for himself.

And since I have mentioned holidays, let me tell you about the Mahashivaratri when Dad started buzzing around his new flower, and as long as I'm talking about that holiday, let me tell you about Diwali and all the other wonderful Shiva Puri festivals.

But, Odessa Piwinski, one of my many, many, many, many editors, is scolding me for shoving such clumsy exposition into a narrative that could very well do without it. Odessa has been transcribing this chapter because I am having one of my worst days. No sympathy from that old tyrant!

"Knock it off," *she snaps, calling me to task.* "What do holidays have to do with advancing the plot?"

I say, "I will, I will knock it off, I mean. Omit needless words, right?"

"Right as rain." *My old friend nods approvingly, smooths my hair, and gets to her feet.* "Just stop trying to be so damned cute, and take out all that extraneous crap."

"Yes, Miss Piwinski," *I promise with my fingers crossed.*

CHAPTER FIFTY-THREE

Holiday Blessings

IS SHE GONE? OKAY, NOW *about those holidays.* In the peaceful year after Major Joe's homecoming, we relaxed into a happy daze of work and rest, plant and harvest, evening satsang and major holidays. We blended the agricultural rhythms of a great farm with the Hindu celebrations-we-sort-of-knew. Sometimes we invented new ceremonies to commemorate momentous events, or just to get two lovebirds caged together in everlasting matrimony.

The Holiday Calendar of Shiva Puri

February New Moon	Mahashivaratri
March Full Moon	Holi Poornima
March 25	Kali Yuga Day
April 30	Offering Day (last day of school!)
May 1	Planting Day

June/July Full Moon	Guru Poornima
August Full Moon	Rakhi Day
October/November New Moon	Diwali
November 1	First day of school
December 15	*My birthday. Ha ha. Just kidding.*
December 25	Christmas

"Might as well be living in the Roman Empire." That's what Odessa said when I asked why there were so many holidays at Shiva Puri. I didn't have my own opinion on the comparison because I never cared much for history, taking after Mother in that regard, but I will tell you, for a fact, we knew how to throw a shindig.

Satsang, our evening program, was every night of the week except Sunday, and was attended by everyone not doing seva. We meditated and chanted, and every Wednesday someone would give a reading from scripture, a discussion, or an experience talk, and on Saturday night Mother would lead us in nritya, the sacred dance. On Sunday morning Mirabai led us in the "Shiva Stotram." Afterward we ambled over to amrit for lunch, or if the weather was nice, we would take a picnic down to Cook's Creek. Sunday afternoons were free time. The adults used the afternoon to ready themselves for the week to come, while we kids ran wild and had a most excellent time fooling around.

Each month, we celebrated *Poornima*, the full moon, with fasting during the day, a special program of some kind in the evening, and a big *bandhara* feast, or as big as Cookie could provide depending on the season and the state of her pantry.

We celebrated every birthday, and because there were more than two hundred of us, that was a lot of celebrating. Nobody ever got overlooked. Most satsangs there was at least one birthday party. Celebrants would sit up front as we expressed gratitude they were born, and a friend would stand up to wish them a long and happy life. The honorees would wear garlands on their heads, and, of course, we'd sing the birthday song:

Om Birthday Jaya Birthday we wish you Ananda Birthday!

Anniversaries were private affairs; divorces were simple. If two people didn't want to be married anymore, they both stood up at satsang and said so. You saw how Mother let go of Dad. Sad, but quick.

Marking the beginning of the year, Mahashivaratri was the first big festival on the Hindu calendar. The old-timers told me New Year used to start on January first, but who picked that day, and why? At Shiva Puri, the new year began at midnight on a moonless night in February to honor Lord Shiva and ask for his blessings. All night and all day we chanted "Om Namah Shivaya," sometimes fast and sometimes slow. Different groups would go into mandir every three hours to bathe the Shiva lingam with water, milk, and honey, to take up the chant from the people who had been keeping it going non-stop. Sometimes those early chanters just stayed where they were all day long. If you chanted with pure devotion, Shiva would wash you clean from sin and destroy your old karmas.

He is the *Destroyer*, isn't he?

The morning after Shiva Ratri, Odessa Piwinski held her annual book faire. The kids from Middles showed off their hand-made books, each one five pages long, front and back, no pictures to take up space. Odessa expected ten pages of solid writing. The kids made a little speech, after which the books were displayed for everyone to make a fuss over. Every book was exchanged for some little treat and then "donated" to the library.

When the day warmed up, we went outside for the races. Each class, Littles, Middles, and Bigs, had their own races through the fields and woods. The day concluded with the annual "Punch and Judy," a fifteen-miler. That race was always won by, you guessed it, Punch and Judy (Max and Mother). Nobody, ever, *ever* beat them.

Until... the big race just before I turned eighteen. Mother and I were barely speaking. Our relationship had always been up and down, but after she dumped Dad for Joe Downing, we were at rocky bottom. I decided I was going to show her up, once and for all.

CHAPTER FIFTY-FOUR

The Punch and Judy

KAVITHA AND I WERE USED to winning every race in our age group. Kavitha was faster in shorter distances, but I could run forever, and I usually beat her in longer races. By the time I moved up to the Bigs, Kavitha was winning all the sprints, and I was champion of the distance events. Even Skyler, a great runner himself, practically killed himself trying to keep up with us, but he always took second place right behind Kavitha in the sprints, and in the long runs, third place behind us wonder girls.

Thinking back on those races, I wonder if Vitha was slowing down so Skyler wouldn't lose face. Why didn't I think of that?

Yes, Kavitha Bose and Janabai Shepherd won every race... except the fifteen-mile Punch and Judy. This year was going to be different.

The race did not start well for us. You know how stupid racers get all wound up and go out too fast, then run out of legs and get chased down? That was Vitha and me, dashing out front as soon as Vic fired the starting gun. After a couple of miles, I looked over my shoulder. Mother and Max were about 200 yards behind, running stride by stride, comfortably chatting. I was drafting Vitha, just off her left shoulder, one of our secret strategies. She would lead and set the pace, and then it would be my turn. I eased up next to her.

"I really, really want to beat her this year."

Vitha cut her eyes at me. "Let it be, Jana. Relax and enjoy the run."

"Ain't gonna happen. She needs to *go down*."

She sighed. "If you say so."

We ran without speaking for a while, saving our breath. Vitha came to a decision. She grinned and wiggled her eyebrows.

"Okay. If you are set on teaching her a lesson, it ain't gonna happen like this."

"How's that?"

"They're waiting for us to burn out, and when we do, they're going to blast by us and leave us in the dust."

I looked over my shoulder. Max waved like "We're still here, don't worry about us."

"What do you want to do?" I asked.

"Turn the tables."

We slowed our pace just a little—we didn't want them to get suspicious—and exaggerated our fatigue and discomfort. By the fifth mile they had pulled up just behind.

"Probably not a good idea to go out so fast," Mother smirked.

"Save ourselves... for the... long... haul," I managed to gasp. *What a little actress!*

"Roger," Max said.

"Ready to let the dogs loose?" Mother asked Max.

Max howled like a wolf.

"*Adios, hermanitas,*" Mother said. "See you back at the village."

They sprinted by. Vitha and I settled into a pace that kept us about a quarter mile behind them. We hit the six-mile mark. Seven miles, halfway, eight miles, nine, ten, eleven, twelve.

"Make our move?" I asked.

"No. Just close the gap."

Thirteen miles. Two to go. We were ten yards behind them.

"Let's push and see what they've got left."

"How are you doing?" Vitha asked.

"I could run forever, you?"

"To the end of time," she answered.

We closed on them. Mother looked back. She said something to Max, and they picked up their speed. Were they playing us like we were playing them? At the fourteen-mile mark, we caught up and settled in right on their heels, drafting, and trying not to show how close we were to collapse. Punch and Judy picked up their pace, but it wasn't much, and we matched them. Two more times they tried to pull away. Two more times we caught up. They pulled, we pushed.

The four of us burst out of the tree line in a tight group. Now, out in the open pasture, we saw the finish line a half mile away. The crowd could see us as well and began cheering.

"Now or never," Kavitha said.

"Now or never," Max repeated.

"*Adios, viejitas!*" I yelled as I sprinted past, taking the lead for the first time, Kavitha right behind.

Mother and Max were pumping hard, but losing ground.

Quarter mile to go. Hundred yards. I slowed down a tiny bit so Vitha could come up right next to me.

"Go for it, Jana," she huffed. "You earned it."

"Oh no, my best friend," I huffed back, "we're winning this *together*."

And that's what we did, stride for stride, side by side, Vitha and I crossed the finish line, Mother and Max the same way, a few seconds later.

Well, it was a big whoop-de-doo, that's for sure. We were the new champs, and no one more pleased than Mother and Max. A little while later, the four of us cozied up to a fireplace in amrit with cups of hot tea, milk and honey, too!

"That was a smart race," Mother complimented us.

"Thanks, Mom," I said, the first words I had spoken to her in almost a year. Funny thing about running; sometimes in the sheer exhilaration, you lose what is false and unworthy and regain what is true and worthwhile. Suffused with happiness, and quite forgetting I hated her, I smiled at my mother. She smiled back and opened her arms for a warm and loving hug. Oh my goodness!

Max interrupted our sweet duet with her typical sour note. "Only gonna pull that stunt one time, you little shits. I underestimated you. Won't happen again."

"Brave talk from an old lady," I said, still holding on to my mother.

Max laughed. "Ten-four," and surprised us with a giggle like she was our age instead of... what was she? Forty?

The four of us sat there in front of the fire, drinking our tea, tired and contented.

Mother put her hand on top of mine, reached out to take Vitha's hand, and gave us a little squeeze.

"I'm proud of you, both of you. Never forget this day."

We assured her we would never forget it, *and we have kept that promise.*

Mother released our hands and stood up. "I've got to get ready for nritya, and maybe a little nap? I'm pooped."

She was speaking for all of us. Vitha and I curled up together on the big pillows and fell asleep right where we were. Late that afternoon, just before dark, I woke up. Vitha was gone. I had just enough time to race to the bath house. Vitha was already there sluiced clean, putting up her hair, fresh as new snow.

"Where have you been?"

She smiled, a kind of smug, heavy-lidded smile I didn't much care for. "Nowhere special." She shrugged.

Hmmm. I tried to ignore her, which is hard to do when she's standing there naked with that long, cocoa body and full bosom looking like some Egyptian queen. I did what I could to make myself presentable. Vitha may be a whole lot bigger, but I'm a whole lot perkier.

So, *pbblffft*, Kavitha Bose, *pbblffft*.

We gathered in the mandir, wearing our best sari, not the men, of course, who do the best they can, being men. Mother arrived gussied up like Lord Shiva, her hair tangled and wild, her neck painted blue to symbolize the poison Shiva swallowed to save the world. She embodied Nilakantha, the Blue Throated One. As the chant grew faster and faster, Mother danced the Tandava Nritya, Shiva's wild dance of creation, while drums pounded and everybody jumped to their feet and joined the divine frenzy, spinning and swirling and stomping, going faster, chanting louder, until we just exploded.

CHAPTER FIFTY-FIVE

Holi Holi Holi

HOLI. HOLI. HOLI. EVERYBODY LOVES *Holi Poornima*, the Festival of Colors. Winter is almost over, and sunny days are here again. Holi is sacred to Lord Krishna, so we chant "Hare Rama Hare Krishna" over and over, and why not? Is there any chant more fun than "Hare Rama Hare Krishna," especially when it gets lightning fast and thunder loud? After the chant, we just go nuts and have a good time. We prank each other, and joke and flirt. You can get away with anything. Hey, it's Holi! We wear our brightest clothes and squirt water and throw colored powders at each other. Later we build a big bonfire and sit around singing. And plenty of messing around, if you know what I mean. One Holi, I saw Max sneaking in from the woods, and a few minutes later I saw Sandra Grimsman sneak back down the same path.

I asked Max, "What were you two doing out there?"

She blushed. I am not making this up. Max BLUSHED!

That gave me a great idea. Where's Skyler? I looked all over, but I couldn't find him. Or Kavitha. All I could think was they better not be doing what I think they're doing. They wouldn't.

Would they?

Guru Poornima comes with the full moon in late June or early July. That's when we thank our teachers for making life worthwhile, for leading us from darkness into the light, for opening the doors within our soul and washing away the useless baggage of our past lives. When people first joined Shiva Puri, back before Kali Yuga, they brought their own *gurus*, hidden away deep in their hearts. Now we bring all of them out into the sunshine. Most photographs of the gurus were lost in the Kali Yuga, but Myron Jefferson painted marvelous new representations of Maharishi Veda, Vyasa, Buddha, Jesus, Krishna, Rama, Hanuman, Meher "Don't Worry Be Happy" Baba, Dalai Lama, Neem Karoli Baba, Sai Baba, Muktananda Paramahansa, Nityananda, Yogananda

Paramahansa, and Pope Francis. On Guru Poornima we sing songs special to these gurus, and some songs we just make up for the occasion.

I love the spirited hymn, "Give Me That Old Time Religion."

> *Give me that old time religion*
> *Give me that old time religion*
> *Give me that old time religion*
> *It's good enough for me*
> *It was good enough for Rama*
> *It was good enough for Krishna*
> *It was good enough for Jesus*
> *And it's good enough for me*

You can put any guru you want in there. Go on, don't be shy.

Diwali is the Festival of Lights. It begins on the darkest night in late October and lasts three glorious days. We clean our houses, workshops, stables, sheds, barns, the amrit and mandir, our meeting rooms, even the guard shacks, top to bottom. Every year at this time, Lord Rama triumphs over wickedness, restoring righteous over wickedness, and then heads for home. But he can't find it. Circling around up in the foggy sky in his swan chariot, Rama doesn't know where to land, so he needs our lights to come down safely. We burn candles and oil lamps so the Lord can bring goodness back to the world. That's the story we tell the little kids, and now I'm telling you.

We are happy on Diwali because the harvest is in and safely stored away for winter, so on the final night of the holiday, we pray to Goddess Laksmi, Divine Prosperity, to thank her for her bounty, and we open all of the windows and doors so she knows she is welcome at Shiva Puri.

Maha Laksmi namostutay!

Christmas. Yes, we celebrate Christmas. Many of our old-timers grew up as Christians, and the holiday is still special to them. Christmas is the one day of the year when everyone in the village gets a present. Back on the final night of Diwali, adults put their names in a basket. If you draw your own name, you have to put it back and draw another, a ritual we call *Secret Siddha*. After the adult names are drawn, each child's name is put in the basket, and adults draw out the kids' names, but if a parent gets their own kid's name, they have to put it back and draw again. Between Diwali and Christmas, we Secret Siddhas make gifts for our chosen one. Most of the adults get to make *one* gift, but the lucky ones get to make *two*, one for another adult and one for a child, and you can bet no effort is spared to make sure every gift is fabulous. Children look forward to the day when they graduate to adulthood, so they too will have the joy of making and giving Christmas gifts. Isn't that the best part of being grown up? To give presents to little kids?

One year G-Mek traded Vic Tretheway for my name and made me a kaleidoscope out of plastic tubes and pieces of glass. I loved it! And I still have his gift in my treasure box. Often I wonder what might have happened between me and G-Mek if I hadn't been so goo-goo over Skyler Jones.

On Christmas Eve we read from the Christian Bible about how Jesus came to earth as the avatar of his age and taught us about faith, hope, charity, and love. There are some parts of the story I don't care for, especially, you know, the horrible crucifixion. Who would do stuff like that? Kali, probably, but Jesus was tortured by his own people! I can't get my mind around it. Hey! Did you know Jesus had a run-in with the demon? True. Says so right in the Bible. One time, out in the desert, Jesus was on his vision quest, and who did he run into? Kali, the old lizard, just waiting to do mischief. I don't know if Jesus was a real avatar or not, but I promise you... Kali was a real demon.

That's all I have to say about the holidays at Shiva Puri. *Odessa is going to pitch a fit, so if you didn't mind too much reading about our festivals, please help me out, and mention it to her.* Yes, I had a lot of fun at festivals that year... except... I so wanted to celebrate each and every one of them with Skyler Jones. I hoped, just once, he would take my hand and lead me out to some pretty spot under the stars, and... well, you know, I was eighteen years old, almost nineteen, and still a virgin.

I decided to do something about that.

CHAPTER FIFTY-SIX

How It Finally Happened

IT FINALLY HAPPENED BECAUSE OF salt. The herds were not doing as they ought, in spite of having plenty of grazing and water. We were growing ample feed, but the critters were listless and sickly. Bill Lemko said the critters needed more salt than we could get around Indian Valley. He speculated the closest natural salt deposits were in the desert over to the east in a place called Nevada.

The council decided to send an expedition to mine the Nevada salt and to explore eastward, and, if lucky, do a little recruiting. Max thought it was dangerous; she didn't like "dividing her forces," but Mother convinced her it was worth the risk, and she was sure Max could figure a way to keep the expedition safe. Max scowled and groused, but, all said and done, she liked being in "command of a mission."

Bill Lemko planned to use the journey to test his oxen teams and the drovers. As it turned out, we were fortunate to have that testing, later, when we sorely needed it.

The caravan rolled out in March, two days after Holi Poornima, when we hoped the old roads would be passable after winter snows, but well before we were needed for planting day. Bill estimated six weeks at ten miles a day for fifteen days to get to find the salt, five days to mine and load it, and fifteen days to return, with an extra week just for "serendipity," by which he meant recruiting, or at least making new friends and trading partners.

Our folk, those staying behind, waved us off with colorful handkerchiefs.

Mother yelled, "Bring back a dentist!"

She can be funny when she wants to be.

We took our twelve best wagons, each sturdy enough to bring home a ton of salt; fifteen pairs of our best-trained oxen; thirty drovers, some seasoned, some learning; and seven of Max's "marines" with Joe Downing as "skipper" and Skyler as "top." Bill Lemko, naturally, was wagon master, still hale at seventy-one, with Vic Tretheway, chief mechanic, as second-in-charge, assisted by George (G-Mek) Sunkari, who kept one eye on the wagons, and the other on my butt. Mirabai was riding on one of the wagons, coming along to give darshan to possible recruits, and, finally, there was me to take care of Mirabai.

Me! Officially, I was Dad's representative, in charge of keeping the travel journal. Unofficially, I was there to make sex with Skyler Jones. I would find a way to pull him down in the grass and give him my woman stuff and have his baby and marry him.

Take that, Kavitha. We were still friends, sort of, at that point, but more like finding fault with each other and making sure the other knew about it. Imagine my vexation when I learned she had connived her way on the adventure by claiming, as herbologist, she was needed to locate sources of medicine we didn't have at Indian Valley. How did Dad agree to this hogwash? Doesn't he know *anything* about women? Herbs? Kavitha, the hussy, was coming along to make sure nothing happened between me and Skyler.

In the end, I guess you could call the expedition a great success in spite of Kavitha never letting Skyler out of her sight, and I guess I should go ahead and get the sulky part over. By the time we got home, safe and sound (sorry to spoil the suspense), I knew Kavitha and Skyler were fixed for life like the pair of skunks they were. I should wish them the best, and Durga knows I have tried, but it is just *too much.*

Deep breath, Janabai.

As I was saying, the expedition was everything we hoped. People we met along the way, good and hardy families, were happy to see us. Everybody received darshan from Mirabai, and there was nobody who failed her "test." It seemed like the folk who managed to hold on this long had learned the important lessons. Take care of each other and get your crops in the earth as soon as the ground thaws. Some people were content to remain where they were, and some started packing up to join us when we swung back through on our return. Fourteen new recruits for Shiva Puri! Mother would be ecstatic. So much new DNA for our village, and yes, I know what DNA is! You don't graduate from the Bigs without picking up a few things.

Along the way, we heard about bad guys up north in Susanville, and down south in Reno, but they had never bothered us, and with Major Joe defending us, they better not try. Still, after those warnings, Grimsman and her marines got real serious about guarding the wagons, morning and night.

One family we found living in the high desert along the old Nevada state line told us where to find the salt, which we did, and, with everybody working, we cut it right out of the ground and loaded it on the wagons in two days. Many hands, happy work. Now that Bill knew the roads were passable, he figured each wagon could carry a ton *and a half,* so we headed back with *eighteen* tons of salt. You'd call it a success, wouldn't you? Even if you didn't make sex with Skyler Jones?

Not that I came home exactly the same, regarding "it," sex, as you have probably figured out. G-Mek was randy as a billy buck, though he was too shy to do much more than mope around giving me looks, so if I wanted something to happen, and I did, mostly to show Kavitha I was as much woman as she was, I had to take matters into my own hands. We were no more than five days from home. Now or never. I managed to lure G-Mek a little ways from camp.

"Help me look for firewood," I said, ever so sweetly, rubbing his arm, making a little "hmmm" noise as I felt his hard bicep.

We walked by the creek. I thought, "This is our opportunity, our best chance, and we're not doing anything but making small talk."

"Pretty big to be a creek."

"Pretty small to be a river."

G-Mek put his arm around me, and I thought, "Okay, here we go." He stepped right up and took my face in his hands, and got close so we were breathing the same air, and he whispered to me, "Every time I touch you, I get the shakes. I can't seem to breathe."

His speech sounded like he had rehearsed it for the Kali play, but in the heat of the moment it was just right. All I had to do was lean forward an inch until our lips were barely touching. I breathed into his mouth, and that's all it took. The next second and we were kissing like it was the last kiss we would ever have, and let me remind you this was not the first time we had made out, me and G-Mek, so we pretty much knew what we were doing. Frenching and all that lip music.

We flopped down on a rock next to the creek, our feet in the water. I pulled my dress up to my knees, just to keep it from getting wet. I could see him stealing looks at my legs, so I pulled the hem up above my knees, but he still didn't do anything, so I pulled it a bit higher until he could see my everything, and still he didn't do anything, so I whispered.

"Stop teasing me, George."

Since I was the one doing the teasing, my whisper pretty much woke him up, so he figured he needed to take charge, being two years older than me, and the man, and he should stop teasing me and get on with it, so, finally he did, and when he got around to it, he was pretty good, as it turned out. Hey, even if it was the first time for both of us, we're farmers. We know where the thing is supposed to go.

He pulled me to my feet and lifted my dress over my head. There we were, together in our altogether. He put his arms around me and pulled me close, and I felt him hard against my belly. As I was on the slender side, I didn't have much topping like Kavitha, but G-Mek seemed to like what he found, and let me know with kisses all over me.

His moans made me feel so beautiful.

"Let me spread these clothes out," I said, prying my mouth loose. I bent down and made a little nest with our clothes, making sure he got a good look from behind. Turning around to face him, I lay down on my back. He stood there looking at me for a few seconds, his thing standing straight up. I remember thinking this wasn't a game anymore. Yes, I was a little scared, but not much, and more kind of, what can I say? Needy? He stood there staring at me, wanting me, no doubt at all, and there's nothing more exciting than seeing the naked proof of how much someone wants you. I could feel my heart slamming in my chest, my breath was coming in quick bursts. What is he waiting for? I spread my legs a bit just to make sure he knew I was ready, and then he was between my thighs, pushing hard.

"Ow!"

"Do you want me to stop?" he asked.

"Just be careful with me."

"Always."

He kept pushing, but wasn't getting anywhere.

"You're too high."

He tried lower, but he was still way off target.

"Let me help." I reached down and grabbed him. He let out a whimper.

"Am I hurting you?" I panted.

"No, no, put me in. Quick."

I got the tip of his thing between the lips of my thing. Got him aimed in the right direction, I was about to tell him to push, push NOW, but he figured that out for himself. George Sunkari may be shy, but he is strong. One hard thrust and he was inside me.

Miss Vee warned me it might be dry and painful the first time, but no worries on the first concern, I was slippery as a river eel; and as to the second part, I was too excited to notice the pain — anyway, not right then, though later, oh mama! Miss Vee also told me the boy wouldn't last long, not if it was his first time, and that part, I will tell you, she got right, because he slid inside, and, boom, I could feel it spurt out of him, one pulse after another.

"I love you," he groaned.

I tried to answer, but I just burst into tears because he was so tender and beautiful, because this was my first time, and because he wasn't Skyler.

I wrapped my legs around G-Mek and held him tight, him gasping, me sobbing.

It was done. At last. Sex.

I liked it fine, thank you, in case you were wondering. I liked having him close to me, inside me, loving me. Such sweet relief I had finally *done it*. I wanted to do it again, right then and there, to go for the big prize, as I had been instructed by Nithinya, but he seemed to think we were done now he had proven himself, to himself, and to all the other men who had ever lived. Wait. Not fair. There was more to G-Mek. We had liked each other all our lives, and he cared for me and loved me. I had a special place in his heart, and he in mine, now and always.

Raising up enough to kiss me, he asked, "Are you happy?"

Happy? I cried like a river. No, cliché. I cried like a waterfall. Lame. Goofball. I cried like a goofball.

"Why are you crying like that?"

"How silly we must look with your butt in the air, and I can't imagine the faces I've been making."

I made one to demonstrate my point.

Resisting the urge to pound his chest, he pulled out of me, oh, whoa, that felt strange (!), and reared back on his knees. Yikes! His penis was covered in blood. What had I done? Did I hurt him? He was smiling at me, so I guess he wasn't in pain. I was. In pain, I mean. Yow. Stars and moons, was I ever stinging! I looked at myself. What a mess, my dress, the one I had been lying on, my only traveling dress, a glistening blot of dark blood as big as my hand, right in the middle. Oh no!

I grabbed the dress and waded into the creek. I scrubbed and scrubbed. G-Mek watched, until, at last, I got the blood washed out.

"Did we get it anywhere else?" I asked.

"Spots on my shirt," he said.

"Give it to me," I said. "No, if I'm going to freeze my butt in this creek, you are too. Get in here. Bring all our stuff."

Together we scrubbed our clothes until they were clean enough.

"Okay," I said wringing out the last item and laying it to dry on the rocks, "I guess we're safe."

He didn't answer. I looked over my shoulder at him. He was standing knee deep in the water, staring at me, a certain look on his face, his thing rigid again.

This time he wasn't shy at all. Nor did we fool around making a nest. I took him, right there on the ground, half in and half out of the creek. My insides were aching. Who cared? I just wanted him buried inside me. It hurt so much, but I wanted him deeper. Is this what *horny* means? He wasn't going deep enough. Then he was *there*, all the way *there*, and he lasted longer, and longer, and longer, and I, and I, and I and… and… and… *Oh. My. God.*

CHAPTER FIFTY-SEVEN

Who? Me?

HEADING BACK TO CAMP, WE split up, G-Mek circling around to come in from the east side, me to the west. The second I walked into the clearing, conversation stopped. Nobody looked at me. In fact, it was obvious everybody was looking at anything, *anything*, except me. De-virginized, de-spoiled Janabai. It didn't help I was sore and stingy and couldn't quite manage my normal walk.

"Stepped on a pricker," I said. "Accounts for why I'm walking funny."

Joe Downing piped up, "A pricker? Did you say you stepped on a *pricker*?"

Now everybody was looking at me. I caught Vitha's stare and gave her the stink eye. She gave me a big, beautiful smile in return, and there was nothing but happiness in her expression, relieved that I had taken my claws out of Skyler and moved on. We'll see about that.

G-Mek walked in from the other side of the clearing, all innocent-like, and said:

"I'm hungry. When's supper?"

Nobody laughed. They howled like mad wolves, shame on them.

So, three nights later, concluding a deeply satisfying sexing with G-Mek, and not stinging at all, except in a good way, I floated back into camp, so happy with the world, and myself in the world, cool beans, that's me, all grown up.

And I want you all to know about it, especially you, Skyler Jones. Are you paying attention?

CHAPTER FIFTY-EIGHT

Oops

 HAT IF I'M PREGNANT?

CHAPTER FIFTY-NINE

Herbs and Blessings

IDN'T TAKE ME LONG TO realize I liked sex, liked it a *lot*, by which I mean I liked it surpassing well, thank you, and I liked it *as often as possible*. Both. And I liked it with G-Mek. After he got over his jitters, he felt the same about the satisfaction he received from me, or so he swore, and G-Mek wouldn't lie about something like that.

Did I imagine I was with Skyler when I was sexing G-Mek? The answer is, yes, of course, sure, but not all the time, and not every time. I was fond of George Sunkari, and I know he adored me; he said so often enough, before, during, and after, each and every time. At those moments I loved him, too, or something close to love, and close to love was as good as it was going to get for this shepherd girl.

In the four months since our creekside de-virginizing, I knew George was mine, if I wanted, and I was his. Probably. Shiva Puri doesn't have much in its herd when it comes to marriageable studs, and I wasn't going to do better. I decided whenever G-Mek worked up the nerve to propose, I was going to say yes.

Meanwhile, we were going at it like rabbits. I even had the ears.

That was my state of mind when Kavitha invited me to go herb gathering up in Foreman's Ravine. On a Sunday afternoon! Those afternoons are special to us, the only free time we have all week, our only time to do exactly what we want. We make serious plans for Sunday; we conduct important private "business," we have our family teas, weddings are planned, and divorces decreed, people meet to say the things that need to be said, so I was surprised to get Kavitha's invitation, as we were barely speaking, and a little put out she would wait until Sunday morning; but there was something so melancholy in her invitation, that instead of telling her to ask me again another time *with more notice*, I accepted.

Okay (sigh), herbs.

Ever since we were little girls, Kavitha Bose, former best friend and current rival, had dragged me along on her pursuit for the elusive pink dandelion. Day after boring day, we tramped through wet gullies and poked under the leaves of the forest floor searching for floral oddities. Vitha couldn't get enough of the "wild thyme and nodding oxlips," a saying she got from *Midsummer Night's Dream*, surely the only Shakespeare she memorized, and only because the speech was about her precious herbs. Herbalism seva was perfect for Vitha, because everyone knew she was going to

212

be excellent at it when she finished training. Already she knew as much about medicinal plants and essential oils as anybody on the medic team. Unfortunately, she liked to show off her skills to anyone who would listen, and unfortunately that was me, on this pretty Sunday afternoon.

We met in front of the number one barn at the mouth of Foreman's Ravine.

"Lead on, mistress of mysterious mistletoe," I said.

"Which way?" she asked.

"Oh no," I said, "this is your expedition," and I couldn't help adding, "Are we hunting the crafty chrysanthemum? Or shall we pursue the precious peppermint? Whatever you choose, I'm sure it will be *ever-so-much-fun*."

What a mean thing to say, the *ever-so-much-fun* part, and I was sorry for it as soon as I saw her wince. But she ignored my snide remark, with the barest hesitation, and rattled along.

"Oh, shepherd's purse today," she said. "Kerilynn needs a fresh bunch. Do you know the important uses for shepherd's purse?"

I gave her my best blank stare. She was not paying the slightest attention and went on without me.

"Shepherd's purse can benefit the pregnant patient in different ways. First by strengthening the uterus during pregnancy, then by reducing bleeding after delivery. It can even be used to treat hemorrhoids."

She looked at me to make sure I was attending her lecture.

"Hemorrhoids!" I exclaimed, my excitement overflowing.

"You can be a real pill," she said.

"Pill!" I responded.

She went on as if I wasn't there, reciting for her own benefit more than mine, but isn't that what friends are for, to put up with you when you light your hair on fire and then pull you out of the flames before you burn to a crisp?

"Those five branches are Chinese Herbalism, Ayurveda, Western Herbalism, Homeopathic Healing, and the Natural Medicines of Native American Peoples."

"PEOPLES!" I shouted with sarcastic enthusiasm. Kavitha bit

her lip and turned away, but not before I saw her eyes fill with tears. Sometimes words fly away, and I just want to snatch them out of the air and shove them back in my big mouth.

We walked along in awkward silence. After a while, I couldn't stand it.

"Okay. Stop. You didn't invite me on this expedition to talk about herbs."

"No."

"What?"

"I miss you," she said.

"I haven't gone anywhere," I said.

"You are my best friend," she said.

I didn't respond. So that's what this is about.

"And I used to be yours," she continued.

"That was before."

"Before what?"

"Before Skyler."

"Yes, I know. But I want you back."

I thought about it. How strange. I'm the one who's been acting like a pig's butt, *still* acting like a pig's butt, and *she's* the one begging me to come back. Is that what I wanted? Back? Yes, oh God, yes, I did.

She went on, "I want things to be good between us like they used to be."

"I'd like it, too," I said, "more than anything, but..."

"But, why but?"

"Too much drama. Too much distance. Too many words we didn't say. Too many words we should have said."

"We can say those words now," she said. "All the stuff we've been holding back. We can haul it out in the light and take a look at it."

"All of it?" I asked.

"Every tiny bit. If we are going to be friends again, if we're ever going to get back to that place, we need to start off by being truthful with each other."

"Completely," I agreed.

"Totally."

"All right. How do we start?"

"First we sit down on the ground the way we used to do with our legs crossed and our knees touching."

"Like we did when we were little."

"Right, and we tell each other every little secret."

We sat down facing each other, and scooted closer until we were kneecap to kneecap.

"You start, Janabai. Tell me what's in your heart."

"Okay, you asked for it." I took a deep breath. Let the floodgates open. I screamed: "How could you do it to me? How could you steal the man I love, the only man I'll ever love? How could you do that to your, what did you call me? Your best friend? All capital letters, question mark?"

"I didn't do anything," she answered. "Please, Janabai, my oldest and best friend, all capital letters, exclamation point, please try to see it for what it was. It just *happened*. I liked Skyler, sure, everybody liked Skyler, but I didn't *do* anything. I never set out to make him love me."

"Why didn't you tell him to go away? Why didn't you say somebody else loved him more than you?"

"Do you think love works like that? We laugh, we cry, we get sick, we fall in love. We're are not in control of these things; they happen, and we do the best we can with whatever love brings."

"Oh yeah? Love? Well, I hoped something would happen to make you break up with Skyler. Sometimes I fantasized you would *die* so I could have him."

Kavitha had no response to this vile confession. So I plowed on:

"How do you think I live, every day watching you two together, looking forward to watching you planning a wedding, knowing you'll have children, making a life, and all the time wishing it was me not you."

"Janabai, do you hate me so much to begrudge my happiness?"

Well, she certainly put a sharp point on it. Hate. Begrudge. She was right, of course, and what good is all our schooling, our spiritual teachings, our chanting and meditation, if we can't see ourselves for who we actually are, and I was seeing myself, oh yes, crystal clear, and I was not liking the picture. Is that selfish bitch in the mirror who I wanted to be? A hater? A keeper of grudges? A petty, pouting priss who didn't get what she wanted and used her anger to hurt her friend, to cast her off, to turn away her love? Looking at myself that way, looking deep, in the bright light of truth, I began to feel immeasurable weight falling away; like I might become so light I would float up into the blue sky and swoop around for the rest of the day just remembering what it was like before... before... I ruined everything. Me. Not Kavitha. Not Skyler. Yours truly.

"What are you thinking about, Janabai? Speak to me. Say something, please."

"I was remembering when we were little girls."

"Yes?"

"We slept in the same bed so many times."

"We drank out of Hanuman's water bowl."

"We pretended to be dogs."

"We played together every day of our life."

"We prayed together," she said.

"We prayed for each other's happiness."

"You always made me feel special."

I didn't answer, and she opened her eyes. I was staring at her with my tongue out. Her eyes went wide.

"Pbblffft," I bloobered wetly.

Kavitha pretended to wipe spit off her face.

"You always made me laugh," she said.

"When strange things happened, you would find me with your eyes to make sure we were going to be okay."

"When you got hurt, I would cry for you."

"You fought Alma Mendez for me."

"You lied for me."

"When I needed you, you came running."

"When I needed to be alone, you never got mad."

"We cut each other's hair on the first day of school."

"We got in so much trouble together."

216

"When I got my period, you showed me what to do, long before MOTHER got around to it."

"We were the best friends anybody ever had."

"Will you come back to me?"

"Will you forgive me?"

"You're not mad at me?"

"No, I'm not mad at you. And I'm not mad at Skyler for falling in love with you."

"What are you so mad at?"

"I am mad at Skyler taking you away from me."

"Oh, darling, he never took me anywhere. I'm right here and always will be. I'm your best friend forever!!! All capital letters, triple exclamation points. Unless you die first. Then I'll find another best friend forever."

"Pbblffft," I bloobered wetly. Again.

You know what's coming next. We grabbed each other as tight as we could and held on for dear life. Eventually, as we started to pull apart, I cupped the back of her head and brought her close where I could whisper in her ear:

"I will find someone else, in time, or maybe I won't, and I have to get my head around that somehow, and stop blaming you for being what Skyler wants, and stop blaming him for choosing you instead of me. I promise."

"You have G-Mek," she said. "Everybody knows he loves you."

"Yes, I have G-Mek, I suppose, if I want him."

"Well, do you? Want him?"

"Not an easy question, but, yes, I think so. Most of the time."

"Are you going to marry him?"

"Probably, but we're not talking about me and G-Mek, are we?" Kavitha didn't answer.

"Look, honey," I said, "you two love each other, you want each other, so why don't you just go marry Skyler and get it over with?"

"I can't."

"You can't?" I almost screamed at her. "You can't marry Skyler Jones, the man you love, the man who chose you over me? Why in the name of the gods not?"

"Because we need your blessing."

Well, that shut me up, and it would do the same to you. I stood there with my mouth open like a bullfrog. Finally, I managed to croak:

"My blessing? Why do you need my blessing?"

"Without it, I will always be looking over my shoulder for you."

Hmmf. Arrow to the bullseye.

"What does Skyler say?"

"He says without your blessing our marriage will be cursed."

"Cursed. That's what he said, cursed?"

"Everybody knows everything about us. 'Kavitha stole Skyler away from Janabai,' that's what they'll say."

"No they won't. Not all of them. Some of them maybe, at first. Oh, who cares?"

"We care. And G-Mek will care."

I chewed on that. If Kavitha and Skyler hitched up, and I went around mopey, G-Mek would figure out pretty quick that I hadn't gotten over Skyler at all and that I had been using him, G-Mek, as a substitute, and teasing him, which, as you know, is the one thing I just cannot stand when somebody does it to me. The last thing in the world I wanted to do was hurt G-Mek. Okay, I got that straight. No mopey girl.

But it left me with the real problem, the *dharma* problem. Did I give my blessing "with my face," as we say at Shiva Puri, but cling to Skyler "in my heart?" Or, could I *honestly* let go of him, for good, for keeps, no ifs, ands, or buts? Let. Skyler. Go.

I inhaled through my nose, deep, deep, deep, and came to rest in that sacred place between breaths. And held there. In the quiet throb of my true self I saw Skyler Jones materialize out of the darkness, smiling at me with great love. *Now.* This was the moment to show my quality, to prove that I had the stuff, right *now*, not later, not some other time, right *now*, in this instant, Janabai, give up the attachment to the "idea of Skyler and Janabai." Let it go... just... let...

I exhaled, and on the outbound breath, my delusions drifted up, and away, and were gone.

CHAPTER SIXTY

Always a Bridesmaid

TWO MONTHS LATER, ON THE third night of Diwali, the Festival of Light, Kavitha Bose and Skyler Jones entwined their karma as wife and husband. Holding G-Mek's hand, I watched the ceremony through a bridesmaid's veil of tears, a few stained with longing, but not many. Mostly I cried with joy, along with every other soul in the mandir, even Max, who tried to cover it up, a funny moment we enjoyed needling her about afterward. As the blessed couple circled the sacred fire, we sang the "Hawaiian Wedding Song," Mistah Tee in the lead with his high island falsetto, Mirabai holding down the lower harmony, and me in the mezzo middle.

I handled the affair pretty well, the perfect likeness of a happy bridesmaid, and most of the time I managed to abide in the witness state, watching it happen without attachment, and watching myself watching it happen. "Oh, look, there's poor Janabai feeling sorry for herself. Isn't she *interesting*?" I observed myself as an actor in a play, a dancer whirling under the heavens. I watched myself letting it go — pain, ego, all of it — letting it flow away on the outbound breath. I was happy for Vitha and Skyler, and, Praise Shiva, clear in my own head. Chilly up here in Janabai's brain box, but clear.

Well, it was a beautiful wedding, and the beginning of wedding season. And babies. Oh my Lord! Every third woman in the village got pregnant at the same time, or so it seemed. Mother said it was proof that our people embraced the future, that we were going to make it, not just survive, but thrive, and grow, and that it was joyous to bring children into the new world.

In the months after the wedding, grace poured into my life like nectar. My friends admired me, my family loved me, I had my *own room* at Shepherd House. I delighted in the love between Kavitha and Skyler, free of the jealous weight, free from the disappointment and anger and hopelessness. Yes, I was free, free at last, mostly free, free *enough*, from my obsession with Mister Jones to get on with my own life, my love life; and believe this, courting was an important seva for us young people, especially on the evenings when I cozied up with you-know-who in the hayloft.

Sometimes our sexing was so intense it actually felt like the earth was moving.

"Wait a minute, George. Stop. No, be still. Holy shit. The earth *is* moving!"

Chapter Sixty-One

Lassen

Suranjini Devi said the old gods rumbled mightily out on the Ring of Fire, a part of the planet I have never seen, and probably never will except on maps; but these days we get our share of shakers up in our foothills. Suranjini had a theory that the big explosion on Kali Night released stresses along the great coastal faults and woke up new faults in other places — like, for example, *here*. She thinks the cataclysm "destabilized" the plates crunching around under the earth. All I can say is I've known earthquakes my life-long days. What's the big deal? Quakes rumble, we grumble, that's what we say. When they stop, we pick ourselves up and get on with whatever we're doing. "Background noise," Mother calls it.

In the summer of 19 AK the quakes piled one on top of the other, gentle reminders we dwelt on a living earth. These were little shakers, not strong or scary; it just seemed that the shivering never stopped. When they started coming so close and so many, we would jump out of bed and run outside. After we got used to them, we'd stay under the covers and ride them out. We'd roll over and keep on snoring. "Rock-a-bye baby," Max would sing to amuse the kids, "in the tree top."

Hardly a day passed that we didn't feel the earth wiggling, and it can positively get on your nerves when the ground won't stay where it belongs. Earthquakes test your faith in the permanence of... well... anything, right? It's a great teaching. Do not the sages say that all form is temporary?

The Devi scientists were worried. Mount Lassen, less than fifty miles away, had a bad reputation for mischief back in olden times, but since it was out of sight beyond the ridges, nobody paid attention. Most everybody else shrugged it off and went about their business.

Not me.

I didn't shrug it off because I had seen signs something bad was coming. Out in the pastures, the sheep were shitting all the time, loose runny yellow stuff; and the goats, willful under the best of circumstance, were impossible. All of the animals—cattle, pigs, birds, all of them—were acting weird. More than that, I could sense they were afraid. And Mirabai, always so centered and serene, was restless at night, keeping me awake. Disturbing.

So I was not surprised when, in the darkest hour of night, October 2, 19 AK, as G-Mek and I were ourselves about to erupt up in the number four barn, less than fifty miles away, Mount Lassen exploded.

The horrifying roar, like thunder louder than you can imagine, kept going on and on. Later, Dad told me the actual detonation lasted less than two minutes, long enough for everybody to jump out of bed (or hayloft), race outside to look at the western horizon, lit up white and orange, only to get knocked to the ground when the shockwave hit. After we picked ourselves up, the council met out in the alfalfa field, surrounded by the entire population of our village. Mother was certain it was Mount Lassen that erupted. Joe Downing cautioned it might be something else. Like what? A bomb. A big bomb like they had in olden times. The old-timers had something else in mind. Only a few actually believed that

221

the cataclysm of twenty years before was supernatural, but they silently mouthed that most dreaded name: Kali.

Whatever caused the explosion, bomb or demon, was not as important as how far away it was and what immediate danger it posed. Mother needed eyes on it right away. Appointing a team of her three fastest runners, Kavitha, Skyler, and me, she sent us racing toward Mount Hough, the highest point near the village, about ten miles away to the southwest. Ten miles wasn't far to us, but only the first three miles are gentle, and after that, it's one un-broken, relentless grind up to the peak. We "scouts" took off at full speed.

I was the first to make the top, no surprise there, arriving at the old watchtower after two and a half hours of running and uphill slogging. Kavitha was next to arrive. Skyler "Thunder Thighs" Jones brought up the rear. Dawn was breaking behind us on the eastern horizon.

From the watchtower, more than seven thousand feet above sea level, we could see Mount Lassen clearly. The entire northern face of the volcano was gone. A monstrous column of smoke climbed miles into the sky. Hundreds of square miles of forests were on fire, hundreds more devastated by the initial blast, great trees shattered into kindling. Closer to home, Canyon Dam had fallen, and Lake Almanor was rapidly draining into its ancient river beds.

I was paralyzed, unable to move or speak. The horrific sight was too much for Kavitha. Overwhelmed by the sheer magnitude of the event, she screamed, not little yelps that climbed into something louder, but all at once and at full volume, ear bursting shrieks of uncontrolled panic. This was the same girl who had thrown herself without hesitation at screwdriver-armed Alma Mendez. Skyler remembered volcanoes from videos he had seen as a toddler, but Kavitha, innocent of movies, television, or Internet, had never seen anything like it except in books. This wasn't like pictures on paper at all. On this day, in this hour, Gaia Goddess was furious.

We stood on top of the mountain in the presence of the Earth

Mother, the might of her wrath unleashed, her titanic roar hurled at the heavens, power and dimension beyond comprehension. Skyler wrapped his arms around Kavitha, stroked her hair, made cooing sounds. I, nearly succumbing to Kavitha's hysteria, caught myself at the last instant, clamped my teeth tight, stumbled to my friends, and put my arms around them both. The three of us clutched each other until we calmed down.

"Where's the rest of it?" Kavitha cried. "It's not supposed to look like that."

Indeed, Lassen looked like a rotting tooth, much of it crumbled into decay, hot pus spewing into the sky. Even fifty miles away we could see lightning exploding inside the column of coal-dust-black cloud.

"Those lightning bolts must be gigantic," Skyler said.

Even as we watched, the morning sky darkened. Winds began to disperse ash between the volcano and our lookout. The clouds roiling and churning in our direction made all three of us nervous.

"Let's get off this mountain while we still can," I said.

"It's downhill all the way," Skyler said. "Shall we?"

"We shall," I answered, spinning away and sprinting down the road.

Flying down Mount Hough, first one of us in the lead, then another, the ten-mile run was child's play for three friends who enjoyed hill running all our lives. Mother and Max were waiting in the lower pasture as we raced up to report.

"Took you long enough," Mother said sharply, but she winked at me as she turned to lead us up to the council room, one of those I'm-proud-of-you winks.

We gave our reports of the eruption. I drew a picture on the big slate board. From the back of the hall, someone yelled it looked like a rotten tooth. Kavitha and I exchanged glances as if to ask, "You don't say?" Skyler took the lead in describing the eruption, Kavitha and I jumping in and out of his recitation to add our own embellishments.

"Did you see the ash cloud moving this way?" Mother asked.

"We saw the air getting smokier," Skyler answered, "down over Lake Almanor, or where Almanor used to be."

"What about Chester?" Dad referred to an alliance of small farms on the shore of Lake Almanor.

"The big destruction is north and east. We should be okay if the southerly wind holds, but Chester could be in big trouble."

The southerly wind did not hold, and within the hour, Shiva Puri plunged into darkness.

Dad sent everyone home with instructions to stay indoors as much as possible and to keep wet cloths over our faces. The animals were led into the barns and pens. Cookie prepared grub for a day, and those cold rations were distributed. Nothing to do but hunker down, and wait, and hope, and send heavenward our best prayers for the people of Chester. By the morning of the second day, the air began to clear, but it was still smoky and smelled like burned eggs. A scant two miles away, Ben Woolsey's rancheria was buried under an inch of ash.

Praise Shiva! The crops were secured in the bins and barns, drying sheds and cellars, but were we truly prepared for two years without a new harvest? We bragged about our "Two Winter Rule," our ability to survive twenty months without a harvest. Now we might be put to the test. Would this volcanic ash be good for the farm? It might render these fields fertile for generations. Or it might contain toxins that poison the land. We wouldn't know until the scientists tested the stuff, and until the Earth Mother gave her blessing by blowing the air clean — or her curse by blotting out the sunshine for years to come.

Dad appointed a team to inventory the resources on hand and make recommendations. Besides himself, of course, he included the Devi family from science seva, Galen Raether for farm, Simone Jackson for stores, Patty Bose for the brats (kids), Bill Lemko for the booger shoes (cows), Radha Mehta for kitchen, and one young shepherd girl for the other animals, from goats to bees, pigs to ducks. Who might that shepherd girl be?

What was my recommendation? *Eat* the animals, *don't* eat the animals, eat *some* of the animals. If I chose the *don't-eat* or *eat-some* options, I have to keep them fed. So, add in the animals' caloric needs to those of the people. Just how much fodder, grain, and feed did I have on hand for the critters? Should we eat our way through the herds and flocks, saving the best breeding stock and the dairy animals until the bells of doom tolled, and only then eat my goats as the last resort? How long before that time came? What would happen to us then?

CHAPTER SIXTY-TWO

Secret Mission

OF COURSE, TO COMPOUND THE stupidity, we didn't tell anyone where we were going or what we were up to, especially Mother.

"Better to say we're sorry after it's over than disobey Azriel Dancer before we even get started. Right?"

I waited until Kavitha nodded. Thus, with her consent, I took over, as usual. Together, the two of us were going to sneak away and rescue Chief Gray Horse, who lived on the old Maidu Rancheria a couple of miles downhill. The elderly Indian would do well to winter with us at Shiva Puri. With volcanic ash covering everything, sulfur gas making it hard to breathe, and the sky so dark all the time, I figured he would have trouble holding on until spring. Besides, he was a good storyteller and knew dirty Maidu jokes.

His full name was Ben Gray Horse Woolsey, but he liked it when we called him Gray Horse. We were happy to oblige. Mother had known him for years, since the time when she and Max first visited Indian Valley. Back in those days there were other Indians at the rancheria, but by the year we arrived, only Gray Horse was left to take care of the tribal headquarters all by himself.

"Some died and some moved away, and some," he whispered, "got grabbed by Kohuneje, the gold-haired ghost who eats human people."

"How come Kohuneje didn't eat you?"

Looking side to side to make sure no ghosts were listening, the old Indian leaned close and whispered, "Bear magic. Kohuneje can't stand bears."

"Well, that explains it."

Gray Horse was getting by with one ancient donkey and a few cows. Each year he planted corn and beans, enough to eke out a living, and though he claimed to be at peace within his solitude, he made a habit of coming up to the village every few days for commerce... and romance. He would bring his shotgun shells for us to re-load, and sometimes he would bring a bag of "corn meal" to trade for vegetables. The bag was just a disguise. He was trading bottles of white lightning he made from his corn meal. Gray Horse came to the evening programs to chant bhajans with us. Afterward he would teach Indian dances, always popular at Shiva Puri. Especially with Miss Odessa Piwinski.

Odessa was smitten. Gray Horse was about her age, and both of them were lonely. It got cold at night, up at Indian Valley, and the old-timers appreciated a warm body to snuggle up to during winter. Odessa wanted him to move up to the village permanently, but Gray Horse refused to abandon his duties as caretaker of the rancheria and leader of his people. What people? Who was he trying to fool? If you just happened to have early morning seva, you would see Gray Horse sneaking back down the valley to his rancheria. Everybody knew about him and Odessa. I was hoping the lovebirds would get the nerve to make themselves known so we could give them a fancy wedding.

Even as I laid the plan, and before we ever left the "wire," there was something worrying me, something unspoken, a foreboding. In the back of my mind, or deep in my soul, I heard a familiar whisper in the dark. I tried to shake it off.

Vitha was saying something. I snapped back from my eerie daydream. "What did you say?"

"Maybe he won't come," she repeated.

"The volcano will give him the excuse he's been looking for to save face and move in with us."

Vitha held her ground. "You don't make that stubborn old Indian do anything he doesn't want to do."

"He might be persuaded—" I smiled "—if Mother promised to dance for him."

Vitha laughed. "Well, if that's what it takes, you tell Ben Woolsey that Azriel Dancer will do the hoochie-coochie right after dinner."

"She'll dance," I affirmed, and didn't give voice to my real opinion, *right after she rips us baldheaded for this scatterbrained adventure.*

Kavitha regarded me with a cocked eyebrow as if to say, "Well, what are we waiting for?"

"O Warrior Sister," I intoned, "let us kidnap the last of the Maidu chiefs."

CHAPTER SIXTY-THREE

The Divine Mister Ponytail

KAVITHA WAS FIRST TO NOTICE the smell, odd and unpleasant, like the faint stench of the slaughterhouse where Bill Lemko dispatched our cows into their next incarnation. I noticed something else. Silence. Usually, the rancheria was a riot of noise: chickens, roosters, ducks, and every bird within a hundred miles flying in for the breakfast Ben always laid out. Custer, his beloved donkey, was quick to bray a greeting. But not this morning. Even the air seemed, I don't know, *thick*, like you had to push your way through it. Bad joo-joo. And no Gray Horse. Usually he was loafing on his front porch in an old rocker, but this day, the chair was on its side, the front door kicked in. Custer was heaved over dead in the corral.

"Ben," I called. "Ben Gray Horse Woolsey, where are you?"

No answer. I heard noise inside the house. Someone came to the door, but it wasn't Ben. A man, big, really big, stood framed in the entryway. He looked like one of the Norse gods, or the way I imagined a Viking might look, arms and chest carved with muscles like that David statue in the olden times art books, a smile like everything beautiful in the universe, and those eyes! Eyes I had seen once before, when I was a little girl, in a clearing beyond the wire, the luminous yellow eyes of a cat.

"Ah," he said, "you've come at last, the blushing bride, and you've brought along your little chocolate maid of honor. How charming."

I should have been afraid, I should have run, I should have done *something*, but all I could think about was how his skin would feel and taste. What was going on with me? Had I lost my mind? It's shameful to write about it now, but back when it happened, I just felt heavy... and hot. You know. Down there.

Lifting his chin, he sniffed the air like an animal.

"Wet already? I can smell you."

Vitha, not impressed with my Viking god, snarled, "What have you done with Gray Horse?"

"Gray Horse. So *that's* his name! I never liked that old Indian."

"Where is he?" Vitha persisted.

He turned his attention to me. "Excuse me, honey pot, I'll be right back."

He stepped down from the porch and crossed the yard to a bicycle leaning against Ben's rail fence. His hair was bright as sunshine. How did he get it that color? His lustrous mane, gathered in a sleek ponytail, cascaded down his back like molten gold, all the way down to his muscular rear end. *Oh my.*

The divine Mr. Ponytail reached his bicycle. He unhooked something from the handlebars. A battle ax like I had seen in books, a blade on one side and a spear point on the other side.

He winked. "It's bad luck to bring the maid of honor along on the honeymoon."

Still smiling, his face began to shift, to melt into something no longer human, his skin stretching to reveal a new shape underneath, some kind of fanged animal, orange and black stripes, the face of a tiger.

Aaaaaaaauuuuuuunnnnnn!

He charged. I had never seen anything move so fast. The man-tiger spun the ax, no, not an ax, it was a claw, no, not a claw, an ax, a flickering claw-ax-claw-ax over his head and brought it down onto Vitha's shoulder, the blade slicing diagonally through her body and whipping out the other side below her ribs. He split Kavitha Bose in half. Her eyes popped wide in shock, then her knees buckled and her body tumbled to the ground in two pieces. She didn't have time to scream. But I did. The tiger man spun around and grinned at me. There was nothing divine about it. I looked into the mad yellow eyes of the demon.

Kali.

His enormous claw rushed toward my face, so fast, so impossibly…

CHAPTER SIXTY-FOUR

An Old Friend Returns

MOSTLY, I DON'T REMEMBER WHAT happened. Splinters of memory like the broken glass in my kaleidoscope. Whimpers and moans of anguish. Rough fur and a dry leather tongue licking my back. Growls and grunts. The suffocating weight of him on top of me, my face shoved into the dirt, his teeth on my neck, his sandpapery phallus inside me. On and on, forever, he pounded at me, and with each thrust I felt my very self tear into shards and spin into eternity, the only thought, the only words, *help me help me help me help me*.

Abruptly, his colossal bulk lifted, his great member ripped out of me. Roars of rage, his and those of some other, buffeted the air and battered against my ears and my mind. On hands and knees, I pulled myself away and curled up against a tree. My tormentor fought with another animal... a bear, a mighty she-bear, almost white except where Kali's talons had gashed terrible wounds. They twisted and rolled, clawed and slashed. They rose to their hind legs, clinching like wrestlers or dancers, biting each other like cannibals or lovers. Then, with a convulsive kick against the bear's belly, Kali separated himself far enough to whirl and leap to safety. A momentary crashing through the undergrowth, and the demon vanished from sight and sound. In the startling stillness that followed his abrupt departure, I heard the bear's heavy breathing. She dropped to all fours and lumbered over to stand above me. We stared at each other. Up close I could see the bear was ancient, her fur matted and shaggy, no longer the sleek cinnamon beauty she had been in the happy days of my childhood. Still, I recognized her.

"You came." I reached out to touch her head.

The old she-bruin opened her mangled mouth as if to speak, and then... illusions and phantoms, dreams and demons...

Later, much, much later, something that resembled reality seeped into my shattered mind. I didn't want reality; I needed to sleep, to burrow into blissful oblivion, but I couldn't breathe. A great weight was pushing me into the ground. The bear? I opened my eyes. No, not the bear. I could tell it was human. Someone was sitting on my chest. Did Kali return to hurt me again? I struggled to focus my eyes. Someone, but not him. Above me, the face of a monster, skin disfigured by disease and decay, grotesque yet somehow familiar. The stench of carrion breath washed over me. I choked on the vomit that erupted up my throat, past my lips, down my chin, and onto my neck.

"Pretty, pretty, Princess Prissy," the monster crooned.

I tried to focus my eyes, to concentrate.

"Alma?"

"I wanted to eat you now, starting with your big nosey nose, but my Kali Man wouldn't like that, no, no, not one bit."

"Your Kali Man?" My thoughts, slippery little fish, darted around in my head. "Where is he?"

"Oh, him run off when you make the bear magic."

"He ran away?"

"So funny I pee myself. Kali Man, him don't like bears, 'fraid of 'em. Him come back, him not be happy."

"Please, Alma, let me up, you're crushing me."

Alma leaned in close until her face was inches away from mine.

"I don't think so," she hissed, drawing her lips back, to expose sharp, triangular teeth.

"What... what happened to your mouth?"

"All the better to eat you with, my dear." She cackled, a witch from olden-time storybooks. "But later. We have a feast. Invite your friends. You'll still be alive... for the first part. I leave you one eye to watch. I take the other out with this."

Alma pulled a long, sharpened screwdriver from her belt.

"Remember her? She's tasted your blood and she wants more."

"Please, Alma, let me go," I begged, tears running down my cheeks.

She ignored me and continued as if I had never spoken, "And your ears. I let you keep one ear so you can hear it all. You won't miss a thing. Now, time to go to beddy-bye while I find my Kali Man."

Holding the hilt of her screwdriver in her right hand, Alma brought her fist with a wicked uppercut onto the lower point of my chin. A gush of blood in my mouth. I fell into darkness.

CHAPTER SIXTY-FIVE

Think, Janabai, Think

ENDLESSLY I FELL THROUGH EVER-NARROWING vortices into screaming nightmares, where taloned paws of striped cats snatched at me, ripped bloody streaks through my legs and back; snake-sharp fangs struck at my face spewing poison into my lips and tongue; a tornado of ratcheting green pulsations squeezed me from all sides, pressing the air out of my chest until I couldn't breathe, couldn't move, couldn't see, could do nothing but scream inside my own mind,

> "Letmeoutletmeoutletmeoutletmeoutletmeoutletmeoutletme
> outletmeoutletmeout."

I hit bottom, a tangled cavern floor of rotting animal fur and bone, tooth and antler, and stench, an abattoir of fetid decay across which I crawled on hands and knees until I bumped into a rock wall and, feeling my way along its dank surface, came to a low chamber, a rough bubble of emptiness just big enough for me to squeeze into and curl up, one small mouse cowering in the innermost cranny of my subterranean refuge, shivering there, waiting for the serpent to slither down, forked tongue tasting my scent, hunting me, this way and that way, but not finding me in the secret place, no, no, not finding Janabai mouse as long as she kept perfectly still, perfectly quiet, curled up tight with her eyes squeezed up; yes, yes, she will be safe here.

Eventually, the pain in my face, and between my legs, roused me. I awoke to find myself still lying on my back under pine trees. I was cold. My coat and shoes were missing. My skirt was up around my waist. No underwear. I was still wearing my shirt, but it was ripped open, all the buttons gone. I tried to reach down to close my blouse, but was stopped by a sharp pain in my right shoulder. Unable to move my arms, I twisted my head around to see what was holding me in place. There was a metal band around my right wrist. The word "handcuff" bubbled up in my mind.

I pulled hard against the restraint, but only succeeded in wrenching my other shoulder. The chain was looped around a tree branch, and the other cuff locked onto my left wrist. I wanted to scream for help. There was just enough wit left to me to realize making noise was a stupid idea. *Think, Janabai, think. Take a deep breath, and think.* When I took the breath, I gagged. What was that stench? Me? Where was Alma? I seemed to remember being carried a long, long way from the rancheria. Maybe not. Could have been a nightmare. With the unending overcast from the volcano, I couldn't even be sure what time it was. It might be getting on toward evening. That would be good.

"The dark is your friend," one of Max's lessons when I was a kid.

"Roger that, Max."

If I could just get out of the cuff, I could slide off into the dark and hide.

"You would be proud of me, Max."

Scrunching up, I brought my face close to the handcuff. My eyes didn't want to focus. I squeezed my left eye shut, opened it, and tried again. A little better. There was a hole in the metal cuff where you stick something to make it open. I didn't have anything to stick into it.

"Think, Janabai, think."

I moved my wrist around inside the handcuff. There was one place where it wasn't quite as tight. I tried to squeeze my hand smaller, twisted it back and forth, felt movement, felt it start to give, felt my thumb dislocating like my hand was coming apart. The pain was blinding. *Push through, Janabai.* I pulled even harder. *Do you want him to come back for more?* Leaning back, using my weight against the cuff. All at once, with a tearing of skin at the base of my thumb, my hand came loose.

I lay on my back panting. When I regained my breath, I pushed myself up until I was sitting with my back against the tree where I could look around. The forest was still. Not a rustle of leaves. Not a bird. I was alone. I examined my free right hand. That hand didn't work like it should, fingers swollen into thick sausages, but

I used it as best I could to pull against the handcuff dangling from my left wrist. The two bones at the end of my arms were stopping me. I spit on my wrist and licked the spit around, put the other end of the handcuff between my feet, leaned back, and pulled again with all my strength. The skin over the bones was tearing, but I kept pulling. *I don't know how much more of this I can take.* The blood seeping out over my wrist was making my hand slippery. *Don't stop now.* One last hard jerk and I was free.

Dizzy from the effort, I wanted to lie down and rest.

"No, no, Janabai, noth yet. No reth. Geth up. Geth up."

What was wrong with my mouth? I swallowed and realized I had bit my tongue. It was swollen huge, and I was having trouble making words.

"Shhhhh. Bether noth talk so loud. He could be anywhere."

I used the tree to pull myself to my feet, looked around, had no idea which way to go.

"Shadows are your friend." Max said that too.

I pointed myself toward the darkest shadow among the trees and took a couple of steps. Lancing pain between my legs brought me to a stop. Bending over, I cupped my vulva and squeezed gently. The pain shot all the way up to my stomach and all the way back to my spine. Breathing hard and whimpering, I took a few more steps. I could feel my pubic hair stuck together, adding to the misery.

"Pathience, Janabai, we'll fith ourselth up later. Now, geth out of here. Shhhh."

One more step and I tripped over something, something squishy, and fell. I pushed myself up on my elbow and turned my head so I could see out of my good eye. It didn't make sense at first. I kept staring until it came into focus.

Kavitha.

What was left of her. Her head was missing. Her organs pulled out and flung around, and most of her flesh stripped to the bone. I started to scream, but the scream was buried in another eruption of molten vomit that exploded up my throat and out of my mouth and nose. I heaved everything I had all over what was left of Kavitha Bose.

I will just say this, at that moment, when the horror was at the worst, when prana failed me, when faith betrayed me, when I begged merciful Durga to take me into the land of the dead, when there was nothing else inside of me but terror and pain, my sister came to me. First as the whisper of a melody, a tinkle of finger cymbals, with the throb of the mridangam drums, the chords of the harmonium, the drone of tamboura, she sang. I knew, somehow, she was with me; my Mirabai, my other half, had not abandoned me. The ethereal strains of "Gayatri Mantra," sung only as my sister can sing, flowed into my consciousness. Grace infused me, grace surrounded me. I knew I was not my tortured body. I was not my hysterical thoughts. I was something beyond those things, and I could surrender of all of those and melt into her song. I let it go. All of it. I was That. And That only. Satyam, Satyam. This is the Truth.

Somehow I got back on my feet and staggered out of the clearing and into the woods. I had one plan, one idea in my head. Get into a shadow, find a darker shadow, find an even darker shadow. I kept moving deeper into the forest. How strange. No matter how dark the shadow was, the next shadow was even darker. How could that be?

It went on for hours. I would catch myself jabbering aloud. Stupid baby talk. Why was I talking to myself? I never do that. Tried to be quiet but kept bumping into things, falling down. How was it I didn't fall over a cliff or step into a hole and break my leg? When I first started making my escape, there was still some light in the forest; then it got pitch dark; now it was getting lighter. Could it be morning already? I recognized black-on-black patterns as tree trunks, branches, bushes, logs. I came out into an open space and realized I was on a road, overgrown and torn up, but manmade. Probably an old logging road.

"Thass a good thing, right? It muth lead thomewhere, why noth home? Where ith the light coming from?"

I looked up. Dim through the overcast, but unmistakable, the moon. It must be an omen. Chandra moon god was blessing me.

"Jai Thandra!"

As I stood there looking at the brightening sky, I discovered I was freezing. My teeth were chattering. I started shaking so hard I had to lean up against a tree to keep from collapsing. I tried to pull the tatters of my shirt tighter around me. Mother was going to be so cross when she saw what I'd done to my best skirt.

"Thorry, Mother, I'm coming home now. Tell Dad noth to worry."

I took one more step and my legs buckled. I curled up in a ball there on the dark road. Okay, Janabai, enough. You've done enough for one night.

Aloud, I lisped, "Reth now. Thleep. Mirabai, thing me that pretty thong."

And Mirabai, my darling sister, did just that.

Chapter Sixty-Six

Marines Have Landed

Mirabai was still singing when gray morning light pulled me out of the sweet nothingness. I heard men talking. Someone was calling my name and gently shaking my shoulder.

"Jana, Jana, wake up. Can you hear me?"

I looked up. Someone was kneeling over me. I tried to focus my eyes.

"Joe?"

He smiled. "And Ben Woolsey. He's the one who found you."

I saw the chief looking over Joe's shoulder.

"He likth when you call him Gray Horth."

"I'll remember that," Joe said. "Gray Horse, go get some help and let everybody know she's alive and safe and we have her."

The old Indian nodded and tried to give me a smile, but his clenched teeth effort was more savage than reassuring. He patted Joe on the shoulder and trotted away.

"Okay, baby girl, you're okay now. You're okay. I've got you."

I threw my arms around him. It all came up at one. Tears and sobs, wailing out loud, in grief and relief, I couldn't catch my breath, crying so hard, I slobbered all over him. He just held me and let me get it out.

"I'm going to take you home to your mommy and daddy," he said. "Would you like that?"

"Uh huh."

"Are you hurt?"

"Uh huh."

"Where are you hurt? Can you tell me?"

"Fathe."

"Face. Yes, I see it. Anywhere else?"

I stuck out my tongue.

"What happened there?" he asked.

"I bith my thongue."

"Ouch. How did you do that?"

"Alma hith me."

"Alma? Who is Alma?"

"Pow. Thee hith hard!"

"You can tell me about it later. Are you hurt anywhere else?"

I held out my hands.

"Not so bad, just skinned up a bit," he said. "Is that all?"

"Uh-uh."

"You're hurt somewhere else? Where?"

"Thween legs."

"You're hurt between your legs?"

"And my buth."

"Your butt?"

"My buth hole."

"Must be uncomfortable. We'll get you fixed up. Before I move you, tell me, does your back hurt?"

I considered that. "Uh-uh"

"How about your neck?"

"Uh-uh."

"Good. Okay, let's see if we can get you up. Do you think you can stand?"

"Hep me."

"Put your arms back around my neck."

He stood, pulling me up with him. As soon as he let go, I fell back on the ground.

"Alright, Jana-bee, here's what we're going to do. Put your arms around my neck one more time. I'm going to pick you right up and hold you, okay?"

"Okeydokey, pokey." I thought that was pretty funny.

Joe chuckled. This time when he lifted me, he swung his arm under my knees and settled me in his arms like a baby. I rested my head against his shoulder. That was nice. I sighed.

"Ready, teddy?"

"Uh-huh. Wanna go thleep," I said.

"Good idea. You do that. I'll just carry you home while you take a little nap."

I was already asleep.

A little while later I woke up. He was still carrying me through the forest.

"Joe?"

"Hmmm?"

"I think I pooped mythelf."

"Thank God," he said.

"Why thank God?"

"All this time I thought it was me."

"Are you making a yoke?"

"I'm trying to."

"Can you find me a plathe to wash up?"

"Might be a creek down there. Let's see what we can find."

Holding me tight against him, Joe sort of slid, sort of hopped down into a ravine. I could hear water running. When we got to the bottom Joe found a place where the bushes were thinner and he could get the two of us knee-deep in the creek. He put me down on a rock.

"I want you to take your shirt off so it doesn't get wet. Do you need help?" Joe asked.

"I can'th do it. My hanth don't work."

"I won't look."

"I don't care."

Joe helped me take off the shirt. He hung it on a branch.

"Now the skirt?" he asked.

"Hep me."

Averting his eyes, he untied the skirt. Disgusting.

"Throw it way," I said.

"Underpants?"

"Don't have any."

"Right."

I saw him clench his teeth. He was breathing hard.

"Hep me into the water."

Joe didn't respond.

"Joe?" I repeated. "Joe, hep me into the water."

He shook his head and closed his eyes, took a few more breaths.

"Okay, honey bun, let's get you cleaned up."

Joe slid me into the creek, not too icy being the end of summer, but still cold enough to make my teeth chatter. I reached down between my legs and tried to clean myself. My hands hurt too much. I looked at Joe.

"Will you do it? Pleath?"

He nodded and put his hand between my legs, and into the shit and blood in my vulva. He gently tried to slosh everything off, sort of fanning water at me, trying to clean me without actually touching me or looking at me. He did that for a while.

"Come on, Joe, don't be thuch a baby. Get thah stuff off me."

He scrubbed harder. A lot of it was matted in my pubic hair.

"Harther," I said.

"I'll hurt you," he said. "If I scrub any harder."

I was almost yelling, "I don't care, juth get me clean."

When he was finished, and the filth washed downstream, he

cupped water over me again and again and did what he could to clean my face.

"How did you get this?" he asked, gently touching the cheek beneath my eye.

"Kalith hit me with his fisth."

"Kalith?"

"Theemon," I said.

"Theemon?"

"Not, THEEmon, DEEmon."

"Demon," he repeated. "A demon named Kalith hit you with his fist?"

"Um-hum."

Joe thought about that.

"Here's what we're going to do," he said. "I'm going to dry you off with your shirt and throw it away. I'm going to take off my coat and slide you in it nice and warm. Then I'm going to take off my shirt and wrap up your legs and bottom real tight."

"Like a papooth?"

"Right. You're going to be the beautiful little papoose, and I am the mighty warrior taking you home. 'Hoorah,' your mommy will say. Your daddy will be so happy to see you all swaddled up."

"Like hith baby?"

"Yep, just like his precious baby. Now see if you can go back to sleep, and when you wake up, you'll be home."

"You're taking care of me, aren't you, Joe?"

"You bet, honey."

"Will you take care of Vithath?"

"Vitha?"

"Kalith hurt her real bad."

"I know. We found her."

"Ith Skyler taking care of her?"

"He's with her now."

"Thath good. Skyler ith Vithath husbanth."

"Yes, he is."

I closed my eyes as Joe Downing carried me home. He picked up the pace, walking fast and running when he could. After a while I heard other voices. I looked over to the side and saw other men running with us. Gray Horse and Vic and G-Mek.

"Would you like me to carry her for a bit?" G-Mek asked.

"Good plan, my shoulders are killing me. Okay, here she is. Careful."

I roused as I was shifted into G-Mek's arms.

"G-Mek?"

"Hi, honeybee."

"Are you gonna hode me now?"

"Yes, for a little while. Then I'll give you back to Major Joe."

"I like Major Joe."

"Me too."

"I like you better," I said, looking up at my new bearer.

"How's that?" he asked in mock surprise.

"You my huthband."

G-Mek and Joe exchanged glances.

"She's in shock," Joe said.

"Righ, G-Mek? You my huthband?"

"Whatever you say, wife."

"Wife," I repeated, and hugged his neck tighter.

He hugged me back.

I drifted away into the fog.

Chapter Sixty-Seven

Baldies

I REMEMBERED THE NEXT DAYS IN flickering, jagged shards; women waking me up, making me drink water. I was too hot, sweating, trying to throw the covers off, and some merciless tormentor was putting them back over me. I was too cold, freezing and shivering, and there were never enough covers to keep me warm.

I woke up once when I felt things crawling on my head.

Someone said, "She has lice everywhere."

They raised me up high enough to cut off my hair as close as it could be, shaved me with a straight razor. It hurt, and I liked that it hurt. They spread my legs and shaved my pubic hair, moved up to my eyebrows. I didn't care. Under my arms. My legs. Kerilynn rubbed disinfectant on me—*and believe me, Kerilynn is not shy like Joe about where she rubs!* Lynda gave me a huge shot of Shakti.cillin in my butt. Now, that hurt! I tried to hit her. They pushed and kneaded me, however they wanted. Like pastry dough. Roll me up, roll me up, bake me in a pie. I wanted someone to wash my head. Not in the bath house; in the creek, the way Joe washed me.

"Where's Joe?" I asked.

"He's out with the others looking for a demon."

"Demon with a *ponytail*," I said.

"That's right. Go back to sleep."

"Wait, where's Vitha? I want to see Vitha."

"What do you remember about your friend?"

"We were..." I started... stopped. The horror engulfed me: the shimmering blade, the flash of surprise in her eyes, the spray of blood, Kavitha, the girl, the woman, my darling, cut through from shoulder to waist, falling to the ground in two pieces. I screamed, again, and again. I would scream forever if it would stop the memory from playing over and over.

"Wrap her in the blanket. Quick now, don't be gentle."

Someone swaddled me up again. Mirabai sang me to sleep every time the nightmares woke me up. I remember peeing in the pot, someone holding me steady; once, at least once, peeing in the bed. Being cleaned up and saying, "I'm sorry, I'm sorry."

I woke up, finally, completely alert. One minute I was in the dark, the next minute wide awake, remembering everything. Simone Jackson was wiping my face with a cool cloth. I wiggled my jaw from side to side. My tongue seemed to have shrunk to its normal dimensions.

"How long has it been?" I asked Simone.

"Three days."

"You've been here with me for three days?"

"No," Simone laughed. "Lots of people have been taking care of you. Kerilynn and Lynda. Your mother."

"Did I tell you what happened, what happened to Vitha?"

Simone bowed her head. Tears ran down her cheeks.

"No. We already knew. Old Ben led the search party back to the rancheria and found her, but you were gone."

"Goldilocks knocked me out and took me somewhere else. Did you catch him?"

"No," she said. "We're still searching."

I shook my head. They weren't going to catch the demon.

"How did you find me?" I asked, changing the subject.

"One hundred and thirty people searched for you all night long."

"Gray Horse found me."

"Yes, he did. With Joe and Vic and some others."

"Major Joe carried me home."

"Yes, he did."

"Blessings on Major Joe," I said.

Simone smiled her sweetest smile and wiped her eyes. "Blessings on Major Joe. He's the hero of the day."

I remembered my hair and reached up to feel my bald head. Weird, but at least I felt clean. "You've all seen me like this?"

"Most of the women, and your dad, of course."

"I must look horrible."

"Without all those curls, people will pay more attention to your beautiful eyes."

"Big deal."

"And they will look in your eyes and think about good things."

"I wouldn't call the things in my head good things," I said.

"Shush. I'm regaling you with this shuck and jive to cheer you up."

"You are?"

"People will look into your eyes and see reflections of themselves, and the reflections will show them a person worthy of love."

"All in my eyes?"

"Would I lie to you?"

"Mmm? 'Kay, so I'm trading curly hair for supernatural eyes."

"Right. Not so bad. Here, let me show you something."

Simone reached behind her neck and untied her scarf. She was bald as an egg.

"What did you do to your hair?"

She didn't answer, but I understood.

"I gave bugs to you too. Oh, Simone, I'm so, so sorry."

"Never you mind about that, honey. I like my bald head a whole lot better. Easier to take care of. My hair was all gray and brittle as straw anyway. Don't bother me at all; don't let it bother you. But there is something troubling me that you can help with."

"What? What can I help you with?" I asked.

"You can get up if you are able and come with me to the bath house. You do, laws a'mercy, smell like a pig's ass, and you need a real scrubbing."

I sniffed myself under the arms.

"Yick."

I also noticed my armpits were orange.

"What's wrong with my pits?"

"Nothing but Lynda's witch's brew liberally applied. Wait till you see your head in a mirror. Okay, up we go. Slowly."

Simone helped me to my feet. Whoa, Nellie, the world was spinning around. I waited until everything stopped moving and settled back into place.

"I don't want people seeing me like this."

"Too late, but here, put this on." She handed me a knitted hat.

"Better?"

"Better."

I looked down at myself, naked with a bright orange triangle where my pubic hair used to be.

"Swell," I said.

Simone wrapped me up in a blanket. She said, "Slide your feet in these Ho Chees." Simone pointed to a pair of sandals, the kind we make out of old automobile tires. Ho Chee Minhs. I didn't

244

know why they were called Ho Chee Minhs, Max's nomenclature probably. I sort of wiggled my feet into them, not bothering with the heel straps.

"Bravo," Simone said, clapping like I had performed a spectacular magic trick. She grabbed a bundle of clothes from the table. "If you're ready."

We walked out into the early morning. There was no one around, but I could hear people talking, and pots and pans clanging in the kitchen. The bathhouse was next to the creek so water had a straight way to come in and go out. The mechanics fabricated a flume up high on the creek that delivered enough water pressure for a real shower, cold, of course. There were two large cauldrons if you wanted to take the time to heat water for a hot bath. Most of us, used to the cold, never bothered, but every now and then, in mid-winter or for a special occasion, someone took the trouble to start a fire and wait for the water to warm up. Someone had taken the trouble this morning. Simone unwrapped the bandages from around my hands.

"Not bad," she said. "Now ease yourself in."

Heavenly. I soaped and washed myself until all the hot water was gone.

"Feel good?" Simone asked as I dressed in the clothes she had brought.

"I may live," I answered. "You know what?"

"What?"

"I'm starving."

Simone laughed. "That's my girl. Let's go see what Cookie has burned this morning."

When we arrived at amrit, people were still sitting at the tables eating and chatting. As we walked in, the room fell silent. Everybody turned to look. Durga Ma! Worse than I imagined. I'm sure I flushed red as rhubarb.

Mother stood up. She was as bald as Simone. Oh no, not her, too. Her long, gorgeous tresses. Then everybody stood.

"Why are they standing?" I asked Simone.

"Out of respect."

Instantly my eyes filled. I blinked and tears poured down my cheeks. I looked around the room. It was hard to see through the tears. Something was off. The men wore black arm bands, but otherwise looked the same. What was different? Scrutinizing the dining hall, I realized all of the women were wearing hats, which, one by one, they removed. Every woman in the village had cut off her hair and shaved her head. All of them, even Odessa Piwinski, who with her pallid pate resembled a shriveled goblin. The room itself looked like an enormous basket filled with speckled brown eggs, men and boys; and pale white eggs, women and girls. Could I have spread my lice to all of them?

"You're bald," I said. "Bald like me." Janabai Shepherd, mistress of the obvious. "Why are you all bald?"

Mother came over to me and took my head in her hands. She didn't mince words.

"When you were violated, all of us were violated. When that monster raped you, he raped us all."

What do you say? You don't. You stand there and let your mother wrap her arms around you. You stand there and slobber and cry with snot running out of your nose and hope you don't fall down. You hold on tight while all around your family is crying with you and loving you.

CHAPTER SIXTY-EIGHT

War Council

THE WAR COUNCIL ASSEMBLED IN the mandir, the most sacred, auspicious location for our grim purpose. If we were going to fight a creature from the underworld, where better to plan it than in the presence of the gods? Galen Raether was there, as was Vic Tretheway, Manoj and Raj Bannerjee, and Dad. Also present,

Max's six best hunters, Sandy Grimsman, Donnie Simms, Jeannie Zarou, Al Rudelic, Govinda Sarin, and Skyler Jones. Mirabai and Joe Downing. Thirteen. Ben Gray Horse Woolsey showed up uninvited. This land was his ancestral home. He had a right.

"I've had enough of that kohuneje," he said, brandishing the cavalry saber he claimed came from Little Big Horn (who was going to argue?) and had been in the family for generations. "I'm going to stick this right up his asshole, and then I'm going to pull it out and cut off that goddamn ponytail."

Fourteen. And me. Makes fifteen. I was there because Mother ordered me to make a complete record of the meeting, the official scribe for the Shiva Puri Council of War. What strange words to write. I have written them in capital letters. How about this? Simone gave me a precious, never-used "spiral notebook" for my scribing, and a pencil! A real pencil. The rubbery eraser thing on the end is hard as stone, but Vic sharpened the other end to a fine point. It was divine. I just wanted to write and write and write. I'd never had a whole pencil before, much less a spiral notebook with a shiny purple cover. I promised Mother I would get it all down, but Odessa would surely take me to task for too many details. Can't you just hear her lecture, "Omit needless words," or more likely, "Take out all that crap."

We sat around waiting. Where was Mother, and, of course, Max, our trusted war leader?

Skyler, setting up a table in the dancing circle, was sending me his sweetest, saddest smile. We had not spoken since… you know. I smiled back to let him know I was okay. Not much of a smile, but the best I could do.

The mandir looked like it was ready for an evening program, smudge burning in the pot; evergreen foliage, washed clean of volcanic ash, in a ring around the lingam; the lingam itself bathed with spring water, goat milk, and honey; Shiva's three-tined sigil applied perfectly with new ash; precious candles flickering; our puja sparkled from top to bottom.

Without explanation, Mirabai chanted:

Hare Krishna Hare Krishna Krishna Krishna Hare Hare

Hare Rama Hare Rama Rama Rama Hare Hare

She sang alone for a while, gently, but with great devotion. Then the rest of us joined her, chanting for some time. Have you ever heard "Hare Krishna Hare Rama" chanted by people who really know how? When the chant was over, the door opened and Mother and Max walked in.

Mother was dressed in rough browns and grays, clothing so unremarkable she was hardly noticeable. That, I learned, was the purpose of her drab attire. To be unseen. Her only ornament a holster across her chest with a Colt Python revolver, grip ready, just below her left breast.

Max was a different vision altogether. The Shiva Puri women had shaved their heads, with one exception: Max. Over the years she had grown her hair long and wore it in a single, glossy braid down her back. I will admit that when I saw that Max, my Max, had not shaved her head like the other women, it hurt my feelings. Yes, I know, pathetic, but it bothered me. As casually as possible, I asked Mother, "Why didn't Max cut off her hair too?"

"She needs it," Mother answered, "it's her *war hair*."

Now, when Max entered, I saw what Mother meant. Max had drawn her hair back in a bun at the nape of her neck, drawn it back so tightly that it seemed to stretch the wrinkles out of her face. Her hair was slicked down with grease or something so that it reflected light, not one follicle out of place. It was mean-looking, fierce.

She was wearing clothes I had never seen, olive green from top to bottom, pressed and starched, sharp creases everywhere. Her boots were shined like black mirrors, so polished you could see your reflection in them. Her belt buckle was made out of some shiny metal. Where had she been keeping these things? On her collars she wore black sigils of some kind, upside down triangles. Around her waist, her own holster with one of Shiva Puri's two .45 caliber automatics. Under her arm, a rolled-up map.

Mother and Max stood there for a moment, waiting.

Joe Downing said, "On your feet, people." He grunted, "Attention," though it sounded more like "ten-shut."

248

Everybody scrambled to their feet. Max smiled.

"Knock it off, Joe."

Mother looked at me. "Is my official scribe ready?"

I opened my notebook.

CHAPTER SIXTY-NINE

Grimsman's Report

" Let's begin with Grimsman's report. Most of you have heard the scuttlebutt, but let's hear it from the beginning in her own words. Sandy?"

Sandra Grimsman, Max's most-trusted "marine," rubbed her fingertips over her recently-shaved head. Most of the women, myself included, did that a lot because our bald heads felt so weird, now that the stubble was growing in.

"Okay (rub, rub, rub). Four days ago, that would have been... (rub, rub, rub)?"

"October 19," Max provided.

"Right. The day after Janabai was... uh... rescued, Max sent me and Al to reconnoiter... what are we calling him? Ponytail?"

"Kali," Mother snapped.

"Kali. Yes. So we were pretty sure Kali was headed to Susanville because of what Gray Horse told us. We pushed hard, running most of the way, and got to the outskirts of town just before dark."

"Remind everybody how far it is from here to Susanville," Max nudged.

"Fifty miles, by highway, but we took back roads which added another ten miles."

"Sixty miles," Mother repeated, "between sunup and sundown." She nodded compliments to Sandy and looked around to make sure we all appreciated the feat. We did.

"Go on."

"We crept up close enough to see a humongous camp all lit up with burning oil barrels. Kali was up on a platform, pacing back and forth and screaming, 'MAWHAM, MAWHAM,' or some shit like that. Whatever it was, I could feel it vibrating in me all the way to my bone. I tell you, he had his people whipped up into a frenzy. They were all drunk and screaming back at him, 'MAWHAM MAWHAM.'"

"Did he have other chiefs or officers or whatever on the platform?" Joe Downing asked.

"Yes. There were two others up there with him, a giant with a horned helmet like a Viking."

"Kumbakarna," Joe affirmed.

"And a woman. Scary. Tall. Jet-black hair that swept down over her face. Long fingers with metal fingernails like eagle talons."

"La Hiena, the witch," Joe added. "This is the same mob that attacked Redding, the ones that call themselves Rakshasa."

"How many?" Max asked. "How many of these... Rakshasa?"

"Hard to tell. The light was bad, and they were moving around a lot, but hundreds. What's your guess?" She looked at Al Rudelic.

"I'd say... at least three hundred."

Nervous moment of silence as the members of the council shifted position and looked around at each other. At best, we might be able to put 150 fighters in the field with the rest; the elderly, the infirm, and the kids hiding in the village behind the barricade. Sandy's report gave rise to another puzzle. If Kali had so many troops, what had he been doing skulking around the rancheria with only Alma in tow?

"Continue."

"We couldn't hear everything, but we heard enough. Kali yelled at them to be ready to ride for Shiva Puri the next morning."

I looked over at Mother. She mouthed the question, "Alma?" I nodded.

Sandy went on, "I told Al to get his ass back here, running all night, to give you this wonderful news. I stayed behind to get a better look in the daylight. Al took off, and I slipped back down the main highway a few miles so I could get some sleep and wait for them to march."

"How long did you have to wait?"

"Let's just say this, they are not the most splendorous troops on parade. It took them till mid-afternoon to stagger by. They looked like warmed-over pig shit."

"Poetic," Max said, "but could you be a little more technical in your description?"

"Roger, boss. Like Al said, there were at least three hundred of them, hard to tell because they were all strung out, no real organization, just a long scraggly line of raggedy-assed drunks on bicycles."

"*Pedaling* bicycles?" Mother asked. "No motorcycles?"

"No, ma'am, but you should see these bicycles, all tricked out with weird shit like skulls and shrunken heads and chrome snakes; and big—not little piddly bikes—huge things, war machines, hand-built for sure, heavy-duty frames, weapons sticking out all over."

"What kind of weapons?"

"I didn't see many firearms, and no heavy weapons like our M60s. These are blade people. Swords, spears, machetes, pikes, knives, battle axes."

"Bows and arrows?"

"Didn't see any."

"What did the people look like?"

"Not much. They're mean looking with lots of tattoos and metal things, rings and chains hanging from hooks in their skin, and stuff like bones jammed through their noses and lips, but when you get a closer look, they're scrawny and diseased. Rashes and sores everywhere. Greasy. Sickly. But, I'll tell you this, they know how to ride. Most of them don't even use their hands. They wheel and spin like rodeo riders. Do not underestimate those bikes."

"Got the picture."

"So, the next day I keep shadowing them, staying just ahead of their column. Lucky for me, they don't send out lead scouts or outriders, like they're not worried about danger, because they *are* the danger. They take their time, and they stop for this and that, and they have breakdowns or get tired, I don't know what. That second day they make better time. I guess they sobered up. And the next day even better. I stayed with them until yesterday evening when they went into camp. I figure they're no more than seven miles north."

"When will they get here?" Mother asked.

"Tomorrow."

CHAPTER SEVENTY

Order of Battle

"Gather around," Max said, "and I'll show you how we're going to destroy these cocksuckers."

Dad looked at Mother.

"Is this dharma? To kill human beings to save others?"

"Why do you pick this moment to ask that question?" Mother snapped. "After what they did to our daughter? Those people are capable of anything."

"One man did that. Not all of them," Dad argued.

Mother glared at him and lifted her chin the way she does. We waited for her to let him have it, but it was Mirabai's soft whisper that filled the silence.

"Arjuna spoke to Krishna, saying 'I shall not fight.'"

Mira recited from the Bhagavad Gita, most revered scripture, verses we had heard many times, yet, on this perilous occasion, as we deliberated the terrifying actions we were about to perform, Lord Krishna's ancient words crackled through the room like lightning. "*You mourn that which is not worthy of mourning. That which truly exists will always be, and that which truly does not exist, can never be. Know that your soul is indestructible. It cannot in any way, in any manner, cease to be. Therefore, do not be afraid to fight!"*

We waited for Dad to respond. He drew in a deep breath and nodded.

"Okay, what's your plan?"

"Simple," Max said. "Trick 'em, kill 'em."

Of course, it wasn't simple at all. Max pointed to the battle map.

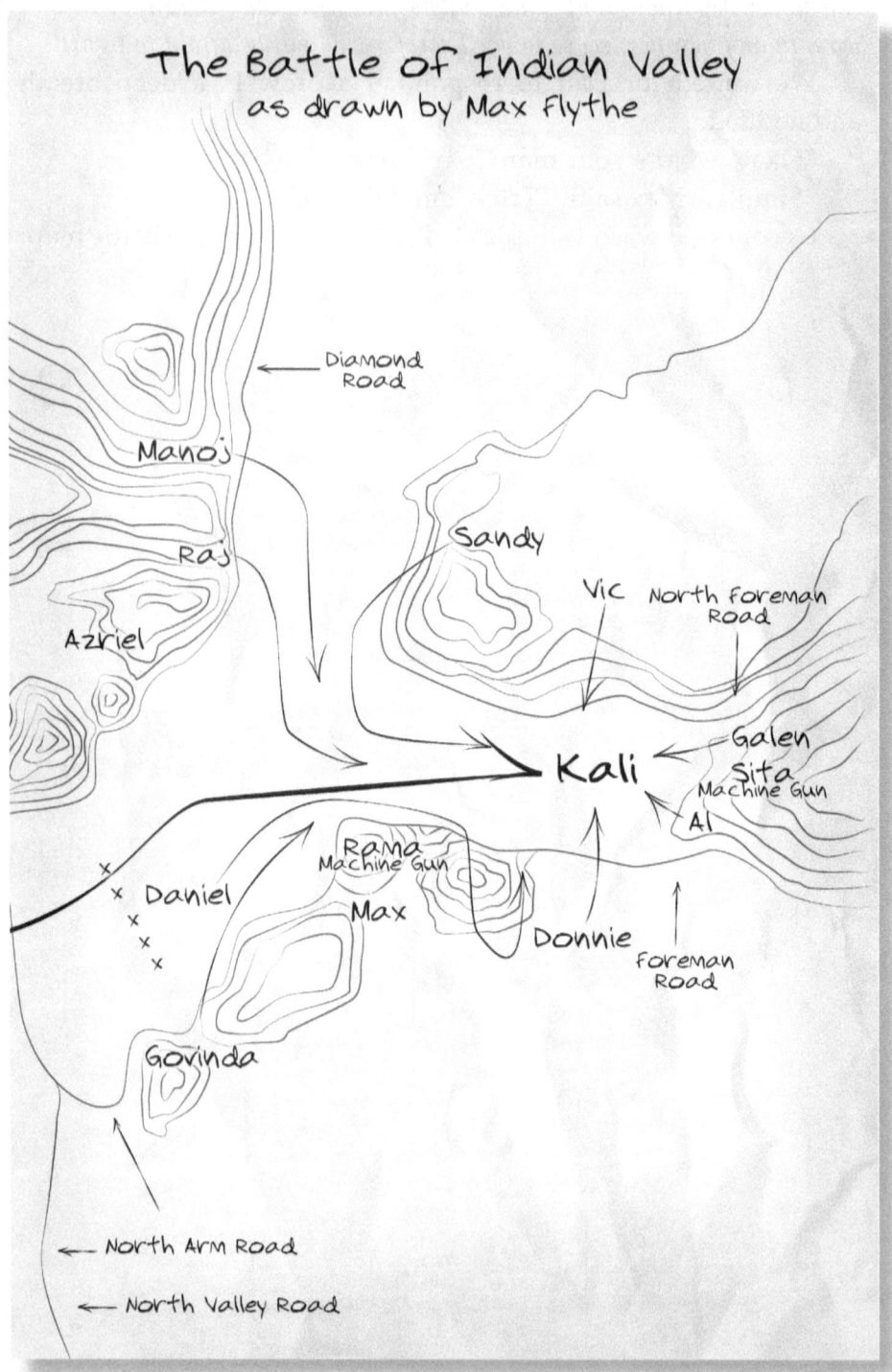

"They have twice as many fighters, but they don't know how many we have. That gives us our first advantage."

She paused and looked at me. I could see the question behind her eyes. *Alma?* I shrugged. She went on.

"It will make sense to them that we defend ourselves here, along the canal. Daniel, you and twenty of our junior fighters will set up behind breastworks so you look like you mean to hold and fight right there. You will emplace all twelve of our bouncing betties ninety feet out in front of your position. You will have eight of our assault rifles and enough ammo to put on a good show. Are you up for this?"

Everyone looked at Dad.

Mother objected. "Daniel is the least experienced fighter, and the least expendable. We need him to do what he does best, to take care of us, to take care of our home, to get the medics prepared for the worst, to make sure the kids stay safe and calm."

Dad was resolute. He did not embrace the enterprise with his whole heart, but he wasn't about to back down, especially in front of Joe Downing. He was deeply grateful to the marine for rescuing me, but there was no love lost between the two.

Dad ignored Mother's objection and spoke directly to Max.

"You said to put on a show and run for the barns." He glanced at Joe Downing. "I can run away just as good as anyone."

"Very well, sir," Max said. "You're the bait to pull them into the trap. Jeannie and Skyler will assist you."

Next to Sandy Grimsman, Jeannie Zarou and Skyler Jones were her most proven hunters. They nodded to Max, and she gave them a look that meant, "You better bring him back intact, or don't come back at all."

Jeannie Zarou said, "Let me see if I got this right. Don't let bad guys kill our village manager?"

"Smart ass," Max said.

Jeannie shrugged like, "Who, me?"

She turned her attention to Skyler. "And don't you get any ideas about playing the great avenger. Keep your head on straight and wired tight."

"I'm going to kill that son of a whore."

"Maybe, but not tomorrow. You bring the big boss man back alive. Got it?"

Skyler answered with a quick nod.

Gray Horse spoke. "I will stand with Daniel."

"Right."

"Daniel," Max resumed, "except for these three heroes, you will only have trainees and kids in your squad. You will *not* stand and fight. Daniel, look at me. You too, Ben. Do you hear what I say? You will *not* fight."

Dad swallowed and whispered, "Yes."

She looked at Gray Horse. "You got it?"

"No scalp'em Kohuneje?"

"Later, you scalp'em, but tomorrow you will fire one volley for effect, then you will fly up the valley like quail flushed from the brush. You will scream like little babies and run like the devil himself is on your heels. He is, for a fact, the devil himself, and he is coming for you. It's at least a half mile to the Pinch, so pace yourself. When you get to Maitreya Hill, swerve right into Foreman Ravine, hook right just past my position, climb straight up through Two Toes, where Donnie's team will be waiting for you in their fighting holes. Do not stop running until you pass right through them. Only then will you turn around, drop into a hole, and reinforce Donnie."

Dad nodded, his eyes big.

"This is where the real fight will take place, in the open ground between the barns and Old Foreman Road. Donnie, get your war face on. You will be the front line. You will have hunting rifles, two assault rifles, and all sixteen of our hand grenades. Daniel, your team will be the second line behind him with your assault rifles. You will be higher and shooting down, over the heads of Donnie's first line. Do not shoot Donnie or his people."

Small chuckle.

"Galen and Al will be in the center with the M60, call it 'Sita gun,' Galen firing, Al feeding the belt. You will have most of the

M60 ammo. When you run out, there is no more. Period. Short bursts. Make them count."

Max turned to Mother. "How are your hands?"

"My hands are fine. Don't worry."

"Not worried. You will be up here in the rocks above Cook's Creek with the 84. You can shoot right across the pasture into Foreman's Ravine. As soon as those people wheel to the right, chasing Daniel, they'll be in your kill zone. Start taking them down from behind, picking off the rear ranks and working your way forward. Don't get antsy and start shooting early. Don't get any ideas about taking out the big juicy officers in front. Don't spook them. Patience, Azriel, patience. As you have taught me, breathe in deep, breathe out long. They need to believe Daniel's team is all we have."

"Got it," said Mother.

"Who's your spotter?"

Mother didn't answer for a moment, then twisted her head to look at me.

"Janabai."

"She's been through a lot."

"She's mad, and she won't flinch."

I smiled. Dad started to say something, then choked it off. The safest place for me would be hiding up among the boulders. Under my mother's wing.

"Janabai it is," Max continued. "I'll be here on Maitreya with the second M60, call it 'Rama gun,' with Cliff shooting, Gil feeding. When the tail end of the Rakshasa formation crosses North Arm Road, when all three hundred are inside the ravine, I will signal Cliff to open up and rake their rear. Understood?"

Cliff answered, "Understood. On your signal."

"Galen, wait until you hear Rama gun, then fire at will, raking their front. But not until you hear Rama. Don't freelance. Wait for Rama. Galen, what are you going to do?"

"Wait for Rama, then kill all the bad guys, I tell you what."

"Perfect. Do not fire too soon and spoil our surprise."

She looked around the table to make sure every eye was on her.

"Now, get this, if you don't remember anything else, get this: when Rama gun opens up, that will be your signal for our general assault. No mistakes here, people. You hear Rama gun, you go to war. What's your signal?"

"Rama gun," we repeated in unison.

"Right. Donnie, you and Daniel will hold in place and fight right here (she pointed at the map) from your holes at Two Toes. You are the anvil. Now we need a hammer. Vic, you and Al will come out of the west woods right here, run downhill, and come out from behind the barns in a skirmish line. You will charge across North Foreman to take them in the left flank. You two gentlemen are the hammer."

Donnie said, "I assume you hammer types will avoid killing my anvil types."

"Spoilsport." Vic grinned at his friend.

"So count 'em up, people. We will have five squads and two machine guns in the ravine. Donnie, Daniel, Galen, you are the long-range shooters."

"Like Henry's bowmen at Agincourt," Donnie interjected.

"Correct. You've been paying attention. You 'bowmen' will kill as many as you can at long range. Al and Vic, you are the heavies. You will smash whatever's left of those people into the dirt. You will destroy them. You will pulverize them. Keep squeezing them up the hill into the shooters. Donnie, Daniel, Galen, hold your ground. Stay in your holes. Let Kali come to you. If he tries to get out the way he came, I will close the door with Rama gun until help comes."

"Manoj, Sandy, you two are the help. You will be up in the valley, here and here, just in case the bad guys turn toward the village. Manoj, you will hide your team in the first gully, just north of Azriel's sniper nest. Right here. You will have the most distance to run, probably a half mile, so I am going to put younger troops in your squad. They are not our best shooters, but they don't have to be with the shotguns. Just get in close. I expect you to cover that half mile in five minutes, no more. Sandy, you will be hidden here, behind the Pinch. Hunting rifles. When you hear the signal, one more time, what is the signal?"

Sandy answered, "Rama gun opens fire."

"Roger. When the 60 lights 'em up, you run to the fight like the devil dogs I know you are. You and Manoj smash into their rear, Sandy on the top, Manoj on the bottom."

"Why does she get to be on top?"

Big laugh.

"Be alert for this, lovebugs. When they start running away, I will fire one green flare. What color?" Max asked.

"Green."

"Right. What does green mean?"

"The enemy is retreating."

"Yes. So now we get to Govinda and his old-timers way down at the bottom with nothing to do. So sad. Poor Govinda. You will be hiding right there behind Laksman Hill. You will stay there, quiet and scared as baby birds. You will not make a peep. You will not try to sneak up behind their main force when they chase Daniel up the hill. This plan will go down the shitter if those people spy you creeping along. They will know it's a setup. They will smell ambush, and we will lose any advantage we have. It will be a big ugly ball of snot, and we will lose this thing. You understand? You will stay out of the fight. Say it."

"Stay out of the fight," Govinda said.

"Unless?"

"We see the green flare?"

"Right. Unless you see the green flare. That means they are beaten and running for home. Then, then, and only then will you hobble out fast as your hairy old stems can manage. You will take up blocking positions along the canal. Be sure you point yourselves so that you are *facing* the enemy when he runs downhill toward you."

There was no reaction.

"That's a joke, Govinda."

"Oh."

"It's funny because... never mind."

"I thought it was funny," Joe Downing said.

"Thanks. Listen up, you badass hell hounds. One more time. If you see the green flare, the bad guys are running away. The green flare means we've won. Govinda, when you see the green flare, your only job is to delay their retreat until everyone else piles into their rear and we crush them out in the open."

"Now for you, Raj Bannerjee, last but not least, I hope. Stay put. I know you want to get into it, but you will stay hidden in the second gully, the gully where Cook Creek comes out, the gully below the gully where your worthless brother will be picking his scabs. *If* you see the green flare, only *if* you see the green flare, come out of your hidey-hole and join the fun. Got it?"

"Like the precious jewel of your virginity, Memsahib," said Raj Bannerjee, "I got it."

Max ignored him and turned to Downing.

"Major, I know how much you want to fight, but I am going to hold you back as our last resort."

Joe Downing did not look happy.

"Don't trust Air Wing?" he asked.

"Wrong. I *do* trust you. I trust you to hold the line and not cave in if this plan gets blown. Because I can trust you to die to protect our children."

Downing sighed and nodded.

"You will guard Shiva Puri itself. You will have the third machine gun, 'Laksman gun' we'll call it, with two belts of ammo, and the nine claymore mines that might still work. If they do, you will have a blast line of a quarter mile, so it's crucial you time it perfectly. Let them get close, but not too close. I'll put markers out in front so you can see when to crank the detonators. Claymores first, then the M60 right behind. Remember, let them get to the markers before you set 'em off. That's going to be a lot closer than you think it should be. You will see them coming and coming, and you are going to want to open up. If you do, you will waste your firepower and have nothing left to stop them. Clear?"

"Crystal."

CHAPTER SEVENTY-ONE

Plan B

"THAT BRINGS ME TO THIS final word. Listen up, and listen good. No battle plan survives the first minute. I don't know what it will be like, except that it will be different than these pretty arrows on my map. So you have to stay flexible. You have to adapt to the situation. You have to keep your head screwed on."

"You are the best and only *infantry* commander we have," said Joe Downing.

"Thanks ever so much for the swell endorsement, but here's where I'm going with this sermon: Plan B. I want you to get this. Plan B. The last-resort plan. If the fight gets away from us, I will fire *red* flares, one after another, as many as I have. If you see a *red* flare, that means we are getting our butts kicked. Everybody, I mean *everybody*, fight your way back to Shiva Puri any way you can. Forget everything else I've told you, and run for home. We may lose the fight in Foreman Ravine and still come out of this okay... *if* we don't panic. You two reserve squads, Govinda and Raj, come up behind them just when they think they've won. That's why we keep you in reserve. To turn the tide. That's your job. To turn the tide."

"We'll save you, boss lady," Raj said.

"We'll be there," Govinda said.

"Yes, yes you will." Max smiled at the two men. "Okay, one more time. Red flares, come a'running. Do not let them get to our children. *Do not let them get to our children!* That's the main thing. That's the whole thing. Questions?"

"Prisoners?" Daniel asked.

"Don't get captured."

Hilarious.

"That's not what I meant."

"I know it wasn't." Max looked at her leaders. "You already know what I'm going to say. No prisoners. I repeat, *no prisoners.*

Not one. Even if he begs for mercy. Even if he looks like your dear old grandpa. What would we do with prisoners? Build a prison? Tell Kali to go away and be more polite the next time. You know what he did to Kavitha Bose."

Max took a moment to stare at Skyler.

"Kali will do the same to us if he wins. No prisoners. It will be easier on the kids and safer for everybody if we finish the job out on the field. Are we straight on this?"

Everybody nodded, except Dad, who still wasn't convinced. Killing to defend family was one thing, killing wounded human beings was murder.

"Daniel, my friend, let this be my karma," Max said.

"It doesn't work that way," he said. "The karma will be for all of us, for the rest of our days."

"So be it," Max said.

"So be it," Dad said.

"Sandy, relieve the posts and send fresh scouts further out. Send Greg, Elicia, and Shana"

"How far?"

"Three miles north, one mile toward Crescent Mills, one mile south, just in case."

"Aye, aye."

"Azriel get to your nest and snap in."

Mother nodded and started to leave.

"Oh, and Jai Shiva, Azriel Dancer."

"Jai Shiva, Durga-Max," Mother hugged her old friend, turned, and departed.

Max looked around at everybody else.

"I want every position put in order, every fighting hole dug, every weapon cleaned, every bullet wiped, both mine fields ready, every field of fire staked. Be sure there is plenty of water at every position. You have six hours until dark. What are you apes waiting for?"

CHAPTER SEVENTY-TWO

Jolene

"ENTER."

I pushed through the curtain into Max's room. Table, chair, beat-up trunk, clothes line, weapons locker, crisply made bed, Max sitting on the bed cleaning her handgun.

"Not a good time, Jana."

I didn't move. She sighed.

"What do you need?"

"Knife."

"Knife? This is a farm. There are knives all over the place. Help yourself."

"No, a real knife, a war knife, to kill a raper."

"Rapist."

"Whatever. Will you give me a knife?"

Max didn't smirk at me, which I expected. She put her weapon on the blanket and stood to face me.

"I understand how you feel, Janabai, but there..."

I interrupted, "No you don't. How could you?"

Max shook her head and gave me a bitter little laugh. "One day, we'll have a long talk, but this is not the day. Today, you need to get real. You're strong and fast, but you're no fighter, and never have been. You couldn't even punch Alma Mendez in the nose when she was picking on you."

"Alma Mendez didn't rape me."

That stopped her.

"You make a good point." She drummed her fingers on the table. "What do you know, what do you *think* you know, about knife fighting?"

"Put the sharp end inside the bad guy."

Max snorted. "Well, I guess you have the basic idea."

"Can you teach me?"

"Not in a thousand years, even if I wanted to, which I don't."

"Why?"

"Because I don't know *how*. Nobody does, not really. You get in a fight with a knife and you get hurt. You cut and you stab, and you *get* cut and you *get* stabbed, and you *hope* the other guy falls down first, and you *hope* you get to the medic before you bleed out. That's it."

"That's all?"

"That, and, oh yeah, stay out of knife fights."

"C'mon, Max, I know you have a trick."

She hesitated, then took one deep breath. "Okay, I'll give you this. Don't let your enemy see that you have a knife. Don't wave it around in front of you like some kind of ninja. Keep the knife hidden up your arm, or behind your back, or in your coat. Get in close, and at the very last second, bring it out and up and into him as fast and as nasty as you can."

"Where?"

"The neck is good, or right here at the shoulder, if you're lucky enough to get behind him, but those are small targets. Chancy. Best bet is in the belly, under the ribs. Aim up toward his rotten heart. You may only get one strike, so make it good."

"I'll make it real good. Thanks, Max."

"Alright, get on out of here and get something to eat."

"Max?"

"What?" she snapped.

"The knife?"

"Oh, fuck it." She knelt down next to a trunk, opened it, slid her hand down one side, and pulled out a large black-handled knife in a leather sheath. She flipped it end-to-end and handed it to me, hilt first.

"Wow. What's her name?"

"Her?"

"War swords always have names."

"You read too many novels."

"No, really, Max, what's her name?"

Max bit her lip, leaned in close, and whispered in my ear, "Jolene."

"Jolene," I repeated, a bit awestruck. "Why Jolene?"

"Because Jolene is an evil slut who cuts off men's balls."

"Jolene!" I shouted, pulling it out of its sheath. I studied the wicked-looking blade.

"Janabai?"

"What?"

"I'm fucking with you. It doesn't have a name."

"No?"

"No. It's a goddamn knife. It's a tool designed for one purpose."

"Killing bad guys."

"That's right."

CHAPTER SEVENTY-THREE

War Paint

"DO YOU HAVE ANY BLUE paint or blue powder or something?" Simone Jackson bit her lower lip to hold back the psychoanalytic mumbo jumbo I knew she wanted to lay on me. Instead, she took a breath, said, "Vishnu preserve us," and narrowing her deep-set eyes, asked, "What do you want it for?"

"Paint my head."

She snorted, "Like the gods of old?"

"Yes, ibu-ma," I said, "like Krishna driving Arjuna to war in the fields of Kurusetra."

She smiled at me. "Got just the thing. Goes on easy, but comes off hard."

"I don't care if it ever comes off."

I was rubbing Simone's sky-blue paint on my face when Mother found me on the steps of the mandir. Taking note of the large, black knife on my belt, Mother closed her eyes for a moment but made no further comment. Sitting down next to me, she reached into the bucket and started painting herself. Over the next couple of hours the defenders of Shiva Puri, every woman who was staying behind the barricade, painted herself blue, from bare shoulder to bald crown, from *vishuddha chakra* in the throat, to *sahasrara chakra* on the top of the head.

Simone's blue stuff, whatever it was, dried fast. When I tried to wipe it off my hands, I knew she was right; it was going to take a long time to wear off. Someone got the idea we should paint three white stripes, Lord Shiva's sigil, across our foreheads. Simone went back to the storehouse for white paint. We painted Shiva stripes on each other.

Mother looked at me.

"Anything else?"

"Bright red bindis between our brows," I suggested.

"Yes!" she said. "Lord Krishna will rejoice when his women destroy Kali's army, when we slaughter every wicked man he brings against us, when we bring the demon himself to earth."

To myself, I added, "When I cut his balls off with my Kali-Knife."

CHAPTER SEVENTY-FOUR

Parley

T HE PARLEY AT THE LOWER *canal as told to me by Skyler Jones. These are his words.*

We hid behind a ramshackle breastwork of ox wagons, hunkered down along the lower canal, and ready as we were ever going to be. Before the sun rose over the eastern ridge, Gray Horse walked in front of our line casting a protective spell. I don't know what he was sprinkling, but it made the most evil stink you can imagine, like a cockroach crawled up your nose and died.

"Bear magic," he said. "Kohuneje don't like bear magic."

I prayed he was right.

So it was, on the morning of October 23, the monster that Gray Horse called Kohuneje, and we called Kali Demon, came against Shiva Puri. His Rakshasa pedaled their war bikes leisurely up North Valley Road like sightseers on a lark. A full two hours, two hours of sweating and waiting, we watched them straggle in, small groups, and in ones and twos. They dropped their wheels under the trees on the far side of the road and settled down for breakfast. Another hour went by as they lounged in the shade, smoking reefer and watching us. They didn't seem to be in a hurry.

Max decided to give them something to look at. She sent us one fighter from each of the upper valley squads as "reinforcements." A distraction, she called it, worried that the Rakshasa would discover Gray Horse's squad hidden behind the southernmost hill, or that someone in the squad would crawl up to the top for a peek and tip our hand. Or that Kali would figure out that it looked too easy.

About mid-morning, three Rakshasa big shots walked out onto the field waving a white flag. One man was a giant, at least seven feet tall with a Viking helmet that added another foot. From Joe Downing's story about the Rakshasa invasion of Redding, I knew this big man had to be the one called Kumbakarna. Beside him, a woman crouched, knife-blade thin, crow's wings of hair obscuring her face, a braided whip in one hand, the other clenched into a claw, fingernails of glittering metal. This one had to be the witch, La Hiena. Next to her, another large man who sported a long, blond ponytail. Kali... the thing who had... murdered my wife. He was holding something along his leg. I couldn't bear to look at it.

He shouted, "You, little people, over there peeking out behind your wall, do you speak for Shiva Puri?"

"Maybe," Daniel shouted back.

"Come out where I can see you."

"I can see you perfectly where I am."

"We show the parley flag. We are at peace. Nobody will hurt you."

"What do you want?"

"You are so rude," Kali said. "What do we want?" He turned to Kumbakarna. "What can I tell this rude Shiva man?"

The giant growled, "Everything. Tell him we want it *all*."

"There, my king has said it. We want everything. All your food. All your animals. All your women. All your men."

"And the children," La Hiena said.

The three chiefs grunted, "Ma WHUM Ma WHUM Ma WHUM." Behind them, across the road, the Rakshasa in the main force took up the "Ma WHUM" chant, slapping their chests with every repetition.

Kali raised his hand, and the chant cut off like he had sliced it in half. He spoke kindly, "Don't worry, Shiva man, it's a joke. We don't eat children... unless we have nothing else. A hungry man will eat anything. Yes? So so so. Here is my offer. Put down your guns. Take us to your town. Feed us and take care of us. We won't be hungry anymore. What you say?"

Daniel didn't answer.

"Not good deal for you? We want everything and offer nothing. Bad manners on us. But, I have a gift for you, even though you have been so rude; something very nice, something you want."

He held up the object he had been carrying along his leg. He held it high to make sure we could see what it was.

Kavitha's head.

"So sorry it's not more," he said, trying to keep a straight face, "but we ate the rest of her, the parts you didn't steal from me. My people wanted to boil it into soup, but I said, no, no, don't be greedy. Gluttony is a vice, and, besides, heads are better for decoration, don't you think? Hang a head here, another head there. Turn a camp into a home. And the aroma? Ah, the fragrance of death when a head gets ripe, like this one."

He lowered the head so the crouching witch could lick Kavitha's face with a fish-belly-white tongue; then handed it to Kumbakarna, who took a step back and launched it toward our wagons. It landed and rolled close to where I stood.

"Steady," Jeannie grabbed my arm as I lifted my rifle. I shook off her hand, but I didn't fire. Breathing hard, in some kind of a trance, I staggered out in front of the wagons and over to the place where my wife's head lay in the dirt. I knelt down and picked her up in both hands. I cradled her against my heart.

"Did you know her?" Kali spoke, his words dripping sarcasm like poison from the serpent's fang. "Was she precious to you?"

I looked into his eyes and saw there the flames of damnation.

"Come closer, boy," he whispered.

I could feel his eyes clutching at me, trying to draw me in, but I was deep in my grief, and hot in my rage. I found the strength to resist and ripped away from his yellow gaze.

Between my clenched teeth, I hissed, "Before this day is over, I'm going to kill you."

He raised his eyebrows in mock alarm. Then he smiled, wider and wider, he smiled. I was close enough to see him... *change*... become something else, something alien and not of this place. His lips stretched wide, like a snake opens its mouth to swallow a rabbit. Curved tusks like daggers unsheathed from his upper gums. The bones of his skull cracked and snapped as his head re-made itself into something bestial and vile.

I screamed, and the demon laughed at me with a voice that shook the mountains. That's not an exaggeration, you heard it too, thunderous peals of laughter that expanded and thickened into those same pulsing waves of pressure I remembered from that night twenty years earlier when I was just a little boy, the night the world ended, and there was no doubt in my mind that the demon was real, that Kali was real, that he was the maker of our destruction, and that he was here, and now, to murder the last of our kind.

"Ma WHUM ma WHUM ma WHUM ma WHUM WHUM WHUM WHUM."

I fell to the ground. Curled tight, a terrified child, I wept and begged the gods for help. Waves of demonic laughter pressed me into the earth, penetrating and violating my every cell with his stink. He swallowed me, shattered and damned, down and down and down...

Jaya Jaya Shiva Shambo.

At first, I wasn't sure I heard her, the barest whisper, the stirring of a fresh breeze.

Jaya Jaya Shiva Shambo.

Mirabai?

Mahadeva Shambo.

Without doubt, the voice of the Songsinger. Our Mirabai. Her chant grew louder, stronger. I sang with her, softly at first, then with conviction. From behind the wagons, I heard Daniel and the others take up the chant.

Mahadeva Shambo.

I got to my knees, pushing against Kali's embrace, struggling to my feet as his reverberating laughter faded and broke into gasps, until there was no sound left in the world except our chant, gaining strength through our communal might.

Jaya Jaya Shiva Shambo.

I picked up Kavitha's head and held her tight against me.

La Hiena screamed, the sound a hawk makes as she plunges for a hill. Kali stood a few yards away, panting and shaking, his demonic aspect grinding and melting back into human form.

He roared, "Stop that fucking yammer, or I will skin every one of you alive, and before you die, you will watch me eat your children. And put down those goddamn guns!"

Our chanting stopped; silence, our answer to the demon's demand.

Alone, I faced the demon. He took one step toward me, stopped, lifted his head, and sniffed. He turned his head this way and that, smelling the air like an animal. Once again, he fixed me with those yellow eyes. From deep in his chest he growled, "Bears!" I remembered the curse Gray Horse made earlier, *"Kohuneje don't like bear magic."* Thank you, Ben Gray Horse Woolsey.

Behind me, I heard Daniel shout one word, "Ready."

The three Rakshasa chiefs backed away.

"Aim."

They turned and ran for the trees.

"Fire."

Max was right about one thing. Her plan did not survive the first moment of battle.

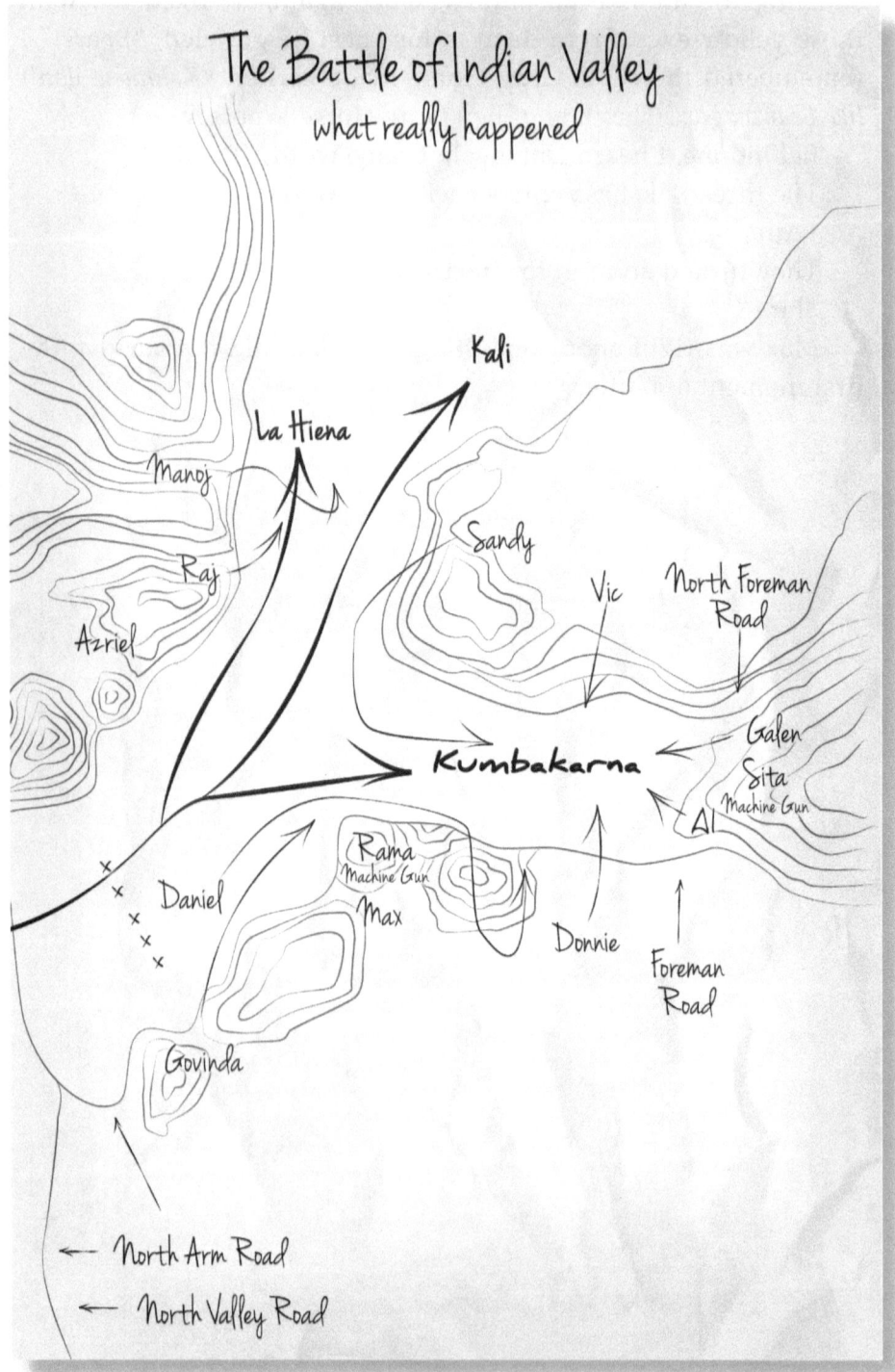

The Battle of Indian Valley
what really happened

CHAPTER SEVENTY-FIVE

What Really Happened

"KALI!" I SCREAMED, AS OVERWHELMING waves of pressure knocked us into the dirt, crushing us flat like a giant rolling pin. In my ears, and in my mind, to the marrow of my bones, I could feel the horrible pulsations.

ma WHUM ma WHUM ma WHUM ma WHUM ma WHUM ma WHUM ma WHUM

"Make him stop, Mommy," I cried, reduced in that instant to a terrified child.

"Hold tight," Mother snarled, "and don't panic."

And immediately, as if obeying her command, another sound, a sweet refrain, rose from deep within me, cool waters against the torrent of Kali's filth.

Shiva Shiva Shiva Shambo.
Shiva Shiva Shiva Shambo.

Mirabai!

Her mantra held against his incantation, then pushed it back, then washed over and drowned it with the stainless purity of her grace.

Mahadeva Shambo.
Mahadeva Shambo.

"Pull yourself together," Mother said. "He'll be coming soon."

She didn't have to say who "he" was.

Taking deep breaths, I calmed myself, but I couldn't help wishing we were further back among the rocks where we started before Mother, frustrated that her field of fire was too narrow, moved our sniper nest out from concealment, so that now only the lower part of our bodies were still hidden in the shadow between two boulders. Together, we built a kind of awning out of feed bags and deer brush to cover the rest of us. Lying side by side, we blended into the hillside, hopefully, with only the muzzle of Mother's heavy rifle extending beyond the edge of our cover. The fall morning was cool, but I felt sweat running out of my armpits and down my side.

"Breathe in deep," she said.

"Breathe out long," I responded and gave her a wink.

She winked back.

A volley of gunfire from the lower valley shattered the peace.

"Here we go," Mother said.

I focused the spotting scope on the canal, a mile below. Tiny as bark beetles, Dad's squad scrambled uphill, but I couldn't locate Dad among the other bugs. His people raced toward the safety of the holes where Max planned to spring her surprise. But Kali had tricks of his own. His army gave chase, but slow and steady, and well before reaching Foreman Ravine, split into three columns. One column, under the war chief Kumbakarna, pedaled bicycles up North Arm road, and into the jaws of Foreman Ravine. Another bicycle column, under the witch La Hiena, split to the left and pedaled up Diamond Mountain Road just below our sniper nest. The main group, Kali somewhere in the middle, dismounted their bikes, more than two hundred on foot, and marched up the middle of the valley. When they came to the mouth of Foreman Ravine, they didn't hesitate, but pushed on uphill, straight through the Pinch, heading for the lightly-defended barricades of Shiva Puri itself. How did they know? How had they figured out Foreman Ravine was a feint and Dad's retreat a ploy to pull them in?

A jumble, a mess, as Max would say, "a total clusterfuck." I saw her signal Cliff to fire a burst from the Rama machine gun to launch the fight in Foreman Ravine. She unloaded the green flare from the pistol, reloaded, and shot four red flares out over the valley. Plan B. In the agonizing minutes it took for her team to shift the machine gun where it could fire up the valley at Kali's center column, it was out of sight around the Spur.

Our sniper position was useless against la Hiena's column. The enemy bicycles passed below us, untouched and unseen, protected by the same outcroppings that concealed us. Nothing to do about that, but we could see the fight all the way across the valley to Foreman Ravine, about a thousand yards away. With me calling shots, Mother concentrated on taking out the rear guard. I gave her the first target, a Rakshasa who had dropped to one knee to clear a jam in his rifle. She put the crosshairs on his spine and squeezed. Keeping my scope on the target, I waited for the two seconds that it took the big fifty-caliber round to scream across the valley and into his lower back, breaking him in half like a rag doll. I gave her another target.

"Five degrees up and one degree west of the one you just got. Blue ball cap."

Lining up her second target, she squeezed the trigger. Another rag doll flopped to the ground. She continued, shooting, killing seven enemy fighters, one after another.

Down in Foreman's Ravine, Kumbakarna's troops outnumbered us two to one, but Donnie and Galen were shooting from prepared positions, and Sita machine gun was raking the Rakshasa front which had come to a dead stop causing the rear ranks to pile into their own formation. In that precious moment of confusion, Vic and Al attacked from the flanks with two skirmish lines of fifteen fighters armed with revolvers and shotguns. They closed with the Rakshasa at short range firing point blank. The Rakshasa had used up what little ammunition they had, and were reduced to flailing around with knives and clubs. As our fighters methodically shot down bad guys, Donnie's team climbed out of the holes and ran in to complete the massacre.

I swung the scope back and forth over the ravine looking for Dad. Didn't see him, but there, in the thick of it, I spotted Skyler. Magnificient! He mowed down the enemy, literally *mowed them down* with a scythe. What was that thing in his other hand? For just a second he held it up where I could see it. A human head. Kavitha's head. No mistaking that hair. The Rakshasa fell back in terror as Skyler fell on them like an avenging angel. He decapitated a man with a single swing of that blade, then another.

"Target!"

"Huh?"

"Target!" Mother repeated, calmly as if she was chatting over a cuppa tea.

I located another fighter, and she took him down. In less than two minutes, most of the Rakshasa were crumpled dead or wounded. Only Kumbakarna fought on, surrounded by his personal guard.

"Do you see him? The giant?" I asked.

"Yes. Range?"

"Two thousand yards."

Mother adjusted her sight.

"Wind?"

"Just a bit out of the west."

She adjusted her windage one click.

"Put your hand on me."

I didn't know why, but I didn't argue. I put my hand on the small of her back.

"That's nice," she said.

I saw her breathe in deep, then let it out half way. She squeezed the trigger.

Three seconds later, Kumbakarna's head burst open in a spray of lava.

CHAPTER SEVENTY-SIX

Bar the Door

THE DECISION TO BAR THE *door as told to me by Maxine Flythe. These are Max's words.*

Their fight was over before the cocksuckers realized they were beaten. Sustained fusillades from our long guns, the sweeping fire of the Sita gun across the Rakshasa front, our wild charge against the exposed flanks, and it was done except for the knot of fighters holding steady around their chief. Our people circled and bit like wolves. For a moment, I thought Kumbakarna would fight his way out to re-join the main infantry; then his head exploded in a burst of blood and brain. Only a heavy bullet could render that damage with a single shot, and there was only one place the bullet could come from. I snapped my head around and tried to locate Azriel's nest on the far ridge.

"Oh my darling," I thought, "that was a shot for the ages!"

Below me, our people mopped up the rest of Kumbakarna's column. But Kali's center force had disappeared beyond the Pinch. I shouted to my team.

"Come on, let's get those sons of bitches."

The boys grabbed Rama gun and scrambled down the hill to chase the main Rakshasa force up the valley. When we rounded the Spur, I called them to hold in place.

"Shit."

Cliff and Gil waited for orders.

"Okay. There's no way we're getting to the village before whatever is going to happen is decided. Don't look so worried. Joe will smash them and send them reeling downhill."

"There's an awful lot of them. Can Joe really hold the barricade?"

"He'll hold because I fucking well told him to hold. Or it won't matter to any of us. Now, we're going to hump this machine gun down to the canal double-time, and we're going to slam the door. Not one of those ass lickers leave this valley today."

CHAPTER SEVENTY-SEVEN

Double Clusterfuck

"WHAT'S SHE DOING?" I SHRIEKED in Mother's ear. "She's running away?"

"Shhh! Trust Max. She has a good reason for whatever bizarre thing she's doing. Stay focused and find me a new target."

I swept the spotter scope uphill looking for Kali's telltale blond ponytail. I couldn't pick him out among the jumbled mass of Rakshasa soldiers, but just ahead, I saw Sandra Grimsman lead her team out of the rocks and form a line across the upper Pinch. She held her ground against Kali's infantry for two or three minutes, then fell back toward the village in good order, delaying the Rakshasa advance as much as possible.

Below the rocks, La Hiena came out into the open where I could see her lash her troops up Diamond Mountain Road. She rode her war bike with one hand on the steering-thing, and her long braided whip in the other, cracking it over her head. Clearly, she intended to flank the village on the north, as if she knew exactly where our weaknesses could be exploited. But she didn't know about Manoj Bannerjee. Attacking downhill, Manoj and his team hurtled out of the Cook Creek gully and plowed through the middle of the witch's column, shotguns blasting, wheeled around, and came at her again. The Rakshasa dismounted and attacked Manoj on foot from all sides. Inexorably, they pushed him out onto the open ground toward the Rakshasa infantry in the center of the valley, a disaster, until Raj Bannerjee came screeching out of the second gully with the reserve team. He tore into the top of the unsuspecting Rakshasa mob, dispatching the witch with a single shotgun blast to her head. Seeing their queen down, the remnants of her column panicked and fled back the way they had come, down Diamond Mountain road and out of the fight.

The Bannerjee brothers met at the mouth of Cook Creek and embraced. I couldn't hear what they said, but it was obvious. Manoj pointed toward the village. Raj nodded. Together with their squads they jogged toward the barricade. It didn't take a geometry wiz to see that the Bannerjees were not going to make it in time.

"Stay here," Mother ordered. She dropped the M84 and raced down through the rocks. I gave her just enough time to get out of sight among the boulders before I disobeyed. Coming out into the valley, I heard her scream at Sandy Grimsman to *"Hold, hold, hold!"*

Sandy's squad retreated in good order, just in front of the Rakshasa center, zigzagging and dropping unexpectedly, as Max had drilled into them, taking advantage of every piece of cover to pop up and fire, drop, roll, come up in another place, all of it asymmetrical and unpredictable, gradually working left in a messy oblique, moving toward the north end of the village defenses in an attempt to draw the enemy after them and expose their flank to Joe's machine gun. Sandy's own fire and maneuver was having an effect. The enemy assault was running out of steam. Rakshasa with working firearms stopped to rest and reload and fire.

I saw three of Sandy's people fall.

Not Sandy, still on her feet. When she got a quarter mile from the barricade she yelled something. I couldn't hear what. Her team stopped running. Only Sandy and four were left standing, two on each side. Greg Pequinot was one. He and the other three pulled in close. Rakshasa broke away from the main body, twenty or twenty-five of them, running ahead and screaming for all they were worth, waving knives and hatchets; but by the time they got up to where Sandy was making her stand, they slowed again, out of gas. Sandy and her four remaining fighters were kneeling and squeezing shots off, careful, smooth, aiming, picking targets.

Behind the barricade women were trilling to give Sandy courage, and themselves, too, because Sandy's squad was doomed. They had been picking Rakshasa off one at a time, so by the time the enemy closed, there were not so many, maybe a dozen, and they were exhausted from marching uphill with Sandy's people killing so many of them. But there were enough left to take her down.

In the end, Sandra Grimsman and her four companions crowded together, back to back. The enemy fighters swirled on all sides, barking like coyotes. Sandy's people fired until the enemy got too close, and then they swung their rifles like clubs. I thought they were going to hold, and they did, until the front line of the main Rakshasa body pivoted in from the right, tearing into her little squad. She kept fighting, but the bad guys pushed in tighter and tighter until nobody could swing a rifle. Then it was knives and hatchets. I saw us go down one by one. Sandy fell, and there was only Greg Pequinot, until they dragged him to ground. Their blades fell like rain, over and over, and I was close enough to yell, "*Stop, stop, stop!*" but they didn't; they just kept hacking them to pieces until Kali himself came up and made them stop, dragging his own men up by the hair and screaming for them to get back in line. They formed up again and kept marching toward the barricade.

Ahead of me, Mother caught up to Al's squad. Donnie and Galen and their people were a little ways behind. There was no energy left for any of us to run, not for Mother, not for me, not, Shiva Be Praised, for the Rakshasa. Walk, stop, gasp, kneel, fire. Mother squeezed off a couple of shots from her Colt Python, but she was out of effective range. Summoning a final surge of energy, Mother sprinted toward the enemy rear. Unsheathing my Kali-Bar, I followed close on her heels. Seeing us out front by ourselves, Al, Galen, and Donnie, their squads exhausted, somewhere found the strength to give chase. We had to, absolutely had to tear into the Rakshasa before they crested the village barricade, before they got in among the children.

Joe Downing triggered the claymore mines. At last! But, of the twelve he had employed, only two detonated, both along the southernmost end of the line, doing little damage. His Laksman machine gun swept the Rakshasa front, forcing the enemy to drop for cover, but when he stopped firing, Kali knew there was only one machine gun, and that it was out of ammunition.

CHAPTER SEVENTY-EIGHT

Durga! Durga! Durga!

THE BATTLE AT THE BARRICADE *as told to me by Odessa Piwinski. These are her words.*

Behind the barricade, Joe Downing gathered everyone together except the children, who were cloistered in the mandir with

Mirabai. Only a few of us had firearms, light shotguns, and .22 single shots, and those provided with meager ammunition.

"We open up with everything we've got left," the major said. "Then we go over the wall and finish them off with axes and clubs."

There was no firearm for me, probably just as well; almost anybody else would make better use of it, my hands swollen as they are with arthritis. I pointed to a hatchet. Simone bound it tightly into my right hand with a strip of cloth. I wondered what mischief Gray Horse, the old fool, had gotten himself into down at the canal. I wished he were here to hold my other hand.

We waited behind the wagons as the Rakshasa front line got to their feet and staggered forward. Out in the open, under the midday sun, the Rakshasa were spent from the harsh climb. We may have been women and teenagers and old people, but we were fresh and rested. We had plenty of water. And we were on fire with righteous wrath.

On such small things, our Sergeant Max says, battles turn.

Joe Downing walked up and down the line, saying "Do not let them get our children. *Do not let them get our children.*" He said it over and over again, but he didn't have to. Never had such faces been seen on Shiva Puri women. Our teeth were clenched, our jaws tight, and on each forehead, the three white lines of Shiva's trident.

No fear.

Fury.

Joe gave the signal. Up and down the line, those with weapons fired every round. In the silence that followed, we could hear the Rakshasa yelling back and forth to each other. I wondered what they were saying.

Downing yelled, "Get ready."

He climbed up on a wagon waving a red and gold flag. A few of the Rakshasa might have remembered the colors of the old Marine Corps, but it was really just a fancy wool blanket impaled on the tines of a pitchfork. Downing screamed at the startled Rakshasa, now only yards away.

"Jai Shiva! Jai Shiva!"

He jumped down off the wagon and began running toward the

Rakshasa, all alone, but just for a second. We poured through the gaps in the barricade. Olivia and Radha, Suranjini and her mother Gayatri, Gayle and Cayla, Nicole and Simone Jackson-Lemko, and even me, Miss Odessa Piwinski, seventy-eight years old. Faces painted the celestial blue of Krishna and his Pandava avengers, we came out from Shiva Puri, hurling our wild war cry into the enemy. "Durga! Durga! Durga!"

The Rakshasa, stunned at the spectacle, stopped and moved a few steps backward, until someone bellowed for them to stop.

"Women. It's women! Take them."

Again, the enemy moved forward. Downing barreled into their front line trying to break the assault all by himself. Before he could thrust his pitchfork into the first man, another Rakshasa, a tall man with a long, blond hair, swept in from the side, so fast, almost a blur, and cut Downing down with a single swipe of a huge ax. Kali.

"Now!" he roared. "Take them now."

But it was too late, far too late for the army of the Kali Yuga. We slammed into them with knives and scythes. They killed five of us before their front line went down under our weight. Lord Krishna's blades flashed in his glorious morning sun.

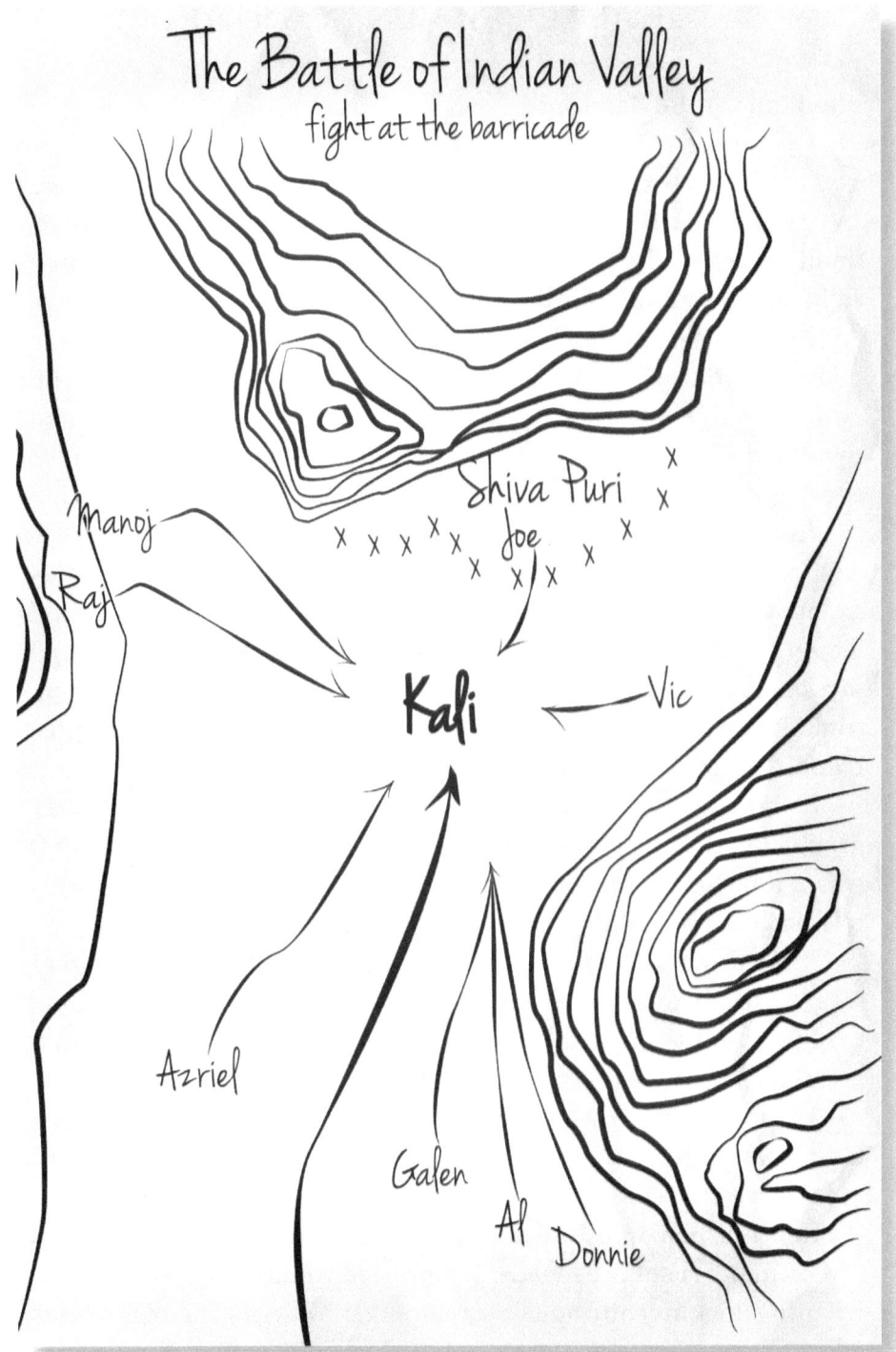

The Battle of Indian Valley
fight at the barricade

Shiva Puri

Joe

Manoj

Raj

Kali

Vic

Azriel

Galen

Al   Donnie

CHAPTER SEVENTY-NINE

The Fight at the Barricade

VIC TRETHEWAY CAME AT THEM from the right, the Bannerjees from the left. The southern squads, Galen, Al, and Donnie, finally reached the Rakshasa rear, and split the enemy formation right up the middle. Still outnumbered, Shiva Puri should have gone down, except the Rakshasa, out of ammunition and spent in body and courage, were done. Our fighters pushed into the fight, now from all sides, firing at point-blank range with shotguns and revolvers. The enemy was pressed into a disorganized jumble, every Rakshasa for himself, and at the center of the melee, Kali.

Aaaaaaaauuuuuuunnnnnn!

Roaring and slashing with great tiger paws, no, that was his ax, no, what was it? Impossible to see clearly, he was whirling and leaping. A distortion of the air enveloped him, like looking through my kaleidoscope, his form broken into facets, sometimes human, sometimes animal, fang and claw and glowing eye, mauling us, blood, and limbs, and severed heads, tearing us to pieces.

Forcing my way toward him, I was jerked off my feet. Somebody grabbed me from behind and threw me to the ground. Thinking it was a Rakshasa, I curled up and covered my head with my arms to ward off his strike. No blow fell. Mother.

"Stay down," she said. "This will be over in a minute." Mother was standing over me firing her revolver, firing and reloading, firing and reloading. I could see Kali bounding toward us, and it seemed as if he was coming on all fours, a great feline shape, now a man, now a tiger, flickering back and forth, back and forth, man, tiger, man, tiger, but always those same unblinking yellow eyes. Mother's bullets couldn't touch him.

Kali crashed into her taking both of them to the ground on top of me. Crushed beneath, I could feel them tangled together, writhing, kicking, hitting. No screaming, no cursing, just the grunts and panting of two powerful beings locked together in a fight to the death. I felt hot blood pour down over my chest. I managed to get my arm out from under me, my grip firm on the hilt of the Ka-Bar. I tried to roll over. No chance. One of the fighters on top of me went limp. Suddenly the crushing weight was gone. Kali bent Mother over backward, with his hands around her throat. She hammered both fists into the sides of his head. I got to my feet and threw myself at them, stabbing down in the hollow where his shoulder meets his neck, over and over I stabbed with the great bitch, Jolene, my blade slicing past the bone and sinking to the hilt deep into the muscle between his shoulder and his neck. He released his grip on Mother's throat and dropped her, whirled around, and batted me away with a backhand sweep of his fist. He was trying to pull my knife out when a bullet hit him in the side, knocking him to the ground. He crawled over to where he had dropped his great ax. Retrieving it, he got to his feet, my knife still wedged in his shoulder. He roared for his men. In seconds, Lord Kali, the Eater of Worlds, and what was left of his defeated army, disappeared into the dust and smoke.

CHAPTER EIGHTY

Alma

As KALI RALLIED HIS REMAINING fighters, I heard Mirabai call for help—not a scream of panic, just the usual serene summons that sounded like soft-struck temple bells.

"Come quickly. Alma is here."

I scrambled to my feet and ran full speed toward the mandir. Bursting in through the door, I saw Mirabai sitting with her back against the lingam, her arms around three frightened toddlers, two screaming babies in her lap. Across the room, Alma Mendez pulled her bloody screwdriver out of the chest of another woman.

Nithinya? I hurled myself at my old adversary, "hard" fist cocked as Max had taught me, twisting from the shoulder, with all my weight behind the punch. Alma turned around just in time for me to land my strike right in the side of her face, knocking her into the wall, but not off her feet. Unsure what to do next, I stood there as Alma shook her head and recovered. Too late, I realized I should have followed up my first punch with many more. Alma launched herself at me, swinging the screw driver down. I grabbed for the weapon, blocking its descent into my heart. Locked together, chest to chest like lovers, Alma swung me around and into the wall, where we stared at each other, eye to eye, the point of the screwdriver now aimed at my throat.

"I didn't think you'd come," Alma said through clenched teeth.

"We have unfinished karma," I spit back in her face.

"That we do," she panted. "Kali Man told me to bring him your prissy twat so he could pick up where he left off."

"Your Kali Man has run away," I said, gasping for air. "I put my knife into his neck... and he's running... for his life. He's gone... and he left you here all alone."

Doubt flickered across Alma's face.

"I don't believe you." She pushed the sharp point closer to my skin.

"Do you hear any more fighting?"

Her eyes flicked toward the open door. It took a few seconds for the silence to register.

"Doesn't matter. I'm gonna kill you and your sister and all these little Yoogies."

Using her weight, Alma leaned into me, one hand wrapped around the hilt of the screwdriver, the heel of her other hand on the metal end cap, driving it down from the shoulder with all her strength behind it. I tightened my grip on Alma's wrists and resisted with everything I had. It was enough. In the years since she had run away, I had grown up. She, who had always seemed so monstrous, was just another woman, and I was now stronger, much stronger. Alma clenched her teeth and bore down on the screwdriver. Easily, I held. Alma panted; the foul saliva from her rotting mouth dripped onto my face.

"Kali... Kali... Kali."

Incrementally, pushing the screwdriver away from my throat, I answered, "Shiva... Shiva... Shiva." My strength was irresistible. In desperation, Alma hooked my ankle and toppled the two of us to the ground, our legs entwined and locked together, Alma on top, but just for an instant. I flipped her over; now I was above. My fingers sank into Alma's wrist, causing her to scream and loosen her grip on the screwdriver, just a little, but enough for me to reverse the direction of the blade so it was now pointing toward her throat. I shoved down on the hilt, using my body weight as well as my newfound strength, to bring the sharpened tip into the skin covering Alma's larynx.

Alma's eyes opened wide in surprise. She smiled.

I paused.

"You can't do it, can you?" she whispered.

"Why didn't you just stay away?" I whispered back. "Why didn't you just leave us alone?"

"I'll eat your sister while you watch."

Alma's threat paralyzed me for a second, and she used the lapse to pull her hands away from my wrists. Instantly, the screwdriver, with all my weight behind it, plunged into, and through, Alma's neck, and deep into the floor. I jerked away and fell backward, scrambled a few feet away, my back to the wall, and watched horrified as Alma dragged her body around in a circle with her heels, hands on the hilt of the screwdriver, her head pinned to the floor. The great meditation hall of Shiva Puri was silent except for Alma's gasps for air. When, at last, I thought it was done, I crawled on hands and knees over to her body.

She was still alive. Her lips were drawn back, exposing the hideous teeth.

"Pri... Pri... Pri... ," she hissed through the crimson froth that bubbled from her throat.

I finished for her, "Prissy."

CHAPTER EIGHTY-ONE

I See You, Marine

KALI'S FAREWELL AS TOLD TO *me by Maxine Flythe. These are her words.*

Fuck me. We should have destroyed them all. I opened up with Rama gun, and Rakshasa started falling, but even in the moment of final defeat, Kali held a few men together. Splitting left and right, they swept around the ends of our position, one of them triggering the last Bouncing Betty. The booby trap hung in the air just long enough for the Rakshasa to realize he was dead. The blast decapitated the motherfucker, the final casualty of the Battle for Indian Valley.

Kali and the dozen who were still alive stumbled across North Valley Road and rejoined the forty or fifty who had run from their defeat at Cook Creek. More terrified of Kali than they were of our guns, they mounted their bicycles and sped off to the south.

All but one.

Kali limped back across the road toward me and into the lower field. He tried to light a reefer, but he couldn't lift his arm. For good reason. The Ka-Bar I gave you was sticking out of his shoulder.

"Hey," he shouted, "give me a light."

I came out from behind the wagon. We stared at each other.

Kali yelled across the field, "Are you a man or a woman?"

I yelled back, "Gunnery sergeant."

"I thought I knew you. The marine bitch. Right?"

I gave him a slow insolent salute.

"Ha. I like you, bitch, even though you tried to shoot me."

"Guess I missed, but it looks like someone shoved a blade in your neck. Does it hurt?"

"Not so much."

"Too bad."

"Say, give a fellow a hand and pull it out, if it's not too much trouble."

"No, I like it just where it is."

The demon laughed and extended the reefer toward me.

"Want a hit?"

"Another time," I answered.

"Sure, we'll sit down, smoke weed, make friends."

"Now there's an idea, but let me ask you something."

"Shoot."

"Before we smoke, how would you like to lick the shit from my ass?"

"Ha. Good one. But before I lick, I will slake my thirst with your blood."

"Yeah," I said, "how's that working for you? Didn't you come here this morning with a great big army for some, what did you call it, slaking? The slaking army I just destroyed?"

"What army? That puddle of piss-ants? Pah! Soon, I shall show you such an army as will fill this valley from side to side. I will come in the spring, and I will take back what is mine, starting with that other cunt, the pretty one I fucked in the woods."

Okay, that was it. I'd had enough of his bullshit. I walked toward him un-holstering my empty .45 and pulling the slide back as if locking a live round in the receiver.

"The .45 talks, and bullshit walks," I bluffed.

Kali pointed at his eye.

"I see you, Marine."

I stopped about twenty feet away and pointed the muzzle of my gun, first at my eye, and then at him, sighting down the barrel at his head.

"I see you, Kali Man."

We stared at each other for a while, wondering who was going to make a move. He nodded, turned his back, and limped across the road where he had parked his bike. One last grin, and the demon pedaled off after his men, his useless arm hanging by his side. I could only watch him ride away, my Ka-Bar sticking out of his shoulder. Damn. That was a good knife.

Chapter Eighty-Two

War Stories

S KYLER JONES RAN INTO THE mandir.

"Azriel sent me to help."

No one answered. He looked around. Blood puddled on the floor of the most sacred place in our village. I was weeping over Nithinya, my friend and teacher. Alma Mendez was pinned to the floor with a screwdriver in her windpipe.

Skyler walked over to Mirabai, who was singing lullabies to the children.

"Are you okay?"

"Jai Shiva," she said.

He came over to me.

"How you doing, Janabee?"

"Have you seen Dad?" I answered his question with one of my own.

"No. He didn't come up the hill."

I began to panic.

"Will you... ?"

"Yes, I'll take care of things here. Go find your father."

I ran back to the field, asking everybody if they had seen Dad. Mother was holding Joe Downing in her arms, moaning like an animal, her head thrown back, the bruises from Kali's hands, a necklace of black finger prints, around her neck. I squatted down in front of her.

"Is he... ?"

I didn't know what to say. All around me the cries of wounded men and women, the stink of shit and piss, the drifting clouds of gun powder. Overhead, turkey vultures circled, the tips of their wings rocking back and forth, back and forth.

"Mother? Mother, look at me."

She raised her head.

"Have you seen Dad? Do you know where he is?"

She didn't, or couldn't, answer, but she motioned with her head in the direction of Lynda Cheng, who was carrying the front end of a stretcher.

"Shiva's blessings on Joe Downing," was all I could manage.

"Thank you," Mother whispered, barely audible. I ran over to the table where Lynda was tending a wounded fighter. Galen Raether. No, please, not Galen.

"Will he be all right?"

"Ask me later," Lynda answered.

"Have you seen my dad come through here?"

"He never left the canal," Lynda said. "He told Jeannie he wouldn't come."

"She left him?"

"Jana, she was fighting for her life."

"Is he still at the canal?"

"Ask Max," Lynda said. "Cliff said she was still down there."

I didn't get far. I saw Dad moving toward me through the battlefield. He walked to one of the fallen, knelt down, said a prayer. Finished, he moved to another body and repeated his small ceremony. I didn't want to interrupt him, so I sat on the bare ground and waited until he drew near. I got to my feet.

"Are you hurt?" Dad asked.

"Beat up a little," I said.

"Your mother?"

"Up there a ways." I pointed.

"Is she okay?"

"She's hurt. Not too bad."

"What's she doing?"

"Holding Major Downing."

"Is he wounded?"

"No," I said. "He's dead."

Dad raised one hand to wipe away tears.

"Aw, no. Not Joe. He was my... brother, in spite of everything."

I grabbed him and hugged him to me like he was the child and I the parent. He cried and howled like an animal. Then it was my turn to let it go and feel the shock wash through me. How long did we stand there shuddering and wailing in each other's arms? I lost all sense of time. The terror of this day was too vast for either of us to comprehend. Eventually, we ran out of tears, and out of breath. Panting, Dad dropped his arms and let go of me.

"I better go to your mother."

"That would be good," I said. "Dad?"

"Hmmm?"

"You don't need the knife anymore."

He looked down at the blood-drenched knife in his hand. He held it up in front of his face and stared as if he had never seen it before, as if he had no idea how it got in his hand.

"Let me take it. Dad? Dad, give it to me."

The way he looked at me, his eyes blank, I could tell he was losing his grip. It took him a few seconds to focus on me.

"Dad. Drop the knife, please, and go help Mother."

He let it fall out of his hand. Forgetting about me, he walked on up the hill.

"Dad," I said, "I love you."

He didn't answer, just kept moving toward Mother. I continued down the valley toward the canal, threading my way through the bodies, Shivite and Rakshasa.

I found Max sitting on one of the upturned wagons. She smiled and nodded.

"Yo, Durga-Max," I said.

"Yo, Janabai," Max answered.

"She's alive," I said, knowing what was foremost in her mind. Max closed her eyes and let out a deep breath. I climbed up next to her.

"You know what I want?" Max asked.

"No. What do you want?"

"A cigarette."

"Never seen one, but if I had one, I'd give it to you."

"Thanks."

"You know what I'd do if I had two cigarettes?"

"What would you do?"

"I'd sit right here on this wagon and smoke a cigarette with you. Wouldn't that be something?"

"Yes, Janabai, it would be quite a sight."

We sat there for a while, watching the sun going down.

At last, Max asked, "How many did we lose?"

"I don't know. A lot. Galen, Nithinya, Manoj, I think, and Joe."

"The major is gone?"

I nodded.

"Semper fidelis," Max said.

"Always..." I tried to respond, but couldn't finish the line.

"Faithful," Max said, "always faithful."

I discovered I still had plenty of tears left. I wept for the loved ones I had lost. I wept for the constant struggle to stay alive, for never feeling safe, for always teetering on the edge of destruction. I wept for our beautiful world, more dangerous, more precarious than I ever imagined. I wept for faith lost and hatred found. I wept, Max's arms around me, until it got pitch dark. Out of tears, again, I wiped the snot from my nose.

"Where was Dad during the fight?"

"I found him curled up in the canal, bleeding from a head wound; didn't seem too serious. His right hand was wrapped around a fish scaling knife, the blade jammed to the hilt in the throat of a Rakshasa. Can you picture that?"

I couldn't.

"Your father was alive, but out of it. We put him on a stretcher to carry him up to triage, but as soon as he felt us moving him, he sat up and told us to put him down. He was okay, he said. He could walk. Put him down. I tried to argue with him. He was waving his knife around like he was still fighting. We put him down."

"Why didn't you take the knife away?" I asked.

"Because he's a grown man," she said, "and it's his knife."

In her mind, that was enough.

"Will Kali be coming back?"

"Don't think so," Max said. "We hammered him today. A few of his men got away. He won't have the juice to come for us. Not till spring. Maybe never."

"Why didn't you kill him?" I asked.

"I wanted to, Janabai, but I was out of ammo. Up close he

would have killed me, even wounded like he was. I wouldn't have a chance. Mean son of a bitch, isn't he?"

"You have no idea," I said.

"Don't worry, honey, someday, your mother will put a bullet in his head."

"Maybe."

"Maybe? Don't you doubt Azriel Dancer. She's got the mojo."

"She saved me already," I said, "up there in front of the barricade."

"Well, there you go. That's what I'm talking about. So, what say you go find your Mother and see what you can do for her?"

"What about you?" I asked.

"I'll just stay here and keep an eye out."

"Maybe I'll just stay here with you. Okay?"

"Hmmm," Max smiled.

We sat there in the dark listening to the crickets.

"Tell me a story," I said.

"About what?"

"About you. Back before. When you were a marine. Tell me marine stories."

"Well, let's see..."

Max told stories about when she went to war in foreign countries. After a while, she got tired.

"Now, it's your turn. You tell me a story from one of your books."

"Haven't you read them?" I asked.

"Not much of a reader. Never have been. Mostly I cut school and went hunting."

"Okay, Max," I said, "how about *The Old Man and the Sea*?"

"Sounds like a good one."

I told her the story, as much as I could remember, and when it seemed to go well, I tried *Of Mice and Men*.

Max told more war stories.

I mangled Poe's *The Pit and the Pendulum*, and we both enjoyed how I changed the ending so the general did *not* get there in time and the bad man fell into the fiery pit, his long golden ponytail whipping around his horrified face.

"Take that, you yellow-haired ass licker," Max said.

"Yeah," I said, "yellow-haired ass licker."

In the darkest hour of the early morning, when my book stories were all told, Max said: "Tell me about Sandy. And don't leave anything out."

I told her about Sandra Grimsman's last stand.

"She saved us," I said. "We could never have held the barricade, too few of us and the babies and the kids and the old people. She stopped Kali long enough for Mother and the other squads to get there. Sandra Grimsman died to save us."

"I'm glad you're the one to tell me," Max said.

"Was she your... you know?"

"Was she my lover? Is that what you want to know?"

"If you want to tell me."

Then it was Max's turn to curl up with her arms over her head and wail. *Don't you dare tell anybody.*

Sometime before dawn, Skyler and Jeannie came down to relieve us. Max and I walked up through the valley, a half-moon and stars our only light. As we got close to the village, we could hear women and men crying over the bodies of their loved ones, one voice louder than the others. Azriel Dancer was keening, like a wolf for her lost mate. Max and I came to stand over her and saw she was not alone. Dad was holding Mother in his arms, rocking her back and forth, Joe Downing's head in her lap.

Chapter Eighty-Three

The Fallen

THE MEDICS CLEANED DAD'S HEAD wound and carried him to his bed. Turning his face to the wall, he rolled over, shaking, his skin gaunt, eyes squeezed shut. He wouldn't, or couldn't, speak. Only Mirabai, sitting next to him, with her hand on him, humming bhajans, brought him comfort. She stayed with him through the night.

The next afternoon he came out of his room, looking like a pale ghost of himself.

"Let's get to work," he whispered.

"Aye, aye, sir," Max said. "Where would you like to start?"

"With the dead. Bring me the names of the dead."

"As you wish."

That evening, Dad posted his final roster, the last piece of business he would ever perform as manager of Shiva Puri Village, his parting gift.

The Fallen of Shiva Puri
Kavitha Bose
Donald Simms
Greg Pequinot
Shanna Wentz
Rhonda Beckwith
Radha Mehta
Abhinav Devi
Gayatri Devi
Al Rudelic
Ted Kealoha
Miguel Dominquez
Kay Escobar
Nicole Loera
Elle Shergill
Gilbert Adams
Charity Masera
Nithinya Varanasi
Marianne Conroy
Taylor Raines
Kelsey Raines
Collin Raines
Mahesh Chowdary
Aaron Magalski

Shivankar Rangarajam
Sierra Reed
Priety Das
Bobby Eversole
Dalisa Gaw
Ashdep Mondul
Kelly Cassio
Suekyung Adams
Cathy Kessler
Mark Wycoff
Manoj Bannerjee
Sandra Grimsman
Galen Raether
and
Major Joseph Downing, USMC

We lost thirty-six valiant comrades, almost as many as we managed to add during the previous twenty years through births and recruitment; we were back to the same numbers as we were at the end of the first Rakshasa winter, two hundred on our feet, another forty wounded but expected to live. None of our kids were harmed. All of the animals were safe. It could have been so much worse.

Karma. How much karma did we make? Who can say? We slew 315 Rakshasa. We took no prisoners. The Rakshasa soldiers, if you can call them such, were a sorry lot, emaciated, filthy, crawling with lice; astonishing so many of them charged all the way up the hill. Our fighters were healthier, stronger, and when our women came out to fight hand to hand, we were more than a match for the exhausted Rakshasa men, but here's the spooky part, something that still gives me nightmares: eighteen of the Rakshasa dead were women. Women. Our sisters. No. Not our sisters. Something else.

Max worried about the dozens who got away, especially Kali. Why did he head south instead of north? Where was he going? When would he come back?

"If he does," Max said, "it will be a different fight. Kali will not underestimate us a second time. He knows who I am and what I can do. He knows I have trained fighters. He knows he fucked up when he split his force into three columns. He won't make those mistakes again."

We didn't know it then, of course not, how could we, but our great victory would lead to an unexpected swerve in the story of Shiva Puri. For all of her visionary powers, her astonishing talent for knowing the road ahead, even Mother didn't see this one coming. We, the women who came over the wall, who followed Joe Downing, who turned the tide of the battle, who fought the enemy toe to toe, became Lord Shiva's warriors on that day. I'm not talking about Mother and Max, of course, and the tough women hunters Max had trained over the years, her "marines," they were already fighters, but also the women cooks and weavers and potters and shepherds and teachers and storekeepers and farmers. Even dear Odessa, our elderly librarian, and I shouldn't say "even." Miss Piwinski will probably be the last of us to fall.

The women of Shiva Puri were changed.

So too the men, but not in the way you might expect.

CHAPTER EIGHTY-FOUR

A New Order

AFTER THE BATTLE, DAD WITHDREW, even from me. He spent most of his time in the mandir, wrapped in his prayer shawl. Raj Bannerjee likewise retreated to the mandir. More and more of the men folk withdrew, and then all of them, spreading their blankets on the mandir floor and sleeping there. We brought them food, which they accepted, and they came out when necessary for sanitation, but most of them were "in silence," so I failed to discover what they were up to in there — and Parvati knows, I tried.

One afternoon, G-Mek came to me. By this time I was the unofficial, but generally acknowledged, village manager, filling in for my father until he found whatever he was looking for. G-Mek told me Dad wanted my sister in the mandir. It hurt my feelings. Why Mirabai and not me? Or both of us? I was Dad's favorite, wasn't I? Mirabai had Max. I had Dad.

No, I *didn't* have Dad, and I missed him like crazy.

I found Mirabai in the goat pasture. G-Mek, stationed at the door of the mandir, politely invited me to deposit Mirabai with him, and, no, I was not needed at the moment. Until I was "required," he said, I should take myself elsewhere. I stomped off in a huff, but it was true, I had plenty of elsewheres to go.

Mother and I, working together as never before, began the hard-nosed labor of getting ourselves sorted out, nursing the wounded, assigning new members to fill gaping holes in seva teams, dragging the Rakshasa bodies to a dry gulch, and, hardest of all, building funeral pyres for departed beloved. The men came out to help, then returned to the mandir without speaking a word. No consolation from them. Our grief, crawling up from unimaginable depths to unendurable heights, the loss of friends and family, parents and children, brothers and sisters, husbands and wives, should have paralyzed us, but we had reservoirs of strength, we women of Shiva Puri.

What were the men up to in there? We had no idea, but we needed them to get their butts out *here*, or we were in serious trouble with winter pressing hard. Losing Galen Raether was terrifying. Karisma, Galen's second-in-charge, was a smart and experienced farmer, but she was in over her head. We had relied on Galen so long, so utterly, to run our farm. Without him, every man was needed; *not* sitting in there doing manly things, or whatever, but out *here*, on the farm, working their manly fingers to the bone.

Please, Daddy, come back.

After eight days of seclusion, G-Mek came to tell Mother the men had concluded their meditation and were coming out to resume their sevas. *Sevas?* What about their *lives?*

We sent runners to summon the women who were out in the

barns and storehouses. Already November winds whipped the valley. I remember shivering and moving close to Mother, who put her arm around me. How good that felt! I put my arm around her. We stood there, the women of Shiva Puri, waiting for our men.

The mandir doors swung open. All the lamps and candles had been extinguished. My father walked slowly out of the dark. He was wearing ceremonial orange robes and carrying an assault rifle in one hand. With the other he was holding Mirabai's hand. What an odd contradiction! Guru and gun. At least he was smiling, as were the other men who followed in procession, likewise wearing the orange robes, and each carrying a firearm.

My father, Daniel Kucinich, fifty-two years old, walked up to the woman who used to be his wife. Mother slid her arm from around my waist and took a step forward to meet him. They stood face-to-face, neither speaking, Dad smiling, Mother without expression. He knelt down and placed the rifle at her feet, stood, let go of Mirabai's hand, and took Mother by the shoulders and kissed her on the mouth, softly, so softly, the kiss of a ghost. As it turned out, that was a pretty good description. Mother accepted his spooky smooch — what else was she going to do, the whole village watching? I was a couple of feet away. *Strange* doesn't come close to describing the moment.

Dad pulled his hands from her shoulders and took a few steps backward, his eyes never leaving hers. One by one, beginning with Vic Tretheway, the men came forward and placed their weapons on the ground at her feet, and, having done so, regrouped behind my father. Last to come was Raj Bannerjee, Mother's most loyal devotee.

"*Et tu*, Brute?"

Later, Odessa told me what that meant.

Raj nodded and dropped his eyes.

"What say you, men of Shiva Puri?" Mother asked.

"Never again will we pick up firearms."

With those words, began the Order of Nonviolence.

I stole a glance at Max, jaw clenched, face of granite. I moved closer to Mother, now sole leader of our people. She was smiling. I touched her arm and she looked down at me.

"Don't fret, Daughter, I have seen this."

Max snapped her head around and stared at Mother for a few seconds, spun on her heel, and walked away, leaving her curse hanging in the air, loud enough for all to hear.

"Pussies."

CHAPTER EIGHTY-FIVE

Nomads

JUST WHAT WE NEEDED. MAX and Mother at odds. We had suffered unimaginable losses in one battle, and our men-folk were... I don't even know how to describe it. Spirits of the air? Renunciants? The word Max used? Pussies? Oh, let's be fair. After their big "renouncement," the men got back to work, harder than ever, and with purpose and energy, as if they had something to prove. Who could complain?

Max.

Down to twelve hunters, all women, eight veterans from Dad's original roster and four "boots" who had taken hunter seva on Offering Days, Max argued we were dangerously vulnerable; we were, in her words, "in deep shit." She had lost five men in the fight and three to the "New Order of Pussies," as she spoke of them scornfully, including, and this was the most bitter pill, Skyler Jones, whom she had previously asserted to be "officer material." Skyler asked to be accepted into the seva of medicine, where he could take Kavitha's place.

"So, you're saying—stay with me, Skyler—" Max sneered "—you're saying if you had to shoot a scumbag Rakshasa to save Janabai, who you say you love like a sister, you wouldn't pick up a gun, stand tall, and defend her? You'd sit there on your innocent, non-violent, sweet little man ass, and let the monster rape and kill and do whatever he wanted to Janabai while you watch?"

Skyler didn't answer. He looked into Max's eyes for a few seconds, lowered his head, nodding just a little bit.

"Wait a minute. What does that nod mean? You *would* defend us? Or are you nodding agreement with my opinion of you as a chicken-shit quitter? Which?"

"Leave him alone," I said.

"No, Janabai, your friend does not get a pass; not from me, not this day. What's it going to be, Skyler? When the time comes, and it's gonna come, can I trust you?"

"I've taken a vow," he said.

"I shit on your vow," Max said.

That evening she asked for volunteers from among the blue-headed warrior women of Shiva Puri. Fifty-one hands went up. Like I said, big changes happening in our village. Now Max had another problem, how to choose from among them.

"Janabai," she said, "I'm going to need your help to sort this out. See who we can switch around."

I was happy to be tasked with the job, anything to feel useful. I needed to get to work. Our village in shambles, who was in charge now that the men, whose "vow" had forced us into a desperate scramble, were drifting around like spit bubbles? Mother appointed new leaders to consist of herself, Max, Jeannie Zarou, Simone Jackson-Lemko (combining stores and kitchens under her sole supervision), Karisma Gupta (our new boss farmer), Deanna Stickles (taking over herds, permanently; Raj Bannerjee, destroyed by the death of his brother, was out of the picture), and Kristen Padilla (cattle boss until Bill Lemko returned from the Cosmic Cattle Roundup in the Sky or wherever he was).

And me, Janabai Shepherd, aged twenty-one-almost, freshly-churned village manager, until my father came to his senses.

Vic Tretheway was the only man to return as boss mechanic.

There we were, the New Council of New Shiva Puri. Mother listened to our opinions, conferred with Max, made the decisions, and turned us loose to make it happen. Though they disagreed on the subject of the Order of Non-Violence, Mother defending the men, and Max thinking the whole thing was the stupidest idea she had ever heard, they finally agreed on one thing.

The necessity for us to pack up and move.

For Mother, an expedition to find good farmland away from the Lassen volcano lined up with her plan to keep Shiva Puri nomadic, flexible, pliable, moving to resources and away from danger. Max, came to the same decision, but for a different reason.

"Our position here is no longer defensible. Kali knows the ground," she said. "Our best chance is to run like hell."

"Then, jump to it," Mother said, looking around at us. "We'll pull out after the last snow, or March fifteen, whichever comes first."

I jumped. Or tried to. But the truth was, I was in over my head and drowning. Managing Shiva Puri looked easy when someone else was making the big decisions and following up on all the little details. Jobs were left unfinished, or not done at all, even though I told someone to do them, and then they said I *never* told them, and I said I *did* tell them, and then I remembered I was *going* to tell them and forgot, and then everyone was mad at me, or so it seemed, and the rabbits didn't get fed for days and two of them died.

Mother pulled me aside. "Janabai, if you can bring your father back to earth, and back to work as well, that would be most helpful."

After Dad dropped his gun at Mother's feet, they treated each other with great tenderness, like beloved little brother and gentle big sister, but she couldn't pin him down. What did he want? What was he going to do? Mother figured I had a better chance of finding out, and she was right. When I talked to him, I would get peeks at whatever was happening inside him. He would be answering my question, stop, freeze, and stare off at something only he could see, no expression, suddenly smile, not a small bemused smile, but a glorious grin of delight. He'd look around slowly until I came into view and stop. I could actually see his eyes refocus on me, one of them, anyway, because I swear he had one eye looking out at me, and the other looking inward at something else. At the same time.

"Janabai," he'd ask in surprise, "when did you get here?"

The other men now regarded Dad as a high priest or something. He was living more on the celestial plane than the material. Sweet, but not particularly useful. Perhaps, he was just was broken beyond repair. One day, I found him wandering with Mirabai near Cook's Creek. They were holding hands, but I couldn't tell who was leading whom.

"Janabai, chrysalis about to fly, is that you?"

"Yes, Daddy, it's me."

"No, I mean is that YOU," he said with added emphasis on the "you" to make sure I knew he was talking about higher consciousness.

"Mirabai," I said to my twin, who was acting more like my father's twin than my own, "help."

She responded, saying, "Tat Tvam Asi."

"True, yes, sister, of course, I Am That, but That is not especially useful way down here on the earthly sphere, in this exact moment, when I am trying to deal with our loopy father."

Officially, Dad "requested" he be accepted into temple seva, where he and Mirabai would assist Annabel with programs. His request was accepted—what else was Annabel going to say? Now Mirabai and Dad were inseparable, morning and night. I felt isolated and abandoned and sick to my stomach.

"Dad," I said, "listen to me. We need you to come back to work as our manager. All of us *need* you. I need you. No one can do it but you."

"There is one hummingbird, and Thou Art That. You can... be there... hovering... Now, quick, fly to the flowers and suck the nectar."

With such floral malarky Dad dumped his seva into my lap. I guess he got his wish after all. I was following his footsteps, the new manager of Shiva Puri. The seva was mine, all mine, and I better step up and learn how to do it. Did I want it? The responsibility? The work? In fact, I did. Simone said I was suffering from severe depression. Seriously? Me? Depressed? Yes! I would work myself back to sanity. I would drown in work, from daylight to nightfall, and even in my dreams, a seva to keep me from thinking about our predicament. Volcanic ash covered everything, the village was critically reduced in people and skills, every one of us suffered from *peetee essdee*, Kali promised to return in the spring, bringing a vast army to wipe us out, and our men had taken vows of non-violence.

What else could go wrong?

CHAPTER EIGHTY-SIX

What I Missed

IN MID-NOVEMBER, I MISSED MY period. It never came, and I was so preoccupied with mastering my new duties as manager, I didn't notice. That's what I mean by *missed* my period. Grieving the loss of so many loved ones, and impossibly overworked, I wasn't paying attention. So December rolled around, my special December because I would be twenty-one years old, and I was thinking I would bust my bubble exactly on my birthday, but the fifteenth came and went, and Christmas too, and a few more days. Not a spot. That's when I got concerned and tried to remember back, a month earlier, to my last period. When did I start? When did I finish? Only then did it snap into focus. I had missed two periods in a row. Holy shit! Dead certain, it's a fact, don't try to kid yourself, Janabai. You are pregnant. Preggers. With child. Caught.

One week after that epiphany, my nipples grew too tender to touch. I experienced unusual sensitivity to light (too bright), to sound (too loud). Morning sickness? You think? And afternoon sickness. Midnight chunks? Four a.m.? Name the hour, and count on me to present you with the steaming contents of my stomach. Deep in my belly I felt that... *thing*... sliding around inside me, writhing and wiggling, sucking at my organs, a worm, a slug, a parasite eating me alive, a malevolent, malignant cancer, growing, festering corruption.

I'd wake up crying, crawl off of the cot I'd set up in Dad's office, dry my tears, and get to work. I drifted through the day like a ghost, going through the motions, not really being in my life; mouthing the words to the evening chants, but not believing them; closing my eyes in meditation, but feeling nothing. Dry as dust, numb to everything around me until some random thing set off another crying spell. I didn't want to talk to anybody, not even my sister, and I didn't want anything to do with men, not G-Mek, and not even Skyler, especially not Skyler, and that's a shame, because he really needed me, and I didn't have anything to give him. When the work day ended, I'd fall back onto my cot, pull the blanket over my head, and cry myself to sleep.

I knew I had to make this disaster known, but before I gathered the nerve to brace Mother, I sought the midwife's advice. Kerilynn said the embryo was way too small for me to feel anything, just a tiny bundle of cells, hanging on the wall of my womb, oblivious and serene, peacefully growing into a beautiful baby. She told me over and over again that the baby was innocent, and that I was innocent. She was wrong, of course. Had I not disobeyed Mother and dragged Kavitha along on that stupid adventure to save Gray Horse? Was I not responsible for getting my best friend killed, for getting myself raped, for the war that followed, for all the death and heartbreak, and for my own disastrous situation? Still, I beseeched Parvati, "O Divine Mistress, what enormous crime have I done to deserve this fate? What unforgivable sin did I commit so foul as to bring this destruction down upon us?"

Kerilynn said that I was prideful, that my ego thought itself so grand as to be responsible for all the miseries of the world. So foolish, she said, to make myself unhappy trying to unravel the mysteries of karma. That perhaps everything that happened to me, and was still happening, was inevitable, and for a purpose, and that I had no idea what that purpose might be, and more so, that the purpose might be good, or even glorious, if Mother was to be believed. Perhaps I served, unwillingly and unknowingly, as the vehicle for divine deliverance, important in some way, and blessed to serve the gods. Sure, Kerilynn, perhaps I would grow wings out of my butt and fly off to heaven and ask Shiva what the fuck he was up to.

The midwife's words were true; I knew this in my mind, but in my heart, I wanted the... *thing*... out of me. I wanted it to die. What if I gave birth and the *thing* was a monster like his father, or worse, and I was the unholy bitch that whelped it into the world? And what of the sire? The old man? The procreator and begetter? The ever-loving daddy? I was terrified. Surely the demon would come back to claim his... child? He would feel it, of course he would, evil reaching out to evil, pulling Kali to me like blood scent draws a tiger. He would be there, always, behind me, in the shadows, waiting for his chance, watching with those yellow cat eyes.

Okay, Janabai, snap out of it. Let's get this done.

"Mom. I need your help. I'm in big trouble."

Chapter Eighty-Seven

My Choice

A LL THINGS CONSIDERED, MY MOTHER took the news her daughter had been impregnated by a demon pretty well. Too damned well, if you want my opinion. Before I could blurt it out, she gave me the shush sign with her finger. She gestured for me to sit at the small table in the small kitchen in the small house where she and Joe Downing had lived until... This was the first time I had been here since Joe was... you know. I sat there in their home and watched Mother moving around, quietly and efficiently, stoking the fire, reheating the tea. Joe's winter coat was still hanging from a peg near the door, his log book on the table, open as if he had been called away for a moment.

Mother brought two mugs and sat down across from me, her face in the steam of her cup, inhaling. I did the same. Maybe I could keep this tea down. We looked up together. Eyeball to eyeball. No turning back now.

"How did you know?" I asked.

"There were several possibilities. You could be sick. Your father might have floated away to the heavens. But from the look on your face, I'd have to guess it's more serious even than that. Go on, Daughter, say the words."

I did.

"Tell me how you know you're pregnant?"

I did.

"Who's the father?"

Gets right to the point, doesn't she? Well, having been, you know, abstinent for as long as I could remember, months anyway, there was no doubt about the identity of the yellow-eyed papa, outlaw, rapist, or demon, or something else, depending on who you asked.

Mother smiled, a small grimace is more like it, and nodded.

"Okay."

"Okay?"

"Okay, I know what's been eating you; and okay, we can handle this; and okay, I know what to do next?"

"And that is... ?"

"Get us some advice."

Mother's idea of getting advice was to summon the people she trusted and have a meeting about "Janabai's situation." She was thoughtful, thanks for small favors, in arranging the benches in a circle so I didn't feel so much like Hester Prynne about to be tattooed with a scarlet letter *P* between my eyes. The assembled advisors were about who I expected: Simone Jackson, Annabel (to make sure we were minding our dharma), Lynda Cheng and Kerilynn Fleenor (who already knew), Max, just because, and

Dad, because, you know, in spite of his astral planing, I was still his daughter. "Hello, Dad? Look at me."

When we got down to it, the decision was simple. I knew the word "abortion." I had read about it, and during those December days after I made the "discovery," I studied every word written about it in the library. I would abort, terminate the pregnancy, destroy the fetus, kill the baby, whatever. Or? Or I could carry the baby and give birth to him or her or it.

Once the options were hanging out there in the air, greasy and fetid, making everybody's eyes sting, we looked at the first possibility. Could Lynda, our boss of medicine seva, perform an abortion? There had not been one since the founding of New Shiva Puri two decades ago. Not one.

"If we go ahead with this," she said, "I will let Kerilynn take the lead, and I will assist."

"You're talking about a D and C?"

"Yes."

"Why not you?" Kerilynn asked.

"You know the territory (she winked at me) better than anybody, and it will be safer in your hands. You know how, don't you?"

"Straight forward procedure, but it's going to be painful."

"How painful?" I asked.

"Plenty," Kerilynn responded. "You probably won't feel too much of what I do after the dilation, but I won't kid you, that first part's gonna hurt."

"Can you knock her out?" Max asked. "Opium?"

"Until her eyeballs spin and she makes personal acquaintance with Lord Ganesha and all the flying monkeys," Kerilynn quipped, trying to lighten the mood.

"So let me understand," Mother said, "you can do this procedure safely, and keep her jacked up on opium enough she can handle it?"

"The biggest risk is infection. We'll dose her with as much Shakti-cillin as we think she can stand."

"Hello," I said, raising my voice, "I'm over here."

"Yes," Mother said, "so you are. What are you thinking?"

"I'm thinking I want to rip my body open with my fingernails or shove wires and sticks up inside until I scrape it out. That's what I'm thinking."

"Alright," Mother said. "Let's look on the other side, the not-having-an-abortion side. First, is there any danger to Janabai if she carries this baby to term?"

"Why should there be?" Kerilynn answered. "She is a strong, healthy farm girl, and there's no reason to think the birth should be anything but normal, unless there is something you're not telling us."

"You mean other than the fact the daddy is a YELLOW-EYED DEMON? You mean that part? THE DEMON PART?" I was screeching.

"That's what you *said*. A demon." This from Simone. "But you have been under unimaginable stress, and what he did to you was horrible, but…"

"BUT?"

I looked at Mother, who cocked her head as if to say, "See?"

But I knew. And Max knew and Mother knew.

"Mother, what do you think I should do?"

"Keep the baby. Love the child."

"Have you seen this? In a vision?"

"Not exactly, but I do know we are at a nexus, a choice point, and what you decide today will bear enormous consequences for you and for all of us."

"Max?" I turned my attention to our trusted marine.

Max, nodded. No surprise there. Where Mother went, Max followed.

"Mirabai?"

My sister smiled. "Your baby will have feet of leather." You can always count on Meera for the odd contribution. But, wait a minute, didn't her off-the-wall remark imply that the child *would* be born?

"Dad?" I asked. "What do you think?" No way he was going along with an abortion, but I wanted to hear him say it.

310

"Mother monkey jumps over a tree with her child holding on to her stomach. In the same way, mother Parvati watches over Janabai, over and over again."

He was quoting obscure poetry from the mystical saint Janabai, my namesake, but I got the point. Keep the baby.

Everyone was looking at me. Simone, and Lynda Cheng favored the abortion. Kerilynn and my parents, both of them, were in agreement, for a change. Keep the baby. Max went along with Mother. Mirabai envisioned "leather feet," whatever that meant. The seconds ticked by.

For all the days of my life, I have cared for living things, fed them, nursed them through sickness and injury. This was my seva, my service. I was Janabai Shepherd, who took a vow to love and protect the creatures of this earth.

I worked up enough spit in my dry mouth to talk.

"I'm going to carry this baby, this *creature* inside me, until it decides to come out."

"Don't worry," Kerilynn said, "we will all help you. It takes a village to raise a…"

"Yes," I interrupted, "I've heard that before. Well, I expect you to keep your promise, you village women, because that's exactly what you're going to do. I'm going to bear this burden, but when I'm done, I'm done. You will take it, and care for it, or kill it, or whatever you want. I'll have nothing to do with it. Nothing."

"You say that now," Mother said, "but when that baby is in your arms, you'll change your mind."

"But I won't raise it."

"You will."

"I won't."

"We'll see."

I started showing early; so big was my baby bump, Mother speculated I was carrying twins, as multiples seemed to run in our family, but Kerilynn, after palpation, after a thorough listen through the fetoscope, probably the last functioning device of its kind in the world, assured me, the proud mother-to-be, my "beautiful baby-to-come" was a single fetus. If true, I declared, it must be a huge monstrosity that would surely kill me when I tried to expel it.

"Don't worry," Kerilynn said, "your baby is perfectly normal. All first-time mothers are afraid they're not big enough. 'Do I have enough room?' They all say that. Let me assure you there is plenty of room down there to give birth. You just need to worry about taking care of *yourself.*"

"I look like a scarecrow that swallowed a pumpkin."

"It just looks big on you because you are too skinny."

I rolled my eyes. Another lecture on the way.

"And you need to eat more protein and drink more milk. I'll tell Simone to get some extra calories in you."

"Don't, please. I just feel sick all the time. I'm not hungry."

"That will pass. Now, more sleep, stop working so hard. Some women subconsciously try to sabotage an unwanted pregnancy by doing stupid things like riding horses."

I looked at Kerilynn like she had lost her mind.

"Okay. That was silly. We don't have any horses, but I know you are *not* going to stop working so hard. What was I thinking? Listen to me, Jana, Jana, Jannajanna bo-banna…"

"Stop it," I pleaded.

"Banana-fanna-fo-fanna."

"Please."

"Mi-my-mo-manna."

"I'm begging you."

"Do you promise to listen?"

"Yes, anything."

"That's better. If you let yourself get anemic, or malnourished, or exhausted, it will be dangerous. Dangerous for you and for the baby."

"Alright, alright. I'll do better."

"Promise."

"Yes, *Shiva, Lord,* I promise."

Kerilynn was also certain the child would be a girl. With none of the olden-time medical thingies available, she resorted to divination. Over my belly, she swung a pendulum, a pearl, on a length of thread. Were the baby to be a boy, the pearl would swing back and forth, back and forth. It might be a subtle swing, and not always accurate, but better than 60 percent; don't ask her how or why, swinging back and forth made for a boy-child. For me, the pearl swung wildly, dramatically, in big clockwise *circle*s, around and around and around, nothing subtle about it. It would be a girl. No doubt. A girl.

Swell.

Chapter Eighty-Eight

Exodus of the Shivites

MARCH 15, 22 AK. MOTHER pointed to a place on the map. Southern Oregon. A town called Klamath Falls. Never heard of it. Did she have a reason to pick that particular spot? Who knows? She said Klamath was at the far edge of our range if we were to arrive in time to get in the spring crops. Max agreed, saying she wanted to put as many miles between us and Kali as we could manage. How many miles would be enough? Who knew? Would we find fertile ground? Who knows? Would we be able to homestead, or would we come in on top of people who had already staked it out for their own? Who knows?

Not me. And by this time, I didn't care much. Five months pregnant and exhausted, undernourished and getting weaker by the day, I just wanted somebody else to be in charge of worrying. I wanted someone else to make the decisions and stand between kitchen and storehouse and listen to their endless complaints about each other.

With great relief, I handed the management reins to Max, who would be our scout; and to Bill, the wagon master; and to Cookie, who would do her best to feed us, on the move, at a different camp every night, for two months. Three months? Four? From now on I was back to being the pregnant shepherd girl, Praise Laksmi, for as long as I could keep on my feet.

Okay, Janabanana, put on that big smiley face! Wagons ho!

Thirty-two Shiva Puri wagons, 98 head of oxen, 190 head of cattle, mixed herds of sheep and goats, all guarded, kept in line, and driven forward with a single purpose by our beloved dogs. No fooling around. The dogs knew this was the real deal, life and death. They got it completely.

Smaller livestock struggled along on foot, or hitched rides on wagons, or complained inside their cages. Us? We walked. Everyone except three elderly and infirm, six still wounded, nine children, and the thirty-two drivers who would sit the boards until it was their turn to walk. The rest of us would walk three hundred miles in two months, a blistering five miles a day, which is flying when you think about shoving Noah's Ark uphill, on broken roads, through the high, cold desert. Pregnant. Did I mention pregnant?

We started west on Highway 36. There, below the mud flats that used to be beautiful Lake Almanor, we found the Chester Alliance camped just off the road. They had been waiting for us less than a day. How's that for timing?

Go back a few months. After the "Chesters" learned about Kali's war against us, we met twice during the winter, to parley about possible opportunities, namely for them to join the Shiva Puri caravan. It didn't take much convincing. Kali's return was a looming threat, and the Alliance barely escaped incineration by the Lassen eruption. They had a bellyful of living at the foot of an active volcano, and they were already planning their own move later in the year. Willing and eager, they hurried their preparations so we could go together. Great tidings! Two villages would make a more formidable road show. And... and... if we could iron out a few kinks between our tribal differences, a permanent merger was not out of the question. Yes, it seemed as if our losses might be reversed, until they told us they planned to keep west all the way to Old Eye Five, then turn north, to find the "Christian Life Brigade" living up in Oregon near Medford. Or so promised a

314

rumor once heard, maybe heard, from an itinerant peddler who was, likely, out of his mind.

"Surely, we Shivites would want to go along?"

"Uh..."

"Surely, that would be best for both groups?"

Mother remained polite, but she wasn't having any. For good reason: she was worried about leaving an obvious trail. People living along the old freeway would remember a great caravan rolling north, you know, the wagon train with a *woman marine* out in front and a raggedy pregnant girl dragging along the rear. Nor did Mother have the slightest interest in throwing Shiva Puri on the mercy of the Christian Life Brigade, whatever that was. The elders of Chester expressed their disappointment, but Mother was not swayed.

Shiva Puri would dodge and feint while the Chester Alliance dashed for Old Eye Five and the relative safety of the Red towns Major Joe had told us about. Hopefully, splitting the two groups would deceive, or at least confuse, Kali's pursuit. That was the plan. Pathetic. Please, don't judge us harshly. We had no eyes and ears, no intelligence about the route ahead; faded old maps, a few rumors, and scouts, on foot and no more than ten miles ahead.

"The Rakshasa may think you're the big party," Max said. "It's pavement all the way to Old Eye Five. After a few days it'll be hard to pick up your tracks. The Rakshasa won't know how many you are, how many rifles you have, or how long ago you passed by. They'll come on slow and careful. If somehow they pick up *our* trail, and they peel off after us, I'll try to make them think we're a decoy."

"Maybe they'll think *we're* the decoy," Pastor Rivenbark, senior among the Chester elders, raised his eyebrows, "and come after you."

After a moment, "Yes," Max said, "they might come after us instead."

Mother added, "They might not even know you are on the move... unless we lead them right to you."

"We appreciate your concern, but we were planning to run before we ever talked to you heathen folk. Don't worry. You're off the hook. Think about it this way: we take a little more risk, and we get a little more protection for as long as you stay with us."

"Are you sure in your heart about this?" Mother asked.

"I have Jesus Savior riding shotgun," the pastor answered.

"I know you do," Max said.

With a straight face.

Our first day together, the Chesters broke trail, and we ate their dust, twenty wagons worth, and scores of livestock. The next day it was our turn to lead — and breathe. Once Mother and Pastor Rivenbark set the order of march and our two tribes started rolling, the Chesters didn't have much to do with us. They camped over there, and we camped over here. Their elders and our council met in the evening, but it was all business. No socializing.

On the third day together, we woke up to snow, thick wet stuff, and Max knew, with the auspicious storm, her opportunity for a grand deception had arrived. Before noon, the ground slippery with slush, Max turned us north across a rocky steppe. We waved as the Chesters continued west toward Old Eye Five.

I hope they made it. I hope their prayers were answered. I hope they found the Christian Life Brigade and were welcomed. Vaya con Dios, Chester Alliance. Go with Shiva.

Here's the amusing epilogue. They left behind two of themselves, a nineteen-year-old girl smitten with Noah Stickles, he of the many nicknames; and a thirty-nine-year-old woman smitten with... wait for it... Vic Tretheway! He's fifty-three years old! Yikes. The old goat!

CHAPTER EIGHTY-NINE

Poop

THE "STEPPE" MAX CHOSE FOR our sideways ruse climbed gently for more than a mile, crested, then sloped down out of sight. At the bottom of the far side an old logging road waited, quiet as a cemetery, and as blessed a vision as you could want, just where the Rand McNally "Easy to Read" road map said it should be. Big olden-times medicine.

"Another day of this snow," Max said, "and it just might cover our tracks all the way from the highway, just in case, you know, you-know-who doesn't wait till spring to come after us. Maybe we'll catch a break and our sign will wash away completely."

"Poop," I said.

She stopped and looked at me.

"What part, Janabai? What part is poop?"

"I didn't mean your plan. I meant, the tracks may be gone, but the livestock will leave behind a ton of poop."

Max took that in. "Right. Okay, Janabai, get every shovel and hoe we've got into somebody's hand. Clean up the entire slope. Not one turd left behind. You're in charge."

Fine with me. Three days of uselessness were quite enough. I welcomed an assignment, even poop patrol.

Thirty-two shovels and as many hoes and rakes made quick business of our "business," from the main highway, over the hill, to the dirt road, in just over an hour; not one turd in sight, not even an itty-bitty rabbit pellet. I, Janabai, swear this is true. Our disappearance from the face of the earth was underway, the door locked behind us, the die cast. I don't know exactly what a die is, but I'm sure if we had one, it would have been cast. We were on our own. Ants on the march under the gray angry sky.

On the second afternoon pushing due north along the logging road, we intersected 44, another highway that is also called 89, I don't know why. It, too, was right where the map said it should be. That intersection perked us up a little bit, knowing exactly where we were, but gosh, I will tell you it was cold there at the foot of Mount Lassen. Cold and wet. Slippery and muddy. Mother was nervous that volcanic flows had destroyed the road, but the lava stopped just short of the highway; you could see it just a little ways off toward the southeast. Toward Indian Valley. Toward home. It made me shiver to think how far we had already come. How far we had to go. To where? A dot on a map called "Klamath

Falls?" Whenever I had those thoughts and started to panic, I took my breath and remembered: *Mother's in charge. She has us in her hands. Where else in this vast broken world would I rather be?*

The April weather improved as we worked our way up to the junction of 299, gradually climbing toward Adin Pass up in Modoc country. The highway crossed two lava tongues separated by fields of soft gray ash, two more opportunities for me to supervise the Poop Patrol and rake the ash smooth. The second lava tongue we had to rake *three* times. Max didn't like the way we did it the first two.

I had an excuse for the sloppy job. Just as we were getting started on our first de-poopilation of the ash field, I bent over to pick up a hoe, not a good move in my condition, felt a bolt of lightning rip up my spine and out through my skull, the world spun around twice, I'm sure it was twice, and I collapsed. Out like a candle in the rain. I was only departed into the world of nod a little while, so I am told, before I came back to the world of heads, a circle of heads ringed above me.

"Why are you standing around?" I asked. "Get to work." *Oh my gosh, I sounded just like Mother.*

Someone suggested they make a litter and carry me back to camp.

"Nice try, but no. I'll be fine. I can boss you around just as well propped up against this boulder. Go. Go!"

Back at the camp, I was crawling under a wagon and into my blanket when the posse arrived. Some traitor, G-Mek, probably, squealed to Mother. Now Mother was here, with G-Mek, Lynda, and Kerilynn in tow, demanding to know what had happened.

"Just got a headache and sat down to rest," I said.

"G-Mek tells it another way."

"And what does G-Mek say?" I grumbled, giving my friend the stink eye.

"I said you screamed," G-Mek said, getting warmed up. "Your eyeballs rolled up in your head and you fell on the ground like a sack of potatoes, out cold, until I revived you by expertly wiping your face with a wet rag. When Skyler said we should carry you home, you almost bit his head off, and made everyone go back to shoveling shit. Yep. That's what I told your mother."

"It's nothing, Mother, really," I said, but the medics checked me over anyway, taking my pulse, and checking my blood pressure with Lynda Cheng's most precious thingy from olden days, the thingy they wrap around your arm and pump up until it squeezes your arm. I had never seen Lynda Cheng look worried when she squeezed the thingy, but I didn't like what I was seeing in her eyes.

"You say you had a bad headache?" she asked.

"The worst."

"It came on suddenly? No warning?"

"Out of the blue."

"Hmmm. Be still a minute." One sluggish minute oozed by. "Hmmm." Again, she hmmmed. "Keri, look at this."

Lynda pinched the skin on the bottom of my arm.

"Hmmm," Kerilynn muttered.

"Now," Lynda continued, "take a close look at the right side of her face and tell me what you see."

"What does 'hmmm' mean?" I asked, getting a bit frantic.

No answer.

Kerilynn bent down. I remember she had been chewing deer jerky. I inhaled and exhaled the smell of spices and wild meat as she examined my face, and her breath evoked the comfort of the Goddess, and I calmed down. After a few more seconds, Kerilynn sighed, so I guess she found whatever she was looking for. She got to her feet, rubbing the back of her neck, silhouetted against the fading sunset. Lynda joined her there, and the two women had a whispered conversation. Silhouettes. Shhhh. Buzz buzz buzz.

"Hey!" I yelled. "Just say it."

Lynda looked at Kerilynn, who nodded, "We think, we're pretty sure, you have a condition called preeclampsia."

CHAPTER NINETY

Preeclampsia?

"Pre... WHAT?" I SAID.

"What does that mean?" Mother asked. I shot her my best "back off" look. I can ask my own questions. Right?

"First off," Lynda said, "it's a complication, under the best of conditions."

"And out here?" Mother asked.

"Mother! Shsss!"

"Out here, it's dangerous."

"How dangerous?" I asked before Mother could butt in.

"Life threatening. You could lose the baby. Or we could lose you. Or both. Or you could have another stroke and be..." Lynda didn't finish.

"I've had a stroke?"

"Probably had a stroke," she corrected.

"I's hah a srok?"

My words came out funny. I caught Mother's worried look.

"A minor one, we think."

I concentrated on forming each word.

"Whah abow... stroke I *probably* already had?"

"The damage to your face may heal itself, most of it, or you will accommodate yourself and do your best to forget about it."

"Whah abow my fass? Whass wrong with my fass?"

No doubt about it, my mouth was sort of weak and loose. Now that I was aware of it, I could speak normally, more or less, if I concentrated.

"It's not too bad."

"Whah you mean, nah too bad?" I said, pressing the left side of my face. It felt odd, numb, like somebody else's skin.

"You've lost some muscle tension in the cheek."

"Wha I look like?"

"You look exactly like yourself… except there's a little sag under that left eye."

"Wanna see. Mirror."

"Later," Mother said.

"No, now. I hah to see now!"

Mother asked Lynda, "Do you have that mirror thing in your kit?"

Reluctantly, it seemed to me, the nurse retrieved the device, a small round mirror with a hole in the center, and handed it to me. I studied my reflection. No "little sag." It looked like the entire left side of my face was melting. Some awful thing was broken. Why was this happening to me? What did I do to earn this horrible karma, and yes, I know karma is not horrible, or wonderful, or anything else, it's just karma, but Goddess of the Earth and Heavens, tell me, I'm begging you, tell me, why did you let this happen?

"Wih I ahways be like dis?" I asked.

"I don't think so," Lynda answered. "In time, I believe your skin will pull itself right back up where it belongs. Maybe not all the way, but some."

That's when it got me. What she was saying, trying to say, was that my face might always be… be what? Deformed? Disfigured? Ugly?

Ugly.

Yes, that's the word. Way down there, deep in my heart, I was terrified I would be ugly. We Shivite women are a spiritual breed, or hope to be, and we try to put vanity behind us; and I know we are farm women, rough from work in the fields, and we don't spend much time primping, but the truth is, we still like to look pretty.

I wanted to be pretty again. Is that so much to ask?

Tears scorched my eyes and overflowed. I bawled.

Lynda put her arms around me. I felt other arms, Mother and Simone and Kerilynn. That's how we stayed, the five of us, holding on to each other, with me in the circle of their love.

In a little while we un-circled ourselves and got around to making a plan. What were we going to do about my preeclampsia?

"First," Kerilynn said, "you will eat and drink protein until you gag."

Such a nice picture.

"You need to build up the iron content in your blood," she elaborated.

"Now lift your tongue... ah... ," Kerilynn said as she squeezed drops of horrible something in my mouth. Yellow dock, dandelion root, and nettle. Yum.

"Next," she said, "you will lay around... how can I put this to you in technical medical language... you will lay around feeling *shitty*."

"Lay round fee shi... shi..." I realized it was the *T* sound that was giving me the most trouble. I concentrated. Tongue to the roof of my mouth. I repeated, "*Shiddy*, feel *shiddy*."

"That's right, you will feel so *shiddy*, you will not want to do seva. You will get up only when you have to pee."

"Pee?" I asked. "Wha dah... *what... sthat*?"

"You've been having problems peeing?"

"Don remember las dime."

"Fourth. Re-hydration. We'll have you pissing like a buck deer in no time."

"I can hardly way."

"Finally," she concluded, "you will get off your feet and ride in one of the ox wagons."

"How long?"

"All the way, or until you deliver, and probably beyond."

I did the calculation. "Rie in wagon FOUR mons?"

"Unless we get wherever we're going first. Pray we get to Klamath soon."

"I'll go ow my mind."

"Try your best not to."

"I wone have anyding do."

"Your mother will think of something."

"No room in wagons," I said.

That did pose a problem. For the entire village. For me to bed down in a wagon meant we were going to have to jettison an equal amount of space and weight in crucial food or equipment. We had no luxuries to throw overboard; everything we carried was essential.

"We have the books," Odessa Piwinski said.

Stunned silence. Odessa loved each and every one of those books, no, not like her own family, if that's what you thought I was going to say. I was her family, and she loved me more than the books; she never thought twice about clearing out a place for me among her Dickens and Poe, but don't worry, she didn't have to. When our folks heard what she was planning to do, every one of them came forward to carry one more of Odessa's books in their own backpacks.

"I'll carry *Twenty Thousand Leagues*," G-Mek said. "And take real good care of it. I know how much you love your books."

"They're *our* books," she protested, "not *mine*."

Sure, Odessa, sure.

"And I thank you, George," Odessa said. "Thank you, thank you. Muchas gracias! Spasibo!"

Okay, Miss Piwinski, enough. We get it. Now please, can I crawl into my little Liberry nest and go to sleep.

That's where I stayed, for another five weeks, in the arms of my teachers: London, and Plath, and Heinlein, and Tolkien, and Bronte, and Chandler and Kingsolver, and especially Kate Douglas Wiggin, who must have been hugely famous because *Rebecca of Sunnybrook Farm* is the most important book I ever read and showed me farm girls like me grow up and have problems and still find happiness, a lesson I so wanted to believe as we thumped and banged down old 44 and up old Whatever, day after day after day, on a cracked and pot-holed road, with iron wheels slamming, always in the rear because the wagon, my wagon, had to stop every hour for me to pee.

During those long weeks my face did begin to tighten back up in the direction of its regular shape, though I expect I will always wear the mark of the stroke under my left eye. G-Mek says it's kinda sexy. If I get shed of Evil Baby, and survive the shedding, I am going to show that sweet boy just what sexy is. Also, I am happy to report that my speech is back to normal. Praise Shiva.

"Hey, Cliff, I gotta go again."

"Whoa," my driver said to the oxen. "Shit," he muttered to himself.

I pulled myself up from warm, snuggly blankets, clambered down the wagon side, waddled over to the bushes, did my business, waddled back, clambered up, and snuggled back down, hoping I hadn't made a mess of myself; and how would I know, not being able to see down there over my ever-expanding bulge?

Evil Baby remained in breech position, showed no willingness to cooperate. Kerilynn prescribed acupuncture to turn the creature, so Debbie needled me every other day. No effect. Breech it was, and breech it remained.

"All the better to kill you, my dear," says Evil Baby, and laughs like a demon.

Chapter Ninety-One

Sadhu

Skyler dragged over a storage box, and G-Mek brought a cushion so I had a comfortable place to sit, and a good bit higher than everybody else. A few people stood in small groups, but most sat on the ground. After supper, we made a little ritual of letting the right and left cooking fires die out, and kept the center fire going. All those not on seva squeezed in around the single fire. We chanted a mantra, or someone would tell a story we probably heard a thousand times. You could tell anything you wanted, except memories of those who fell in battle. We tried that one night, a special program of remembering, and freaked ourselves out. Probably too soon for that kind of thing, and let me tell you something true, out here in the high desert, alone as we are, with the wind blowing cold from the northwest, with a billon stars pressing down on us, it is a terrifying place. We certainly don't need melancholy sighs and open weeping to bring us further down. Anything else you want to tell is okay, especially if it's funny, or about sex or farting, stuff like that, or pregnancy jokes. Ha ha, they think they're so funny. I swear I am going to put a snake in Vic Tretheway's bedroll.

"I have to tell you," Vic began, "that our little Janabai has gotten herself pregnant. So pregnant. Real pregnant."

And Bill Lemko, or another witless ally, would set Vic up, as expected, with, "How pregnant is she?"

"Janabai is so pregnant she looks like a stick that swallowed a watermelon."

"Janabai is so pregnant..." And on and on.

I'd shake my head and pretend to be annoyed, when inside what I felt was gratitude. And everybody knew it. The sour slice of Shiva Puri pie is that everybody knows everything about you. The sweet slice is exactly the same: everybody knows everything about you, so it doesn't do you any good to try to keep secrets, and when you understand that, you don't worry about trying to keep them, secrets, I mean. Just let it all fly out, like startled sparrows bursting from cover:

I'm pregnant and everybody knows. Check.

The thing inside me is a child of rape and everybody knows. Check.

I don't want the child and everybody knows. Check.

I'm grumpy and whiny and everybody knows—oh believe me on that one, I've made sure everybody knows about my pain and woes.

I am having a difficult and dangerous pregnancy and everybody knows.

I may die and everybody knows.

I think I am well-grounded in the truth. I know that when we try to hide something, we just dig ourselves in deeper. How many times do we have to learn and re-learn this? Tell the truth. Know the truth. Be the truth. There's nothing to be afraid of.

Oh. Kali. Yes, you can know the truth and still pee down your leg if the demon comes after you, yellow eyes, lips curled, claws slashing.

Whoa. Stop, Janabai. Shake it off. What am I writing about? Oh yes...

I was sitting high on my Throne for a Pregnant Princess, as Vic helpfully dubbed it, *thanks a lot*, where I could gaze out over the heads of the people, and through the gaps between wagons, and into the featureless darkness. That's all I was doing, breathing, ignoring the thing slithering around in my womb, trying to ignore it, gazing, drifting, and worrying about Mother and Max and wondering about the mysterious goings-on. Why did we pull up so early yesterday? Why did we stay here another full day? Where were Mother and Max with the answers?

That's when I saw the scarecrow.

He must have walked among the goats and cattle without raising alarm, wafted past the unseeing eyes of the night watch, through the great outer circle of wagons, and into the center of the Shiva Puri firelight. My first thought: why didn't the dogs bark? What's wrong with the dogs?

Paying no attention to any of us, the scarecrow stalked to the edge of the fire pit and stared into the flames. We see strangers from time to time, but none *stranger*, if you take my meaning. Gangly, emaciated, tendons like rawhide cords strung along his bones, shrunken cavity where his stomach should be. His hair was a matted bird's nest, sticks intertwined with his topknot to keep the arboreal habitation aloft. I don't know what was living up there, amongst the hair and mud and twigs, but I can tell you, it would be roomy enough for a pack rat. Oh yes, how could I forget this? The scarecrow man with the hair nest wore only a loincloth of rags held above his skeletal hips with a piece of rope. The rest of him was naked as any naked thing you have ever seen... except for what seemed to be a face tattooed on his chest.

"Oh my God," G-Mek whispered. "Is he for real?"

Normally, when strangers come to us, we offer tea and polite conversation while someone fetches Mirabai. She is brought in, casual and soft, a pretty, plumpish, blondish, blind woman, and introduced to the stranger. She holds the unsuspecting newcomer's hands for a few minutes, a "telling" as we now call it, after which the stranger is made to depart, awkwardly or forcefully; or, if the telling goes well, invited to hang around while we "court" each other. Be sure of this, it's Mirabai who is making these invitations.

"Come."

I heard my sister calling for me, her silent summons, no doubt about it. I snapped my head around looking for her, saw a movement to the right, and here came Mirabai feeling her way through the crowd toward Skeleton Lizard Scarecrow Tattoo Man.

"Help me down," I said to Skyler.

With two hundred pairs of eyes on me, I lumbered across the circle, both hands under my belly, mustering as much dignity as I could, which wasn't much, more comical than regal.

"Let me see him," she said when I reached her.

This should be interesting. With the massive baby-boulder sticking out below my rib cage, Mira wasn't going to be leaning back into me, so I squeezed in sideways until I could get my chin on her shoulder, my flesh against hers. The stranger watched calmly, standing with his arms straight by his sides.

I gestured for our "guest" to come over. He obliged, though he must have thought us a most exotic sight, two women, side by side, cheek by cheek, one blind, the other pregnant.

We "looked" at him, Mirabai and me.

A while later, Mother and Max pushed through the circle and came into the firelight. I thought they would do something or say something, or click the rifle safeties to ready, something, but they just stood watching.

Having seen what she needed, Mirabai nudged me away. Holding out her hands, she took a step toward him. He stepped in and took her proffered hands. Remarkably, up close he didn't smell bad. The opposite. About him I smelled familiar odors of wood fire, and dirt, of course, but also something like perfume. I know about these things. It was perfume, I swear. Once, when I was little, I smelled the stuff myself.

Face-to-face, Mirabai and the stranger stood there holding hands. How long? I don't remember, and that's for good reason. Something was happening, between them, and from them, flowing out and penetrating each of us. Oh, honey, I will tell you, the Shakti was rolling throughout the caravan, and we were all going places, up in the sky, under the sea, exploring magical cities, in the arms of our one true love; whatever it was that gave us bliss, there we were.

Sometime later, he pulled his hands away from my sister, knelt down, bent forward and felt for her feet, and touched his forehead to the ground. After a few seconds, he raised his head and sat back on his heels, looking up into her opaque blue eyes.

"Bless me, holy one," he said.

"Holy one!" I didn't say it aloud, but Mirabai heard me.

She swiveled her head in my direction. "He is a *sadhu*." Her words reverberated among the cacophony of my thoughts.

Sadhu? Like in the tales elderly Indians tell about olden times across the sea, this scarecrow is a sadhu? My thoughts caught his attention. "Humph," he said. I raised my gaze from my sister and up into his eyes, remarkable, wise, and gentle eyes. He held out his hands to me as Mirabai had done for him. I placed my hands in his.

Kaboom!

I thought the Shakti coming from this man was already hot, just being near him. Now I was standing in the fire itself. His heat raged through me, into my extremities, swirling around my heart, and down, down into the core of my being and through the walls of my womb and into... that... that... creature. With a puzzled look on his face, the first expression I had seen, the sadhu placed his long bony fingers on my belly as if warming himself on a stove. He bent down to study my bulge; looked again into my eyes. The corners of his mouth turned up, and up, and up, into a grin. He threw his head back and laughed. Without knowing what was funny, the people of Shiva Puri joined the laughter, and soon everybody was laughing just because everybody was laughing. You know how it gets sometimes? I suppose we were an amusing sight to the people of Shiva Puri, Mirabai kneeling like a suppliant in an old painting, the holy man guffawing at the heavens, and me, grinning my head off and feeling better than I had in months.

How much cannabis did I eat this morning?

Mother held up her hand. "My friends, I want to introduce, well I don't know his name, but I have thought of him as 'Baba,' and he hasn't objected so far. I trust him, and it's plain to see he's made Janabai happy."

"Mmmm hmm," I hmmmed.

"Good," Mother said, "real good, because tomorrow, Baba is going to lead us to our new home. Right through the middle of the Mausoleum."

CHAPTER NINETY-TWO

Mausoleum

MOTHER LET THE WORD HANG there in the smoke. Mausoleum. Solemnly she turned in a slow circle, making sure everybody was paying attention. She needn't have worried. She grinned.

"I know you are chomping at the bit to find out what's going on, and some of you have just enough misinformation to send interesting rumors flying all over the place, so let me bring you all back to earth and tell you the truth about our new... what shall I call it?"

"Shit storm," Max offered.

"Opportunity," Mother corrected.

Everybody laughed. It couldn't be too bad if Azriel and her marine were joking around.

"Yesterday, the first scout team returned early. They found

something up ahead, something they thought I should see before we drove up on it unprepared."

The first scout team, Mother's eyes and ears, departed camp at daybreak, ran ahead for two hours, turned around, and ran back to report. A second team left two hours after the first, and the wagon train got underway an hour later. And so on throughout the day. Coming and going, at least three teams were always out in front, leapfrogging each other and reporting back. That's four hours of running for each team, but any Shiva Puri kid over ten years old can do it without breathing hard. With decent footing and lots of precious calories, our scout teams can get out ten miles and ten back in under three hours. On this morning, they didn't have to. The wagon train was barely underway, less than an hour, when the scouts loped in with disturbing news.

Moving cautiously, the scouts encountered abandoned automobiles and trucks, singly, and increasingly in clusters, tangled and smashed together, and finally, cresting a hill, they saw great heaps of demolished vehicles blocking the roadway altogether, an impenetrable mass of rusting debris.

"When I heard their report," Mother continued, "I called a halt while Max and I ran ahead to see this... Mausoleum."

"Clusterfuck," Max offered. This time Mother gave her a certain look that needed no words.

Max, shrugged. "Aye, aye, General, putting a stopper in it."

"Well," Mother said, "I think, after twenty years of arguing and guessing, we may finally get the answer to the big question, the gorilla in the Kali closet. What happened to all the people? Tomorrow you may be seeing the graveyard of civilization, the final resting place of humanity. So many bones, the bones, the dry, bleached bones of our kind. I think the people fled the cities, those that could get out before the fires came up, and headed north to Oregon where they thought they would be safe. Some of them made it up here before they ran out of gasoline. They probably raced up 97 through Weed, and east from Medford along 140, and on 66 through the Siskiyous, only to collide with their counterparts fleeing west on 140 and south on 139. Here, on the outskirts of Klamath Falls, they ran out of open road. They ran out of hope. They ran out of time."

"How many?" someone questioned. "How many cars?"

"You'll see for yourself. It's all mashed together."

"How will we get through?"

"Hold the reins, I'm getting to it. Max and I ran ahead, leaving Bill to move the wagons up into this bowl and wait. We worked our way into the... necropolis. Five hours later we realized two things: first, we were completely lost, and second, we were in trouble. Climbing on top of the tallest pile, we looked around in a circle. Metal carcasses stretched as far as we could see. To the south, sticking up above the catacombs, we could see this hill where we are now, but it was miles away, and we had no idea how to find the path back."

"Oops," Max said.

"Yes. Only a lot worse than oops. We decided to hunker down for the night. We built a fire from sagebrush and whatever flammables we dug up from nearby cars or lying around on the ground. We shared our water and some of the food Max had thought to stash in her coat."

"At least someone was thinking."

"After it got dark, the wind began to pick up, to whistle through the metal, a mournful funeral dirge for the dead. About midnight the wind stopped altogether and left a silence as deep as a tomb—and I don't know which was scarier, the moaning, or the absence of it. The only sound, and I was grateful even for that, was the crackling of sagebrush in our fire.

"When Max saw him, our guest was standing at the edge of the firelight, like a skeleton, watching us. Max ever so casually reached out for her rifle and snicked off the safety. Out in the middle of that cemetery, the snick was just about the loudest sound you ever heard."

"What happened?"

"I told him to advance and be recognized," Max said.

"He advanced," Mother said. "Max greeted him cordially, saying, if I remember correctly..."

"Who the fuck are *you*?" Max filled in.

Another laugh. Punch and Judy are hilarious when they're on a roll.

"He didn't answer except to make popping sounds with his lips, like *bah bah*. There was something familiar about him, but I couldn't put my finger on it. I was sure I had seen him before. 'Namaste, stranger,' I said. 'Pleased to meet you. Will you have some food? There's not much, just some oatcake, but we're happy to share.' I got up and walked around to his side of the fire, breaking off a piece of cake and squatting down to give it to him. He looked at it like he had never seen food before, and judging from his skeletal appearance, my opinion was not far from the truth. He leaned over and sniffed the offering, smiled, looked up at me, and, before I could do anything to stop him, tapped me right between the eyes with one bony finger. My head exploded like fireworks."

"What do you mean?" someone asked.

"You know how it is with Mirabai?" Mother answered. "When she's giving darshan and she touches you and you go off to la-la land? Like that. I was completely aware of what was going on; I could hear Max behind me getting into a better fighting stance, but I was transported, utterly blissed out."

"What did you do?"

"Nothing. I was frozen. Happy as a clam, but paralyzed. He spoke, breaking the spell, or trance, or whatever, saying 'Bah-bah' and taking the food from my hand. When our guest finished chewing, I pointed at him, repeating his one word, 'Baba,' by which I meant, 'Is that your name? Baba?' He considered my question for a minute, and confirmed, 'Bah-bah.'

"I suspect the word may be the extent of his vocabulary, because it's all he would say when I asked him anything else, though he seemed to understand me. I asked where he lived. Bah-bah. How did he get here? Bah-bah. Did he have any people? The same. Again, déjà vu. Where had I seen him? It was right on the edge of my memory.

"I told him we were lost, we were trying to find a way through the jumble of wreckage. Did he know how to get to the great

Klamath Lake? He stood up and walked to the edge of our little junkyard clearing, stopped, stared at us as if waiting. We looked at each other, Max and I.

"'Okay, boss lady,' Max began, 'let's Oscar Mike outta here with the...'" She stopped. 'Ah, that's it! Now I remember. The first year in Graeagle. Late at night. The guards woke us up, and took us out the north road toward Quincy...'

"'And he came dancing down the road...'

"'And you called him Mister Bojangles...'

"'And you gave him your coat...'

"'And he had a tattoo on his chest!'

"'Baba,' I said, 'do you mind lifting your shirt so I can see your chest?' I didn't know if he understood, so I pantomimed lifting my own.

"He smiled with delight, his wide grin exposing teeth so perfect and white, I thought, 'Now here's a man who knows a dentist.' He pulled up his shirt, exposing his chest. There it was, the face, the blue tattooed face, faded, wrinkled, but unmistakable, with the index finger of one hand on the lips, shushing all who looked upon him, and below the face, the caption I now remembered: 'Don't Worry, Be Happy.'

"'Hey, Baba man,' Max said, 'Pull your shirt down and lead on.'

"There was enough starlight to see where we were going, at least enough light to avoid bumping into things or cutting ourselves to ribbons on metal jags sticking out everywhere. Twice we lost sight of Baba, but each time he returned to find us and lead us onward. Over the next two hours our eyes adjusted to the dark and it got easier to follow him. We came to a wall of vehicles that seemed to have melted into a solid mass, but he squeezed through a crack we couldn't even see. Emerging on the other side of the narrow crevice, we came out into the open—in front of us, the forest; above us the Milky Way; and beyond the trees, the night sky reflected in the calm waters of Klamath Lake. I don't know when I have taken a deeper breath of relief. Just to be out of that place, that... Mausoleum, was one of the best moments of my life. I turned back to thank our guide, but he had disappeared."

"Fucker's good," Max said.

"We slept rough for the rest of the night, cuddled tight under a pine, right along the shore. Oh, wait till you see it, the most beautiful lake in the world. And wait till you see it with the sun coming up at dawn and the mist rising and coiling over the water like smoke. I know you are going to love it. I know we are going to be happy there."

"She's seen it in a *vision*," Max exaggerated.

"Max, will you please shut up."

"Urk," Max said, "shutting up right now."

"Of course," Mother went on, "we had one small problem. We were on one side of the Mausoleum, and the rest of you were still up here on this hill, with the world's biggest graveyard in between."

"Did you find it?" The questions were flying. "The special place?" "Our new home?"

Mother looked at Max for confirmation, but her friend just raised her hands, shook her head, pressed her lips together, and made unintelligible sounds. I'm sure she was mumbling something like, "You told me to shut up." Another nice laugh. Just too funny, Max.

"You can decide for yourself," Mother answered.

Questions flew.

"How far to the lake?"

"Four miles as the crow flies."

"How long to get the wagons through?"

"Probably six hours, and the rest of the day for the livestock."

"What about the kids?"

"What do you mean?"

The parents were worried about the carnage the younger children would see on the passage. Perhaps the kids should be blindfolded?

"No," Mother said, squelching the suggestion. "Let the children look. Let them learn."

"What should we tell them?"

"The truth."

CHAPTER NINETY-THREE

Passage

C RESTING THE HILL, I SAW a vast expanse of... I don't know what... stretching east to west until it faded into the shimmering air. As we drew closer I determined it to be a colossal repository of disintegrating motorcars, a dumping ground, a junkyard from hell. Every machine was covered in rust and buried in dirt up to the doors. No real color. Dun, maybe, the color of death. Dusty yuccas and creosote brush grew between the piles of metal, and even inside the crumbled wrecks, branching out through roofs and windows, the high desert working day and night to reclaim itself.

We passed through an opening in the southern edge of the mausoleum. Following the tracks of the leading wagons, we snaked among shambles of broken glass and jagged iron mixed chockablock into mounds, burial mounds; and each car or truck was like its own burial chamber, its own casket, its... what's the word? Sarcophagus! The funeral vaults of my species, and inside those metal coffins, I saw what remained.

Corpses.

After twenty years in the bone-dry weather of the high desert, the bodies had yet to collapse in on themselves, dead people sitting up and driving to nowhere, chalky fingers clutching steering wheels, car loads of papery cadavers, more than I ever needed to see if I lived a million years. Intact bodies, many of them, and also pieces of... pieces of... people dissolving into the earth like compost, and some in monstrous, horrible heaps, all smushed together with relics of olden times: artifacts and curios, suitcases and children's toys, the pitiful fragments of the dead and gone.

And Mother wanted the children to see this?

It was a terrible passage through the Desolation of Klamath, one of the names I thought up, along with the Plain of Kali, and City of Bones, and Final Resting Place of Human Kind—only not totally final, because some of us are still here, right? It made me wonder, did all these people just sit here and die, quietly and politely, hoping the gov'ment would come to the rescue? Did some of them get out of their dead automobiles and wander away to starve — as might have happened to us? Did some of them perish like the Donner Party? Did they run out of gasoline and get stuck here? Did they run out of food and start on each other; millions and millions of cannibals, eating each other, even their babies? Maybe this is where the Rakshasa came from, right here, from this nasty place, normal people who turned into murderers and rapists and flesh-eaters.

Dust, skulls, carcasses, chaff, ashes, remnants, tatters, and bones, bones, everywhere, the dry bones, and the wind whistling through the tombs like the screams of the damned.

Chapter Ninety-Four

Homecoming

Last through the jagged teeth of the Mausoleum, Mother, Max, and the goats. Then teams of oxen dragged shut the maw behind them.

While we rested along the lake, Mother sent scouts in all directions, this time looking for the *right place*, the sacred ground for our new home. They found it, not on the near side where we were camped, but on the east side, where there was rich farm land, more than we would ever need... and protected by high mountains. To the west we would be guarded by the vast lake itself. To the south? Between our farm and the abandoned city of Klamath Falls, a ridge came right down to the water, leaving barely enough room to squeeze by. That natural pinch was the only door to the south, and Max wanted to slam it shut and lock it.

Our oxen dragged cars, busses, tractors across the only southern approach. Soon, there would be no passage at all.

To the north? Mother wanted the road left open. Just in case.

We arrived on the banks of the Williams River, a tributary to the great lake, after fifty-eight days of walking, many losses of livestock — and six people: one by drowning, two from lingering wounds sustained in the battle, one gored by a bull, one by unknown causes, probably a heart attack, and one just got sick, fell down, and died. We who survived took stewardship of thousands of beautiful acres adjacent to the old Jen Weld Window Factory, a treasure house of saw blades, metal of all kinds, glass, and lumber. The main building was big enough to get the whole village out of the weather and, later, to provide a ready-made winter barn for the livestock. Lapping the shores of our farm, the gentle waves of Klamath Lake. Lake Klamath. Lake *of* the Klamath. I couldn't get used to it, not even seeing it every day. I was astonished and overwhelmed by its grandeur... and I still am. Wowie.

True, the Jen Weld factory could shelter all of us, but the weather was turning nice, so most of us chose to sleep rough outside. Me? No such luck. I had to stay in the back of the library wagon all afternoon while they fixed up something special for me, a corner somewhere out of the way, where I could lie in the dark, all by myself, with no company, and no friends. Poor Janabai. Finally, just as I smelled the cooking fires for the evening meal, they came for me. I waddled across the factory parking lot holding on to Skyler and G-Mek, Mother and Dad leading us up the hillside along a winding path.

"Do you think you can make it?" Mother asked.

"How far?" I panted.

"One hundred yards," Dad answered.

"Two hundred," Mother corrected.

"Is there a bed for me there, or any place I can lie down without being bounced to pieces?"

"We can do better than that," G-Mek winked.

"Then I can make the climb," I said aloud. "Hopefully," I muttered to myself.

We came out into a little clearing, a sort of flat shelf perched on the side of a steep hill. Max was there, and the midwife, Kerilynn. Simone was holding open the entry flaps of our only big tent, the one the council used for meetings while we were on the road. I stood amazed, and deeply moved that these people, exhausted as I was, and without seeing to their own comfort, were taking care of me first.

"We thought you would be more comfortable in your own space," Skyler said.

"And we don't have to listen to you complain," G-Mek added.

"Or listen to you scream when you go into labor," Max said, of course, being ever so cheerful.

"Well, come on in," Simone said.

The floor was dirt, but swept clean of every twig and pebble. Boughs of aromatic foliage hung in the corners, and over the exquisitely soft-looking cot... an oil lamp for reading! Next to the cot, an upended box from the factory, covered with a cloth. Somebody's last clean towel. The tent flaps let in lots of light, and even more wonderful, lots of breeze. The space practically shimmered with sweet vibrations, a delicious energy I could taste on my lips. You can't imagine, *but go ahead and try*, what it's like to get used to the thick smell of a wagon train, and then, suddenly, you're taking a breath of fresh air, high up on a hillside, in the shade of great pines; that's what it was like, sort of like. I inhaled deeply. The cool, clean air smelled like... freedom.

I haven't even told you the *best* part. They had pitched the tent so I could prop myself up in bed and look between my rather gorgeous pregnant breasts, and up, up, up the colossal mound of my belly, and there, sitting right on top of my navel... the lake. The enormous expanse of it stretched to the faraway shore. Lake of the Klamath People. I wondered if any of them survived the Kali Yuga, and I wondered where they were, and I wished I could meet some.

I was ever so grateful to my loved ones who had brought me to this magic place, and I wondered if they made it so special because they knew I'm going to die here and they wanted it to be nice.

I was pretty sure God lived here. Lord Klamath, I decided to call him.

CHAPTER NINETY-FIVE

A Dying Wish

"**D**ID I REALLY CALL YOU my husband?"

G-Mek had been sitting with me most of the night, a long, agonizing, sleepless torture for both of us, me trying to get comfortable, pillow under my big belly, rolling this way and that way, passing gas endlessly, cursing and letting the universe know how angry I was at it and everything in it, including G-Mek, who was wiping my face with a cool cloth, rearranging my pillow, enduring my ill-humor, and my farts, trying to distract me with the story of my rescue from Kali.

"Yes, that's exactly what you said. 'You my huthband,' you said with a lisp that I remember as charming. Back then. Not now. There is nothing remotely charming about you right now."

"I'm sorry. Honestly. And thank you for staying through the night."

"Welcome. How's the book coming, I mean the whole thing?"

"Great, I think. No, not great, like wonderful. How would I know? I mean it's great because it's almost done. And a miracle, too."

"Why do you say that?"

"Don't bullshit me, George Sunkari. Give me some water."

G-Mek held a cup to my lips, wiped my face again.

"We've been friends too long. I know, and you know, and everybody knows I am not going to make it. This baby is killing me. I'm going to die with my legs spread wide, with the bloody monster crawling out of me."

"Shut up, stupid. You're not going to die. We're not going to let you. The baby's not going to be a bloody monster. You're going to have a fine baby girl. She's going to be beautiful and perfect, and you're going to love her and be a wonderful mother. You're going to be happy again. Healthy and loved and blessed. That's

339

the way it's going to be. I'm telling you, with all my heart, that's what I believe. Are you hearing me?"

I turned my face away and didn't answer.

Skyler breezed in through the tent flap, pretending as if he didn't have a care in the world. He saw the expression on G-Mek's face, stopped, and gave him a questioning look. G-Mek shook his head.

"I was just coming to tell you," Skyler said, "Simone is running late and she'll be here in a little while, so I'm going to relieve you until she gets here."

"Okay," G-Mek said, "I'll get myself over to breakfast. Rest well, Jana-bumble, and don't worry so much."

"George, wait," I said, shifting position so I was looking at my two friends. "I want to ask you and Skyler something."

"Uh... okay."

"What's this all about?" Skyler asked.

"She's in a state," G-Mek answered. "Gloom and doom. She thinks she's going to die, and she's trying to, what can I say, put things right? Get everything in order? I already told her, don't be ridiculous, nothing is going to happen."

"It's not ridiculous, is it?" I was looking at Skyler. "You'll tell me the truth, won't you? Look me in the eye, Skyler Jones. I deserve the truth. Now answer me, am I going to die?"

Skyler knelt next to me. Taking my hand, he said, "You *might*. That baby is one great ox of a girl, and she should have turned long before now. When you go into labor, Kerilynn is going to try to turn her so she's facing the right way. If she can, it will help a lot, but..."

"But what?"

"You are such a little thing. I don't know. It's serious. It's..."

"Dire?"

"Good word."

"Thank you. You heard him, George. You're my witness. Dire, he said, dire. So I'm going to ask you both to grant a dying woman her last wish. Right?"

Skyler closed his eyes and nodded.

"Come here, close to me. Closer."

Skyler leaned over me. I put my arm around his neck and drew him close.

"George too," I said.

G-Mek leaned in, and I pulled him down with my other arm. Holding my dearest friends close, I whispered, "I want you to promise me something, both of you."

"Yes."

"Anything."

"If this baby is a monster, you will take it out to the middle of the lake and give it back to the gods."

Chapter Ninety-Six

Deliverance

" Honey, I need you to *stop* pushing."

"Keep pushing?"

"Pay attention, Janabai." Kerilynn used her no-nonsense midwife voice to snatch me back from the incoherent daze where I was hiding from the pain.

"It's too soon to push. You'll bash her head against your cervix until it gets so swollen she'll never come out. You don't want that, do you?"

"That," I panted, "would be... a *bad* thing."

"Yes, it would. A very bad thing. The baby would die, and so would you."

"I don't care. Make it stop... please... just make it stop... I can't do this anymore. I don't care what you do... just make it..."

I screamed as loud as I've ever heard anyone scream.

"Okay," she said to Simone and Masha, who were serving as doulas, "let's get her back on the floor."

Kerilynn didn't care much for the birthing chair, preferring to get "down and dirty" on the floor with the lucky mother-to-be, but she was at her wit's end, having tried everything else to induce labor: nipple stimulation and traditional medicines, black and blue cohosh, cotton root bark, and finally membrane stripping, a *procedure* best left to your imagination.

"Episiotomy?" Lynda Cheng, who was assisting, asked.

"Not yet. She can do this."

Finally, after twenty-one hours, at five a.m. on the second day, it started. A whole fire team showed up to help. Besides Kerilynn, Lynda, and the two doulas, the little Prymak girl, still nursing her own baby, was standing by, *just in case*, and Mother and Dad, and Max. My next of kin.

And me, of course, the star of the show.

"Ten centimeters?" Lynda asked.

"Close enough," Kerilynn answered. "She's crowning. Janabai, I can see your baby."

I was too exhausted to do anything but moan.

"Jana, are you hearing me?"

"Uh-huh."

"Now is the time to push. You got to push that baby out right now. You've been begging for this, so let's get it done. Push, push, push that kid out RIGHT NOW! One... two... three... PUSH!"

I did my best. They told me it was going to hurt, but this was worse, much, much worse, than I ever imagined. I was ripping open, tearing apart, splitting down the middle, but I wasn't going to scream, wasn't going to scream, wasn't going to...

I screamed.

"Here she comes, your little girl."

Then, "Oh shit."

Like a lightning jolt, panic in the room.

"Oh shit what?" I screeched.

"Sorry for the bad word, honey. The baby's stuck a little bit. Don't worry, I'll get her out."

But I saw the look Kerilynn flashed Lynda.

"Stuck? What's wrong?" I asked.

"It's called shoulder dystocia. Don't worry, happens all the time. Easy to fix, no sweat, but I need you to work with me. Can you get up on your hands and knees? Do you think you can do that? Hands and knees?"

I was thinking, "Bitch, you gotta be shitting me," but I was coherent enough to keep it together and whimper, "Help."

Simone and Masha lifted me from the bed down to a mattress on the floor and into, how can I put this, a most unflattering position, on my elbows with my butt in the air, Kerilynn crouching behind. Not that I cared what I looked like.

"The little squished-up face is squinting right up at me," Kerilynn said.

"Turning purple," Lynda said.

"Yeah, I can goddamn well see that," Kerilynn snapped.

"Cord around her neck?"

"No. But she's got her left shoulder wedged on top of the pelvic bone. And she's trying to go back inside."

"Go back?" I asked.

"Trying to pull in her head like a turtle."

"Turtle?"

"That's what we call it. Grease, please, both hands. 'Turtling,' isn't that funny?"

"No… not funny."

Kerilynn took one look around, as if drawing strength from her team.

"How much time?" Lynda asked.

"Maybe five minutes."

"Okay, Janabai, this is going to be the most fun you've ever had in your life. I'm going to put both hands inside you and get the baby loose. Want to hear the good news?"

"Good news?"

"I have really tiny hands. It's better for midwives to have little hands. Ready?"

"No."

"Too bad, here we go."

After all the acupuncture, palpations, tinctures, chanting,

prayers, and spiritual mumbo jumbo, to get me to this point, it came down to one woman, Kerilynn Abigail Fleenor, standing between me and the end of my life. With all her concentration, her forty-six years of experience, with the fingertip sensitivity of two hundred deliveries, closing her eyes, relying solely on feel, shutting out the world, shutting down her own fears, her guilt for not being more, having more, doing more, softly she worked both hands up inside me, somehow found enough room to get her fingers around the baby's head, searching for and finding the baby's shoulder.

"Got it. Now… going to lift her up a bit… uh-huh… there we go… and rotate her from anterior to posterior… mmm-hum… and stretch her out a little bit… just a little bit more… there."

Kerilynn paused, opened her eyes, and breathed.

"Why'd you stop?" I panted.

"Letting the baby rest and reintegrate for a moment. Me, too. Okay, deep breath, last part, Janabai. I'm going to corkscrew her around this way."

I screamed again.

"That's right, honey, let it out. There we go, a little shimmy, some wiggle, do the hokey pokey… and… now, one more push. Come on, Jana, push… yes, yes, good girl. Here she comes, the little booger… got her!"

Eureka! Kerilynn held the baby in her hands.

Whew!

No. No whew. Not over. Not even close.

"Baby's not breathing."

And I thought, "Merciful Shiva, thank you."

Pulling the infant further away so the umbilical cord stretched out, Kerilynn nodded to Lynda. "Clamp and cut."

Lynda leaned in to tie up the cord with string, high and low, snipped it, and handed the surgical scissors to Simone.

"Good enough for now."

Kerilynn held the limp infant upside down along her thigh until the fluids started draining, then brought her upright to give her mouth-to-mouth. Two hard puffs, and the baby, with an ear-piercing squall, announced her arrival into the land of being. Kerilynn handed her to Lynda.

My heart hammered in... what? Anguish, joy, hope, guilt?

"Okay, Jana, let's get rid of the placenta. One more big push. C'mon, push."

I pushed. I felt a gush of blood.

Kerilynn grabbed the cord, squeezed tight, and pulled.

"A little cord traction, and... here we go. Push again."

This time I ejected the placenta.

"Right on time," Kerilynn said, and looked over to Masha. "Help your pal roll over on her side," but before Masha could step in, I hemorrhaged, and don't believe for a minute you can't feel it when you hemorrhage.

"Oh my God," Masha said, "she's dying. Do something."

"Shut up, Masha," I, the dying woman, hissed through my clenched teeth.

"Yes," Kerilynn said, "shut your trap, or I'll ask Max to throw you out on your ass."

Big-eyed, Masha put her hand over her mouth.

"Here," Lynda said, handing Masha the caterwauling baby, "make yourself useful and clean her up. Simone, you keep those cool cloths coming."

"Janabai," Kerilynn said, "I'm going to press down on your abdomen with my right hand and push up on your cervix with the other."

"Why?" I gasped.

"I'm going to help your uterus contract so the bleeding will stop."

"Hurt?"

"Not much. It's probably going to feel good after what you've already been through; some pressure, that's all, and it's going to deflate like a balloon."

She didn't add, "I hope," but I could tell that's what she was thinking.

"Okay, here we go, baby chick. Be over in a minute."

Again Kerilynn closed her eyes, doing everything by feel. She found the place inside me she was looking for, stopped, pressed, and held, and held, and held. With her other hand she began kneading my belly, feeling for and finding the top of my uterus, which she began to work downward toward my birth canal. She worked from side to side, but always pressing down, trying to squeeze me shut between her two hands.

Simone passed a cool, wet cloth across Kerilynn's forehead, and the midwife, dimly aware someone was wiping her face, nodded a quick acknowledgment and continued to concentrate and press, my life in her hands.

I looked down and saw I was lying in a puddle of blood. When did that happen? Something shattered in my chest. I choked and tried to speak.

"Am I pushing too hard?" Kerilynn asked, leaning over; her face, her giant face stretching wider until it filled my vision. I could see her mouth move, but her voice was coming from down the hall.

"We're losing her." The words reverberated: "ooosinginginginging herherherherherererrrrrr."

Oh, my. I'm going out. This is really happening. I'm going. Do you know how much I love you? I love you all so much. Om Namah Shivaya, Om Namah Shivaya.

Faces above me and leaves and trees and sky melted together, bright green and gold; and blue shards faded into white, glaring white, hard-to-look-at white. I saw myself floating above a sea of milk, endless white, liquid, without feature. Why was I still holding on to the last little piece of Janabai? Take me, take me now, I thought, or did I say it aloud? No of course not. I had no body, no... what were those things? Lips! I had no lips to speak the words, and it didn't matter because all I needed to do was let go, surrender the last little bit; and I wanted to, but in the final second, I saw far below me, the white sea was no longer flawless. Some disturbance on the chalky surface whirled around itself and drew me down into the vortex, where I realized the singularity had rendered itself as milk, and sea, and flaw; but the true disturbance was not a *thing*, it was a *sound* that rose and enveloped me. Music. Someone was singing.

I knew that voice. Mirabai! My sister, was reaching out for me, again, like the time Kali took me. Mirabai held me and would not release me. I told her, "Let me go," but she laughed and kept on singing:

Shiva Shiva Shambo

Janabai.

Shankarah

Wake up.

Hara Hara Hara

Janabai come back.

Maha Deverah

And I hear others singing from outside.

Shiva Shiva

It must be everyone in the village singing.

Shambo

Come on, Jana, you can do it.

Shankarah

That's my mother.

Hara hara hara

I feel hands on me, on my shoulders, and legs, and belly.

Maha Deverah

Goddamn it, Janabai, open your fucking eyes.

Shiva

That would be Max. What's Max doing inside my death?

Shiva Shambo

Alright, Alright, I'll open my eyes if it will make you so happy.
I opened one eye. A single tear rolled down my cheek.
"She's back."
"We have her."
The singing died away.
"I'm sliding," Kerilynn said. "Help me."
Max jumped over and encircled Kerilynn's waist to brace her
and take up some of the weight.
"Better?"
"Yes. Thank you."
Seconds dripped like dirty sludge.
Finally, Lynda whispered in Kerilynn's ear, "Let's see if it
stops when you release a little pressure."
Moment of truth.
Slowly, slowly, Kerilynn relaxed the pressure, cocked her head
as if listening.
"The bleeding stopped?"
"I think she's holding," Kerilynn said. "For now. Don't let her
move. I'm dizzy. I need to sit down."
Max lifted Kerilynn to her feet and helped her over to the bench.
"Suture?" Lynda asked.
"Wait. When I'm sure the bleeding has stopped for good, I'll

do it, but not now. Masha, give her a dose of Shepherd's Purse and the other thing we talked about."

Masha handed the baby to Simone. She reached into the placenta and tore off a piece.

"Hey, pal," Masha said.

I tried to speak, but my throat was so swollen from screaming.

"Water," I managed to whisper.

"Sure.

She held a cup to my mouth until I swallowed a few sips.

"Now, I want you to chew on this."

"What is it?"

"Magic medicine with lots of… ?" Masha looked at Lynda.

"Oxytocin," Kerilynn supplied the answer.

"Oxytocin," Masha answered. "It will help your uterus cramp up and stop bleeding."

Allowing Masha to slip a piece into my mouth, I mumbled, "Tastes like chicken."

I thought that was pretty funny, and tried to laugh, but it came out like *huff huff.* Everybody laughed with me, too loud. Wasn't I funny? Lynda gave me an amused look and resumed doing whatever nurses do after babies come. She took the baby from Simone and tried to put it on my breast. I pushed her away. She said the things I guess women are supposed to say, "You have a healthy girl child. Look how strong she is. What a fine baby," and all that shit, but I wasn't having any. I turned my head, didn't want to see the baby, didn't want it near me.

"Take it away. Give it to Mother. She wants it so bad."

"Don't you want to nurse your baby?" Lynda asked. "Give it a try. It will be good for both of you. The sucking will help contract your uterus."

"I told you," I snarled, "no nursing. Get it away from me."

What could they do? Lynda gave the baby to Kimberly Prymak, my emergency wet nurse. The rest of them gathered around to take a gander at the new arrival. I suppose it looked like any other waxy newborn. Simone and Masha got me back on the cot and began cleaning me up.

"Simone," I said, "get Max."

Max came over and knelt down.

"Closer," I whispered.

"Yeah, big girl, what do you need?"

"Cigarette. Got any cigarettes?"

Max chuckled. "No. No cigarettes, but if I did have one, I'd fire it up for you. You deserve it."

"How about a joint?"

"Maybe later," Max said. "I think I can requisition a medicinal spliff from Vic's private stash."

"That would be good. Now do me a favor."

"What's that?"

"Get everybody out."

"Everybody?"

"You can stay."

Max winked at me. "You got it." She stood up and turned to the others. "Okay, everybody out, and by everybody, I mean you doting grandparents also."

Mother and Dad looked up from where they were making grotesque grandparent noises over the baby.

"Out?" Dad asked, bewildered.

"Yes, as in, go away. Now."

He did.

"Will she be okay by herself?"

"Hey, what am I," Max asked, "chopped liver?"

Mother gave me one more pleading look. I closed my eyes, just far enough to peek out from under my eyelids. Shaking her head, she left. I can't even imagine what she was feeling.

"And the baby," I said.

Max jerked her head at the wet nurse, who followed the others leaving the room in blessed silence.

"Okay," Max said. "They're gone. What's going on?"

"Max?"

"Yeah, I'm here."

"Am I going to die?"

"Yes, baby girl, you are. I hate to be the one to break the news, but you can trust me to give it to you straight. Indeed, Janabai, it's the truth. You are going to die. Someday, you are going to die."

"Shut up."

"Someday, but probably not today. Probably not this year, or next year, but some day, even you, Janabai Shepherd, are going to die."

"Thanks a lot."

"Don't mention it."

CHAPTER NINETY-SEVEN

The Official Report

I got a question for you. Why do I have to write all the Burke-Kucinich birth reports? Me, of all the goddamn people left in the world? I've never had a baby. What do I know? In case you haven't figured it out, this is Max, you know, Sergeant Max, a.k.a. Janabai's godmother, reporting as ordered, to make the Official Report of the Delivery because of my "superior observational skills," or so blathered Azriel when she sucked up to me, you know, twisting my arm into doing this.

Well, here it is. My official report, dutifully transcribed from Janabai's recitation and my own creaky memory. Janabai refuses to give the baby a name, so I'll just call her Baby.

Baby weighed... how the hell would I know? She was a big girl. How long was she? Who gives a shit? But I will tell you this: Baby has the blue throat, same as her mother, and yellow sparkly eyes, same as her father... only not scary.

Semper fi, y'all.
Maxine Flythe, USMC
July 15, in the Year 22, After Kali

Chapter Ninety-Eight

Fresh Baby

So I didn't die after all, not that day.

The *thing* was a girl-child, as predicted by Kerilynn, and huge, like the monster who put it in my belly. In the days that followed, Simone kept bringing *it* to my breast to feed, though I would rather cut off my nipples than have the abomination suck on me. Actually, I'd as soon someone with a sharp knife *did* cut off my nipples. My breasts felt like hundred-pound bags of rocks, swollen, painful, hot, super tender. But I pushed the *thing*, the baby, away.

"Okay, look," Simone said, "this is not doing you, or the baby, any good. You are suffering, and she's fretful with Kimberly — you know, your pal who is trying her best to nurse her. That baby wants her mother. She wants you."

"I don't want her," I said.

"You might try being more humble. You've been through a lot, but you can't keep using that as an excuse for being such a bitch."

My eyes welled up to hear Simone call me that word.

"You don't have to hurt my feelings."

"I'm not through," she said. "You can't let your unhappiness swallow you and make you into someone you're not. I know you, Janabai Burke-Kucinich Shepherd, down to the marrow of your bones, and you are not a person who turns her back on some little creature who needs you, and this baby needs you, needs you so desperately. If you can't take *joy* in this child, at least take some *comfort* from her. Please, Janabai, please."

"Okay, okay," I said. "I give up. Bring it in."

Simone sent Masha to fetch the *thing*. In less than a minute, Mother came in holding the *it* in her arms and making cooing sounds. That's a sight you don't see every day. Simone pulled down the blanket, and Mother shoved the *thing* into my arms before I could do anything about it. She dragged a stool up next to me.

"She's tough," Mother said, abruptly. "She survived the long march like we all did. She deserves your respect."

"Respect!"

"Did you lose your hearing along with your compassion? That's what I said, respect."

"And now I suppose you're going to give me your *every-life-is-special-in-these-hard-times-because-there-are-so-few-of-us* lecture?"

"No, you already know that one by heart. What I want you to hear is your own child calling for her mother. Listen."

In the silence, I became aware the baby was mewling like a kitten, little unhappy baby sounds.

"Look at her," Mother said. "Look at this precious bag of bones. Look at her."

I looked. The scrunched-up little face looked back at me. We studied each other. Dad used to say that I was born wide awake. This creature was like that. As if she were trying to say something, she made little popping noises, opening and closing her mouth. Leaning closer, I saw the tiniest spit bubbles on her lips. I inhaled her baby smell. Dimly, I was aware Mother was speaking.

"She's the sweetest thing. See? She has your chin, your father's chin."

"The eyes," I said.

Deep in the baby's dark eyes, yellow sparkles, and around the edge of the iris, a thin yellow corona. Beautiful. Ancient. Have you ever heard the expression 'an old soul'?

"What do you see?" Mother asked.

"Him."

"Yes," Mother said.

"Kali is there, inside her. She is of him."

"She is. And one day, in the years to come, when she grows to womanhood, she will be the pride of Shiva Puri."

"How do you know this?"

"Because I am who I am."

What do you say to that?

"Here, let me help you," Mother said as she untied my gown and slipped it off my breast. "Cup her head and bring her to you."

Without hesitation the baby began to nurse. At first it was agonizing, lightning bolts of pain, and then heat, as if my breast was running a fever, but when my milk began to flow, I felt a wave of utter pleasure ripple through me. Extraordinary. Humbling.

She was strong, hungry, greedy. She put her tiny hands on by breast, gurgling and smacking her mouth. And that gaze, drawing me in, making me her own.

"What will you name your daughter?" Mother asked.

"I'm not going to name the *thing*."

"Your child is a *girl*, not a thing. She requires a name."

"You name her."

"You're giving me naming rights?" Mother asked.

"Yes, naming rights and anything else to do with this *thing*. This *child,* if you prefer."

"Alright, as you wish. I name her Azriel."

"Azriel? You're giving her your own name? Isn't that rather vain?"

"No concern of yours; you gave up naming rights."

"Yes, I did."

"And for your information, I have my reasons."

"I don't care. Do what you want with it."

"No, you don't shrug her off. You don't throw her away."

"I don't want it... her."

"You've made that clear."

"Good."

"But. You. Will. Listen. To. Me. Now."

When Mother spoke in *that voice*, you listened, you listened as if the world depended on it, and it might, because that voice demanded that you listen on peril of your life. That voice reminded you that my Mother, Azriel Dancer, was the big boss of Shiva Puri, and where she pointed, you go. She had the Shakti, the divine imperative, not Mirabai's tender Shakti, but lethal, as if Durga the Destroyer was speaking through Mother's mouth.

She said, "You *will* take care of her. You *will* nurse her and hold her and clothe her and tell her you love her even if you hate her. This baby is blood of your blood. In the sight of Lord Shiva, you will do dharma to her. *Do. You. Hear. Me?*"

"Yes, Mother."

She leaned over. I thought for a moment she was going to bite me.

"I was not the best mother to you, Janabai, but I did love you. I *do* love you. I will tell you this, *satyam,* the truth. Someday you will come to love this child — in a short time, or in a long time, perhaps — but some day you will know her, you will understand her purpose, and you will acknowledge her as your beloved daughter."

I felt my heart crack open.

"Stop it, Mother. You're making me cry."

"Don't be afraid. I will help you. Max will help you. Your sister will help you. Skyler and G-Mek and all of your friends will help you. Even your Dad, whacked-out as he is, will help you. Lord Shiva will help you, and all of Shiva Puri will help you. You're not alone."

"It feels like it," I said.

"I know."

She leaned down and kissed me. That surprised me more than if she had bitten me. She stroked the baby's head, got to her feet, and walked out without another word or look. Now it was just me and the baby and Simone.

"I'll leave you two alone to get acquainted," Simone said. "I'm going to bed, but somebody will be nearby if you need anything."

She gave me one of her sweet smiles, a look of such unconditional affection.

"I love you, honey chile," she whispered as she tiptoed out, closing the door behind her.

We were alone. Me and it, her, the girl, my daughter, Azriel the Second. I maneuvered her mouth to my other nipple.

"This is called my left tit," I said. "Get to work."

She did. That big girl can suck.

As I watched her feed, it seemed as if she was, how can I put this, *blooming*. As if she was *becoming* a person, right there and now, against my breast. Oh, sure, she looked like any nursing baby should look... only this one was mine, and that made her different in ways I cannot express.

"Oh, my baby, whatever am I going to do with you?"

LEATHERFOOT

Daughters of the Kali Yuga continues in Book Three

Azriel Leatherfoot's Third Recitation, August 15, 51 AK

B EFORE WE GET AHEAD OF ourselves, I better go back and recite me about Indians. Back in thirty-two we was already set down east of Klamath Lake near the old Kla-Mo-Ya gambling hall, and we had been here ten years. Eleven years? No, ten, 'cause we came here in twenty-two, isn't that so, the year I was born? Right. We had been here ten years when Shoshone moved in from the north and come poking around to check us out. They didn't want anything to do with us, but pretty much decided we was harmless. We would see them from time to time off in the distance, just above old Chiloquin Town on the Sprague River, the men riding beautiful ponies and the women washing clothes and grinding meal and such. We ignored them and they ignored us, but it gave both people comfort knowing our backsides was guarded, us on the south, Shoshone on the north, Lake Klamath on the west. These was real Shoshone, too, not the Bannocks from up in Idaho at the Fort Hall reservation. Our Shoshones was an offshoot. They had some trouble with the Bannocks, I don't know what it was, and they don't say, but they drifted around until they hunkered down just across the Williamson River. It wasn't like we stole their land. We was here first, this time.

One morning when I was nine years old I showed up on our side of the Williamson River, uninvited, a dirty-faced, matty-haired little white girl with a .410 shotgun. I had heard about Indians, of course, and I wanted to meet some. There was a bunch of women and girls on the other side, washing and doing chores and singing. I waded across the river and said hello. The singing stopped.

One old woman seemed to be in charge. I was guessing she was the grandma, and it turned out I guessed right. She stared at me and said something in Indian to one of the girls, a hard-faced girl not much older than me. I found out later she was the old woman's granddaughter. The girl give me a hateful look, swung up on a horse, and pulled me up behind her. She rode me back the nine miles back to Shiva Puri without saying a word. Wasn't that something, me riding into the village behind a Shoshone? The girl pushed me off where I landed on my butt in front of everybody. I was grinning my face off. Dancer just shook her head. Mother rolled her eyes. The Indian girl nodded to my people, wheeled her horse around, and galloped away.

"I want a horse," I said. "I really *need* a horse."

We didn't have any horses in those days. It just wasn't something we did, growing horses, or, speak the truth, had the slightest idea how to do. We had started with goats, added sheep along the way, and we adopted cows we mostly raised as oxen to pull the wagons and fertilize the fields, some pigs, rabbits, chickens, and ducks, that's about it. Me asking for a horse was like asking for a air-o-plane from olden days. There was only one place I knew I could get a horse.

I traipsed back to the river the next day. The hard-faced girl walked right up to me, snatched the shotgun out of my hand, and pushed me down. I was not expecting that. It was not a good thing for her to do.

"Girl," I said, "I'm going to throw some fight on you."

I came up off the ground and went after her. She was older and bigger than me, and I surprised her, being fast and strong like I am. I head-butted her right in the nose—you know how much that hurts. Then we was into it, slapping and punching and hair pulling. She tripped me and I pulled her down on top of me. We rolled around screaming at each other and trying to hit each other anyways we could. Some women pulled us apart. We stood there breathing heavy and hating each other.

Old grandmother walked over and looked me up and down.

"*Gojoi*," she said in Shoshone, then in English, "You wash. You stink."

Two women took me by the arms and dragged me into the water. They stripped off my clothes and scrubbed me from one end to the other with soap root. One woman washed my clothes while the other one washed my hair a bunch of times. That wasn't too hard because I kept it hacked it off just above the shoulders. That hard-faced girl just stood there on the shore smirking at me.

The old woman spoke to the girl.

"Fix her hair," she said.

The girl made a mean face at her grandmother and stood with her arms crossed. The other women waited, looking back and forth between the old woman and the girl. Grandmother didn't say a word. She lifted her chin, just a little bit. The girl dropped her eyes, let out a breath, and stomped over to where I was dripping. She pointed to a rock. I sat down and she sat behind me. The girl tugged and pulled and combed my curls until she managed to get out all the snarls, probably for the first time ever. I wanted to cry because it hurt so bad, but I set my teeth and let the tears roll down without making a sound. Then the girl tied up my hair on both sides of my head with strips of rabbit fur so my hair sort of hung down behind my ears like two straggly corn shucks. From that time on I always wore my hair that way, even after it grew out long enough for me to sit on—two dirty blond pony tails tied up with cord. It was my look, and I never found one I liked better. I called it my "Indian hair."

I admired my reflection in a pool of water, looked at the girl.

"It's nice," I said. "Thank you. How do you say 'thank you' in Indian?"

The girl didn't answer.

"*A'ho*," said Grandmother. It was my first lesson in Shoshone.

"*A'ho*," I said to the girl. "What is your name?"

The girl said nothing.

"Tell her your name."

"Bu-u-he'gap," the girl said.

"A'ho, Bu-u-he'gap," I said.

She sniffed and turned away, but I thought I saw her smile, just a little smile. The other women and girls was not so stingy. They was all smiling at me.

Bu-u-he'gap picked up my gun from the ground and gave it to me.

"A'ho," I said. The girl lifted her chin just like her grandmother and walked off to wash in the river.

Grandma took a liking to me, I don't know why. Her granddaughter Bu-u-he'gap was slow to come around, but the rest of them women put up with me. Maybe they figured I'd just keep coming back if they chased me away. They was right about that. From that time on, I spent more time with the Shoshone than my own people. Since I wouldn't go away they figured they might as well teach me Indian ways. They didn't know what to make of me. I looked like a girl. I acted like a boy. Also I had my own gun. That gun gave me great face. The Shoshone didn't have but a few old broken-down guns, and no working ammo to speak of. My .410 was something no girl child should be carrying around. It was a big medicine. Also I could outfight anybody my size, even the boys, except one, Bu-u-he'gap's cousin, who was called Ogwifi; that means "thorn" because he was so sharp and pricky. That boy was mean. He was the fiercest fighter you ever saw. He did not like me one bit, and he did everything he could think of to hurt me and make fun of me. We had some terrible dust-ups, me and Ogwifi, scratching and biting and hitting and rolling around until some grown-up pulled us apart.

I asked Bu-u-he'gap why Ogwifi was so mean to me.

"Maybe he likes you," she said.

"Likes me?"

She just smirked her nasty little Bu-u-he'gap smirk.

Them Indian boys refused to have anything to do with me, so Bu-u-he'gap made pow wow with Ogwifi, who was the leader or chief of the boys or whatever he called himself. All of them boys was afraid of Bu-u-he'gap, her red-hot temper, and because she was speaking for Grandmother Dai Ta-zumbi; but taking a girl with them, a white girl, was just something they wasn't doing. Bu-u-he'gap just shrugged and give up.

"Maybe you should just be a girl," she said.

"I don't want to be a girl," I said. "I want to be a warrior."

"Maybe you can give Ogwifi a present."

"Like what?"

"Like your gun. Ogwifi would like to have your gun. I have heard him say this."

"He's not getting my .410," I said.

"Even his big brother does not have a gun. Such a present would give Ogwifi great face."

"I have seen Weda Mukua with a gun."

"It is broken, and also, he does not have any bullets."

"I already told you, Ogwifi is not getting my gun. Weda Mukua is not getting my gun. You are not getting my gun. Nobody is getting my gun."

"And I have spoken enough about this, and you are too stupid to understand these things. Go home where you are wanted."

When I went home and told Grandmother Dancer about this problem, she said she would think about it and tell me what to do. The next day she called me into her room. Max was there with her.

"Max is going to teach you how to shoot a new weapon."

Now that is the kind of thing I like to hear.

"What kind of weapon?"

"Show her."

Max unwrapped a small bundle. A handgun. I knew it was called a revolver because I had seen Max shoot it before and it had this round thing that turned around every time it fired. We don't use handguns at Shiva Puri because they are no use for hunting, and why else would you want one? You have to remember, I was still a child in those days.

"What is it?"

"This is a .357 Colt Python," Max said.

"Can I hold it?"

"In due time."

"You will learn how to shoot it," said Grandmother. "Then

you will take it to Ogwifi and teach him how to shoot it. You will present it to him as your gift."

I looked from Grandmother to Max and nodded. They are so smart, those two old women. Ogwifi would have the revolver, but I would have the bullets.

Max started teaching me that same afternoon. By the next day I was a better shot than she was. That will not surprise you.

"You're just as good as your grandmother used to be," Max said, "a natural."

Her words lifted my feet right off the dirt. Forgive me for bragging. You know how I am.

I spent more time learning how to break it down, clean it, and take care of it than I did in learning how to put a bullet in the target. Besides learning maintenance and marksmanship, the other parts of learning handguns is, first, how and when to use it, and secondly, not to shoot your own self with it or one of your friends. Handguns is tricky. If you don't keep your mind on it, you will suddenly find the muzzle pointing at somebody else or at your own foot. Surprise. Don't shoot. That would hurt, ha ha.

Let me tell you, Grandmother's plan worked just like she knew it would. Ogwifi didn't believe me at first when I showed up with the Colt Python. I asked him if he wanted me to show him how to shoot it. You bet he said that he already knew how and no girl had anything to teach him. I gave him the gun and he pointed it and pulled the trigger. Nothing happened, of course, because it wasn't loaded.

"No good," he said. He threw it at the ground at my feet.

"That is no way to treat your gun," I said.

He was walking away when my words sunk in to his thick head: "*Your* gun." He stopped. Ogwifi turned around and walked back to me. He stared into my face trying to tell if I was funning him.

"You have to treat your weapons with respect," I said. Ogwifi knew this, of course. He would never have thrown his own bow on the ground like that.

"If you want it, pick it up and give it to me. I'll show you how to clean it, how to be careful with it, how to load it so it will fire when you squeeze the trigger." I smiled at him. He scrunched his face up. He was embarrassed because he knew he should have checked to see if it was loaded before he made a fool of himself. He nodded once. He bent down and handed the gun to me, muzzle pointing at my heart.

"First lesson. Never point it at a girl unless you plan to kill her. Are you going to shoot me?"

"Maybe later," he said. Was that a little smile at the corners of his mouth?

"Until then, let's get it cleaned up from you throwing it in the dirt."

I took the revolver from him. We sat down in the shade. I unrolled a cloth and took out the cleaning brush and rod.

"If you try to shoot it with dirt in the barrel, it will explode and blow your hand off." I went on with my lesson. Ogwifi listened to every word. I might be a girl, but this was warrior talk, the most important matter in the world to him. Ogwifi is mean and horrible, but he is one smart Shoshone. He was taking it all in. After cleaning, I showed him how to carry it safely and how to load it. Then we started shooting. First, I put six rounds into the circle he carved on the side of a dead tree. Then he shot, missing the whole tree. But he got better, real quick, and soon he was getting almost as good as me. Well, that's what I let him think. I was catching on to this handling a boy stuff.

When we had shot that tree to death, we cleaned the revolver again. We stood up facing each other. I turned the revolver around, presenting it to him, muzzle down, hand grip toward him.

"Ogwifi, of the Bear Clan, I give you this Colt Python to have as your own."

"Azriel of the Shivas, I accept your gift, but you are still a worthless white girl. You know nothing of Shoshone ways. I will teach you so you will not be in my way all the time."

After that Ogwifi let me come along on hunting parties and showed me how Shoshones track and stalk and kill. I learned how to read signs, how to stop and listen—hard for me, you know, Azriel Ants-in-Her-Pants—how to close my eyes and smell the air, I mean really take the air in and roll it around on my tongue, and how to recognize what I was smelling, how to move through the land so quiet and smooth not even a badger noticed when I passed by, how to read the wind and use it to mask my own scent, how to string and pull the powerful bows they made from mountain sheep horn. Those bows was only about three feet long and not very good at distance, but they could pack a wallop from close in, say from horseback into a buffalo, if I had a horse or a buffalo to shoot at, which I didn't. I learned how to fly the arrow, following the shaft all the way into the animal, and what part of the animal to hit for a quick death. Speak the truth, I was never that good with the bow and continued to stand by my shotgun, but for silent hunting, nothing beats Shoshone arrows zipping out of the shadows.

The women showed me how to trap fish and rabbits and how to grind pine nuts and acorns. As I got older they taught me how to manage my female stuff out in the wilderness, and you men have no idea at all how hard and messy that is without paper or cloth or medicine, especially when I am trying to hunt and every animal can smell me for five miles, or what it's like on a long trek by myself doubled over with cramps in the rain. Let me give you this piece of advice, for free, when I am having my time of the month, stay out of my sight.

The only Indian kid who really wanted me around was Yagaichi; that means Crybaby. He stood out odd just like me. I was a girl who acted like a boy, he was a boy who acted like a girl. He wore girl's clothes and fixed his hair like a girl and sashayed around camp like you never saw anything like it. He was funny, too. Crybaby made everybody laugh with his foolishness. The people put up with him and loved him, and I did too. He was the most kindest and most sweetest boy I ever knew, and when he grew up, he was just the same. Crybaby was my first real friend among the Shoshone, or here at Puri, for that matter.

By the time I was twelve I had learned enough Shoshone ways to make myself the go-between for the Bear Clan and my own people. The Shoshone didn't want to get all buddy-buddy with us, because, speak the truth, they didn't trust white people and they blamed us for the Kali and all the troubles that came after. But they did want some things we had, our most valuable trade goods, wool cloth and Shakticillin.

Just after Mother was born, is that right, when we made Shakticillin? Yes, in 3 AK, we learned how to grow antibiotics. When I say "we" I mean Suranjini Devi, our genius scientist. First she had to figure out how to keep stuff cold. She did that with some kind of gas, and along the way, she also learned how to make ice, and that is good for a lot of things, but mostly ice cream. Everybody called her the "mad scientist," but she was always nice to me and didn't seem mad about anything. Her daddy and mom was the Old Shiva Puri scientists, so I guess being smart just run in her family. Suranjini Devi kept working away growing one batch of nasty after another until she found a way to grow the good stuff she wanted. She didn't know if it was penis-cillin or moxi-cillin or what, so she called it Shakticillin. It didn't always work, and every now and then made you even sicker, but mostly it cured you from infections and fever. Shakticillin. God's grace-acillin, that's what I call it.

Wool cloth was our other trade specialty. From the time she was a little girl, Mother and the other women was learning how to weave from a book she had brung out of Old Shiva Puri. They was weaving clothes mostly from stuff they could salvage, but after we added sheep to Mother's herds, they learned how to shear and spin wool. Then the weavers really got rolling. Shiva coats and bliss blankets was just about the best trade goods you could find.

So I traded our medicine and wool goods to the Shoshone for stuff they knew how to get: roots of all kinds, wild onions, strawberries, and tobacco, poison for fishing, and arrowheads, dried meat from elk, antelope, and bighorn sheep. Baskets and beautiful bead work. But not horses. The Shoshone never, and I mean never, traded horses. They have bad memories about being cheated by white people that go way, way back. Shoshone wealth is horses, speak the truth, Shoshone soul is horses.

The December I turned thirteen, I showed up at their village with a 12 gauge, double-barreled shotgun. You probably guess how I got it. Let's just say some old lady slipped me a birthday present when Mother wasn't looking. I kept buckshot in one barrel and a solid slug in the other. At close range it could take down a buffalo. I learned how to fire the 12 holding it straight out with one hand. None of them, not even the biggest men, could do that. Break your wrist if you don't know how. Of course it helps to have a light load in your own shell. You put a heavy load in the shell you give the big man. That is my little trick, ha ha.

The shotgun give me face among the Shoshone. Not enough face for a horse. Never enough face for a horse. Oh, who needs a horse anyway? I wouldn't take three of them if they came dressed in war paint and feathers. That's a bald-faced lie, of course; I would shoot you dead in your tracks for one old sway-back nag.

I didn't have a horse, but never mind. By then I had learned how to walk. That sounds stupid. Everybody can walk. What I mean is I had learned how to walk real good, walk for days, through the mountains and over the deserts and across rocks and in the canyons. My bare feet growed tough as cow hide. For two years I walked all over south Oregon. I was the walkingest girl anybody ever saw. Then I started running. Don't know what got into me. Maybe I was late for prayers. I just started running, longer and longer. Running for hours. Running for miles. I run more than a hundred miles one time without stopping except to pee. That sounds like bragging. Okay, I'm bragging.

Two years later on one summer afternoon just before dark, I ran into Grandmother's village hoping I was in time for supper. I was planning to spend the night because New Shiva Puri was still nine miles off, and speak the truth, I was filthy and beat from a eighty-mile trot up to hang around with some Nez Perce, good folks who knew some things. I washed my feet in the river while Shoshone women sat around on the rocks to hear my Nez Perce gossip.

"You have the ugliest feet in the world," said Bu-u-he'gap, never one to pass up a compliment. "They look like old leather and they smell like old leather."

"A'ho, Sister, your tongue is sharp like your manners is poor."

The other women laughed, and Bu-u-he'gap snapped her head like I was some kind of bug buzzing around her ears.

Later that evening, I was surprised when it was her who come to fetch me from Grandmother's lodge where I was trying to rest and ignore my grumbling stomach. "Why was supper so late?" I asked her. She just smirked and shrugged. When we come to the main lodge, everyone was there, even the men, and dressed in their best, looking just splendid in the firelight. I was embarrassed with the way I looked, my clothes dirty from the trail. The musicians began playing drums and flutes and shaking rattles. The women sang a sweet tune I had not heard before. When they finished, Grandmother came to me and led me into the middle.

"This girl, Azriel of the Shivas," she said, "is known to the Shoshone."

The people murmured in agreement.

"But how shall the other tribes know her without a proper name? How shall she be respected among the Hidatsa and the Arapahoe, the Cheyenne and the Crow without a Shoshone name?"

More murmuring. Louder. Lots of head nodding.

"It is not right for her to go through the world without a proper name. Tonight we give her the name that she shall carry among the Nations. Does this girl have friend among the Shoshone to give her a name?"

There was a silence that seemed to go on and on. Then Bu-u-he'gap walked into the circle.

"I am her friend," she said.

Well, that kicked the feet out from under me. Her friend?

"Do you have a name to give to your friend?" said Grandmother.

"Her name is Leatherfoot. Azriel Leatherfoot," said Bu-u-he'gap.

Grandmother grinned. "From this day she shall be known to the Nations as Azriel Leatherfoot." The Shoshone women trilled their assent and the men shouted my new name over and over. There was singing and dancing and feasting in my honor, the most fun night of my life.

Leatherfoot. Azriel Leatherfoot. My name. I was fifteen and

I finally had a name, no longer Azriel Yet-To-Be-Named-By-My-Mother. Leatherfoot. Mother won't like it. No, Mother won't like it at all when she finds out someone else took charge of a thing she had planned for herself.

Hey, I've got an idea. I've been flapping my tongue so long, it done wore out. What say I put it to bed for this evening and we get off our butts for some dancing? Max, get Paw Paw's fiddle and wake him up. Auntie will you call the figures? All right! Well, what do you say? Let's have us a hoedown!

GRATITUDE

"Ass in chair, keep it there," as oft-quoted by the guru of American haiku, Steve Sanfield, is not the important discipline. By now, I should have mastered AICKIT. Nossir, the real discipline is sitting down to *re-write*. That reminder arrived just in the nick of time from novelist, John Woodbury. Thanks, John. I was sagging between draft four and draft five, or six, or eight, or whatever. I needed the pep talk.

Editor Cate Hogan badgered, bullied, and buttered me up as needed to keep this Rube Goldberg contraption clattering down the track. "In a novel called 'Janabai Shepherd,' the title character must be the *heart* of every scene." Duh. I had to hear that sermon again and again. When I foolishly let the action drift, the fault is mine. When I occasionally got it right, the credit is hers.

Once again, my street team, Azriel's Angels, came through to help lift this endeavor off the ground. More than forty Angels turned up for the launch, and if I tried to list them all, I'd certainly leave someone out, and then that someone would have hurt feelings. I know. That's what happened with *Azriel Dancer*. I'm still apologizing. So, all y'all Angels, you know who you are, I send you my Eternal and Celestial Appreciation.

Professional proofreader, Stacey Kopp, cleaned up after me. I'm grateful, and I know you readers are, too. Or should that be: "I know you readers are, *as well?*" STACEY! HELP! By the way, Stacey didn't proof these acknowledgements, so don't blame her.

Glendon, Tabitha, and the artists at Streetlight Graphics devised the layout and cover. It's such a pleasure to work with them again.

My goombah Brian "Conrack" Conroy dispatched the typos on the final draft. Mille grazie, consigliere eccellentissimo!

Readers have asked how I managed to write convincing pregnancy and birth sections. With expert consultation, of course. One of the finest midwives in our Sierra foothills, Jessica Mairs, gave generously of her knowledge. To Jessica, I posed this predicament: let me get our heroine into the deepest possible trouble... then you rescue her. I thank you, and Janabai thanks you, for coming through.

Without Christine Jenkins' shrewd critiques, patience, support and belief, there would be no "Janabai Shepherd." Thank you, Darling, forever and ever.